# A DISTURBING NATURE

# A
# Disturbing
# Nature

## Brian Lebeau

ISBN: 978-1-95386549-6 (Paperback)
ISBN: 978-1-95386550-2 (eBook)

Library of Congress Control Number: 2022900429

Any references to historical events, real people, or real places are used fictitiously. Names, characters, and places are products of the author's imagination.

Books Fluent
3014 Dauphine Street
New Orleans, LA
70117

*This novel is dedicated to my family, who provided endless inspiration and support, and to the great men and women of our armed forces, past and present, some of whom I had the distinct privilege of working alongside for nearly a quarter-century. Their professionalism, trust, and friendship, directly and indirectly, afforded me the opportunity to write this novel.*

# ACKNOWLEDGMENTS

Thanks to Julie Schoerke and Marissa DeCuir at JKS Communications for putting together a great team to turn my dream into a reality, Hannah Robertson and her team at Books Fluent for their experience and encouragement, Lana Allen, Angelle Barbazon, Jeizebel Espiritu, Brittany Kennell, Erica Martin, and all the great folks at Books Forward for their planning and foresight. Recognition also goes to the efforts of Diane O'Connell at Write to Sell for pointing me in a better direction with her honest critiques and spot-on recommendations, and Alex Cody Foster for his tireless support and reassurance during the process of crafting this novel and navigating the publishing process. Notes of appreciation are extended to Basil Wright from Salt & Sage Books for helping me avoid some common misunderstandings and misinterpretations through her comprehensive sensitivity reviews, Jim Davis from TypeRight for his contributions correcting my many writing flaws, and Joseph Borden and Emily Colin for their detailed copy and proof editing.

A big shout-out also goes to my team of editors, artists, and administrative personnel at Tangent Inspired Stories. This novel would not exist without Nicole, Rea, and Stephanie's collective creative talents and immense dedication. I'd also like to thank the students and staff at Bryant University (formerly Bryant College, where I taught as an adjunct faculty member in the early 1990s) and the fine people of the cities of Boston, Providence, and Fall River, as well as Fauquier County, Virginia. They made our team research visits worthwhile and enjoyable. And I'd like to thank my immediate and extended family and friends, who inspired the best attributes in the characters that make up this story.

Finally, I want to express my sincere appreciation to all the wonderful people who read the multiple iterations of this novel over the past four years, particularly those who had to trudge through the encyclopedic first draft: Anita Quagliani, Ann Pinning, Brenda Johnson, Coral Adamson, Fran Keenan, Jason Cox, Leah Cullen, Margie Hicks, Stephanie Rae, and Steve Pinning. Their inputs along the way proved instrumental to what appears on these pages.

The efforts of all these individuals and more have helped improve the story and writing immeasurably. However, with that in mind, any remaining deficiencies, omissions, oversights, inaccuracies, or outright errors are entirely the result of the author's personal limitations as a writer.

# AUTHOR'S NOTE

*A Disturbing Nature* primarily takes place across the great states of Rhode Island and Massachusetts in 1975, with several scenes set in Seattle, Washington, and Salt Lake City, Utah. In addition, a number of 1975 scenes and numerous flashbacks and memories extend to Fauquier County, Virginia, several tourist destinations in the White Mountains of New Hampshire, and Boston's neighboring cities. While I have sought to ensure historical accuracy in geography, locales, weather, terminology, and events, certain liberties were taken to weave the fictitious characters in this story into the applicable events, as necessary. In addition, "mass murderer" is used throughout in place of "serial killer," as the latter identification was not coined until the late 1970s or publicly recognized until the early 1980s. The story presented here is fictional, and any similarity to actual incidents or persons is entirely coincidental.

# Map of New England

1 - Bryant College (Changed to Bryant University in 2004)
2 - Podunk Dive (The Girl Who Moved One Stool Over)
3 - Providence Police & Fire Headquarters
4 - Palmer's Apartment at One Boston Place
5 - The Country Club (Brookline, MA)
6 - Grandparents' Home (Palmer)
7 - The Old Man of the Mountain (NH)
8 - Clark's Trading Post
9 - Bennie's Barbershop
10 - Smithfield Inn
11 - Langford's Home (Slatersville, RI)
12 - Kay's Home in Hillcrest Estates
13 - Stepstone Falls
14 - Capron Pond
15 - Olney Pond
16 - Roger Williams Park & Zoo
17 - Lincoln Park (Dartmouth, MA)
18 - Georgiaville Pond
19 - Hunt's Mill
20 - Cook Pond
21 - Harvard University

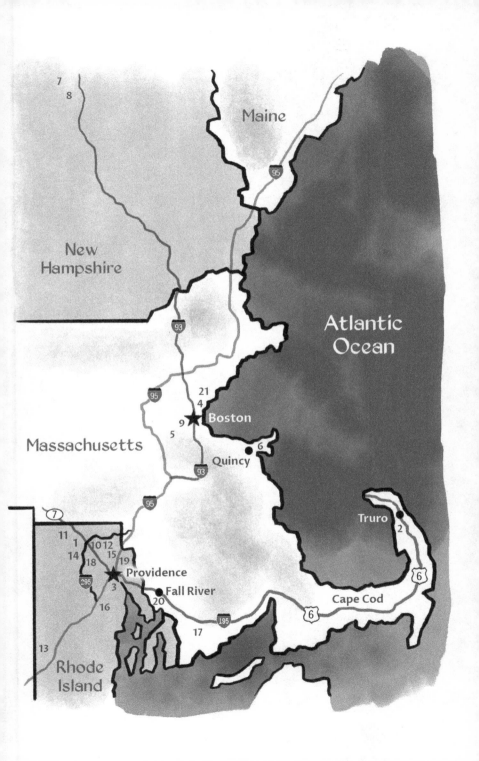

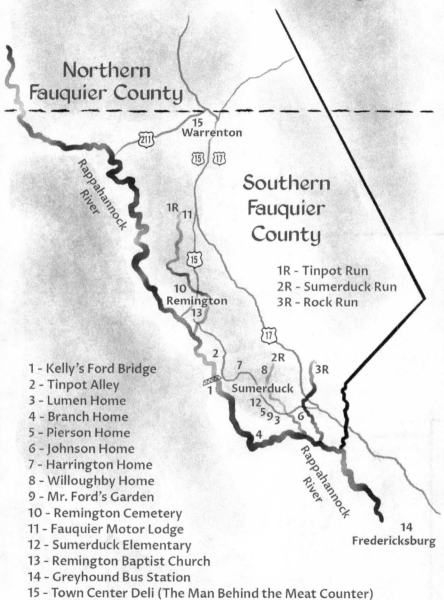

# Map of Fauquier County

**Northern Fauquier County**

**Southern Fauquier County**

211

15 — Warrenton

15   17

1R   11

15

10 — Remington

13

1R - Tinpot Run
2R - Sumerduck Run
3R - Rock Run

17

2

7      2R

1      8      3R

Sumerduck

12

5  9  3      6

4

Rappahannock River

Rappahannock River

14
Fredericksburg

1 - Kelly's Ford Bridge
2 - Tinpot Alley
3 - Lumen Home
4 - Branch Home
5 - Pierson Home
6 - Johnson Home
7 - Harrington Home
8 - Willoughby Home
9 - Mr. Ford's Garden
10 - Remington Cemetery
11 - Fauquier Motor Lodge
12 - Sumerduck Elementary
13 - Remington Baptist Church
14 - Greyhound Bus Station
15 - Town Center Deli (The Man Behind the Meat Counter)

*We begin in the process of dying, and we end up dead. Of this, there can be no doubt. Two beginnings and two ends. Conceived in obscene and ejaculatory fashion, suffering a human birth similarly vulgar, we descend a preordained path toward physical irrelevance and fear an unceremonious spiritual expiration. We cannot abort our own birth. We cannot escape our own death. This is to be understood that we may accept our human frailty and reject spiritual indifference—our first death dictated by the former, our second death subject to the latter, leaving only the fine line between hunter and hunted as negotiable. On this, we shall not disagree, lest we risk a grave misunderstanding.*

*– Reverend Arthur Leslie Bainbridge*
*Remington Baptist Church, Remington, VA*
*Sermon Excerpt, 17 March 1963*

# Part I

# THIRTY-SIX HOURS

# GHOSTS

## TUESDAY, 21 OCTOBER 1975

T*he third time Mo collides with Palmer, their worlds are unraveling,
and twelve young women are dead.* He tenses as Palmer navigates
his chair closer. Casters straining against linoleum tiles spin and
squeak in objection, stopping when the distance between the two
men suggests an intimacy they do not share.

Palmer's breathing is rhythmic, his words unsympathetic. "Okay,
then, Mr. Lumen, one final question. If none of the scenarios we've
discussed here seem likely in your estimation, are you the killer
known as the Pastoral Predator?"

Shaken by the question, Mo leans back, shifting his eyes away
from the chief investigator's glare. Staring at Palmer's fresh-lit cigarette in the ashtray, he sees willful abandonment in a silent bed
of ashes. Smoke rivulets that earlier suggested memories now harbor only ghosts. A small stack of baseball cards rests in his palm.
Unfurling his fingers, he inspects the one on top. Worn edges represent tangible evidence of a two-hour interrogation, time passing
at the pace of a dying man's desperate crawl. It has all led to this
moment. He refocuses on Palmer but cannot offer an answer.

Palmer, inching closer, rephrases the question. "Maurice Lumen, are *you* the Pastoral Predator?"

Mo understood the question the first time. He's asked himself
the same several times over the past week. Still, he cannot answer.
Again, he looks away. On the opposite side of the table, Agent Lowe
recedes into the arsenic-green drywall—a spectator bearing silent
witness to his mentor's cool competence. Mo seeks encouragement
in Lowe's eyes but finds indictment in their reverent anticipation.

Attention returning to the stack of cards, Mo studies the one on top and notices a new crease in the cardboard. His mind drifts to this evening's crucial game, irresistibly drawn to the simultaneous hope and despair it may deliver. Sitting in this unwelcome space and facing accusation, he's filled with anxiety on two fronts. He prays the next thirty-six hours will bring an end to the uncertainty, providing relief in both cases.

Unable to answer, Mo stares at a crack in the wall behind Palmer. He'd noticed it earlier, but it's grown during the interview. With this last question, it appears somehow larger, more sinister—a crooked smile mocking him. Afraid of its condemnation, he looks down, observes the movement of the second hand on his Timex, and considers the alternatives. Across an eternity comprised of fifteen measured ticks, a decision is made. He straightens himself, looks his accuser in the eyes, and responds. "No, sir."

Retrieving his cigarette, Palmer flicks the ashes, showing no emotion as he settles back. "Well, Mr. Lumen, I believe we'll be talking again, but, for now, you are free to go." He gestures in the direction of Agent Lowe, his subordinate's color resurfacing. "We'll continue our investigation with the help of your responses, evaluating your proximity to the crime scenes and relationships with the other primary suspects." A disingenuous smile emerges. "Thank you for your time and stay close to home until you receive confirmation the investigation is closed, or we bring you in for further questioning. Do you understand?"

Mo responds politely, as he always does. "Yes, sir."

Following a long drag, Palmer exhales. A dispassionate cloud of white consumes remnant blue streams still rising from the ashes.

# Part II

# THIRTY PUNCH BUGGIES

- 2 -

# THE BEAST

## SATURDAY, 16 AUGUST 1975

*The Beast inside Francis Palmer is familiar with monsters.* Ted may no longer be terrorizing Seattle, but FBI Chief Investigator Palmer knows this monster isn't hibernating. So his bloodshot eyes stare at the alarm clock in his hotel room, and its fractured red numbers stare back, each silent digital toll one minute closer to his weekly status call to Boston and, he fears, one step closer to bringing The Beast back home.

This morning, the phone beside the clock is Palmer's last refuge. When 6:59 turns to 7:00, time becomes irrelevant, and sound takes over—the sound of ringing in his ears. And when it stops, Murphy's voice brings him back. "Hey, Francis."

"Dick."

"Whatcha got?" Special Agent in Charge Murphy's voice has always helped Palmer heal, but this morning it's laced with remorse.

With Murphy's first few words, Palmer knows he's bringing back baggage. Still, he'll play it out. "The computer queries spit out twenty-six names that match the list of suspects. You know I believe he's in Utah and has been prowling around Colorado to throw off the scent."

"I know. You've been trying to get that ticket to Salt Lake for two months."

"He's overdue. He shits about every month like clockwork."

"I understand that, but time's run out."

Palmer squeezes the receiver tighter. "You can't! Not now!"

"Sorry, Francis, Washington's stepping back, there's been no request from Utah, and Colorado isn't certain their cases are connected."

"That's bullshit, and you know it."

"Doesn't matter what I think or know. It's time to come home."

"I can't. I just can't. I've got him. He's trapped inside me."

"No he's not. He's in Utah. You said so yourself."

Palmer grasps the hand that grips the receiver. "You know I'm right. Let me go. I can get the bastard."

"I can't. No matter how much you beg, I can't do it. My hands are tied."

"Fuck this shit. I'll head there myself!" Palmer slams the receiver down. Through the initial set of rings, he stares without answering. When it starts ringing a second time, he picks up.

Murphy's voice is calm. "It's time to come home."

Following several deep breaths, Palmer sighs. "I can't," he mutters.

"Agent Palmer, come home! That's an order! Don't throw away your career for this. They'll get him. Your time there's been productive, but it's time to come home, so you can get this motherfucker out of your head and heal."

Palmer acknowledges with a grunt.

"Try to catch the red-eye tonight or first flight in the morning. I'll see you tomorrow."

Palmer runs his fingers through his hair. "I'll see what's available." But he knows there will be no seats left because he won't check. He'll spend tonight and tomorrow just as he has the past six months—The Beast roaming free on Saturday night, with Palmer regaining control on Sunday. No, Palmer does not fly on Saturdays.

"Alright, Francis, I'll see you first thing Monday morning."

Palmer's aware Murphy knows him too well. He holds the receiver long after the click, running down the unusual circumstances surrounding the case: a Volkswagen Beetle as a mobile morgue, the unheeded calls from Ted's girlfriend, and the geography. In his mind—now the mind of the killer—it points in one direction. But the littering of bodies around Seattle ended just as they picked up in Utah and Colorado, Ted staying just out of reach. Palmer knows The Monster's mistake is close.

The shower's been the worst part of Seattle—cracked tile sealed with mold and a showerhead that spits on any setting—but Palmer will pay the extra night and spend the evening downtown. He's gotten used to the clean air and local flavors, acclimated to the views of Puget Sound and Sunday afternoon breakfasts, and familiar with the layout of the city and the pulse of the nightlife.

Calling the airline, Palmer secures a ticket for the Sunday red-eye. After hanging up, the phone rings while he's dressing. "Hello?"

Washington State Police Detective Hawley is on the other end. "Morning, Frank. Hope I didn't wake you."

"Nope, just heading out for breakfast. What's up?"

"I hate to bother you on the weekend, but thought you'd want to know." Hawley hesitates. "Utah Highway Patrol picked him up early this morning."

Palmer sits on the edge of the bed. "What happened?"

"Well, we haven't gotten many details, but they brought him in on evading a police officer."

"What was he doing?"

"Again, we don't have much. They just picked him up a few hours ago. He was driving through a residential community in Granger with his lights off. Sped away after he saw the cruiser. When he finally did stop, they noticed the passenger seat was missing and found a crowbar, ice pick, ski masks, and other stuff that might be used in burglaries."

"Anything else?"

"They also found handcuffs. They're going to search his apartment. That's it. That's everything we know right now."

"Thanks, Pete. I appreciate the call."

Palmer lays back on the bed, feeling a tiny weight lifted. Ted will be on the radar now. But will they find more incriminating evidence in his apartment? Will they have enough to hold him? Will they be able to get this bastard off the street? His stomach aching from hunger and unease, he finishes getting dressed and heads out.

Palmer eats lunch at Clark's Crabapple before dropping pennies into the Bellevue Square wishing well. In the well's false assurance of water, he sees broken promises made to his daughters, the constant travel and associated distance causing him to miss Pauline's maturity into adolescence and Peggy's college years. He's made the trip here every Saturday morning for the past six months, making the same wish each time. He misses his daughters all the time, on each investigation and across every mile, but he never goes back without resolution. Never. It's the only way he knows how to protect them, wherever he may be.

Standing under the shade of a large madrona, Palmer leans over the edge of the well. Staring at the cement bottom, he sees wishes piled up in the form of copper, nickel, and zinc. He tosses nineteen pennies into the historic well, one for each year of his marriage. Here, he counts the cost. On the prowl tonight, he'll pay the price— Marilyn's face atop every skirt seated on a barstool.

When he arrives back at the Sorrento, the front desk clerk waves him over and hands him a message scribbled on hotel stationery:

*Mr. Palmer, Room 719.*
*Detective Hawley called.*
*Insufficient evidence to detain.*
*Subject released on own recognizance.*

Palmer growls in the elevator. In his room, prepping for a Saturday Night at Lacey's Bar, he boils. It's feeding time for The Beast.

10

# AN ISLAND OF ISOLATION

## SATURDAY, 16 AUGUST 1975

O*n the day Maurice Lumen leaves Virginia for the second time, it will be for good.* He reluctantly sets off for Rhode Island, all his memories tucked into his father's old duffel bag. Wearing the accumulated stress of five weeks' uncertainty, he wedges his knees against the seatback in front of him and leans his head against the window, feeling as constricted by the seat as he is by his clothing.

As the bus pulls away from the Fredericksburg Greyhound station, Mo does not see the Branch family's station wagon, Mrs. Harrington's sedan, or Earl's pickup. He also does not see Jake waving, Sam smiling, or Dion's silent stare. Instead, he thinks about what he's leaving behind—accusations, a half-brother, and an inhospitable cot.

When the bus merges onto 95 North, Mo retrieves his duffel bag from the overhead and rests it on the empty seat beside him. After more than three decades, the black letters have faded into the olive drab canvas, but he can still make out his father's name and the year—*Lumen, Kenneth L.* and *1944*. He runs his finger across the American flag stitched next to the words, recalling the texture of a much larger one draped over his father's casket six months earlier, Earl Johnson crying as a single trumpeter played *Taps*.

Ken and Earl were friends long before the Second World War, sharing Fauquier County's schools and interest in many of the same local girls. Having spilled blood on battlefields and alcohol in barrooms, they fought, worked, and drank together, their military experience marking them with a sincere brand of patriotism that could only come from deployment, duty, and disarmament. On his sleeve, Ken Lumen wore his love of country, and under his shoulder, he strapped a badge of honor collected from the battlefield in Germany—a Nazi SS Waffen Walther P38 9mm pistol.

From the time he could open the refrigerator and bring his father a beer, Mo would listen to their war stories, Ken seated on his recliner talking with Earl about "pushing them sons-of-bitching Nazis outta Europe." Before his schooling began, he had already lost count of the times his father reminded him he was named after Major General Maurice Rose, commanding officer of the Army's Third Armored Division. Knowing Ken was a patriot, hero, and all-around man's man, Mo understood he was expected to fill his father's shoes.

Mo stares out the bus window and spots several deer grazing in the woods along the highway. In the wheezing of cool air pressed through pinhole vents overhead, he hears his father's quiet encouragement on a cold, damp early evening in October 1958, just before his eighth birthday. It was the one time he went hunting with his father and the only time Mo saw him fire a weapon.

The smell of whiskey enveloped Mo's cramped space, where he knelt between two scrub oaks and behind some elderberry shrubs still ripe with dark purple fruit.

"Whatcha waiting for?" Ken whispered through the leaves. "Shoot, Son."

Shaking from steady rain and the beseeching of his father, Mo struggled to keep his rifle's sight focused on a mature doe. He wanted to oblige his father but saw only innocence in the doe's alarmed stare.

Ken leaned closer, helped Mo steady his weapon. "Go ahead. Take your shot."

Mo could feel his hands sweating despite the cold. "I don't want to kill her, Daddy!"

Earl sighed. "He ain't ready, Ken. He's thinking of Bambi or something."

"Dammit, Earl, keep your voice down." Ken confirmed the doe's position. "This is the first good one we seen all day."

Mo felt his father's hand cup him around the neck, causing his spine to arch and quake.

"Look at the target." Ken placed his other hand on Mo's chest. "Settle down, Son. Steady your hands and hold your weapon up." Pointing at the doe, his hand stretching over the elderberry shrubs, Ken's fingers did not waver despite the weather and approaching darkness. "Aim for the body, so you have a better shot. It ain't gonna feel a thing."

The rifle shook in Mo's hands, his high-pitched voice quivering. "But how do you know?"

"Done enough killing to know." Ken winked at Earl. "Go on. It'll be okay."

With the last twinkling of daylight weeping through the trees, Mo saw the deer's breath no different from his own. He sat back on a clump of weeds, pulling the rifle to his chest. "Daddy, can we please go home?" Darkness harboring cooler air, he was shivering and wet. "I want to see Mommy."

Pulling Mo up, Ken helped him steady the rifle, frustration in his voice. "Aim the gun and pull the trigger." The doe lifted her head a little higher. Her front legs twitched.

"I can't, Daddy. I don't want to." Mo began crying, the deer's attention focused on his sniffling.

Earl took another swig of whiskey from his flask. "I'm telling you, he's too scared to shoot." A cough caught in his throat, startling the doe.

"She's gonna bolt!" Ken yelled, rising to his feet. Reaching inside his coat, he drew the Walther, raised his arm, and pointed the gun.

The first shot whistled through the doe's knee, ending her attempt to escape. A second blow, more precise and damaging, felled the animal, her final breath leaving a temporary white mist that evaporated as it rose through the rain.

Mo slumped into the brush, eyes and mouth agape.

Ken slid the Walther back into its holster. "Can't be wasting good table meat!" Turning to Mo, he gave him a pat on the back. "Don't worry, Son. You'll get one next time."

All light removed, Mo trembled, feeling colder than before. The men walked in darkness, guided by an indiscriminate flashlight, and tended to their kill, indistinct whispers fading into the boundless night. Mo sat, huddled and alone, wishing he were at his mother's side and wondering why death is a necessary part of life. Brushing away thoughts too serious for a young boy, he unfolded his arms to wipe away the mixture of rain and tears from the sides of his nose and mouth.

Late afternoon sunlight weaves through the trees, bounces off the silver panels of the bus, and shines on the highway sign welcoming passengers to Maryland. Reaching into his duffel bag, Mo pulls out a small, gift-wrapped box and an oversized shoebox. He places the unopened present inside the shoebox alongside several family photos, a stack of old baseball cards, a well-read paperback novel with dog-eared pages, and other reminders of his time in Virginia. Positioning the shoebox in his lap, he stares at the contents until he falls asleep, slouched on the duffel bag.

An hour later, Mo's shaken awake by a young man about his age with a mustache, beard, and long, wavy light brown hair.

"Is anyone sitting here?" The young man's blue eyes shine like a cloudless sky.

Staring, Mo lifts his head off the duffel bag, his Timex leaving a red circle imprinted on his face.

"Do you mind if I sit here?"

Mo nods, then shakes his head, checking the time on his wristwatch. "Where are we?"

"Baltimore." The young man places Mo's duffel bag in the overhead.

*Baltimore?* Mo thinks. *Sam played for the Baltimore Elite Giants.*

"I'm Abraham. What's your name?"

"My name's Mo."

Abraham points to the small, gift-wrapped box. "I see you've got a present there." His voice remains calm, ignoring items of greater concern in the shoebox. "Are you headed to college?"

Mo places the cover back on the shoebox. "Yes, I'm going to be an assistant groundskeeper. I like being around flowers and trees, so Mrs. Harrington thought it would be a good job for me."

"Cool, I'm finishing up at Columbia this year. Is Mrs. Harrington a friend?"

Mo runs his hands along the cover of the shoebox. "She was my sixth-grade teacher and best friends with my mother from when they were little."

"Did Mrs. Harrington come with your family to see you off at the station?"

"Mr. Branch dropped me off at the bus station, and Mrs. Harrington came to say goodbye just before I got on the bus." Mo lowers his head, voice cracking. "My mother died a long time ago, and my father died in February."

Abraham places his hand on Mo's shoulder. "I'm sorry. I lost my mother many years ago and couldn't imagine losing my father. He and I are very close. People say we share a kindred spirit. Do you have any brothers or sisters?"

The warmth of Abraham's hand blankets Mo. "My brother Jake lives with the Branch family." He's comfortable answering Abraham's questions in a way he hadn't been with Mr. Branch.

"Were you living with the Branch family, too?"

"Yes, but then I had to leave."

"Why did you have to leave?"

Mo turns to face the window. Gripping the shoebox, he places it between himself and the cold metal of the bus. "I'm sorry. I'm tired, and I don't feel like talking anymore."

"I understand. I'll be right here by your side if you need anything or just want to talk."

Forehead pressed against the bus window, Mo gazes out and considers Abraham's questions. Though different from Dr. Winchester's two days earlier, they lead to the same painful answers—answers he seeks to understand when praying. He wonders if people in Rhode Island will question him about his family and Mrs. Harrington and the Branches. Will they ask how his parents died? Will they ask about Jake? Why he came to Rhode Island? Why he had to leave Virginia?

Will they believe his answers? He wants to tell the truth. He wants to put his troubled past behind him. But he worries the truth will raise more questions. And his troubles will resurface like carcasses in the river, coming back to haunt him in his new home.

He looks across the highway to cars traveling the southbound lanes, in the direction of Virginia, wishing he were in one of those cars headed back home—back to a time when he was young, and his parents were both alive and in love.

And he was happiest.


Mo was too young to understand the circumstances surrounding his parents' marriage, Ken Lumen and Sarah Cleveland's court-ship and subsequent union having been considered scandalous in rural, post-war America, her fifteen and he a decade older. The condemned couple, their son born out of wedlock in late 1950, reconciled the pressures of biblical law and familial persuasion not long after Mo's birth. Other residents of southern Fauquier County were less forgiving.

Nestled between Warrenton and the Rappahannock River, Southern Fauquier marks the northern boundary of the Bible Belt. The seven primary towns are blessed with an abundance of pastoral beauty and rural charm. Likewise, they are plagued by their share of secrets and proverbial sins. Sinewy backroads across serene land-scapes weave a pattern of quaint indifference, delicate indulgence, and overt intolerance; God looming over the flock in the form of country spires and tutorial ministers. For deep within the recess-es of Southern Fauquier's gently rolling hills and peaceful valleys, a collection of grievances worthy of judgment rest heavily on its God-fearing inhabitants.

Whether the result of cruel fate or, as many locals believed, God's wrath, immediate misfortune descended upon the young family. The spring after Mo's birth, Sarah began experiencing mus-cle aches and fatigue. Bedridden by the time she was twenty-one, Sarah found inspiration in her only child and comfort in weekly visits from the country doctor.

On the first Friday in June 1959, eight months after hunting with his father and Earl, Mo walked home from school near the end of second grade, stopping to look into a neighbor's garden. Stretching across Mr. Ford's front yard, nestled within a white picket fence, were clusters of hyacinths and daffodils. He crouched down and placed his nose against a mass of lavender bleeding through a fence post and broken picket. He pulled the flowers to his face, the scent reminding him of a day years earlier when his mother could still stand, and his parents danced in the kitchen, Mo tucked between them. His mother's blond curls cascaded around him as he rested his head on her shoulder, the smell of lavender filling the room.

"Ouch!" Mo cried, feeling a pinch on the back of his right hand. Falling backward, he sniffled, checked the small red inflammation, and pulled out the stinger. Tears welled in his eyes as he ran home, reminding himself that gardeners love lavender for its smell, but bees need pollen to survive.

Nearing his house, Mo saw his father's pickup and a car he knew belonged to Dr. Cross in the driveway. Drying his eyes on his sleeve, Mo entered from the back porch and tiptoed through the house, stopping outside his mother's bedroom. He peeked in, finding her asleep and his father talking to the doctor.

Ken paced at the foot of the bed. "I'm not sure what all this medical mumbo jumbo means. Just tell me plain, Doc, how's she doing?"

Dr. Cross put on his glasses. "She's doing well as can be expected. Right now, I'm concerned about the weakness in the muscles that help her lungs inflate with air. She says she's in pain when she does any deep breathing and is having trouble swallowing."

"I'm guessing that ain't good?"

Dr. Cross looked at Sarah, watching the uneven rise and fall of her chest. "This is the normal progression of the disease. She's fought hard for you and Mo, but as post-polio syndrome takes hold of more and more muscles, it eventually works its way to the critical functions."

"So, what you're saying is she don't have much time?" Ken waited a few seconds for a response that didn't come. "Doc, I'm gonna need you to give it to me straight."

Dr. Cross shook his head, his eyes still fixed on Sarah's face. "No, she doesn't have much time left. We're looking at weeks, maybe a month, at best."

Mo slid down the wall until he was seated on the floor, hugging his knees, squeezing his eyes shut, and hoping the doctor was wrong. Walking by moments later, Dr. Cross tousled Mo's hair. Mo retreated to his upstairs bedroom before his father came out.

Later the same evening, after readying himself for bed, Mo came downstairs to give his parents each a goodnight kiss. Seeing the light off in his mother's bedroom, he walked to the kitchen table, where his father was seated, head in hands. He stood by his father's side until Ken looked up.

Redness surrounded his father's eyes. "Sit down, Son. We need to talk."

Mo sat in the nearest chair. He had never seen his father look so dejected.

Ken wiped a tear wedged in the corner of his eye. "Your mama's dying. Ain't nothing you or I can do about that."

Witnessing his father helpless for the first time, Mo felt a sharp pain, as if his heart and lungs were being pulled out of his chest through his mouth, and he'd have to swallow them back down.

Ken choked through his words. "She made me make three promises to her." Jaw quivering, his mouth twisted. "Your mama sure does love you, Son. She wants me to be sure and bring you to church every week. I know I ain't been good about churchgoing up to now, but I'm gonna make sure you get your Bible schooling." He looked down, rubbing his eyes. "She also wants you to talk proper. Not like me. Don't know how much I can do about it but tell you not to listen to how I talk. Don't be cussing and listen to your teachers." He turned his head, staring into Mo's eyes. "And she says she wants you to get an education. Now, Son, I don't think she's meaning practical smarts like hunting and fishing and working. But I ain't much good at book learning, so we'll just have to figure that one out as we go." He laid his head back in his hands. "Now, go on and get to bed. And don't be disturbing your mama."

Mo hugged his father before walking upstairs, where he let his sorrow collect on the pillow. The cool dampness of the pillowcase pressed against his cheek as he pleaded with God to help his mother heal and his father cope.

A week later, his mother was dead.

Mo's eyes open when he's jostled awake by a heavyset man. Abraham's gone, and the bus driver is leaning over him with his hand on Mo's shoulder. "Welcome to New York, young man."

Mo stumbles to his feet, grabs his duffel bag, and settles into the station with a dozen other less-fortunate travelers. It's a little before midnight, and his next bus doesn't depart until morning. Finding no comfort on the station's long benches, Mo surveys restless travelers spread out on the floor with their heads on their luggage and arms wrapped around their bodies. It reminds him of the cold cement in Mr. Branch's office.

Mo shudders at the thought of those nights alone with Dion, each summer evening starting out hot and sticky before growing cold and damp in the early morning darkness. He would pull a lambskin blanket close to his body and listen to Dion's relaxed breaths. Lying on his cot—an island of isolation—and forbidden from touching anything, Mo spent long, anxious nights awaiting his fate.

# THE GIRL WHO MOVED ONE STOOL OVER

## SUNDAY, 17 AUGUST 1975

P*almer's an enigmatologist.* By age eight, he and his mother would work together at the dining room table assembling 1,000-piece jigsaw puzzles. On Sundays, he'd sit on his father's lap, helping with the newspaper crossword until he could do them himself. To this day, there's always a puzzle in process on his own table, an unfinished crossword on his nightstand, and more significant problems occupying his mind: sexual predators, child molesters, and mass murderers. Monsters.

Palmer views the world around him as a giant riddle, each individual a piece of a puzzle, a square in a crossword. Those he encounters offer clues: a number, an article of clothing, or a significant feature. In his efforts to protect society, he does not see the humanity, his preoccupation with the villains and the victims, not the bystanders. When he does remember a name, it's out of repetition or dependence. He has few close friends.

Early evening, Palmer peels himself out of bed, showers, and packs his bags, arriving at SeaTac three hours before departure. Grabbing a newspaper, he sits at the airport bar. Two dozen crossword clues and three shots later, the pair of glistening pink lips at the other end is winking. But it isn't Saturday night, and he hasn't had enough liquor. He slides the bartender a twenty and points in her direction, figuring she got what she came for.

Walking through the terminal, he reaches into his shirt pocket and grabs a smoke, stopping a flight attendant rushing by to ask for a light. She strikes a match and holds out the flame. He steadies her hand, pulling on his cigarette while returning her gaze. She hands him the matchbook. They exchange fleeting smiles and knowing glances. Yeah, he hopes he comes back to Seattle. There's a monster on the loose, but he's dormant. Palmer can't get the bastard out of his head.

Shuttling through first-class, passing by the privileged passengers with their cocktails, Palmer's throat feels dry as the well in Bellevue Square. The passenger in 14D, a big guy with a crew cut and blood-shot eyes, stands, permitting Palmer access to his middle seat. When 14D sits back down, the seat rest feels like it's going to give.

The middle-aged woman with savagely tapered eyebrows in 14F lets out a small yelp. Settling back with her crochet hook, she resets a wayward length of yarn. "It's a hat for my grandson. My daughter named him Darren."

Palmer nods, setting his coffee in the cupholder between them.

14F's hands spin and tug, her eyebrows resting like a boxer be-tween rounds. "She lives in Quincy. Her husband's got a good job, you know, an accountant for some very important men." Nudging Palmer, she winks, her weaving unaffected. "Met him when I went out there for the wedding three years ago. Seems nice—tall, dark, handsome, quiet type. My daughter calls every week and sounds happy. All a mother could ask for."

Palmer smiles, hopelessly scanning the plane for an empty seat. He releases the chokehold on his coffee cup, pulls his elbow out from under 14D's side, and lifts the pack of Marlboros out of his pocket, his fingers fumbling for the matchbook.

"Oh, dear, I wish you wouldn't." 14F's brows flatten under the creases in her forehead. "My husband died of lung cancer five years ago. I quit smoking, but it's still hard for me to talk to someone when they're having a cigarette without wanting one myself."

Palmer stares at the unattached and still unlit match, his fingers twitching as he turns to her. Eyes resigned even before they catch the interwoven gray in her hair, he drops the match, checks his watch, and folds his arms.

Visits from a Nordic-looking stewardess with polyester lashes are too infrequent, her conditional attention and prerequisite smile what he desires most. He hands her an empty cup or crushed napkin with the same emotion as if money were changing hands in a hotel room after the lights come on.

Ninety minutes into the flight and 14F's monologue, he excuses himself, tapping 14D's shoulder. 14D opens his eyes, frowns, and steps into the aisle, pulling the seatback in front of him as he rises. A balding man with ferret eyes looks back, swallows his courage with a nervous gulp, and resumes reading. Palmer thanks 14D as he squeezes by.

The rear of the plane is a sanctuary—a respite from the confined quarters and deep-rooted apathy his assigned seat dictates. Standing in the back of the plane, he knows there's no rule or sign posted suggesting a two-cigarette limit. It's more of an informal understanding between the flight crew and passengers. Palmer decides this once he'll go three deep. Polyester Lashes, uniform snug and charms apparent, is fluttering with intent and mercifully sparse with her words. He reaches for a fourth, but the Italian stewardess with sausage eyes bumps him from behind with the breakfast cart. He knows it's too early for a morning meal but takes the hint, heading back to his seat.

Aware 14F's watching him buckle, Palmer feels the anticipation in her staggered breaths as he fumbles with the belt.

Like turning an engine, a click starts her back up. "I hope it's not as humid this time. I went to the wedding three years ago, and it was so humid, the frosting on the cake was sweating." She chuckles.

Still gripping the buckle, Palmer turns and smiles. "I'm sorry, what was your name?"

"Agatha, dear. Agatha Rothschild."

"Hi, Agatha, I'm Francis. I apologize for talking your ear off. I should—"

Her eyebrows rise. "But, dear, you haven't spoken a word."

"Yes, but I've kept you from your business there." He points to her ball of yarn.

"Oh, this?" She chuckles again. "I can do this with my eyes closed."

"I believe you can." Palmer nods. "I'm sorry, but I need to review some documents for a morning meeting; otherwise, I'd love to keep chatting with you through the remainder of the flight."

14F stows her chuckles, eyebrows pained. "Oh, dear, I'm sorry. I get so nervous when I fly, and I get chatty. My husband would tell me all the time." She unwraps her finger, patting Palmer's hand resting on his cold cup of coffee. "You go right ahead, dear."

Palmer watches her fingers reset, the ferocious arch in her brows returning. He wonders how many hats her grandson will need.

Reaching down to retrieve his briefcase, Palmer pulls out several folders and turns on the reading light. From the list of twenty-six probable suspects, King County detectives and Seattle police had their pools, a little side action for potential profit off others' losses. He had his eye on one highlighted name.

Opening another folder, Palmer flips through the victim profiles in Washington and Oregon. Then the next, looking at the young faces of girls dead or presumed dead in Utah and Colorado, one only twelve. Pauline was just a year younger when he took the girls to the grand opening of Disney World.

Palmer had been detoxifying after a brutal case and some poor judgment on the Cape. Marilyn, recovering from the aftereffects, needed some space. He understood his wife was the real wounded warrior in the family: absorbing his long absences, emotional torment, and combat fatigue—each case a different battle in an unending war. He put on the stripes; she put on the miles.

Palmer remembers Pauline's smile, her auburn hair long and straight like her mother's as she twirled around in the teacups. He struggled to keep his focus on his girls as Peggy spun the wheel faster. With all the pain and uncertainty surrounding him at the time, he refrained from drinking the entire week and cherished each moment until the next psychopath emerged, when he'd once again be called upon to descend into depravity.

Flipping from one photo to the next, Palmer sees a reflection of his daughters' faces in the eyes of every victim, feels Ted's anger and maligned motives each time his thumb presses against an image, and senses the Monster's wrath in the air—even in the stale, recirculated air of the plane. He hopes Ted's tail stays attached. And he fears for any girl crossing The Monster's path. But he'll be back in Boston in two hours, not in Seattle or Salt Lake. Mumbling to himself, he closes the folders, the voice in his head responding. *Fuck!*

Two hours later, Palmer's not asleep. His eyelids are half-closed, but he's not sleeping. Enough light penetrates the lower half of his pupils to catch two nips in front of his face. Opening his eyes, he smiles at Polyester Lashes, taking the mini bottles from her outstretched hand and placing them in his lap. She smiles back. Focusing on the bottles, she gives him a slight nod. He turns them over to find a telephone number scribbled on the back of one. Looking up, he raises his eyebrows. She smiles wider, nodding more pronounced. He winks. She heads back to the rear of the cabin. His eyelids return to half-mast.

A few short minutes pass before Palmer, still restless and hearing rhythmic wheezing, checks on 14F out the side of his nearly shut eye. Satisfied she's asleep, her brows at peace, he looks out the cabin window, discovering city lights just south of the plane. Toronto shines like a beacon. He recalls a friend from school, a Toronto native, who lit up every campus social event and college mixer. With two nips of whiskey in his lap, a full pack of Marlboros in his pocket, and 14F snoring like a stoned weasel, Palmer decides to throw a small party over Lake Ontario. He doubts 14D will much care, and there isn't enough liquor for the big guy anyway.

Celebration over quickly, Palmer pushes 14F's crochet hook aside to squeeze his finished cigarette into the ashtray before slipping the empty bottles in the seat pocket in front of him. He stares at the caps peeking up, thinking back to the only other time a woman paid for his drinks. It was years ago, but it feels like last night. She clings to him everywhere he goes, into every bar and back to every hotel room. And she changed his view of everything.

The bar was empty, late enough on a Monday night that even the regulars had stumbled home from this Podunk dive. She moved just one stool over. He didn't budge. She talked too much, the little mole above her lip hopping to the local plumber-turned-lounge-singer's interpretation of Mel Tormé, but Palmer wasn't using his ears. Not in *this* joint and not with *that* singer. Pretending to laugh at her anecdotes—the ones he couldn't hear anyway—he tossed back a few worthless lines about some nine-to-five office job he'd read about and accepted her charity: a string of Glenmorangie shots he'd never tab up for on a Monday night—any night for that matter. Her outfit was tight, looked straight off a Paris runway, and her jewelry set a proud papa back more than a few of the finest bottles in his private wine cellar. The offspring of excess, Palmer wondered why this girl would be in this dump at any time, but why, of all nights, a Monday night.

By one thirty, the lounge singer was back in his bed tossing and turning through some pipe dreams, the jukebox was skipping through *Rags to Riches* with Tony Bennett, and Palmer's lady friend was signing the tab—daddy's good faith extending even here. As they walked out, he knew he'd not soon forget her scent of lilac and leather, eyes of a cheetah, and hair that spilled off her shoulders like the silk tassels of a brown throw draped over a chair. He also knew it was better she was leaving with him than risk some night-crawler without a proper strategy. He'd take her home and treat her nice—nice enough to make her papa proud—maybe make him proud enough to pop open one of those expensive bottles of wine.

She drove his car, saying she'd get a ride back in the morning. She didn't live in a dorm. Not out there. No dorms that far along the neck where she lived. And it didn't matter if she wasn't in college. He was educated enough for both of them. He'd be happy to share his formal education. But he didn't need to; she had home-schooled smarts. By the time the apartment door clicked shut, her lips were locked as well, and the remnant oral mix of dirty martinis and pretentious scotch created an exhilarating Rob Roy with vodka chaser, further fueling their desire.

When he woke up five hours later, she was asleep on the bed face down next to him and their clothes were comingled on the floor in the aftermath of a lust-driven tornado, her jewelry intertwined with his keys on the bathroom counter. He emptied the tank he hadn't drained last night, checked the bite marks on his neck and chest, and got dressed. Walking through the living room, her ride back stood by the sofa in a morning coat and curlers, mouth agape, coffee spilling from her mug. He gave a quick nod as he passed, thinking better of The Girl Who Moved One Stool Over. *Maybe this wasn't who she was,* he thought. *Perhaps she was overcome with grief—a death in the family, dumped by a boyfriend.* It didn't matter, though. He left knowing this was a one-night excursion—one never to be repeated and one hard to surpass. He didn't get her name, didn't try to remember the street. But he couldn't forget her scent, her eyes, or her hair, even if he wanted to. And he didn't.

The disturbance caused when 14D gets out of his seat is sufficient to snap Palmer back into the present but not enough to break 14F's snoring. Palmer lights a cigarette and looks out the window. He knows they're somewhere between Syracuse and Albany, maybe near Utica. It doesn't matter. It's not where he should be. It's someplace between Seattle and Boston. Someplace between where he was and where he's going. Someplace between where he wants to be and where he has to be. And it's just a city, or a town, or a Podunk bar in a place he's not supposed to be.

Watching the smoke rise from his cigarette, Palmer contemplates the life he might've had with The Girl Who Moved One Stool Over. She was exciting, exotic, and charitable. She was perfect— perfect for that night. She was drunk, desperate, and nowhere. She was trouble—trouble down the road. Palmer looks over 14F's ball of yarn into the empty darkness pressing against the plexiglass. He's somewhere, but it's nowhere that matters to him—like the girl and the stool and the Podunk dive. They're somewhere. And it shouldn't matter to him. But it still does.

- 5 -

# THE MAN BEHIND
# THE MEAT COUNTER

## SUNDAY, 17 AUGUST 1975

M*o leaves Manhattan at dawn.* Climbing aboard the Greyhound to Providence after a sleepless night, he pulls a sandwich from his bag, staying awake long enough to see the 'Welcome to New England' sign as the bus crosses into Connecticut. From there, he sleeps straight through. He sleeps the uncomfortable sleep that comes with sitting on a bus. He sleeps the uneasy sleep that comes with a new home. He sleeps the terrified sleep of being alone. And he dreams. He dreams of what Rhode Island will bring, his hopes and fears conditioned by pleasant and unpleasant memories from Virginia.

For all his anticipation and anxiety, Mo is unaware that exchanging Virginia's pastures for Rhode Island's piers will subject him to relentless interrogation. Residents of the Northeast, steeped in legend and folklore, are hearty and suspicious, welcoming newcomers only after sufficient scrutiny. From the fisherman yarns in Stonington to the witch trials of Salem, New Englanders exalt in their piety, revel in their iniquity, and preserve their distinctions with prejudice. Every forest harbors a mythical creature. Every stream offers a chilling tale of resurrection. Into this boiling pot of incantation and indulgence, he unwittingly commends himself.

Spending just enough time at the Providence station to walk off the disorientation from his sleeping and dreaming, Mo finds himself alone on the connecting bus to Smithfield. He sits in the last row, staring out the rear window at the city skyscrapers he's leaving behind. The bus pulls onto the same 95 North as the first Greyhound in Fredericksburg as he journeys ever closer to a new home. Will he find happiness here or more sorrow? Will the residents of Rhode Island accept him or treat him differently? Will this be a new beginning or lead to more of the same misunderstandings, accusations, and abandonment?

Pulling his knees to his chest, resting his heels on the seat cushion, and wrapping his arms around his legs, Mo parks his questions in Providence. With the early morning sandwich contributing to an unsettled stomach, he starts a car game he and his brother would play in the front seat of their father's pickup. Wishing Jake was there, he pounds his fist into his own hand, counting thirty punch buggies by the time the bus pulls into Smithfield Station.

A middle-aged pirate draped in a red, oversized bellman coat stands near the bus door holding a small, whiteboard sign. Scribbled at the top is Mo's name; beneath, in much smaller printed letters—*Smithfield Inn*. Mo waves as he approaches.

Unenthused, The Pirate nods. "You Maurice Lumen?"

"Yes, sir." Mo wrinkles his nose.

"Need any help with your bags?" Without waiting for a response, The Pirate retreats, carrying just his sign. "Hurry up!" he says. "It's about ten minutes to the inn."

Mo opens the rear door. A pile of dirty clothes and the stench of sour armpit spill out. "Can I sit in the front seat?"

"Sure. Where you from?"

"Virginia."

"Mm-hmm."

With that, the conversation ends, and an uncomfortable silence settles in.

Absorbing the landscape, it appears to Mo every bit as pretty as Virginia, just as Mrs. Harrington promised five days earlier in the Branches' dining room. Although she was excited to deliver the news of his new job in Rhode Island, Mrs. Harrington did not seem well. He felt her weight lean against the back of his chair as she spoke. Her body shook when she struggled to rise after crouching down to comfort Jake. Later, as they spoke alone outside, Mo helped her regain her balance when she stumbled on the gravel. She assured him she was fine. It had just been a busy week, and she was very tired. But the unevenness of her breathing accompanied by a strange rasp in her voice made him doubt her words for the first time. Both understood the circumstances surrounding his exodus were troubling.

Predating the American Revolution, the Smithfield Inn is a colonial gem, albeit a shadow of its former glory. Curled paint and rusted nails suggest the passing of many unyielding seasons. Looking up at three stories of white clapboard and green shutters, Mo can't help but compare the Smithfield Inn to the only hotel in southern Fauquier. An eight-room, single-story motel with all the charm of a laundromat, the Fauquier Motor Lodge had been an enticing roadside stop in its early years after World War II before turning into a local refuge for the afflicted, disparaged, and abandoned by the early 1960s.

Ascending the stairs to the Smithfield Inn's wraparound porch, Mo recalls the time he and his father retrieved Earl Johnson from the Fauquier Motor Lodge the day after Earl's wife threw him out. Told to keep the windows up and car doors locked, Mo waited while his father went inside and talked to Earl.

When they emerged from the hotel room, Mo saw Mr. Johnson's reddened face and unsteady walk as he approached the car, his father helping Earl into the front seat. Looking over Mr. Johnson's head, Mo saw a woman wearing only a bra and panties leaning against the door of another room. She held a cigarette in one hand and a half-full bottle in the other. The Fauquier Motor Lodge and The Woman Leaning Against the Door would become enduring images of despair.

Years later, lying on his cot in Mr. Branch's office, aware the Branch parents wanted him to leave, Mo would worry about ending up at Southern Fauquier's only motel. He enters the lobby of the

Smithfield Inn, feeling the scars of his abandonment and hoping the well-worn clapboard of this hotel holds more promise than the red brick of the Fauquier Motor Lodge.

Standing beside the counter, a man with a worn smile and ill-behaved eyebrows wears colonial attire. "Good afternoon, sir. Checking in?"

"Yes, sir. My name is Mo, uh, Maurice Lumen." Noticing the man's gray skin and many wrinkles, Mo pictures him as a skinny elephant in the circus before the hotel was built.

The man's unruly eyebrows rise and fall as he turns the pages of a reservation tablet. "Here we go. I have you here for one night in a nice room with a double bed on the third floor. It's prepaid, so if you just sign here, our bellman will show you to your room and help you with your luggage."

The bellman, a skeleton as old as the hotel, guides Mo into a gilded, caged elevator where an egg-shaped man of similar vintage sports a faded blue jacket and stubby round hat. The elevator operator wobbles like one of Jake's Weebles as they ascend to the third floor. Mo wonders if the people who work in this hotel are ghosts or live forever.

Setting Mo's luggage near the bed, The Skeleton dangles a key with one hand while offering the other palm up.

Noticing The Skeleton's bony fingers, Mo thanks him and takes the key.

The Skeleton runs his hand across his shirt. "Just ring down if you need anything," he says, turning to leave.

Mo places his hand on The Skeleton's shoulder. "Excuse me, sir, where can I get something to eat?"

The Skeleton peers over his shoulder, staring at Mo from the edge of his lifeless eyes. "There's a restaurant on the first floor. Meals are included with your room, so you'll just have to sign the check." He continues out the door, his droning voice hanging in the room with the scent of incense. "Maybe you could remember to tip the waiter."

Watching The Skeleton lumber down the hall, shirt puffing out of his baggy pants, Mo wishes his clothes were as comfortable.

Closing the door, Mo ponders what it means to 'tip the waiter.' He had seldom eaten at a sit-down restaurant after his mother died and not at all from the time he got hurt. Instead, he and his father would often stop by the deli to get sandwiches. After greeting the man behind the meat counter, they'd share a few laughs before his father would reach across to collect the packages. Was something his father said, maybe 'thanks,' considered tipping? The Man Behind the Meat Counter always seemed happy to see his father, except the last time—the one time his father did not thank him.

Considering the restaurant downstairs and still uncertain what tipping is, Mo imagines the waiter and himself facing each other at the end of the meal like the Nazis in his father's favorite war movies: clicking their heels, holding out their palms, and bending at the waist.

After lunch, Mo heads out to the walkways weaving through the hotel property. Crossing a wooden bridge that separates the hotel's parking lots and open fields from its wooded boundary, he sees fathers and sons fishing in the stream below. Mo and his father had a favorite fishing spot under Kelly's Ford Bridge on the Rappahannock River. They went many weekends with Earl before Jake was born. One particular outing, on the last Saturday in September 1959, several months after his mother's death, occupies Mo's thoughts as he enters the woods.

Ken attached a lure to Mo's hook and cast the line. "Mo, d'ya know how the Rappahannock got its name?"

"No, sir."

"It was named by the Algonquin Indians and means 'river of quick-rising water.'" Ken leaned Mo's fishing pole against a low-hanging branch and wedged the handle against a rock. "It floods about every ten years and sure wreaks havoc." Popping the top off a fresh beer, he took a gulp. "Gets pretty bad down here in the slums. Water goes right up over this here bridge and backs up into Tinpot Alley. When it's real bad, like it was four years ago, you can't even see the houses no more. That's why the Coloreds and poor White folk live down here." He looked at Earl. "Yeah, Kelly's Ford Bridge here's only good for fishing under and driving over to Culpeper."

Earl cleared the suds from his throat. "The local Negroes have some voodoo legend about a dragon that lives in the river near here and rises up, flooding everything when it's angry. They say God blesses the land, or something, in order to absorb the waters."

"Dunno about that, and don't think it does the Coloreds down here no good." Ken shook his head. "My daddy," he pointed the top of his bottle at Mo, "your grandpappy, and his daddy before him, would tell me stories about how they'd come down and see the critters here in Tinpot Alley all tangled up in them trees on that little island in the middle of the river right there. Hair on those critters not brown, though. No, sir, black as coal—black-haired critters, they was." He winked at Earl. "The local White folks would cut 'em loose and let those carcasses float downriver. Smell that stench all the way to Fredericksburg, and then it'd be gone. But it's never gone from here in Tinpot Alley, and you can smell it even when the river's not flooding."

Mo knew the smell of animal carcasses along the water from a big flood four years earlier. He tried to think of animals with black hair: Earl's Labrador, a few horses on Old Man Southerland's farm, skunks, and maybe some dirty, old rats. He wondered why the brown and light-haired animals were able to avoid getting hung up. He wondered if, with his black hair, he'd get caught up in the trees if he lived in Tinpot Alley. And he wondered whether his father would save *him* if there were a flood.

"No, sir, the Rappahannock ain't done the Blackies no good," Ken said. "But it's sure been treating us right. The Flood of '55 been keeping all us construction folks going strong." Ken raised his bottle, and Earl joined him. "In fact, with the extra hours and doctor bills paid off, I been able to save a little over the past few months." He paused. "Earl, how about that business thing we been talking about?"

Mo had heard his father talk to Earl about going into business for the past few months and liked the way Ken's eyes brightened when he did.

Earl grabbed another beer from the cooler, his voice shaky. "Think we can do it?"

Ken's eyes followed the ripples of the water downstream. "Dunno, but seems like a good time to give it a try. Eisenhower says the economy's downright strong, and it's gonna keep on that way, so if we're gonna do it, then we best be doing it sooner rather than later."

Earl straightened up. "You know what? You're right. No time like the present."

"Alright, then, we'll give notice on Monday." With the Rappahannock reflecting in Ken's brown eyes, they shone their brightest in months.

Earl pulled the bottle from his mouth. "M-Monday?"

"Well, it's almost October, so if we're gonna do this, we have to get some work lined up before winter sets in."

Eyes wide, Mo pushed away from the tree. "Daddy, can I come to work with you and Mr. Johnson?"

"Not just yet, Son. Maybe next summer or a Saturday after me and Earl start working for ourselves." Ken's gaze passed by Mo as he looked across the water.

"I'd like to come along." Standing up, Mo puffed out his chest. "I'm big enough now to help with the tools."

Earl laughed. "Might need him to do some work at that."

Ken nodded, smiling at Mo. "Reckon we just might."

Mo sat back down and watched his line, leaving the men to drink their alcohol, strategize, and philosophize.

"I got an idea." Ken set his beer down. "You know how I been going to church every Sunday with Mo and Sarah's mom?"

"Yeah?" Earl tossed his empty bottle near the others collecting at the base of a tree.

"Well, I promised Sarah I'd take Mo to church every Sunday, so we been going to Sumerduck Baptist. Been getting to know some of the folks there pretty well after services."

"So, you think you could talk to some of them about some work?"

"Yeah, but I got a better idea." Ken picked up a twig, started tapping it on the ground. "If I drop Sarah's mom off at church here in town, Mo and I can rotate to each of the other Baptist churches in Fauquier and get to know folks at all of 'em." He pointed the twig at Earl. "*You* could do it, too."

Earl stopped mid-swig. "Ken, you know I don't do the church thing."

Ken laughed. "C'mon, Earl, it gives us *both* a better reason to go to church. Might even do you some good."

Earl guzzled the rest of a nearly full bottle. "Well, if you think it'll help, but I ain't the talker you are."

"That's okay. We'll get K&E Construction painted on our trucks and include our phone number, too, so they at least see us around. It's just good advertising."

A wide smile crossed Earl's face. "Why not E&K Construction?"

Ken scratched the inside of his ear with the twig. "Cuz it sounds dumb. Now I think about it; plum makes sense to post a letter of advertising on each of the bulletin boards of those seven churches." His brows furrowed, he turned to Mo. "I wonder if your mama knew what she was doing when she made me make that promise."

Back on the Smithfield Inn's wraparound porch, Mo relaxes in a rocking chair after dinner and reflects on quiet afternoons in Virginia and his time spent sitting along the Rappahannock behind the Branch home. Watching the river flow, he'd contemplate who else might see the same ripples farther downstream, speculate whether they felt as alone as he did in those hours by the river, and wonder if they'd join him on a raft as he floated by.

Rocking and thinking, despite other travelers sitting nearby, Mo once again feels alone, just as he did even when Dion sat next to him along the bank of the river. He misses his home—not the Branch house, but his parents' home. And he wishes he were back where he was born.

Mrs. Harrington had been there for his final moments in Virginia. She attracted his attention as he stood in line to board the bus. Approaching her, he observed the frailty of her body, the thinness of her blond hair, and caked red blush on her cheeks. He noted how his grandmother looked the same when she was sick. Following a comforting hug, Mrs. Harrington kissed him on the cheek, wished him luck, and said goodbye. He checked the boarding line, hoping the bus would leave so he could stay with her family. When he turned back, her hands trembled as she gave him the present. He returned to a much shorter line. Smiling from the sidewalk, she waved as he placed his belongings in the overhead. The glare of another bus passing erased her. When it was gone, so was her smile. Mo scanned the sidewalk, his heart racing, but she had disappeared.

Resting in his rocking chair, Mo hopes he'll see her again. And as daylight turns to darkness, his rocking chair slows before becoming still.

# 6

# MURPHY'S ALLERGIES

## MONDAY, 18 AUGUST 1975

*almer does not mistake the Boston skyline for Seattle's.* Descending into Logan, he looks out over the city and laments. Buildings here are square, bland, traditional, remnants of a puritanical bias toward simple conformance, minimalist architecture, and lack of creative risk-taking. There's no Space Needle piercing skyward, nor Kingdome under construction. Hell, the city's professional football team plays home games at a nondescript cement trough in a cow field an hour away.

The dim morning light and early offshore cloud cover settle between the red brick and brownstone facades, hiding grimy downtown streets and seedy alleys, but Fenway Park still shines. Boston and its residential suburbs have been home to Palmer since childhood, though this does not blind him to its corrupt political infrastructure, neighborhood violence, and systemic racism. Still, Boston's where his apartment is. And even if it no longer feels like home, there's something to be said for the city's history, emerging subculture, and ethnic diversity.

Wheels bouncing along the runway, 14D grips the armrest so tight Palmer can take his pulse through the big man's elbow. Palmer smiles at 14F before holding a napkin to his nose as passengers rising from their cloth seats release six hours of pent-up anxiety. Noticing the twist-on caps still staring at him from the seat pocket, he pushes the empty bottles down and follows 14D to the exit, preferring to buy his own drinks.

It's two miles from Logan to the FBI Field Office as the crow flies, but more than twice the driving distance on Boston's antiquated inner-city streets. It's not a scenic drive any time of day. At six in the morning, it's depressing. Narrow one-ways are littered with delivery and garbage trucks—and litter. Palmer thinks back to trips into the city with his father to watch games at Fenway. He doesn't remember so much trash in the late forties when Ted Williams reigned. He opens his morning paper to check on the Red Sox and to block his view.

Murphy's office is almost empty. His nameplate looks to be the last item to go in the box sitting behind his desk. It rests near his arm as if one simple swipe and he'd be off. The only other thing he owns in the room is the smoke tinting the ceiling tiles.

Palmer owes his habit to Richard Murphy, following his boss up the ranks for two decades. This morning, when he enters, he sees Murphy rubbing his cheeks and staring out the window.

Murphy points with his thumb at the desk behind him. "Help yourself to a smoke." Continuing to look out over the city, he sighs. "Sorry, Francis, it was out of my hands. Seattle's pressing its authority, and the big boys are trolling from their new Hoover palace in DC."

Palmer shakes his head, pulls out a Marlboro. "When did you start smoking lights?"

"Ah, my wife's been on my case since the doctor said my blood pressure's too high." Murphy's voice is coarse.

"Damn, Dick, what's she worried about?" Palmer taps the tobacco end of his cigarette on the desk. "You're gonna live to a hundred."

Murphy turns his chair. "That's what she's afraid of." His thick, white eyebrows separate. "She's planning on making it to a hundred-and-twenty. Says she already lived enough years alone." He coughs into his hand, a soft wheeze followed by a full-blown, phlegm-driven duck call—a cough resulting from self-diagnosed allergies. The rest of his doctor's concerns won't be shared. Neither is fooling the other amid the fog in this room.

They laugh. Palmer remembers when Murphy's eyebrows were

black, and his voice could match Sinatra note for note.

"They want you to submit." Murphy presses half a cigarette into the ashtray. "Director's demanding it."

"He can demand all he wants." Palmer releases a narrow white stream toward the yellowed ceiling light. "I'm not interested. I saw what this job did to you." He takes another drag and exhales. "He can threaten to break me. I don't give a shit. I like it right where I'm at."

"Where's that, Francis? Where you at?"

"I'm right here with you, Dick, living the dream."

Murphy lights another Newport. "They couldn't hold him. You know that, right?"

Palmer squints, his dark-blue eyes turning black. "Yeah, I know, evading an officer. Really?"

"Well, at least he's been flushed. Truly believe it's him?"

"I'd stake my career on it."

"But there's nothing to pin on him."

Palmer taps his finger on the desk before standing. "Not yet, but it's there. I'm certain."

Murphy turns to the window. "I don't doubt it."

Palmer heads to the door. "I need to get out there. I'll find what we need. If they'd have let me trail him for a month in rentals, I'd have caught the prick red-handed. Small price to pay to save some college girls' lives." He turns back before leaving. "I'm gonna go over your head. I need this. I can't get this sick son of a bitch out of my head."

Murphy pulls at the hair under his chin. "You won't be going over my head in a couple of weeks, but I'd still advise against it." Turning to face Palmer, he wastes another cigarette in the ashtray. "They're gonna be so pissed, you'll be lucky to get out of there with your badge."

Palmer laughs. "Sometimes, I think you're being serious." He exits, drafting a cloud of smoke through the office cubicles and knowing he'll take Dick's advice. He almost always has.

# 7

# SUITE FIFTEEN BARRINGTON

## MONDAY, 18 AUGUST 1975

*M*o *paces the deck of the Smithfield Inn's back porch a full hour before an escort from Bryant College is scheduled to arrive.* After multiple trips to the lobby bathroom, and with saliva pooling in his mouth, he uses one of the hotel's distressed columns to relieve his anxiety, picking at flakes of paint and watching them collect on the decking. Many years ago, he grew impatient waiting for his father in K&E's first new truck out front of a customer's house.

It was the summer of 1960, and a minuscule hole on the dashboard above the glove box drew his attention. At first, he used his fingernail to pull the vinyl over and close the hole, but as he tugged, the hole grew. Vinyl gave way to foam cushion, and it became easier to dig down. He decided to find out how far he could dig before hitting metal.

By the time his father came out, the almost imperceptible pinhole had become large enough to wiggle his finger around and deep enough to bury a knuckle. He would remember that hole, and his father's belt, each time he noticed something that needed mending around the house.

Mo's hard work on the hotel column clears a sizeable area down to bare wood in little time. A hotel staffer offers him something to drink, politely requesting he not disturb the woodwork. Nodding while he takes the glass, Mo blushes as he sits in a rocking chair.

Twenty minutes later, just before nine, a white pickup arrives. A tall, sturdy man in blue chino pants and matching shirt steps out and walks over, smiling and pointing as he gets closer. "Maurice Lumen?"

Standing at the base of the stairs, Mo nods. Along with the man's name patch—*Boss Griffin*—the 'B' on his baseball cap reminds him of Sam. He wonders if this Black man also played for the Baltimore Elite Giants.

"My name is Derek Griffin." He clasps Mo's hand in an uncompromising grip. "I'm the head groundskeeper at Bryant College. I'm here to bring you back to the school. I was told to look for a very tall, young White man." He shakes his head, eyes wide. "Man, they weren't lying."

Mo smiles, thinking maybe the 'B' stands for Bryant. "Hello, Mr. Griffin." He notes his new boss is also tall, though several inches shorter than himself. "I'm Mo, and I'm going to work really hard for you." He's surprised by the welcoming sincerity of Griffin's handshake. It doesn't seem at all like Mr. Branch's two days earlier.

"I'm glad to hear it. This yours?" Griffin tucks Mo's duffel bag under his arm while inspecting his new worker. "Son, you're gonna come in handy when it comes to moving rocks. C'mon, get in the truck." He tosses Mo's bag in the bed of his pickup and climbs in. "You like baseball?"

Mo settles into the passenger seat. "A little. My dad used to listen to the Washington Senators sometimes."

Key at the ready, Griffin holds it near the ignition. "Well, you're in Red Sox country now, and we all don't much like the Orioles, Tigers, Indians, or Brewers, but we downright hate the Yankees."

Mo is attentive, ensuring Griffin is done with all his disliking and hating before speaking. "I haven't followed baseball since I was little."

Griffin chuckles. "Son, I don't expect you were ever little, but you're gonna start following now. Sox are in a good position. I think this might be their year. Been more than fifty years since we won us a World Series, back when Babe was in Beantown, but I got a feeling this year." He turns the ignition and raises the radio volume.

Sports talk on the truck radio, Mo's eyes are drawn to Griffin's hand on the wheel, the pink of his palm peeking out between the black of his hand and the dark-blue steering wheel.

Sam never drove the work trucks when he worked for Mo's father in the early 1960s. He didn't even own a vehicle. One of Sam's neighbors would drop him off at the Sumerduck store, leaving him to walk the last quarter mile to the Lumen house. Sometimes, Mo would meet him at the store, and they'd walk together, Sam telling stories about his days in the Negro Leagues and the great Black ballplayers of the forties, fifties, and early sixties.

Mo last saw Sam on February eighth, the day Mo's father was buried.

Sam stood by Mo during the short memorial. He wasn't wearing his Baltimore cap.

Mo could see patches of his hair graying.

"I'm sorry about your dad," Sam said when the service ended. "He was a good businessman."

Mo wanted to smile but struggled with the paradox of joy and sorrow, choosing instead to nod.

Sam pointed at Jake. "Who's this with you?"

"This is my brother, Jake."

Sam gave Mo's younger brother a nod. "How d'ya do, son?"

Jake waved and walked to Mr. Branch's waiting station wagon.

Sam scratched his head, his eyes following Jake. "That the boy born to your daddy and that Clara lady?"

"Yes, he's eleven."

"Hmm, he done near all grown up. Crazy how fast time flies, huh, Mr. Mo?"

Despite his sadness, Mo couldn't help but smile at Sam's use of his old nickname. "How have you been?"

"I been okay. Got a masonry job up in Warrenton. Been there near about ten years. How about you? You got a job?"

Mo thought Sam looked smaller, but his voice sounded the same, and his eyes were still bright. "I help my brother with his paper route."

"Well, if you ever need a job, just let me know. I'll put in a good word with the boss." Sam took a step back, rubbing his chin. "Geez, you're built like a plow horse. Bet you'd be right useful moving brick and block."

Mo shook his head. "My brother needs me to help deliver all those papers."

"Ever get a chance to play ball?" Sam's eyes filled with hope.

"Nope. Dad never did let me."

"Not in high school or nothing?"

"I didn't go to high school."

"That's too bad. Bet you could have hit the ball a country mile." Sam pulled his tattered cap from his back pocket and placed it on his head. Mo noticed the torn stitching, the red 'B' curling at the edges. "Yes, sir, I'd like to have seen that." Then, Sam turned and walked away.

Mr. Branch didn't stand by the grave for the ceremony. He said he didn't like the cold, choosing instead to wait in the car with the engine running. He came over just after Sam left, rubbing his coat sleeves. "Who's that, Mo?"

Mo's eyes followed Sam. "He used to work for my father."

"That was a long time ago, huh?" Mr. Branch looked at Mo from above his elongated, black-rimmed spectacles. "You don't see him anymore?"

Mo turned to Mr. Branch. "No, sir. He was a friend of mine."

"So, he *used* to be your friend?" Mr. Branch's placid brown eyes aligned with his pencil-thin nose. "That means he won't be coming around the house, *right?*"

"No, sir."

Mr. Branch nodded. "Okay, let's go home. Your brother's already in the car."

Mo climbed into the backseat of the Branch family station wagon, wishing Sam could still be a part of his life. He looked out the rear window, watching Sam's figure get smaller as the car pulled away until he disappeared altogether.

Mo emerges from his thoughts when Griffin lowers the radio

and informs him they've arrived, the trip to Bryant College being a short one. Driving by the school's entrance, Mo marvels at the wide, brown sign.

At the end of a long, wooded road, Griffin points to a sprawling brick building with a large glass dome. "There's the Unistructure up ahead. It's where all the classrooms and faculty offices are located. It also has the library, theater, game room, dining hall, and student gathering area called the Rotunda."

Mo leans forward, holding his hand up to shield the sun. "It's so big. It looks like a hospital."

"I suppose there's more than enough academic heartburn and indigestion for students in there." Griffin chuckles. "At least Student Health Services is there, too." He points out the driver's side window. "That's the central campus pond. The fountain's forty feet high."

"Wow, this whole place is a school?"

"Sure is." Griffin points out the passenger window. "Student dormitories and the new gymnasium are over there." Parking in front of the Unistructure, he leads Mo along a brick walkway at the edge of the pond to a wrought-iron archway with open gates. "Students don't pass under this arch until they graduate. Legend says it's the gateway to their future. But, if students walk through it before they graduate, it becomes a portal to their past." He winks. "The boys and I sometimes walk under it during the summer when nobody's looking."

Smiling, Mo hides his fear of what *he* might see from his past if he walked through the archway.

Griffin pats Mo on the back. "Alright, let's see about your housing." He leads Mo through the main entrance of the Unistructure.

Mo's eyes open wide as he passes through the glass doors into the Rotunda. "Am I living in *this* building, Mr. Griffin?"

"No, son. Not here." Griffin laughs. "No one lives in this building. We're here to find out where you'll be living."

Mo likes Griffin's laugh. It's different, nicer. Not at all like Emily's laugh or the other teenagers laughing at him back in Virginia.

At the end of a long corridor, they enter an office where Griffin retrieves Mo's house key from a middle-aged woman wearing an emerald turtle brooch.

"We're pleased to have you here, Mr. Lumen." Her syrupy voice and gentle demeanor are reminiscent of his grandmother. "I trust you'll keep the grounds beautiful and safe."

Mo straightens up, feeling a surge of responsibility. "Yes, ma'am, I will."

A fragrant blend of fresh paint and cleaning agents welcomes Mo as he crosses the threshold into Suite Fifteen Barrington. Looking up the staircase and down the hall to the left, he counts the doorways. "It's so big."

"You'll be sharing it with four seniors," Griffin says, passing Mo in the hallway to open the first door on the left. "I think this may be your bedroom here."

Mo hasn't had a bedroom of his own since Jake turned two. Until his father died, he'd shared a room with his brother at home. When they moved into the Branch house, he roomed with Jake, and later Paul, when Jake moved into Peter's room. Over the final two months, banished to Mr. Branch's office, he bunked with Dion.

"I'm guessing the others will share the bedrooms upstairs, but you won't know for sure until after they get here." Griffin gestures for Mo to follow him. "Come on, let's see what else is downstairs. Then, I need to get back to the office."

In the hallway, Griffin inspects the closet door under the staircase and the bathroom to the left before entering the community space: a combined living room and dining room with a kitchen in the rear of the unit. Along the back wall are sliding glass doors exiting to a patio and a narrow strip of grass running up to a small stream with trees and shrubs on the opposite side. Looking through the glass, Mo likes the appearance of his reflection floating on the water.

Tour complete, Griffin hands Mo the townhouse key. Mo locks the front door behind them, realizing he's never had a key before. His parents' doors were never locked, and Mr. Branch gave Jake a key for them to share. For the first time, independence is not equated with exile.



Cutting across campus, Griffin and Mo are greeted by a tall, clean-shaven man; his short, espresso-brown hair parted to the left using gel. "Derek, good morning," he says.

With his dignified air, slim-fit, blue-striped seersucker suit, and two-tone saddle shoes, Mo wonders if the man is a movie star from one of his father's old gangster films.

Griffin waves. "Well, good morning, stranger. How's your summer been?"

The Movie Star places his hand on his chest. "Excellent. Went with some friends to Europe—Paris, Venice, Rome, London, Dublin—and took in a few lectures on medieval art. Should provide some wonderful classroom material." He points at Mo. "Who's this strapping young lad?"

"This is Maurice Lumen. He's our new junior groundskeeper." Griffin pats the Movie Star on the back. "Mo, this is Professor Langford from the humanities department here at the school. He's also quite the angler."

Langford strokes his chin. "It's been a while, hasn't it? When *is* the last time we went fishing?"

Griffin scratches his head. "You know, I'm not sure. Was it last spring?"

"We should head out one of these Saturdays coming up." Langford gestures toward Mo. "Maybe your new apprentice here would like to join us. Do you fish, Maurice? Can I call you Mo?"

Startled by the professor's questions, a period of awkward silence passes before Mo nods. "My dad and Mr. Johnson would take me when I was little."

Griffin, nodding, looks from Mo to Langford. "Sounds like a yes to me."

Stepping back, Langford points a finger gun at each and clicks his tongue. "Let's plan a trip to Georgiaville Pond for the Saturday after next. I'll swing by the Shed next week so we can square away the details."

"I'll be expecting it."

With a thumbs-up, Langford turns and walks away. "Nice to meet you, Mo. I look forward to seeing you again." After several accelerating steps, the professor's cadence is measured and brisk.

Having never met anyone as well-educated or who uses their hands so much to communicate, Mo wonders if he will have to learn a new language.

Walking several hundred yards further, Griffin points to an oversized gray barn at the southwest edge of campus. "There's groundskeeper central. It's called the Shed. Everything we need to keep the campus in tip-top shape is inside that building. There's even a locker room and showers for you to clean up if you need."

Unlike Old Man Southerland's farm in Fauquier, Mo's disappointed to find no animals in Griffin's barn. He follows Griffin through an open garage door and into an office just large enough for a metal desk, a green footlocker, and two swivel chairs. Griffin hands Mo three pairs of blue chino uniform pants along with matching shirts. Staring at the "Lumen" in green stitching on the left breast patch, Mo hears a voice coming from the locker room. "Hey, boss, who's the newbie?"

Griffin motions to a scrawny Latino, whose face is peppered with pockmarks and sparse chin hair. "Come here, Juanito. This is Maurice Lumen. He's joining our team." He places his hand on Juanito's shoulder. "Juanito's one of our newer guys." He looks at him. "Been about six months, right?"

Juanito clicks his heels and salutes. "Aye, aye, captain." He smiles at Mo. "It's kinda cool here. Maybe a little less cool when it's freezing out, but there's also a lot of cute young chicks around most times if you get my drift." He winks.

Mo smiles back, confused why the little man would be interested enough in baby birds to point them out. "Our neighbor had chickens that ran around our yard when I was little."

Juanito laughs. "You're funny, man. I like you. Got your uniforms, huh? Did you get your work gloves too?"

"Thanks for reminding me." Griffin opens the footlocker. "Here, try these on." He flips Mo a pair of mustard-colored canvas gloves with black coating on the palms and underside of the fingers.

Mo struggles to work the gloves between his fingers. "They're kind of tight."

Griffin straightens up. "They're the biggest we got. They'll work themselves out. At least there won't be space for thorns to get in. You'll get used to them."

Mo continues interlacing his fingers in an attempt to mold the gloves to his hands. The tackiness of the black, rubbery sections pulls his hands together as if in prayer. When he went to church with the Branch family, Emily would sit on the opposite end of the pew. Sitting beside Mr. Branch, he felt isolated from all the children, including Jake, even as he appreciated the distance between himself and the Branches' ill-tempered teenage daughter. Clenching his hands, he wishes he'd had gloves like these to help separate him from Emily's anger and spite.

# - 8 -

# DEMONS

## MONDAY, 18 AUGUST 1975

P*almer pushes his apartment door open with the key still in the knob.* Six months of stale, pent-up air swarms the hallway and infests his nostrils—a bitter greeting following a prolonged absence. Suitcase wheels echoing off bare walls, his two daughters smile at him from their easel-backed five-by-sevens. He shuts the door with his foot and heads to the shower.

Water dripping from his hair collects around his feet, the sting of leaving Seattle's acid rain mixing with the anguish of returning to Boston's polluted harbor. He wipes the walls and squeegees the glass, clearing the mist, but leaving the grime. Staring into the mirror as he shaves, Palmer sees The Monster. Still in his head. Still on the loose.

It feels twelve hours later than it is. Palmer closes the curtains to shield himself from the unforgiving midday sun, turns on the television to drown out the vehicular fist thrusts and extended fingers of Boston traffic, and props up a pillow to receive his aching head. Nothing worth watching, he shuffles to bed and stares at the phone on the nightstand. He knows not to call—she'll be at work, and the girls will be with their friends. He reaches for the receiver, grabbing a cigarette instead. Sitting at the edge and lighting, he takes an extended drag before resting his head in his palms.

The contrived tension of a soap opera playing in the living room and the heated burbles of Mr. Coffee working in the kitchen serve as background noise to Palmer's rambling thoughts. Why did Osmond have to go on vacation *now*? Why would he fly home on a Monday? One more day isn't so bad, he assures himself, but it's been over a month since Osmond left Seattle. They've talked on the phone once since then, but Osmond didn't mention anything about a vacation at the time. This is the longest stretch they haven't worked together in eighteen years, all the way back to when Osmond was hospitalized.

Palmer knows Osmond kept him safe when the nightmares started. He protected Palmer when The Beast tried to take over, succeeding almost every time Palmer sought to explore the darker path. He shared the responsibility with Marilyn for bringing Palmer back to the respectable world of a white-collar family man. Palmer walked the edge, and Osmond held his hand.

Again, Palmer looks at the phone. This time he knows there's no point—Osmond's on a flight back from Antigua. Pulling himself from the edge of the bed, he staggers to the bathroom, dumps several Valium down his throat, and checks the red clouds forming on the outside edges of his eyes. Are Ted's eyes bloodshot, too? Juggling law school and nighttime activities? How many more young girls?

Palmer scoops the excess foam from a can of shaving cream on the counter, smearing it across the mirror. He sees the lines in his forehead and the creases in his neck, nothing in between. This time, Ted's eyes do not stare back. Palmer knows he must have closure. He must take down monsters like Ted before they get to his daughters. And he must purge his mind of The Monster's depravity.

Eyelids almost closed, Palmer crawls back to bed and slides under the covers. He imagines Osmond poolside, sharing a rum punch with his wife. Marilyn and the girls are swimming in the pool while he works on a crossword puzzle under an umbrella with a scotch mist. And he's himself again until the Valium wears off. And the demons return.

# FATHER'S SHADOW

## MONDAY, 18 AUGUST 1975

M o sits across from Griffin at lunch, looking out the cafeteria picture windows. The floor-to-ceiling glass is a lot like the two walls of solid glass in Dr. Winchester's office, where Mo had gone four days earlier. However, the hard, plastic chairs in the dining hall are functional, unlike the soft, leather chair in the doctor's office. He thinks about the doctor's big words and short questions. Why were his questions so important? How had he passed the doctor's test so he could be here, in this dining hall with Mr. Griffin, and starting his new job far from Virginia? What questions will he be asked in Rhode Island? Can he answer them well enough to be accepted? Will he be believed here? Allowed to stay?

After a few silent minutes, Griffin folds his newspaper. "How do you like the campus?"

Mo smiles. "I like it. It's big."

"What was your home like in Virginia?"

Mo pulls the onions out of his Italian grinder. "I liked my house, but then my dad died, so me and my brother went to live with the Branch family."

"How old's your brother?"

"Jake's eleven, but we have different moms."

Griffin unwraps his sandwich. "That's a pretty big age difference. Was your father married twice?"

"No, my mom died when I was eight, and Jake was born when I was thirteen. His mom didn't stay."

"How did you and your brother end up living with the Branch family?"

"Mrs. Harrington helped us move in with them."

"Did you like living with the Branches?"

Mo shifts a little in his chair, sets his grinder down. "I was with my brother, and I liked Paul and Dion and the backyard with the river."

"Did they have any daughters?"

"Yes. Mary's seven. Emily's fourteen."

Griffin nods. "Must've been quite a change for you. How did you like living in a house with girls?"

"Mary was fine. She just liked to play with her dolls and hang around Mrs. Branch all day." Picking his grinder back up, Mo takes another bite.

"What about the older sister? Emily?"

Mo grips his grinder; oil gushes out the bottom. "I tried not to talk to her. I tried to stay away."

"I can understand that. Teenage girls can be pretty unpredictable." Griffin tears open a bag of chips, stares at his plate. "My oldest daughter just turned thirteen. You'd think the world revolves around her sometimes."

"Emily didn't like me."

Looking back up at Mo, Griffin smiles. "Oh, I'm sure she liked you just fine. Girls that age like one or two boys and believe they have to dislike the rest."

Mo hangs his head. "No, she *really* didn't like me. She kept trying to get me in trouble."

Griffin pats Mo's hand. "I'm sorry, Mo. Sometimes girls can be mean at that age. It must be hard to adjust from having just your dad and brother to a house full of kids, even harder with a teenage girl." Pulling out his wallet, he shows Mo a photo. "My wife and I have five kids. They're a handful, that's for sure." He smiles as he takes a last look before putting the photo away. "My wife always says she wouldn't take a million dollars for any one of them; wouldn't give a penny for one more." He chuckles. "So, your brother's gonna stay with the Branch family?"

Mo sighs. "They all like Jake. They're going to adopt him."

"Maybe they'll come visit you."

Mo nods with a hollow smile. "Yeah, maybe someday."

After lunch, outside the Unistructure, Griffin climbs into his pickup truck. "Alright, Mo, enjoy the rest of the day. I'll see you in the morning. I get here about seven thirty, and we start work at eight. Make sure you're on time." He turns the ignition. "Okay, you got your key, your uniforms, your gloves. Anything else you need?"

Mo shows Griffin his items. "No, sir." The noonday sun shines off the townhouse key onto Mo's forehead.

Griffin waves.

Mo sees Griffin's smile reflected in the side view mirror as he pulls away.

The warmth of the key feels good in Mo's hand as he walks to the townhouse. On the landing, he slides the key into the lock. Turning it back and forth, he listens to the click several times before opening the door.

Inside, he goes to the downstairs bedroom and tries on a uniform. For the first time in years, his clothes fit. The uniform feels so good he doesn't take it off. He thinks he may never take it off. Folding the clothes Mr. Branch gave him, he places them on a shelf at the top of the closet, sliding them out of view. He hangs his other uniforms on the closet rod and leaves the door open. Unpacking the rest of his bag, he sits on the bed with his father's shoebox full of Virginia memories by his side. His hand resting on the shoebox, he reflects on the events of the last nine months leading to his arrival here at his new home, far from Fauquier County.

Mo stares at the shoebox—the box in which his father's personal belongings were delivered several days after the funeral and the box his father's final new pair of work boots came in about the time Jake was born. Besides his brother, the items inside represent the only tangible evidence of his life in Virginia.

Rubbing his hand across the cover of his father's paperback novel, Mo works his way back to how it all began—the event that changed everything and started his path to Rhode Island. Mo hasn't wept for his father since that day—the day after Thanksgiving when Mrs. Harrington visited the Lumen home for the last time.

Mrs. Harrington stood startled at the back door. "Boys, have you read these papers?" She pointed to two documents posted on the door—*Notice of Foreclosure* and *Notice of Eviction*. "Do you know what these papers mean?"

Jake tapped a spoon on the table. "I think it means we may have to move soon."

Mrs. Harrington placed a grocery bag on the kitchen table and went back to the door to remove them. "These notices are very serious. They mean you *will* have to move in the next month."

Mo watched Mrs. Harrington drop the notices on the table before hurrying into the living room to chat with their father.

Mrs. Harrington's voice grew louder, more desperate. "Ken?! Ken?!"

When Mo walked in, Mrs. Harrington was shaking his father. The smell of vomit, urine, and excrement hung in the air.

Mrs. Harrington held her hands over her nose. "Ken?! Wake up!"

Stunned, Mo and Jake stared from the hall. Their father did not move.

Mrs. Harrington looked back. "Boys, how long has your father been like this?"

Mo pushed his trembling brother back into the kitchen. "I don't think he's been out of his recliner in a couple of days. He didn't eat any of the Thanksgiving dinner Aunt Elizabeth sent yesterday, and the beer Mr. Johnson drops off is stacking up outside."

Mrs. Harrington went to the phone and picked up the receiver, but it hadn't been working for six months. "You boys stay here. I'll be back in a few minutes."

When she returned, there were several police cars and an ambulance following. Mo watched as his father was placed on a stretcher and slid through the rear doors. The deafening sound of the siren seemed loud enough to wake the dead. Mo paced the front lawn, rubbing his arms and asking God to help wake his father. On the front steps, he saw Jake crying in Mrs. Harrington's blouse.

She placed her hands on Jake's cheeks. "Come on, boys, let's get in the house. You'll catch your death of cold." She winced, unable to pull the words back.

Less than a week after his father's funeral, just two-and-a-half months after Mrs. Harrington's fateful visit, an officer brought his father's shoebox to the Branch home. Having never talked to a police officer before, Mo was surprised by how apologetic the officer was as he handed him the box.

Mr. Branch walked in while the boys laid their father's things on the bed. Clapping his hands, he reached for the box. "Oh, no, not in this house!" Scooping everything up, he took it away.

When their father's shoebox was returned, the items Mr. Branch found offensive had been removed. Mo and Jake distributed the remaining items between themselves. Sharing the photos of their father or Grandma Cleveland, Mo kept the ones of his mother. Jake got the wallet with the expired license and credit cards, while Mo took a small stainless-steel medallion about the size of a quarter that was inside. Jake took almost all his father's books, with Mo keeping the paperback copy of his father's favorite novel.

Between the center pages of the paperback novel, Mo slid a sealed envelope addressed with his handwritten name. When she gave the envelope to Mo, Aunt Elizabeth explained the letter inside had been written by his father several years earlier. Ken handed the envelope to Grandma Cleveland for safekeeping, instructing her to give it to Mo in the event anything should happen to him. Grandma Cleveland gave the letter to Aunt Elizabeth with the same instructions before she died. With his father in a coma, Aunt Elizabeth gave the letter to Mo.

Two days after receiving the unopened envelope—two days after Christmas—Mo saw his father for the last time. He lost his shadow as he walked into Ken's hospital room. The shadows of Aunt Elizabeth and Jake were also lost. He had seen their shadows in the corridor but saw none in his father's dimly lit room. Yet Mo's father was a shadow, silent and motionless in the room's unnatural and unforgiving light.

Mo could not see promise in his father's clean-shaven face, ghostly white and glowing, nor encouragement in what appeared to be his father's detached head, neck buried beneath a square chin and the angled corners of a hospital pillow. He could not hear optimism in the hissed breaths of a ventilator—the rhythmic sucking of a man's marrow. Nor could he find reassurance in the pulsing beats of a bedside monitor—the cadenced grinding of a man's measure. And he could not smell hope in the sterile air, cleaning agents, and witch hazel masking the foul odor of disease, despair, and death.

Preferring to remember his father as he had been before all the mistakes and misfortune, sorrow and suffering, punishment and pain, Mo did not linger. He laid a handmade card on the bed before leaving, choosing to picture his father at his best.

The news of Ken's passing came on the first Wednesday in February. Few attended the Saturday morning funeral. Fewer still braved the cold for the internment at Remington Cemetery, where Ken's body was laid next to Sarah. Besides Ken's sons, mourners included Aunt Elizabeth, Mrs. Harrington, Earl, and Sam. Mr. Branch waited for the Lumen brothers in the warmth of the family station wagon.

Paying for the coffin and burial of his lifelong friend, Earl also secured a veteran's flag to place next to the headstone. He was the only attendee to shed tears—a lifetime of laughter and hardship, joy and pain captured in a few earthbound drops of saline.

Opening his father's paperback novel later that day, Mo stared at the sealed envelope. Too depressed, he decided not to open it until the following Christmas. By doing so, he left one final surprise from his father as a later present. The envelope continues to sit, wedged between the pages of the paperback novel inside his father's shoebox, undisturbed, among the words his father so enjoyed.

Alone in the townhouse, laying across his bed in a new home under the reassuring shelter of afternoon sunlight, Mo slides under the covers for a nap, filled with conflicting thoughts of newness and sadness. The world he knew—three days ago, nine months ago, seventeen years ago—now seems like a distant memory. For the first time, he's fully conscious of his loss. Squeezing his hands together under the pillow, he drifts into cautious slumber.

# -10-

# OSMOND'S BETRAYAL

## TUESDAY, 19 AUGUST 1975

P*almer's head is ringing the following morning, part of the standard post-investigation purge: several weeks of daily Valium followed by long nights of sleep and morning headaches.* But this headache is different. This one's still running around the campus at the University of Utah.

Lighting a cigarette, Palmer massages his head before opening the curtain and staring down at an empty street. *Three thirty in the morning is the only quiet time in Boston,* he thinks. But he's been asleep for fourteen hours, so he turns on Mr. Coffee, changes the channel to a *Dragnet* rerun, and counts the minutes to six—until he can call Osmond to set up a time for breakfast.

S tew's Breakfast Bowl sits twelve at the bar and another forty at tables. By seven, customers line up outside. Palmer shows up at six thirty and squats at a table by the bathroom. When Osmond arrives at seven thirty, Palmer waves him over, holding a chair away from the table.

Osmond grabs a menu. "Hey, Frankie."

Palmer notices Osmond's face is tanned. "Good to see you, Harry. Your coffee should be here in a minute. Did you have a good time?"

"Yeah. What about you? Any luck?"

"They screwed me over." Palmer slides the sugar dispenser in front of Osmond.

"I heard about the Salt Lake request."

56

Palmer takes the coffees from the waitress, places one in front of Osmond. "I needed *one* month. One!"

Osmond tips the sugar dispenser to the edge of his cup. "You know how hard it is to get funding on speculation. I heard they had to let him go."

Palmer nods. "I kept telling them all the footprints tracked to Utah. If they'd have let me go, I'd have followed this bastard every minute and caught him in the act."

"So, how you gonna get this scumbag out of your head?"

"We need Utah or Colorado State Police to call us in." Palmer leans his back against the window. "Or we need the son of a bitch to make a mistake. At the very least, we need a new case."

Osmond raises his eyebrows. "There may be no 'we' on this one, Frankie."

"What's that supposed to mean?" Palmer grabs his Marlboros off the table.

Osmond strikes a match, holds it in front of Palmer. "I put in for Dick's job. They're waiting for you to submit, but I know you won't."

"You gotta be shitting me, Harry." Palmer leans in. His eyes, like wet beach pebbles, reflect the flame. "We always laughed at the desk jobs. Said we wouldn't sell out."

Osmond blows out the match. "I know, but the kids are gone, and my wife wants me to spend more time at home with her. Maybe take a vacation now and then."

Palmer gives Osmond a dismissive wave of his hand. "Ah, you ain't gonna get it anyway. They got their eyes on Humphrey, been grooming him with desk jobs for the past three years."

"You may be right, Frankie." Osmond nods. "You usually are."

# 11

# TINPOT ALLEY

## TUESDAY, 19 AUGUST 1975

M o waits on a tree stump outside the Shed, gazing across the access road to the woods forming a natural barrier around the campus. Early for work, he hears chirping in the trees and scuffling in the undergrowth but doesn't see any wildlife. The sun beating stronger on his face, Mo closes his eyes and collects a memory, tranquil and unimpeded. Back home, wide-eyed and communing with nature, he had always been the observer. Here, eyes shut and seated alone, he's observed.

Interrupted by the sound of tires crunching stone, Mo opens his eyes and turns toward the disturbance.

Stepping out of his truck, Griffin waves. "Good morning, Mo." A box is wedged under his arm. "Were you able to get some sleep?"

Mo walks by Griffin's side. "A little bit. I saw a deer last night."

"There's a whole lot of whitetail out here." Griffin pushes against his office door. "Darn thing's swollen from heat and humidity, sealed tight as the lid on an old jar of pickles." He wrestles with the knob, kicking the bottom panel to nudge it open. "Come on in. Gotta get that fixed." Griffin tosses the box on his desk along with the morning paper, pulling a clipboard off the wall. "We need to check the schedule before the boys get here. Let me see," he says, talking to himself, "King and Theo...okay; Sarge and Sprinkles... alright; Flatbush and Juanito...yup." He lowers the clipboard. "Mo, you and I are gonna collect the trash and take it to the incinerator."

Mo sits, bewildered by the flurry of odd names. "Yes, sir. What's an incinerator, Mr. Griffin, sir?"

Griffin smiles. "It's a large furnace where we take all the campus trash and green waste to be burned."

"What's green waste?"

"Green waste is everything we collect from landscaping: grass cuttings, leaves, weeds, plants, dead flowers, stuff like that." Griffin turns back to the desk. "Okay, that's enough questions for now. You'll pick it up as you go. First things first, though." He hands Mo the box. "These are for you."

Mo recognizes the box from the one under his bed. "Thank you, Mr. Griffin, sir."

"Same size as I wear. Hope they fit."

"These are really nice, Mr. Griffin, sir." Mo addresses his boss as Sam had Mo's father.

"You're gonna have to stop that, son." Griffin's tenor doesn't change, even in a moment of mild irritation. "Either call me sir or Mr. Griffin, but don't call me both." He smiles. "Sounds all distinguished. Just show respect by doing what needs to get done. Don't need any fancy titles. Most of the boys just call me boss."

"Yes, sir." Mo's new boots are a bit tight, but he's not one to complain. His shoes have always been undersized, so he's learned to like them snug. "Thank you so much."

A voice calls out from the office door. "Morning, boss. This the new kid?"

Griffin turns his attention to the doorway where a man in his late thirties with short, black hair, coarse, dark skin, and hazel eyes is standing. "Yes, Sarge, this is Mo Lumen. He's gonna be my sidekick, so I can train him up."

Thomas Moore's nickname is the result of a twelve-year enlistment. He's begun to lose the battle of the waistline but is otherwise fit to serve. "Hi, Mo. Nice to meet you." Sarge points to the breast of his uniform. "We got a rule around here says you don't get your real name patch until you show you can hang. It's kinda like earning your stripes."

"Sarge's right. You gotta earn the nickname on your name patch."

"Rest of us are outside, boss, waiting on instructions." Sarge heads out.

Griffin and Mo follow.

"Hey, Griff, who's the lumberjack?" The name patch on Stephon Johnson's shirt results from a constellation of freckles running across his nose and cheeks.

Griffin rolls his eyes, conceals a smirk. "That's a good one, Sprinkles." He raises his hand. "Alright, everybody, listen up. Mo here just arrived from Virginia a couple of days ago. He's gonna saddle up with me until he learns the ropes." He pats Mo on the back. "I suspect he'll come in handy when it comes to heavy lifting."

"Hi, Mo. Good to meet you." Sprinkles rolls his wrist in Mo's face. "Slip me some skin."

Mo stares at his palm. "Good morning. It's nice to meet you, too."

Sprinkles pulls at the front of his shirt. "You got that mostly right…it is *great* to meet me."

Sarge and Griffin snicker while shaking their heads. A chorus of laughter joins from behind.

Mo recognizes their playfulness as similar to the K&E crew's banter. It doesn't seem to be mean as it had often been in the past when others laughed at him, so he joins in.

Griffin points to Sarge and Sprinkles. "Alright, you two, you're gonna get out to the playing fields today." He shifts his attention to a Black man about his own age and another who looks like he's still in high school. "King and Theo," he calls out.

They step forward, the younger one flicking the butt of his cigarette on the ground.

Griffin points down. "Theo! Pick that up and throw it in the trash where it belongs. These grounds are not your ashtray." Sighing, he shakes his head. "You know they're no good for you, anyway."

"Yes, sir." Theodore Harris does not smile as he approaches Mo, his name patch reading simply, "Theo." "You're from Virginia, huh?" He nods. "You ever see the Squires play when Dr. J and The Iceman were together a couple years back?"

Mo's response is a blank stare.

"Come on, man," Lucius Branch says, breaking an awkward silence. He's in his late thirties with a receding hairline. "Ain't no

White people watching the ABA." He looks Mo over. "But, man, this guy would be a beast at power forward." Situated proudly above his name patch, 'KING' stitched in bold, is another ebony patch shaped like a guitar, the name 'Lucille' inside with a crown above it.

Looking at his second patch, Mo wonders if King's wife also works at the school.

Griffin claps his hands. "Alright, guys, that's enough. We got work to do. You'll need to throw your tools in the truck and get to the flowerbeds." He peers around King's thickset build. "Get over here, Juanito. We start at eight, not ten past."

As he passes, Juanito greets Mo with a nod and a sheepish smile.

Retrieving his cap from his back pocket, Griffin pulls it on. "You and Flatbush finish those stones around the pond."

A middle-aged, dark-skinned Latino leans against a faded, orange car watching the discourse without comment. A product of Brooklyn, Jericho Gonzalez is a part-time employee who works Tuesdays and Thursdays, his face and neck lined with years of toil across many unforgiving Northeast seasons. Unlike the others in their uniforms, he wears a white tank top and jeans. "Nice to meet you, kid." With those few words, the man they call Flatbush ambles by.

Mo watches the workers make their way to the garage, thrilled to be part of a team.

When everyone has left the Shed, Mo helps Griffin attach the trailer to the pickup. They hop into the truck. Griffin's radio is tuned to his favorite news and sports station, as always. Behind the dining hall, Griffin navigates the trailer within a few yards of two dumpsters.

"Put your gloves on, Mo," Griffin says, "and grab the box of bags."

"Yes, sir." Mo's nose wrinkles at the smell of five-day-old trash. The rank, depressing odors—a mix of sour milk, rotten vegetables, and rancid meat—remind him of the stench along the Rappahannock after a flood, the decaying flesh of animal carcasses prevailing for several weeks.

Griffin tosses the bags at Mo's feet. "Here, just throw them in the back of the trailer."

Mo points to a clearing in the woods. "*There's* some deer."

"Pay attention, Mo." Griffin pulls back the bag in his hands. Standing, he wipes the beads of sweat racing to his shirt collar with the back of his glove. "They look all pretty until they get in the way of some car or truck. You must be used to seeing them down in Virginia."

"Yes, sir. My dad took me hunting once. He would kill them for us to eat. I never shot one, though."

"It's okay if you're gonna eat them, but some people kill animals just for sport, and that's not right. If you're being attacked, it's okay to shoot an animal, or if you intend to eat it." Despite repeated swipes, the droplets of perspiration on Griffin's face and neck band together, resulting in a breakthrough on several fronts, sweat stains creeping all around his shirt.

"Sometimes people shoot other people, right?" Mo asks.

"Sometimes, I guess, when they're being attacked." Lifting his cap, Griffin wipes his forehead with his sleeve. "What made you think of that?"

"My dad was in the Army. He said soldiers shoot at each other in war." Mo nods. "He said that was okay, too."

"Oh, yeah, your dad's right. It's okay because they're attacking each other." Griffin arches his back, stretching his arms over his head. "No fun getting old, son. Alright, that's enough conversation. Let's finish getting these loaded on the trailer so we can get the trash at the dorms."

By the time they reach the incinerator, Mo's listened to enough news on the radio to learn it will be hot and humid for the next month with occasional rain, the Red Sox play a night game, and citywide busing in Boston will require a lot more police ahead of expected riots, though he's not sure who will be doing the rioting.

Smelling like Grandma Cleveland's sourdough left out on the counter to rise, the incinerator doesn't have the foul odors of the dumpsters back at school. Bulldozers plowing trash through the incinerator doors look like gigantic versions of Jake's Tonka trucks—toys the boys would play with on the back porch while Grandma Cleveland hummed and baked bread.

Mo's already been sweating for a couple of hours when they head back to campus. Despite the dashboard air conditioning, he feels perspiration lines make their way down the slope of his back and under the elastic waistband of his underwear—a gross, sloppy feeling made more uncomfortable by Griffin's foul odor.

Mo's familiar with the sweaty smell of men working on hot, humid days while driving in the K&E trucks with the windows down, but it will take time to get used to the smell swirling in Griffin's truck cab with no outside air. Mo hadn't worried about how he smelled during his outdoor lunch conversations with Sam but now fears he may leave his own stench in the cloth seat covers. So, he sits in his pool of sweat, listening to the radio and praying he doesn't stink.

Griffin lowers the volume. "We're heading over to Tony's Pizza for lunch."

"I love pizza!" Saliva pools under Mo's tongue. His stomach wailing like a bear in the throes of labor, he wraps his arms around his belly.

Griffin releases a solitary chortle. "You *must* be hungry."

"Yes, sir. I could eat a burrowed beaver, as my dad would say."

Griffin no longer suppresses his laughter. "Not sure we have many establishments serving up beaver around here, but I think you'll like the pizza."

Mo nods, face red from squeezing his tummy so tight.

"We can't always agree on burgers, or tacos, or fish and chips, or pizza, but everyone agrees on beer." Griffin looks back at Mo, his head at an angle, forehead creases exposed. "You drink beer, Mo?"

"No, sir." Mo slumps in his seat. "My dad let me try it a long time ago, but I didn't like the taste." He feels for his father's medallion. "He said that was alright because drinking beer never did nobody no good."

Griffin turns the pickup into Tony's parking lot. "Your dad's right. At best, beer is just a waste of money or makes us look foolish. At worst, it can wreck a man's life." He nods. "Yup, he got that right." The engine lets out a final gasp. "No worries, Mo. I don't let the boys drink but two beers during lunch. You drink whatever you'd like."

Seated with a Sprite, Mo waits for his coworkers to indulge, watching the first pizza disappear before the second hits the table. He takes a slice, listening, along with Griffin and Flatbush, to the others chat about sports, politics, and music. He enjoys several slices before being asked a question.

"What about you, Mo?" Sarge motions for him to pass a napkin. "You got a favorite team?"

Mo grabs another slice of pepperoni. "My father used to root for the Senators."

"That's right; you came from Virginia. Where did you live there?"

"I lived with the Branch family."

King looks up from his plate. "Hey, that's my last name. Guessing they're White?"

Mo swallows his bite. "Yes, everyone back home in Virginia is White. But my dad did have a Black worker, Sam, who would tell me all about baseball and the great Negro League players."

King nods. "Should've known that. Lot more White than Black Branches, I suppose."

Sprinkles scrunches his eyebrows and cocks his head back. "They ain't *all* White, is they?"

Realizing he's the center of attention, Mo lays his slice down. "Back home in Sumerduck, all the people at church, school, and around town are White."

Sarge mumbles through a mouthful of pizza. "Where do the Black folks live?"

Mo works the seat of his pants into his chair, his face pale. "My dad told me they live in Tinpot Alley or down in the bad parts of Fredericksburg."

"What's Tinpot Alley?"

"It's the slums at the end of Sumerduck Road, where my dad says the Colored and poor White folk live." He adjusts his chair. "It's the lowest part of town along the river and floods bad when there's lots of rain."

Looking around the table, King scowls. "Sounds about right."

Griffin stands up, glaring at King. "Okay, guys, we get the point. Let's change the subject." He pulls a chair next to Mo and sits down. "You wanna come to dinner at my house Friday night? I can pick you up at the townhouse about thirty minutes after work. You interested?"

"That sounds nice." Mo's face brightens.

"Alright then, I'll pick you up at five thirty." Griffin rises. "Wrap it up, guys. Let's get back to work."

On the way out, Juanito gestures at Mo's feet with a nod. "See you got your new pair of work boots from Boss Griffin."

"I like them," Mo says, though his toes sting.

"You should. I bet they fit you good. I had to get used to walking around with duck feet."

Sarge pats Mo on the back. "We pitched in and bought him a red wig and ball nose to go with them."

Juanito grabs Mo's arm. "No, seriously, walking in mud is super hard. If I don't tie my boots up over my ankles, they just slide off."

Stopping in his tracks, Griffin turns. "You can always get your own."

Juanito shrugs. "Yeah, but that be costing green."

Griffin nods. "That's right, and don't you forget it."

Even if his workbooks are a little too small, Mo appreciates Griffin's charity. Knowing they're the same as everyone else's makes Mo feel like he fits right in.

# 12

# FATHER'S FINAL ROUND

## THURSDAY, 21 AUGUST 1975

*P**almer's bored by Thursday.* The space between cases is filled with the mundane: paperwork, meetings, phone calls, and more paperwork. He hates paperwork, sees it as dues paid by the younger agents, though he's not enamored with training the greenies either. Palmer likes comfortable. Murphy, Osmond, and Ross are comfortable. Can't blame Murphy, but Osmond's going to go and fuck things up.

Taking a break from editing his Seattle reports, Palmer sits at his desk fingering through the first 725 pages of the FBI files from the Julius and Ethel Rosenberg investigation. Released twenty-two years after their execution for treason, the files are more compelling than anything in today's newspaper or the stack of papers on the side of his desk. He was in college when the espionage case dominated the news for several months in 1951 and again in 1953.

Palmer took two years off after high school to intern with his father at the law firm, filing papers, running documents, and filling coffee mugs. The second Friday in August 1950, he sat at the bar with his father, several of his father's close friends from the firm, and a buddy from the Bureau named Richard Murphy. There had been some liquor spilled, but Palmer abstained, busy pushing peanuts around the bowl.

Mr. Edmunds patted Palmer on the back. "You must be excited about heading off to Harvard next month, huh?"

Tossing several peanuts in his mouth, Palmer nodded.

"Pulled some strings through Hawkins in Legal Accounting," Palmer's father said, lifting his mug. "Got a full scholarship."

Palmer pressed the brass footrail down hard with both feet, mumbling to himself, "I earned that on my own."

His father held his mug just below his mouth. "You say something, Son?"

Palmer shrugged, forcing a smile while still trying to detach the footrail.

Murphy placed his hand on Palmer's shoulder. "Aren't you excited, Francis?"

Palmer's father grabbed his shoulder. "Sure, he's excited. Who wouldn't be excited about attending Harvard for pre-law?"

Palmer slammed his fist on the bar, grazing the edge of the bowl. Unable to contain them, the words spilled out before the peanuts hit the polished oak. "I'm not going to be a lawyer." He felt the heat of ten eyes burning into him. Hanging his head, he sighed. "I'm sorry, Dad. I'm not interested in law."

Palmer's father glared, his eyes growing larger. The other lawyers and Murphy shuffled in their stools, gaping at each other and holding their mugs to their mouths, waiting for the eruption. But it didn't come. Not here at Finnegan's anyway. Placing his mug down, Palmer's father fiddled with his wallet. He dropped a twenty on the counter, turned, and walked out.

Palmer took a taxi home. When he walked in at midnight, his father was waiting, nestled in his favorite chair with a book, reading glasses resting on the tip of his nose.

His father's voice was soft, measured. "You had to embarrass me in front of my colleagues. We couldn't have talked about this alone, here at the house?" He removed his glasses.

Standing by the door, Palmer held the knob. "Dad, I've tried to talk to you a dozen times, but—"

"No 'buts,' Son. You wanna be a man?" His father draped his book on the armrest of his chair, laid down his glasses, and stood up. "Then have the balls to stand up for yourself."

Gripping the doorknob tighter, Palmer said a silent prayer as his father approached him. It would be the second to last time he would pray.

His father got to within a foot of him. "You can let go of the doorknob. I'm not gonna hit you. I've never hit you, have I?"

Palmer shook his head, letting his hand fall from the knob.

"You've been talking about being an FBI agent since before your mother died. She's the one that wanted you to become a lawyer. I've been trying to be true to her wishes, but I've also been waiting for you to show some passion."

Pulling his son in for a hug, Palmer's father patted him on the back. "I'd have preferred you expressed it to me alone, but the guys already knew I was waiting for you." He pulled away, looking into his son's eyes. "Your mother would be proud no matter what you do, just like I will be. Don't be afraid of candor and conviction. Say what you mean and mean what you say." He rubbed his hand along Palmer's arm. "Tonight, I'm proud of you, Son. I'll always be proud of you."

That would be the second to last time Palmer would shed a tear.

Two weeks later, Palmer was just settling in for his first weekend at school. His roommate and several new friends were getting to know each other over a few pints when there was a knock on the door. Heading downstairs to the operator's room, he picked up the phone. Mr. Edmunds was on the other end. Palmer heard only two words—*father* and *dead*.

Palmer's father had been enjoying an afternoon round at The Country Club in Brookline with some friends. On the thirteenth green, he dropped to his knees, then down on his side. The ambulance left the course in silence.

Darkness creeping into Palmer's line of sight, he drifted through the hallway and into the first-floor restroom to mourn in solitude.

He didn't let anyone witness his grief that evening, during the funeral, or at the burial. He didn't cry when Osmond was shot, when his daughters were born, or when Marilyn left with the girls. He's never allowed himself to shed a single tear to this day. Murphy became a surrogate father, checking in on him for four years at

Harvard before helping pave his path to the Bureau. Palmer's seen all sorts of heinous crimes and remains unemotional, stoic. Some say ice flows through his veins; others believe it's Jack Daniel's.

Palmer closes the Rosenberg files, dropping them into the lower drawer. Walking over to Osmond's cubicle, he crumples a twenty and drops it on his desk.

Watching the bill unfurl, Osmond shakes his head. "You don't pay out on bets, Frankie."

Palmer walks away. "You'll get it, Harry. I frigging hate you for it, but you're their man." He stops at the hallway door without looking back. "I'm headed down to Finnegan's if you're thirsty. It's your turn to pay."

# THE JOGGER AND
# THE DEER

## THURSDAY, 21 AUGUST 1975

**M**o *notices a few early arriving students smile and wave at him as he walks to the dining hall.* He likes the attention. Smiling and waving back, he wonders if the Bryant College logo on his uniform makes them friendly. His first two days of work left him exhausted in the evenings, but Thursday, Mo is finally ready to take advantage of Bryant's natural blessings.

After dinner, he explores the grounds, discovering three sets of primary walkways on campus: an inner ring around the pond, a central ring around the main campus, and an outer ring bordering the woods. On this night, he chooses to investigate the full perimeter of the campus along the outer ring.

About an hour into his journey, a young female with dirty-blond hair passes by, her ponytail bouncing from shoulder to shoulder as she jogs. She trots in place before taking a hard right onto one of the school's many woodland paths. Following her, Mo notes the serene density of the surrounding trees and abundant undergrowth. Putting his gloves on to engage some prickly shrubbery, he encounters the paradox associated with the intimacy of nature and the disarming sterility of his gloves.

Mo runs his protected fingers across the bushes and vines lining the path. When The Jogger returns, she acknowledges Mo's presence, creeping towards him with a finger to her mouth. Motioning him to remain still, she points in the direction of a doe staring at them. The woods are filled with shadows of dusk, allowing just enough light for Mo to see the flurry of small flying insects and particles of plant matter between them.

Moving closer, The Jogger whispers. "Isn't she beautiful?"

Mo *is* struck by The Jogger's beauty. Though her hair is several shades darker, there's a similarity to his mother when he was very young. He turns his attention to the doe as The Jogger gets within a few feet—close enough for him to smell the aromatic mix of deodorant and sweat. Stumbling over a vine, The Jogger falls into him, causing a commotion that ripples across the ground cover. The doe reacts with a swift jolt and a hurried set of leaps to distance itself from the disturbance.

Her face red, The Jogger finishes their one-sided conversation, "Wasn't that amazing?" before pulling herself up and making her way back to the outer walkway.

Though The Jogger doesn't stay for his response, Mo nods, feeling a gust of buoyant air fill his lungs. He thinks to himself, *She was amazing.*

Encroaching darkness compels Mo to retreat to the solitude of his new home. Nights alone in the townhouse are scary, and he's anxious with every creak in a wall or settling of the floor. So each night, he turns on the television in the living room and turns up the volume to eliminate any other distractions. Never having had a say in what was watched at night when living with the Branches, he enjoys checking out all the channels before settling on *The Waltons.*

When John Boy, Mary Ellen, and the rest of the Waltons say their goodnights, Mo reflects on his youthful home, retrieving his father's shoebox from the bedroom and returning to the sofa. Having allowed the suspense to build as long as he could, Mo opens Mrs. Harrington's present, discovering a sterling silver necklace and medal with an etched face that shines in the lamplight. Retrieving his father's stainless-steel medallion from his pocket and inspecting its indented red heart, Mo imagines his mother wearing it around her neck before his parents were married. He threads the chain from Mrs. Harrington's medal through a hole in his father's medallion before hanging both symbols of love around his neck.

Daily discussions with Mr. Griffin rekindling his interest in baseball, Mo watches the evening news each night to see if the Red Sox won. Waiting for the sports report, he pulls out his old baseball cards from the shoebox. Shuffling through them, he notices their frayed edges and rounded corners. Sam gave them to him when he was much younger, and Mo spent many long nights studying the profiles and statistics on the backs of each card. He can picture Sam reaching into his pocket, handing him a small stack with a big smile, and asking him to read aloud the player accomplishment blurbs. Not long after his thirteenth birthday, his baseball conversations with Sam ended. It seemed when Sam left, his brother, Jake, took his place. And his father's sickness began.


Work spiraled after Jake's birth. Sam had to be let go three weeks later, just after Thanksgiving 1963, and work wasn't fun for Mo anymore. On the morning of Mo's last day in the public school system, the first day of June 1965, Ken and Earl sat at the Lumen table conducting their final business meeting.

Ken's scandal took a terrible toll on K&E, with work drying up over the twenty months since Jake was born. Selling all but one of the company trucks and most of the equipment, Earl returned to Cardinal Construction, leaving Ken to respond to the few remaining service calls. Ken took a second job as a night watchman at a department store down in Culpeper. It would have been easy for Earl to blame Ken for K&E's demise, but he knew the business was built on Ken's twin ships—salesman and craftsman—and he had enjoyed the ride.

Mo was feeding Jake in his highchair, while Ken grumbled to himself as he dug around Jake's sippy cups in the cabinet, trying to find two coffee mugs. The screen door creaked as it opened and shut before yielding to the familiar sound of Mr. Johnson's heavy boots.

Earl took off his hat and pulled up a chair. "Morning."

Mo's father let out an unenthusiastic growl.

"Long night of work?"

Ken filled both mugs before falling hard into a chair. "They're all long nights. I gotta head over to the school today. Principal wants to talk about Mo. Just need something to keep me going until I can come home and sleep."

Ken opened the front page of the morning paper, handing the sports section to Earl. They read while sipping coffee.

Mo made faces, and Jake's giggles hung above the kitchen.

Earl's stomach rumbled, and he cleared his throat to disguise the noise.

Ken looked at Earl above his newspaper. "I'd offer you something to eat, but Anne's out at the store getting groceries. We're outta just about everything. I swear, these boys eat almost the whole paycheck themselves." He paused before muttering, "Damned minimum wage don't take us too far."

Earl tapped the table with his folded paper. "Don't worry about it. I'm on a diet anyway. The wife's pushing me to lose a few pounds."

Mo knew Mr. Johnson was lying. Earl had always been a little heavy.

Ken raised his coffee mug to Earl before taking another sip. "Well, tell her I appreciate you dropping off dinner as much as you do. Can't be relying on Anne to do it all. She's getting older, you know. And with this night job, my schedule's off. Hard to be much help with the kids when I gotta be sleeping."

By that time, Mo knew sleeping and drinking were synonymous.

Unsure of what to say and unable to keep his stomach quiet, Earl finished his coffee. Getting up to pour a refill, he glanced at the open newspaper in front of Ken.

Ken noticed Earl reading the headline—*Vivian Malone First Black to Graduate from the University of Alabama.* "Can't pick up a newspaper nowadays without seeing something the Coloreds ain't celebrating. Always full of that Negro nonsense."

Earl chuckled. "I guess most anything counts as news these days."

"Not sure who was celebrating that Malcolm X fella." Ken jerked his hand in anger, coffee spilling onto the floor.

Jumping off his chair, Mo grabbed a dish towel.

Ken looked down to where Mo was wiping. "Not sure if the Coloreds didn't like his being Muslim, or the Muslims didn't like his being Colored. Either way, got himself shot. Then they try and make a martyr outta him. Got sick of reading that shit a few months ago." He slammed his mug down, splashing more coffee onto the floor. "That ain't no tragedy," he muttered. "Us talking about shutting down K&E? Now, *that's* a goddamned tragedy."

When Ken swore, Mo knew his father was talking politics, taxes, or Coloreds, though he never understood the connection. Ken was often bitter and angry by that point, so Grandma Cleveland would ask Mo to pray for his father. It was about then Mo started preferring the times his father was sleeping.

Earl stared into his mug. "Yeah, I sure miss working together. Being back at Cardinal just ain't the same without you. We had some good times." He downed the rest of his coffee. "I think it might be time to sell the rest of the tools and call it a day. What d'ya think?"

Ken pushed himself back from the table, scraping the chair along the floor tiles. "Ahh, I guess it's time. Just a crying shame, though. Only good thing about it's not having to deal with that damned civil rights equal pay bullshit."

Jake began crying. Mo threw the dirty dish towel in the sink and scooped up his brother. Heading to the living room, he saw Mr. Johnson get up from the table.

Earl waved to Ken. "I best be going."

Crumpling the newspaper, Ken threw it in the trash. "That's all that's good for."


Medals dangling from his neck, Mo squeezes his baseball cards. He doesn't have as many as he did fifteen years ago, but each represents a connection to an important childhood friendship. He wishes he had the rest but knows they continue to speak to him through Sam's colorful stories and enduring smile. He also wishes Sam was nearby so they could talk baseball with Mr. Griffin. He didn't get enough time with Sam—not quite four years—but he clings to the joy Sam brought him, just as he does his mother, father, and Grandma Cleveland. Sleeping again on the sofa, where the noise and light from the television are comforting, he says his prayers and closes his eyes, knowing people seldom get enough of the things they truly cherish.

# THE OLD MAN OF
# THE MOUNTAIN

**FRIDAY, 22 AUGUST 1975**

P*almer exits the city unnoticed, though he knows there are always witnesses.* Clark's Trading Post is a two-hour drive from central
Boston, ninety minutes if he leaves by five. So, as he does each year,
he takes a Friday off in late August, leaves by four thirty, and heads
north to New Hampshire. Driving quickly through the early morning darkness, he can't see the road signs. He doesn't need to see
them. He's visited Franconia Notch and looked up at his father's
favorite mountain for more than thirty years.

The sun rises over the peaks as he walks to the edge of Profile
Lake, several miles north of Clark's and just below the Old Man
of the Mountain. Palmer tosses a penny into the lake, as his father had before him. This is where they would go fly fishing each
summer. He can still picture his father carrying the tackle box as
he followed with the rods. He can see his father out on the lake in
waders, casting and explaining the finer points of hooking a brook
trout by emulating the movement of a fly in the water. Some of his
best childhood memories came on this lake. And his worst.

In the summer of 1945, several weeks after the bombings of
Hiroshima and Nagasaki, one week before the end of World War
II, and two days before his fifteenth birthday, Palmer's father had
them on the lake early to beat the heat and humidity. Though a
bit late in the year, the trout were jumping. His father was always

excited to be on the lake spending time with Palmer, but today he seemed subdued. He held Palmer's arm out to the side. "The wrist, Son, you have to keep your hand back and hold the line at forty-five degrees."

Palmer felt the cool water seeping through a tear in his waders. He watched his father cast again and leaned his body back, trying to emulate the proper position. "Like this?"

"That's better, Francis. Now, remember what Mr. Ouimet taught you and adjust to the strong hand. It's a lot like a golf swing, just a different angle."

Palmer wanted to make his father proud, so after several attempts following his advice, they were casting and working the current with their lines in rhythm.

They fished together all morning in a quiet spot before making their way back to shore for lunch. Palmer's mother wasn't feeling up to the drive this year but still prepared the basket. Sitting at the edge of the water under a sycamore, Palmer talked to his father about the upcoming school year and his chances of making varsity baseball the following spring. With the food all gone, Palmer got up to grab the equipment so they could head over to Clark's, as they always did.

His father brushed away a few leaves, running his fingers across the soft dirt. "Hold up, Francis. I need to talk to you about something. It's about your mother."

Palmer laid down his fishing rod and sat cross-legged a few feet from his father. "What about mom?" He noticed his father's downcast eyes were moist.

His father looked up into Palmer's eyes, lips pursed as if he couldn't stomach the words. "Your mother's very sick. She's got breast cancer, Son, and it's untreatable. She's dying."

Unable to feel the breeze lifting the hair from his forehead, Palmer's world stood still. After a few moments, the upper half of his body began quivering. He felt for the ground, but it seemed to be moving as well. "Why?" is all he could utter.

Swallowing the emotion rising in his throat, his father shook his head. "There's no reason. It just happens. God takes us when He wants, and we can't understand." Motioning Palmer to stand, he welcomed him into a hug.

Pulling away from their embrace, Palmer stared at the dampness left on his father's shirt. He knew the stain would disappear, but the pain would not. "Did the doctor give any idea of how long?"

"Doctor says maybe a year, but he's not certain. I'm gonna need you to be a man, Francis. You need to enjoy every moment you can with your mother and don't let her see you sad." His father patted Palmer on the sides of his arms. "You need to be strong and keep a smile on your face. It'll get more difficult as time passes. I need you to promise me, Son."

Rubbing his face with both hands, Palmer nodded.

After picking up their gear, his father slid an arm around Palmer's shoulder, guiding him along the trail back to the parking lot. When they arrived at the pickup, Palmer tossed the rods in the back, watching his father pull down the tailgate and slide the tackle box in the bed.

Taking off his fishing cap, his father ran his hand across his forehead.

Palmer leaned against the side panel. "We don't have to go see the bears."

Palmer's father closed the tailgate. "I knew you'd say that, Son, but we need to learn to go on like always. Your mother's preparing a nice dinner for us when we get home. We wouldn't want to disappoint her by showing up five hours early, would we?"

Palmer scratched his head, nodding before opening the passenger door.

Palmer's father smiled as they drove to Clark's and all during the bear show. He smiled that night over dinner and at every dinner for the next ten months until his mother was taken by ambulance. When he and his father returned from the hospital that evening, dinner was cold and somber. Three weeks later, as they lowered his mother into the ground, he watched a part of his father go with her. Though his father often smiled after that day, it would never be the same.

Thirty years after that promise to his father, Palmer stares into Profile Lake and tosses a second penny, this one for his mother. He follows the lake's edge to his father's favorite fishing spot. He didn't bring a pole or a tackle box. He has no lunch basket or son to teach. And he hasn't fished at the lake in a decade. Instead, he sits alone, thinking back across the years.

Palmer brought his girls every summer, but they were more interested in the amusement parks up in Jefferson and Glen. They never liked fishing—thought it was boring, and hated seeing the fish filleted. The Old Man of the Mountain became just a passing attraction on the way to Santa's Village, Storyland, and Six Gun City, but he made sure they always stopped at the lake, and he always looked up.

He heads over to Dottie's Diner for breakfast before catching the first show at Clark's. He leaves early afternoon, knowing he'll hit more traffic on the way back. Driving south on Route 3, he sees the profile of the Old Man of the Mountain on every road sign, a silent witness as he passes each exit. He knows the old man is staring back.

And he likes it.

# GRIFFIN'S COLORFUL NEIGHBORHOOD

## FRIDAY, 22 AUGUST 1975

M o surveys the landscape, allowing Griffin's truck to transport him. Late afternoon Friday, with the passenger window rolled down, he's headed to Griffin's home for dinner. Unlike the country mouse from a children's book his mother read when he was young, Mo discovers his surroundings grow more intimate. Quiet country roads weaving through well-manicured suburban estates and sprawling farms give way to congested municipal highways slicing between bland commercial buildings and well-lit parking lots before surrendering to charming little houses and sidewalk-lined streets.

Entering Griffin's neighborhood, brightly colored bicycles enliven small patches of sunburnt grass in front of identical Cape Cods, and chalk drawings decorate uneven squares of cracked pavement. In the shadow of aligned brick homes bounded by chain-link fences, Mo feels a sense of community he hasn't had since his days at Sumerduck Elementary among his childhood friends and teachers.

Nearing Griffin's house, Mo's nostalgia is disturbed by an ice cream truck, its creepy interpretation of a familiar childhood tune attracting a mob of enthusiastic Black children. Paying greater attention to pedestrians walking along the sidewalks and crossing streets, Mo is alarmed to discover he's in a Colored neighborhood. Recalling Tinpot Alley and the bad areas of Fredericksburg, he rolls up the window.

Griffin parks on the street in front of his house, the family station wagon occupying the lone space in the driveway. Though an older model, the Griffin family car appears more welcoming, with its scratches and dings, than the unblemished one in the Branch family's driveway. Before Mo can exit Griffin's pickup, he's swarmed by a gaggle of children eager to collect tonight's dinner. Once the food is laid out, the Griffin children flock to the dining room with a zest reminiscent of the Branch dinner table, where Dion was always first to arrive.

From the base of the staircase, Mo sees family photos running up the wall. Like the rest of Griffin's modest home, they are cluttered and well-worn. Inspecting the crooked and chipped frames with the smell of restaurant-prepared food and freshly laundered clothing engulfing him, Mo already feels more at home here than he ever did in the Branch family's much larger house with its perpetually tidy appearance, proper homemade dinners, and phony aerosol scent.

Mrs. Griffin waves to Mo, gesturing him to join the family in the dining room. She's a robust woman with a warm smile and gentle disposition. "You must be Mo. Welcome to our home." Her words drenched in sincerity, she holds his gaze in an earnest attempt to make a connection, motioning Mo to be seated. "Pay no mind to the children. They're so unruly when Derek comes home with dinner. Best get yourself some chicken before it's all gone."

"Thank you, ma'am." Mrs. Griffin's hospitality reminds Mo of his grandmother.

"Oh, it's no bother. You must be starving."

"Yes, ma'am."

"Here, sit yourself down and eat to your heart's content. I'll make myself busy with the children."

Griffin retreats to the bathroom to wash up before returning to address the fracas in the dining room. "Settle down. No need to act like a bunch of hyenas." He turns to their guest. "Welcome to Casa Griffin, Mo. It ain't much, but it's all we need."

Mo smiles through a mouthful of food.

After dinner, the family plays board games. The children ask Mo questions about his parents, siblings, and friends, where he's from, and why he came to work with their dad. He politely answers each, proving he's a suitable fit for their father's workplace and family game night. Not one to meddle, Mrs. Griffin does not pester Mo with personal questions, content to listen as he engages with the children.

On the drive home, Mo notices the colorful chalk and children's bicycles have been replaced by loud clothing and decorative hats igniting the dark streets. With his father's cautionary words running through his head—*Don't get yourself caught in a Colored neighborhood any time a day, but never after dark*—Mo presses down the door lock knob.

Back at the townhouse and once again alone, Mo repeats the same pattern as the previous evening, though filled with a sense of belonging he hasn't known for many years.

# GRANDFATHER'S COMMON FOLK

## SATURDAY, 23 AUGUST 1975

P*almer heads south to Quincy on the twenty-fifth anniversary of his father's death.* He drives to Saint Mary's Cemetery to visit his parents' graves. Dwarfed by the Palmer Family Mausoleum, two unassuming, gray-speckled obelisks stand out front, his parents' initials carved into their bases. He reads the information on their granite markers before sitting on the marble bench in front of the mausoleum.

Despite coming from wealth, Palmer's mother didn't crave an ostentatious lifestyle nor desire opulence in death, her self-worth dictated by a strong fundamental belief in self-sacrifice, commitment, and charity. She made her husband promise she'd be buried in a grave with a simple marker when her time came, her significance resting in her life's body of work and not in death's chamber. She made her son promise he'd honor his father through hard work and integrity, and pay tribute to his mother through generosity and love. When Palmer visits Saint Mary's, as he does twice a year, he's impressed by the family mausoleum and enjoys the bench out front but cherishes the values his parents instilled in him.

Sitting on the bench, staring at his parents' obelisks, Palmer allows his thoughts to wander to one summer day he visited his grandparents, now entombed in the building behind him. His grandparents' estate sat half a mile south of Adam's Shore on Sailors Snug Harbor at the end of a road named for his family. It was the setting for many Sunday gatherings with lunch or dinner served on the rear terrace overlooking Town River Bay. And if young Francis sat on the far northern end of the terrace, he could see the twin masts of his grandfather's vessel at the venerable Town River Yacht Club just across the bay.

It was a hot, sticky day in the Summer of 1936, seven years into the Great Depression, three and a half years into President Roosevelt's New Deal, and one year into Palmer's schooling. On the lunch menu were tuna steaks and fennel-and-citrus salad, with passion fruit cheesecake for dessert. Palmer didn't always like the food, but he loved the smell of cinnamon pipe tobacco on his grandfather's blazer, the feel of the smooth ivory on his grandmother's backgammon board, and listening to his parents talk with his grandparents.

On that second Sunday in August, the discussion transitioned from the Olympics in Germany to Jesse Owens and his gold medals to Hitler and the Nazis before arriving on the subject of young Francis and his education.

"Really, Son," Palmer's grandfather bit down on his pipe, "Francis must attend Milton Academy. All the Palmer men have since my grandfather."

Palmer's father gave a polite nod. "We live in Brookline, and Francis goes to Pierce School. When he gets old enough, he'll go to Brookline High School. They're quality schools, and he likes it."

Palmer watched his mother's face. It never changed; she just smiled. Even as his grandfather's temper was tested, his father's voice never rose, and his mother continued to smile.

His grandfather slapped his hand on his knee. "But your son deserves the best education. Wouldn't you agree?"

"Yes, sir, I do." His father grabbed hold of Palmer and tussled his hair.

"How can you say that when you're sending him to school with common folk?"

"Why are they common? Because they don't live in fancy houses or drive expensive cars or sail in beautiful yachts?" His father gave Palmer a gentle kiss on his head, got up, and stood by his grandfather's chair. "Is the choice to be uncommon limited to the size of one's savings account?"

"Hmph, this what they teach at Harvard now? That we should all strive to be common?"

Palmer's father shook his head. "I don't understand. How can an educated man who sees the extraordinary in the achievements of Jesse Owens also condemn an educational system striving to be a great equalizer? How can that same man not support an education system operating for the common good on common ground? The public school that Francis attends is right for him, not because it separates him from others, but because it teaches him to thrive in a diverse environment. I very much appreciate having had the opportunity to attend Milton, but I need my son to be exposed, not isolated. To be empowered by understanding and empathy, not entitled by privilege and prejudice." Turning to his son, he nodded. "Francis won't be uncommon because he's sheltered from what's common; he'll be exceptional because he's exposed to issues of equity and equality, opportunity and justice."

Palmer didn't understand all his father's words, and he didn't question his father when they walked to their car. On the drive home. Palmer sat in the back seat, watching his mother's approving gaze fall upon her husband. He understood they made each other better. He knew his father listened to his mother when it came to the home and raising their son. And he knew his mother listened to his father when it came to business and providing for their family.


Palmer picks up a twig and rises from the marble bench, tapping headstones as he walks back to his car. He wonders how his parents would judge him today. It's unfair to compare his marriage to their perfect union. Unfair to be compared to *any* marriage, really. And therein, he thinks, may lie the issue. In his thoughts and comparisons, would he not be guilty of the same prejudice between what's common and what's uncommon? Would his father be proud of his work? Would his mother be proud of his work-life balance? Would they approve of his personal choices? What would he say if they questioned the way he treated his family? How would he answer? But he knows they would not ask, nor would they judge. That was not their way.

His car phone ringing, Palmer hustles the final few yards. "Yeah?"

"Hey, Frankie, it's Harry. You busy?"

"Nope. What's up?"

"We were wondering if you want to come over for dinner. My daughter's bringing her husband, and the wife's making lamb chops, mashed potatoes, and gravy. Thought you might be interested."

"Hey, sorry, Harry. I do appreciate it, but I'm gonna be busy tonight. Tell your wife I'm sorry I can't enjoy some of her cooking. I need to get over there one of these nights."

"C'mon," Osmond says, his voice cynical. "I know what busy means for *you* on Saturday night. Why don't you come eat and play cards with us? You'll have a good time."

"Thanks, but I got plans."

"I'm sure you do. Why don't you change them and spend the evening here?"

"Wish I could, but I can't change these plans. Maybe next time."

"Alright, I know you got a date with Jack and whatever female friend he attracts. You know I'm always here, buddy."

"I know that, uh, Harry." Palmer almost lets the word 'dad' slip out. "I gotta go. Thanks for the call. Tell Irene I appreciate the invite." Palmer fumbles with the receiver as he slides it into the slot. Why had he almost said 'dad'? Was his father speaking to him through Osmond? Was his mother asking his father to intervene? Why tonight? It's the same as any other Saturday night. Why *this* Saturday night?

Driving over the Neponset River and reconnecting with 93 North, Palmer sees the Dorchester exit signs. To his right, houses of the privileged look out over Squantum Point and into the channel. On the opposite side, across six lanes of traffic, the residents in some of Boston's toughest communities look out for their children. He thinks back to his grandfather's words. He wonders if his grandfather's term—*common folk*—includes the children of middle-class and hardworking blue-collar families. How would his grandfather describe families trying to eke out an existence amid the dangers present in Dorchester, Mattapan, and Roxbury's worst neighborhoods? How would he describe the whores and the pimps, the dealers and the junkies, the neighborhood bullies and the local vagrants? How would he see the minority populations in Boston's ethnic districts? Palmer knows how his parents would see them— uncommon. He slides into the outside lane and opens up the engine, ready to socialize with his grandfather's common rabble.

# FOUR HORSEMEN

## SATURDAY, 23 AUGUST 1975

M*o deposits his gloves into the rear pants pocket of his work uniform, fingers dangling out as he had seen Flatbush do earlier in the week.* Standing on the front door landing of the townhouse just after dawn, he surveys the landscape, preparing himself for a long morning walk. Several minutes later, entering one of the many paths mazing through the woods around the campus, he feels the residual cool, moist air pressing against his face.

Mo runs his hand against the bark of an oak tree and squeezes a maple leaf between his fingers. He rubs the leaves of a bee balm and inhales the scent of oregano and thyme. He endures the sting of a Japanese barberry thorn, encouraging him to seek refuge for his hands. Working his fingers into the gloves gets easier each time, creating an immediate separation—an unexpected indifference he's learning to appreciate. Forming a fist, he crushes a New England aster. Wiping the residue on his pants, he feels no sense of loss, any associative connection removed by a crafted patch of cloth, a length of latex.

A gunshot pierces the early-morning silence—dew strewn on groundcover ripples in its aftermath, disrupting the delicate balance ordained by nature. Into the seam created by this unnatural disturbance, Mo walks unsuspecting, startled by its cruelty and lingering just long enough to contemplate the consequences. His lone hunting experience, from many years before, ensures he always considers the viewpoint of the predator and misfortune of the prey. Here, in Rhode Island, he doesn't seek to resolve these conflicts. When his walking is done, he steps across the threshold and enters the townhouse.

Mo works his way down the corridor, surprised to see his bedroom door open and hear laughter fill the community space in the rear of the townhouse. Closing the door, he continues to the living room, where a young man sits on the sofa. "Hey there, you must be the new guy."

Mo hears a female voice from the kitchen. "Hi!"

"That's my girlfriend, Kay." The young man says, walking toward Mo. "I'm Carlton." He jerks his head back. "Wow, you're even taller than I am." Carlton Eugene Dufresne is clean-shaven with medium-length, mousy brown hair drifting across his forehead just above his amber eyes. "What's your name?"

"I'm Mo." He looks at Kay, then back at Carlton. "Are you both going to live here?"

Carlton chuckles. "No, this is an all-male townhouse. Kay lives off-campus with her family and works at her dad's hardware store in town."

"Hi, Mo," Kay says, wiping her hands on a dishtowel as she walks over. She extends her hand. "It's nice to meet you."

Embracing Kay's hand, Mo feels the hair stand on the back of his own. "You're very pretty."

"Why, thank you," Kay says. Kayleigh Ann Thompson's crystal-clear blue eyes are warm and inviting, drawing attention away from her mildly askew nose—a minor dent on the bridge from a childhood skating mishap.

Carlton nudges Mo in the ribs. "Whoa, big boy, she's taken."

Mo steps back. "Oh, I'm sorry, she reminds me of my mother."

"Well, that's okay, then. She reminds me of my mother, too. Sometimes." Carlton jabs Mo in the chest with his long, muscular arms. "I'm just teasing. I know she's pretty, and everyone else does, too. I'm also required to say she's intelligent and caring." He winks at Kay. "My mother says she has a heart that matches the color of her hair."

Kay places her hand over her heart. "Oh, Carlton, sometimes you can be so sweet." Glancing at Mo, she rolls her eyes.

Carlton puts his arm around Kay's shoulder, turns to Mo. "So, they tell me you're working here at the school?"

Mo nods. "I'm working with Mr. Griffin as a junior groundskeeper."

Kay moves out from under her boyfriend's arm, tosses the dish-towel on the counter, and takes a seat on the sofa.

Carlton watches Kay's progress before refocusing on Mo. "How did you score a senior residence on campus?"

"I don't know. Mr. Griffin took me to the housing office, and the lady there said I was living here."

Kay waves Mo over and pats a sofa cushion. "Where did you come from?"

Mo sits next to her. "I was living in Virginia with my brother and the Branch family after my dad died."

"I'm sorry to hear that. How did your father die?"

"He was sick for a long time. My grandma took care of me and my brother until she died last year. Then, an ambulance took our dad to the hospital, and he died there."

"Oh, that's awful. Where's your brother? Did he come with you?"

Mo lowers his head. "Jake's being adopted by Mr. and Mrs. Branch, but they didn't want me."

Kay taps Mo's hands. "Well, we're glad to have you here."

Carlton pulls Kay up from the sofa. "Yeah, I think you'll fit right in. The other guys should be here this afternoon. We're gonna head upstairs to take a nap." He winks.

Kay gives Carlton a soft slap on the arm. "Stop that."

"I'm just kidding. We got off to an early start, and it was a late night, so we'll catch you on the flipside."

Stretching out on the sofa to read, Mo is elated with the arrival of his first housemate. Earlier in the week, to help get through the lonely nights, Mo borrowed several books from the library at the Unistructure. With his new friends upstairs, he continues reading *The Trumpet of the Swan*. He loved listening to Grandma Cleveland read the E.B. White classic to Jake, pretending not to pay attention while playing solitaire. He always liked Sam Beaver, the kindhearted eleven-year-old nature lover helping Louie, the voiceless trumpeter swan, learn to communicate. On those long afternoons by the river waiting for the Branch children to come home from school, Mo hoped Louie would come floating down the

Rappahannock, trumpet in hand, and teach Mo how to play so he could communicate better with the Branches.

Early afternoon, Mo's startled by the front door slamming against the wall. "Lucy, I'm home!" Two young men storm into the living room with boxes, bags, and violent thirst.

The one with short, curly, red hair and freckles across his orange-toned cheeks drops his baggage with a thud. "Grab me a Bud, will you?" Heading out for another load, The Redhead spots Mo lying on the sofa and stops in his tracks. "Who the hell are you?"

His friend, sporting a full mustache on an otherwise clean-shaven face and short cinnamon brown hair, stands at the end of the sofa staring at Mo. "Hey there, are you in the right house?"

An avalanche of long legs cascades down the stairs and rushes through the hallway. "Hey, guys," Carlton points to the sofa, "that's Mo. He's gonna be in the downstairs bedroom." He slaps The Redhead on the back. "Mo, this is Jim. We call him 'Bozo' when he's drinking, and 'Nancy' when he's hungover and irritable." He snickers.

Jim pushes Carlton away. "Shut the fuck up." He points to The Mustache. "Get that Bud, would you?"

"T, will you grab me one too, please?" Carlton uses a single letter to refer to his closest friends. He nods at The Mustache. "That's Trevor. He's the brains of our little operation here. He's on a full academic ride."

Trevor points at Mo. "You want a beer?"

Mo shakes his head.

Sitting next to Mo, Carlton starts lacing his shoes. "You guys need some help unloading? Where did you park the car?"

"I thought it was just the four of us living here," Jim scowls, "and, pronounce your Rs, you pretentious Boston asshole."

"I got a call from housing last week. They said there was a worker about our age coming to the school that needed housing, and if we took him in, it would reduce each of our housing costs by twenty-five percent." Carlton puts his arm around Mo. "Say hello to our new housemate."

Mo remains silent, wondering if they're deciding whether to keep him. As Kay enters the living room, Mo catches her smiling at him. He's too nervous to smile back.

Jim pulls the tab on his beer. "You made a decision affecting all of us without asking?" Guzzling, foam escapes from the sides of his mouth.

Carlton places his unopened beer on the footstool. "It didn't impact you or Trevor, other than reducing your cost. I gave Brian a courtesy call because we were supposed to have singles. He was cool with it."

"Shit!" Finishing off his beer, Jim stomps out of the room, shouting as he leaves, "Anybody else gonna give me a hand unloading the fucking car?"

Carlton follows Jim. "Hey, watch the language. Kay's here," he says. "And for Chrissake, pronounce your G's, you self-righteous hillbilly," he mutters to himself.

Trevor stops in front of Mo on his way out. "Jim's okay, just gets kinda ornery when he needs a beer."

Kay sits beside Mo. "You'll be alright. Jim takes some getting used to." She taps his knee several times. "Why don't you go give the guys a hand?"


After the dust settles, Trevor and Jim head upstairs, Carlton and Kay go to lunch, and Mo returns to reading and napping on the sofa. A little after four, he's disturbed by a knock at the front entrance. Opening the door, he finds a young Black man wearing a white tee and Levi jeans holding a gunny sack over his left shoulder and a guitar case strapped on his back.

The young man stares at Mo with wide eyes. "Holy cow, you're huge. You must be the new guy. You gonna play on the football team?"

"Yes...uh. Um...no," Mo scratches his head. "Are you going to live with us?"

"Yeah." The young man drops his gunny on the floor and looks upstairs. "Any of the other guys here yet?"

"They're sleeping."

Carlton approaches from the parking lot. "B, that you?"

"Yeah. Who's the defensive lineman here?"

"That's Mo. He's the new guy taking the downstairs bedroom I told you about. It's good to see you, bud." Carlton hugs his friend. "Mo, this is my roommate, Brian."

"Nice to meet you, Mo," Brian says.

Kay squeezes through the congested doorway, rolls her eyes, and continues down the hall without saying a word.

Brian watches her pass. "Good to see you, too, Kay."

Without looking back, Kay throws a half-hearted wave. "Sorry, wouldn't want to disturb your little love-fest."

Brian turns back to Carlton. "Man, it's nice to be back. What a summer!"

Carlton pats him on the shoulder. "Throw your stuff upstairs, and let's catch up."

Brian pounds on Trevor and Jim's bedroom door as he heads back down.

Minutes later, Mo is sitting in the living room with his new roommates. Though they ignore his presence, he enjoys the sound of their voices after a week of silence.

Kay says very little, sometimes looking over at Mo with a smile or a wink or shrug of her shoulders.

Mo smiles back. Crushed beer cans piling up on the coffee table, he notices Carlton, Trevor, and Brian apply a simple hourglass-style squeeze when they finish a can, similar to his father and Earl Johnson in the past, while Jim pounds his fist down to flatten it when he's done, an aggressive ritual that surprises him. After a couple of hours, the collection of tin on the table spills over to the floor.

Carlton kicks a can resting near his bare foot. "Let's get this mess cleaned up. In fact, let's go over house responsibilities while we're all together."

Brian raises a beer. "Hear! Hear!"

Carlton slams his nearly full can onto the table, spraying several streams of Schlitz onto the carpet. "Four Horsemen, come to order." He speaks as though he were running for office. "J, you get weekly beer runs. Everyone's responsible for filling the beer jar—twenty dollars a week. T, food. Everybody, twenty-five dollars per week in the plastic envelope on the kitchen counter. If you want something else, edit the list and leave T additional money to cover it, or go get it yourself." He places his hand across his chest. "I've got parties. I'll collect money as needed and hang notices at the Rotunda. We can all contribute with word of mouth. B, you got chick schedule. Let's get it posted on the refrigerator. In an emergency, make sure there's a sock on the doorknob."

Mo scratches his head, still curious about the seemingly widespread interest in baby birds. "Where do we keep the chickens?"

Even Kay is unable to keep from laughing as the room breaks out in howls and hoots. Mo blushes.

Scratching his belly, Jim lets out a wailing belch. "Damn, you're one stupid son of a bitch."

Carlton looks at the other boys with a wry smile before turning his attention to their newest housemate. "Mo, you get the most important job. You get to keep the place up. Every night, you get rid of all the trash. Once a week, or when necessary, you vacuum the community area, mop the kitchen and clean the hallway bathroom. You'll also be responsible for keeping the refrigerator clean and doing the dishes. I want this place kept spotless." He points at Mo. "You got that?"

Mo beams with a surge of importance. "Yes, sir."

"Stay out of our bedrooms and bathroom upstairs. Those are off-limits."

Kay pulls on Carlton's pant leg. "Carl, that's not very nice."

"Why? He's happy to do it." Pointing to the coffee table, Carlton snaps his fingers. "Chop, chop, Mo! You can start by getting these beer cans out of here and getting us another round."

Jumping to his feet, Mo retrieves five cold cans and a trash bag from the kitchen. Jim extends his leg as Mo passes by, but Trevor kicks it out of the way, glaring at Jim.

Interpreting Jim's action as playful, Mo smiles. "I'll keep the downstairs clean. I promise."

An evil smile crosses Jim's lips. "You'll do fine. We're all gonna make sure you do."

When the housemates finish their beer, they lob the empties at Mo, Jim's hitting him on the side of the face. Mo smiles as he wipes off the suds.

Early evening, everyone heads to McGuinn's pub for dinner and a few pints. Once the plates are cleared, the drinking begins in earnest, as does the inquisition.

A rapid accumulation of beer settling in his stomach, Jim looks across the table and addresses Mo. "So, what's your story, big guy?"

Surprised, Mo looks up from his Sprite. "I'm sorry, what story?"

"Like how'd you end up here at Bryant? Living with us?" Jim pushes a beer bottle into Mo's shoulder. "How'd *we* get so lucky, huh?"

Mo checks his shoulder. "I came on a bus from Virginia to work as a groundskeeper, and Mr. Griffin showed me the house and gave me a key."

"Okay." Jim points the neck of his beer bottle around the table, "But why *our* house? Did we win a lottery or something?" Pointing at Trevor, he shakes his empty bottle.

Kay rests her palms on the table. "Come on, Jim, leave him alone."

With a look and a nod, Jim sends Kay a silent but strong suggestion, *Fuck off, bitch*. He proceeds to grill Mo. "How come you came here alone?" Reaching across the table, he takes a long swig from Trevor's beer. "Doesn't seem like you should be traveling by yourself."

Sitting back, Kay folds her arms.

Mo shakes his foot under his chair. "My brother and I went to live with the Branch family when my dad died, but they're adopting him and not me."

"There's a surprise." Jim looks around the table with satisfaction. "Guessing your brother's not like you?"

"No, he's a lot younger and not as big. He has a different mom and darker skin than me." Mo's hand begins to shake.

"One that's smarter, no doubt." Jim chuckles. "Is his mom Black?"

"Don't answer that, Mo." Kay nudges her boyfriend. "Carl, stop him!"

"Come on, Jim. Leave him alone," Carlton says, smirking, "or at least wait until Kay isn't around."

"Carl!" Kay glares at Carlton.

Jim speaks faster, louder. "So, why didn't they want *you*?"

Mo feels the tension rising in his chest. "Emily didn't like me, and she told lies about me, and then I had to sleep in Mr. Branch's office until I came here."

"What kind of lies did she tell about you? That you're smart?"

Mo avoids Jim's glower. "I don't like to talk about Emily."

"Why not? If you're gonna be living with us, shouldn't we know why you got thrown out of your last home?" Jim slams his hand on the table. "C'mon, Mo, tell us about this girl."

Mo stares at his Timex, bouncing his knee faster than the sweeping of the second hand.

"What was her name again?"

Carlton places a hand on Jim's arm. "Seriously, man, stop."

"Hey! Answer me, asshole!" Jim roars, his bourbon-colored eyes now molten.

Mo stands, arms by his side. Hands clenched, he stares down at Jim, voice louder than before. "I said I *don't* want to talk about Emily!"

The full measure of Mo's physical stature before them, an uncomfortable silence descends upon the group. Sliding his chair away, he walks outside.

Nodding, Jim sneers at Carlton.

Trevor returns in time to witness the final stages of the exchange. "Let's take these back with us." He hands Carlton and Brian two bottles each. "You're done, Jim. Let's get you to bed."

Jim shakes the empty bottles on the table, sucks out a few drops from each, and grunts.

Driving back to the townhouse, the boys chat as though nothing has happened. Mo and Kay are silent. When they arrive, Kay exits first, heading straight to her car. The rest of Mo's story will have to wait.

# -18-

# PHANTOMS

## THURSDAY, 28 AUGUST 1975

P*almer's partial to Jack.* Alcohol's permitted in the field office on three occasions: celebrations, workdays after six, and weekends. Murphy always has a bottle or two of top-shelf, single malt scotch whiskey in his drawer. Today's a celebration—Murphy's retirement—and Palmer's preference aside, he's not afraid of a little old-country hair.

Murphy's speech is short, as expected, almost as short as Debbie the admin's skirt. Her cups have been in Palmer's face all afternoon, but he's never been interested in her typing skills or the bearskin rug in front of the fireplace in her apartment. For him, work and play don't mix. Not during the week. Not even on Saturday nights. He slips away while she refills, finding Osmond and Ross in Murphy's office one final time.

"Hey, Frank." Ross raises his glass. "Good to see you still standing."

Palmer tosses his empty cup in the trash. "Takes more than cheap bourbon and one of the girls from the admin pool to lay me out. Heard you've been running donuts for Barnhart down in Brockton. How's that treating you, Gerry?"

"Always the asshole, right?" Ross shoves a bite of cake into his mouth.

Murphy points behind Palmer. "Close the door. I'm down to my last bottle here."

"Jesus, no." Palmer waves his hand in front of his face. "You guys need to let the air circulate in here."

"You missed the taco bar at lunch." Ross chuckles, his face red as a bottle of Campari.

Osmond nods once in Palmer's direction. "How you feeling, Frankie?"

"I'm fine." Palmer sits on the edge of the desk, lights a cigarette. "I'm sure I'll release some anxiety over the weekend."

Murphy hands him a shot of Glenlivet. "Here, no plastic for us. Feeling better they slapped suspicion of burglary charges on your boy in Salt Lake late last week?"

Palmer stares into the glass. "Yeah, but the bastard's daddy bailed him out." He spins the scotch before downing it, handing the tumbler back to Murphy. "At least they've got a tail pinned on that jackass."

Murphy pours another shot and hands it to Palmer. "They found all that shit in his trunk. Asshole had an excuse for everything."

"Son of a bitch can't hide now." Palmer swirls and pounds. "It may stop the killing for the time being, but they haven't got enough to hold the bastard." He slides the glass back to Murphy.

"Slow down, Francis." Murphy pours a half-shot. "They've got him now. It's only a matter of time."

Palmer shakes his head. "I wanted to help build that case."

Osmond pats Palmer on the back. "Relax, Frankie, you were right. You had him pegged months ago. That asshole, Bundy, ain't gonna hurt any more girls now."


An hour later, Murphy's waiting for Palmer outside the bathroom. "Hey, Francis, I wanted to talk to you alone for a minute."

Palmer shakes his hands before tapping a cigarette out of his pack. "What's on your mind?"

Murphy taps Palmer's elbow. "Well, I know what's on yours." He grabs the cigarette before Palmer can light it, snaps it in half, and drops it in the trash can. "You need to give these damned things up. Now, listen to me."

Palmer nods as he reaches for another cigarette.

"I called in a favor this week from an old friend in the Salt Lake Field Office. He pushed a few buttons with the Utah State Police, and we got a request for profile and forensics support. They asked for you by name."

Palmer lights, blowing the smoke behind him. "Thanks, Dick. I really appreciate this."

"Yeah." Murphy sniggers. "They did it for the sorry old man who's leaving." He winks, his eyes glassy. "Don't you believe it. They were getting ready to ask for you anyway. Bundy sold his car two days ago. They confiscated it yesterday. Gonna be tearing it apart."

Palmer smiles back. He knows Murphy's not being completely honest, but it's what he's always loved about him—Murphy takes care of his own. "I'm gonna miss you, Dick. Where you leaving for tomorrow? Word around the office is there's a big trip planned."

"Oh, yeah, well, Helen and I aren't going anywhere right now. I've got some tests the next two days; then we'll start planning a nice vacation around Christmas." Murphy's smile doesn't fade, even as he tells Palmer the truth. "I wouldn't be worried about that. You have your own trip to think about. You fly out Tuesday morning after the holiday."

Back in the office, Palmer looks at his friends on Murphy's last day: Dick retired, Gerry not far behind, and Harry moving up to his final position. He doesn't see himself retiring for years—two decades, maybe three—and doesn't expect to last long after he's done. Staring at his now-former boss, he's fully aware that Dick's frequent coughing has grown increasingly violent over the past several years. Palmer knows Murphy's will be a brief retirement followed by a prolonged period of mourning for his wife.

Alcohol still warm in his throat and stirring in his belly, Palmer thinks about Marilyn: how she endured his long nights, the phantoms he brought back from investigations, and the escalating sins of his obsession. She had been so loving and patient, tending to the girls' needs and his when he was recovering. He wishes he still had her love and patience, even if he knows it's selfish. He'll work until there's no retirement, and Marilyn's mourning will be much shorter. He'd made damn well certain of that.

# VERONICA

## FRIDAY, 29 AUGUST 1975

M o's filled with excitement as he heads to the townhouse after work. With a letter from Virginia and his first paycheck tucked in his rear pocket, his pace is brisk. He holds the sports section from Griffin's morning paper out in front of him, memorizing the baseball standings as he hustles home. Spared decades of disappointment, his budding interest in the home team lacks perspective. But he will learn. Late summer in New England is predictable for its heat, humidity, and the fading optimism of Red Sox Nation.

This afternoon, as Mo marches and reads, all is well. Despite sweltering conditions, the Red Sox are still leading the division as August draws to a close. Heading back to a townhouse filled with new friends, weighed down only by a jingle in his pocket and an envelope on his mind, life could not be better.

Outside of birthday cards from his Aunt Elizabeth, Mo did not receive mail in Virginia. Seated on his bed, he examines the stamp, post office imprint, and return address before opening. Unfolding the sheets of paper, he finds two letters, each with handwriting on one side. He reads the shorter one with better penmanship first.

*Mo,*
*Hello from all of us in the Branch family. We hope you are doing well and adjusting to your new job and surroundings. Jake misses you.*

*Sincerely,*
*Mr. and Mrs. Branch, Emily, Mary, Peter, Paul, and Dion.*

Uncertain how he'd reply, Mo raises a single brow and places the letter down on the bed. He turns his attention to the second letter, recognizing Jake's handwriting even as he unfolds the paper.

*Big Brother,*
*Hi! I hope you're OK. It's been so hot here and I miss you a lot. Paul says hi. We play with the hose out back but it's not as much fun and Dion's lonely without you here. School starts in two weeks, so we had to go with Mrs. Branch to get some clothes yesterday. It took all day, which wasn't fun, but we got to eat pizza at the mall, so that was cool. We had a lot of rain last weekend and the river was moving fast on Sunday morning. I wish you were here to see it. I miss you. It's time for dinner, so I'll stop here. I love you. Jake*

*P.S. Mrs. Harrington is real sick. Sorry for the bad news. She went to the hospital last Tuesday and mom says she has cancer and may not live too long. She went home yesterday and we went over to see her. She's skinny now and looks yellowy and everyone seems sad. She asked how you're doing.*

The postscript hits Mo hard. Reading it several times, he pleads with God to help Mrs. Harrington feel better. When Grandma Cleveland had cancer, she got skinny and yellow at the end, dying almost eighteen months after they told her. He wonders if Mrs. Harrington only has that long.

Mo reaches for a sepia-toned photograph sitting on the nightstand by his bed, an enduring image of Grandma Cleveland standing over his mother and Mrs. Harrington at the dinner table. Taken by his grandfather on one of the first Polaroid Model 95 cameras when his mother was thirteen, the photograph was given to Mrs. Harrington before his mother died to hold on to until Mo was older. Mrs. Harrington gave it to him after Grandma Cleveland's burial last April. Standing guard by his bed, Mo's most beloved possession watches over him while he sleeps. As he often does, particularly in times of despair, Mo flips the photograph around to read his mother's inscription on the back—*When we do not harbor bitterness, we only have room for bliss.*

Sometimes, when Jake was tiny, Mo would kneel with his brother by Grandma Cleveland's bed, asking her why their father was angry. When they got older, after praying, they'd ask why he was so sick. She would smile, telling them God had not abandoned their father and explaining that life is like a great river: easy to navigate in calm waters, but some folks come to see only turbulence, grow bitter, and lose their way. She would implore them to keep God near as their compass. With the help of Mrs. Harrington, they bought their father a compass for Christmas one year, placing it on the folding table beside his empty cans. But he seldom left his chair by then. And he never really woke.


On the night of Grandma Cleveland's funeral and burial, with the sepia-toned photograph resting on the nightstand by his bed, Mo went into the living room at eight to watch the Dodgers play the Braves in Atlanta on Monday Night Baseball. A little after nine, Mo raised the volume as he watched the celebration. Fans were giving a Black man a standing ovation in the Deep South for breaking the most cherished record in sports.

"What's that?" Ken grumbled, rubbing his eyes. "Why's that so loud?"

Mo sat at the edge of the sofa. "Hank Aaron just passed Babe Ruth as the all-time home run king."

"Figures." Ken's voice was hoarse. "Don't change nothing. Ruth's still the greatest home run hitter." Ken shifted to his side, closed his eyes. "Now, shut that crap off and get to bed."

Upstairs, Mo looked in the mirror as he brushed his teeth, dogged by questions he could not answer. Why was his father so bitter? Why was he so sick? Why did God have to take Grandma Cleveland when they needed her? Was his grandmother watching the game? Was Sam watching? Grandma Cleveland always liked Sam. When he finished brushing, he checked his teeth, wondering why God makes some folks White and some folks Black, and why it would matter. Had his grandmother already asked God why? Did she know the answer?

Lying in his bed so many miles from Virginia, Mo realizes Mrs. Harrington was always there: by his mother's bed, at school, in photographs, and through her actions. Mrs. Harrington was *always* there. Even now, as he touches the medal on his necklace, he knows she's with him.

Despite his sadness, Mo looks back at Jake's letter and notices a reference to Mrs. Branch as 'mom.' It stings. Acknowledging the cursory tone and inclusion of Emily's name, Mo tears up Mrs. Branch's note, squeezing the tatters in his hands before tossing them into the wastebasket.

Mo rolls off the bed, places Jake's letter in the nightstand drawer, and uses the envelope to stow his savings in his father's shoebox. Resting a photograph of Jake on the nightstand between the ones of his parents, he prays for Mrs. Harrington and hopes Jake won't become a memory.

Returning from dinner and laundry at the Unistructure later that evening, Mo's happy to find Kay at the townhouse with the boys. They're collected in the living room along with a young brunette seated on Brian's lap. Mo has learned to ignore Brian's female guests, having yet to see one twice.

Mo walks behind the sofa, leans into Kay, and hands her a twenty. "I got my first paycheck today. Can you buy me a transistor radio at your father's store, please? I want one so I can listen to the games in my room."

Turning, Kay smiles. "Sure, Mo, that's a good idea. Can you put it on the counter next to my purse?"

Mo nods and heads to the kitchen.

"Hey, Mo! Did I just hear you say it's *payday*?" Jim taps Trevor's arm. "Wanna play cards?"

Sitting up, Carlton slides his arm out from around Kay's shoulder. "Yeah, that's a great idea. You'll need some money, big guy. Shouldn't need more than twenty bucks. We can make change if you don't have any."

Following an excited nod, Mo heads to his bedroom.

Kay nudges her boyfriend. "Carl, don't."

Mocking confusion, Carlton looks back at Kay. "Why not?"

"Carl?" She glares at her boyfriend. "I'm gonna leave if you're gonna take advantage of him." She points at Trevor. "*You* should know better."

The Brunette empties a bottle of wine into her glass. "He lives here, right? Let him play if he wants to."

With an air of disgust, Kay removes herself from Carlton's side. Passing Mo in the hallway, she pats him on the arm. "Good luck. Don't let them take all your money."

Confused by her sudden departure, Mo watches Kay exit, and Carlton rush by to say goodnight. Mo returns to the living room, occupying the spot Kay just vacated. "I can't stay up too late. I'm going fishing with Mr. Griffin and Professor Langford tomorrow morning."

With a mischievous smile, Jim taps Trevor's beer can with his own. "That's fine. It shouldn't take long for us to clean you out."

Upon Carlton's return, the housemates teach Mo how to play five-card stud. The pots don't exceed two dollars, and Mo has some early success. But as the evening progresses, the bidding increases and Mo finds winning more difficult, twice going back to his room to retrieve another twenty. While there's the occasional outburst by one of the players, Mo remains silent with an enthusiastic smile throughout.

Just after eleven, The Brunette, seated on the armrest of Brian's chair, tugs at the hem of his sleeve. Ignored, she taps Mo's elbow with her foot. "So, you like it here?"

Mo's eyes remain focused on the stacks of change in front of him. "Yes, ma'am."

"Do you go to school here?"

"No."

"I didn't think so." The Brunette nudges Brian. "You don't seem like the college type. How old are you?"

"Twenty-four."

The Brunette points her wine glass at Mo. "How'd you get so big?"

Mo shrugs. "I'm not sure."

"Was your father big like you?"

"No."

"Did you have a nickname at home?"

Mo fidgets with his Timex. "Not really."

"C'mon, everybody's got a nickname."

Brian places his hand over her mouth. "Let it go, Veronica."

She pushes his hand away. "Let him answer."

"'Slow Mo.'" Wincing, Mo glances at Veronica while scratching the back of his neck. "My dad said it's because I'm so big, and I run slow."

Veronica releases a wicked laugh. "I don't think that's it, Mo."

Trevor's head is hung over his cards. "Veronica, stop."

"What? He should know why they call him that." She continues to giggle.

"Come on, Veronica. We have to live with him." With his eyes, Carlton motions Brian to get rid of his date.

Veronica tosses a dismissive wave. "I guess if you guys don't mind living with a big idiot, it's no matter to me. You just keep patting yourselves on the back for taking the retard's money."

"Hey, knock it off!" Trevor glares at Brian, "Take her upstairs. Educate her. Disrespect her the way you do. She deserves it." He slams down his cards. "I'm done with this."

Grabbing Veronica's arm, Brian escorts her upstairs while she volleys expletives in Trevor's direction.

Dejected, Mo picks up empty cans. "I'm sorry."

Trevor helps him with the trash. "Don't be sorry, Mo. It's not your fault. *She's* the idiot."

Carlton pulls a twenty from Jim's pile and his own, placing them in Mo's. "Here's your money back."

Jim sweeps several empty beer cans off the table. "What the hell are you doing?! He lost that fair and square. I agree with Brian's white trash."

Carlton clears the cards from the table. "T, for the love of God, please get Nancy to bed." He motions to Mo. "You can clean up in the morning. Why don't you head to bed. It's been a long night, and we got a little drunk. It's all cool. You're cool."

Trevor stands over Jim. "C'mon, let's go."

Jim gives Carlton a dirty look and the finger, pushing Trevor away as they head upstairs.

Back in his bedroom, unable to erase Veronica's insensitive words and her high-pitched laugh, Mo lies in bed rereading Jake's letter. He stares at the paper. Two words stare back—*mom* and *cancer*. After saying his prayers, Mo asks God why Mrs. Branch gets Jake, and Mrs. Harrington gets cancer. Was Mrs. Branch like Emily when she was young? Why do Mr. and Mrs. Branch treat Emily better than the other children? Why do they always believe *her*? Are Veronica's parents like Mr. and Mrs. Branch? Is that what makes girls like Emily and Veronica so mean? He rests the letter on his side table, recalling the first time Emily confronted him.


During his first ten weeks in the Branch home, Mo learned to stay away from Emily. But on a Saturday afternoon in early April, six days after Easter, Emily caught Mo and Dion alone in the upstairs hallway. Her face was shriveled up like an old dish rag. "Do you know why the kids call you 'Slow Mo?'"

Mo, surprised Emily was addressing him, answered with a smile, "It's because I'm slow at running and stuff. My dad told me."

"Is that so?" Emily stood there, hands on her waist, eyes glowing, her tone incensed. "Well, your daddy was lying. They call you 'Slow Mo' because you're an idiot—brain damaged or something." Her head rocked back and forth, mocking him. "What happened? Did your mommy drop you when you were little?" Her ocean-colored eyes turned cobalt as she threw her head back in laughter.

Mo's cheeks began to itch. His mouth went dry, unable to respond.

Emily pointed at him, one hand still on her waist. "You're only here because my parents saved you from the nuthouse."

Mo's body shivered, his leg muscles tightened. His hands felt for the wall. From the doorway to his room, Dion bore silent witness. Though his face showed no emotion, Mo knew Dion felt his pain.

"Jake's okay, but you're a giant retard, and *we* all have to deal with it." Emily let out an angered grunt. "I hate you! So does everybody else."

Mo felt the burning along his spine as he slid down the hallway wall, burying his face into his forearms and knees. "That's not true. Why do you want to hurt me? What did I do to you?" He looked up with tears smeared across his cheeks.

Glaring, Emily hovered over him. "I hate you! You ruined my life!" She walked to the top of the stairs before turning back. "Because of you, I lost my room! You embarrass me in front of my friends! We'll keep Jake because he's okay, but you need to go. We all hate you!" She descended the stairs.

Resting his head back into his arms, Mo clenched his hair in his shaking fists. Dion sat at his side and laid his head against Mo's shoulder.

Five hundred miles from the Branch home, Mo again feels the sting of hurtful words. Hands shaking and feeling the familiar rush of heat to his cheeks, he presses his fists into the mattress. Finding Emily and Veronica's faces interchangeable, their scornful voices and sinister laughs equally disturbing, he rests his Timex on the nightstand, reaching under the bed for his father's shoebox. He pulls out several items, including a picture of his mother smiling. Placing them under his pillow, he feels the extremes of warmth and coolness as he struggles to calm his growing anxiety.

# -20-

# PAULINE'S VISIT

## SATURDAY, 30 AUGUST 1975

Palmer's drive to South Shore Country Club in Hingham is scenic. It takes him along Boston Harbor and south to Quincy and Hingham Bay. Excepting Brookline, South Shore was his father's favorite course. A start time before seven on weekends is less expensive, so his foursome tees off at six fifty. Between himself, Osmond, and Ross, Palmer's the best golfer. Murphy's absence allows a single to join them at the clubhouse, with the investigators soon discovering the young man plays scratch golf. At the seventh, Ross is assigned to Scratch, and they play a beer a hole against Palmer and Osmond.

The fairways are soft after heavy overnight rain. Osmond keeps to the cart path while Palmer manages the cooler—two fresh Millers every third hole. Work's not discussed on the course—a time-honored rule. But today, their conversation turns to their longtime coworker and friend.

Osmond steers the cart to the path indent for the eleventh green. "How did Dick look to you Thursday?"

Palmer pulls his putter from the bag. "Ah, he just looked run down. You know Dick, he's fine."

Following Palmer to the green, Osmond swipes at the tall grass with his putter. "Yeah, I guess so. I just hope he can enjoy some travel. I was talking to my wife last night, and she wants me to retire if I don't get the promotion. Says I should take a security job."

Palmer stands between Osmond and Scratch as Ross takes a second chop from the bunker. "Makes sense, but you'll get it, Harry. You don't have to worry. I'm sure Dick's recommendation will carry weight with the board."

Osmond steps back to allow Ross's ball to scoot by. "With the youngest headed off to college next year, it's just gonna be the two of us. She wants me to start slowing down. Can't blame her."

Palmer nods as he bends down to fix his ball mark. "Well, I think she'll get her wish."

Standing behind Palmer, Osmond waits for him to rise. "You know I'm going with you, right?"

Palmer spins around. "What?"

"I'm headed out to Salt Lake on Tuesday. We're on the same flight."

"Why?"

"Someone's gotta make sure you come back."

"Well, that's bullshit, but it'll be like old times." Palmer pats Osmond on the back. "Tell your wife she doesn't have to worry. I'll take care of you."

After Ross chips his sixth stroke to within five feet, Palmer kicks the ball back, lines up a birdie putt. He thinks about Osmond's wife and wonders what Marilyn would be telling him right now with Pauline headed to college in a few years. Their youngest was always the fearless one. She'd hang from the tree branches in the backyard when she could barely walk, go with him on the scary rides, while Peggy would watch with her mother from the safety of a park bench. Sometimes it concerned him how little regard Pauline had for her own safety, like the day she tried to feed a peanut to a kinkajou through the fence at Franklin Park Zoo. As he stands over his putt, Palmer's concentration is upset by the memory of Pauline's scariest adventure—the one that really hit home.

Pauline had run away. Palmer got the call from Marilyn on a very late Friday night in early June. Pauline left a note saying she wanted to see Dad. She was headed to Boston. Almost twelve, her parents knew too well what could happen to a young runaway. He boarded a plane for Cincinnati at dawn, raced up to Middleton to settle Marilyn down, and read Pauline's note before heading to the bus station.

Pauline had gone to see a movie with several of her friends the night before. Sometime during the film, she went to the bathroom and never returned. Her mother found the note after a frantic parent called, the other girls having realized their friend was missing. Her father knew she walked out to the street to catch the local bus to the Greyhound station.

Palmer was at the Dayton Greyhound station by eleven and sped to Columbus. An attendant there had seen a young girl with brown hair and tan glasses dressed in blue jeans and a green sweater boarding the bus to Youngstown just twenty minutes earlier. Knowing the bus stopped in Canton, then longer in Akron, Palmer hustled to the Columbus airport to catch a commuter. In Youngstown, he was standing outside the bus as Pauline came down the steps. Dropping her bag, she ran into his arms.

"Hi, Daddy," she said, smile wide and eyes bright. "I was coming to visit you."

Palmer crouched down to accept her hug, "I know. I read the letter you left your mother."

"I miss you so much."

Palmer pulled her tiny body into his chest. "I know, sweetie. I miss you, too."

Holding her head back, Pauline squeezed her father tighter. "Can I go home with you?"

"That's for your mother to decide. We need to get you home. She's worried sick." He drew her in for another hug. "I was terrified. What were you thinking?"

"I wasn't afraid, Daddy. I stayed right near the bus station people and told them you work for the FBI, and you get the bad guys."

Palmer couldn't help but laugh. He scooped her up, grabbed her bag, and hailed a taxi. Pauline was back in her bedroom a little after ten, falling asleep minutes later.

Marilyn closed her daughter's bedroom door, poured Palmer a cup of coffee, and made up the sofa for him to spend the night.

Pauline jumped on her father in the morning, smothering him with a barrage of hugs and kisses. Observing from a distance, Peggy sat on the ottoman and smiled. Marilyn made pancakes, and they enjoyed breakfast together. For a short time, it felt to Palmer like he had a family again. At nine, Marilyn took the girls to church. Palmer headed to an empty airport. It was the last time he saw Pauline.

Palmer pulls the putter back and swings through cleanly, but a poor read results in the ball lipping out. He taps in with the back of the putter. Watching Osmond hover over his putt, Palmer's attention drifts to a weeping willow in the background. Wind off the bay rustles the tree's sagging branches, and he sees Pauline's hair as he would push her on the swing in the backyard. Not yet three, she would giggle, begging him to push harder. He realizes he's always pushed harder for his daughters.

# 21

# LANGFORD'S SHADOW

## SATURDAY, 30 AUGUST 1975

M*o opens his eyes just after dawn, and though his bed is much bigger and more comfortable, last night's restless sleep had an eerie similarity to his final six weeks in Virginia—anxious nights spent on the tiny cot in Mr. Branch's office.* He drags himself out of bed, trying to focus on the excitement of his first paycheck, Jake's letter from home, and playing cards with his housemates, but his thoughts turn to Mrs. Branch's insensitive note, Mrs. Harrington's cancer, and Veronica's hurtful words. Later, striding through the woods, Mo wears gloves to protect his clenched fists from the cold reality of his anger. After three hours, he yields to the scorching heat and gunfire at close range, having resolved, at least temporarily, his inner turmoil.

When he returns, Mo takes a quick shower, brushes his teeth, and inspects some fresh scratches on his neck. Having been clawed by limbs as he wrestled with nature, he rinses his wounds with cool water before waiting on the front landing for Griffin's arrival. Following the ten-minute drive to Georgiaville Pond, Mo sees Professor Langford waiting in the parking lot as they arrive.

Stepping out of the pickup, Griffin grabs Langford's outstretched hand. "Hey, Michael, good to see you. How long you been waiting?"

"Not long." Langford waves over the cab of the truck. "Hey, Mo, how are you doing? Ready to catch some fish?"

Mo is beaming. "Hi, Professor Langford. I sure am!"

"There's no 'professor' here. Just call me Michael or Mike."

Griffin collects two fishing rods, a tackle box, and a cooler from the bed of the truck. "I picked up some nightcrawlers and shad."

"Perfect," Langford says, handing Mo a fishing rod. "Here you go. You'll need this. You can keep it. I picked up a new one a few months back. This one's just taking up space in the garage."

Reaching for Langford's present, Mo's eyes grow wide. "Thank you, Professor Langford."

"Please, Mo. It's Mike."

"Yes, sir. Thank you, Mike."

Griffin pulls the bill of his cap down. "You still gotta call me Mr. Griffin. Can't have my workers getting too comfortable." He winks at Langford. "There's no 'professor' in front of my name."

Mo nods, studying the 'B' on Griffin's cap. Knowing it's a Boston Red Sox logo, he hopes to get a team cap himself one day.

When they arrive at a suitable location on the pond, Langford shows Mo how to release the fishing line from the spin-cast reel and thread it through the guides, attach a hook and bobber, and secure a nightcrawler. Mo practices each step with Langford's help but doesn't like the feel of the nightcrawler in his hand or skewering it alive. Putting on his gloves, he fumbles with the oversized maggot, oblivious to the irony that his concern for the worm doesn't extend to the plight of the fish. After numerous attempts, he weaves the hook through several times.

Langford helps Mo stand his pole against a large, square rock with the handle wedged at the base of a tree. He leans his pole next to it. Releasing a little extra line on each, he places a small rock across the excess and winks at Mo. "A little trick my father taught me. When a fish takes the bait, we'll hear and see the rock fall off." He stands over Mo, casting a shadow across the water in front of where Mo's seated. "So, you mentioned you went fishing with your father. What do you remember most?"

Mo watches Langford's shadow linger, shimmering rather than floating on the water. "Just him and Mr. Johnson talking and drinking, I guess." He raises a finger. "Oh yeah, I do remember one of his sayings." He changes his voice to the way he thinks his father sounded. "He'd say: *Some people live life like a hooked catfish—they flounder a long time before they die.* And then he'd say: *Don't be a dumb old catfish, Son.*"

Looking at Griffin, Langford smiles. "Now there's a

thought-provoking observation. I may need to look at adding it to one of my lectures."

Griffin rolls his eyes, lowers his cap.

Langford grabs a Budweiser and Coke from the cooler. "Why don't you tell me a little about yourself," he says, sitting next to Mo.

Mo takes a sip of Coke, allowing a few thoughtful seconds to pass. "What would you like to know, Mike?" He feels important using his new professor friend's first name.

"Tell me about your family. Where are you from?"

"I came here from Virginia. I lived with my brother and the Branch family. My brother, Jake, still lives with them. My mom died when I was eight, and my dad died earlier this year. He was sick for a long time, and Jake helped me take care of him after our grandma died last year."

Langford shakes his head. "Sorry to hear you've endured so much tragedy. I lost my mother when I was very young, too. I was three when she died of complications from pneumonia. My father raised me in Rochester, New York, where he still lives." He pulls the tab on his beer can. "Did you enjoy living with the Branch family?"

Langford's body language and cut-to-the-chase approach remind Mo of Dr. Winchester, though he likes that Langford also shares his story. "I liked the river out back and being with Jake, Paul, and Dion."

"So, why did you leave?"

Mo's body tenses, his words spilling out. "Emily was mean to me, and her mom and dad always believed her instead of me, so they sent me away."

"How old's this Emily?"

Mo speaks through clenched teeth. "Fourteen."

"What mean things would she do?"

Knowing this is a sore topic, Griffin cuts in. "Hey, Mo, did you listen to the game last night?"

Resting his Coke on the ground, Mo smiles. "They won!"

Griffin lifts his cap. "Made a few baserunning mistakes, but they still won handily."

Humidity curling the points of his shirt collar, Langford presses them down with his thumbs, looking over his shoulder at Griffin. "I'm not much of a baseball fan. They're doing pretty well, though, right?"

Griffin pushes himself up. "Yes, Michael," he says, winking at Mo, "we're doing alright."

Mo discusses the Red Sox chances with Griffin for an hour, Langford mostly nodding, before enjoying a lunch of the professor's turkey pesto paninis with a side of Mrs. Griffin's three-bean salad. Acids and enzymes feasting like a pack of scavengers, his friends become as silent as their fishing poles, so Mo decides to explore the paths along the pond. Drawn by the sound of Langford shouting his name, he returns ninety minutes later, drenched in sweat with mud stains on his elbows and knees, his hair a mess, and his work shirt untucked.

Langford's voice is hoarse. "Mo, where have you been? I've been calling you for the past fifteen minutes."

Mo takes off his soiled gloves, shoving them in his back pocket. "I'm sorry. I got lost."

Griffin shakes his head. "I wasn't worried. But Michael here..." Rolling his eyes, he points with his thumb. "I thought he was gonna start crying."

Mo rubs his neck. "I'm sorry."

Langford reaches his hand out. "Why's your neck so red?"

Putting his hand up, Mo pulls away. "I got some scratches when I was walking this morning, and I'm all sweaty now."

"I should have something in my glove box to help with that," Langford says.

Griffin picks up his tackle box and cooler. "Alright, no harm done. Let's get back. My wife's gonna need a break from the kids."

Langford helps Griffin with his poles. "Hey, Derek, I can take Mo back to his townhouse. I'm headed that way, and you're headed south."

Griffin looks at Mo. "You good with that, son?"

"I'm okay. I like Professor Langford, uh, I mean, Mike." Mo

114

appreciates when Griffin calls him 'son,' wondering whether it will be on the name patch of his uniform one day. His first outing in Rhode Island has resulted in a new friend and a renewed interest in fishing. A day anchored by two cleansing walks shelves his anxieties for the time being.

# 22

# A HOUSE BUILT BY THIEVES

M*o has never seen a car like Langford's.* Low and wide with two colors splitting it in half, it's very different. It also doesn't look very big, but Mo's surprised by the roominess once he's in the passenger seat. He rolls down his window, allowing fresh air to replace the smell of vinyl protectant. "I like your car, Mike," he says.

Langford rubs the dashboard. "Thanks. I bought it a few months ago. It's a brand-new model. I think they'll become popular."

"It's so shiny and clean."

"I try to take care of my things," Langford says, glancing over at Mo. "My house is a little ways north. Would you like to join me for dinner?"

"Sure!" Mo looks at his Timex. "Can you bring me home by eight, though?"

"Not a problem. What's happening at eight?"

"I don't want to miss *All in the Family*. It was my father's favorite show."

"Alright, I'll get you home in time."

Situated at the corner of two rural routes in Slatersville, about fifteen minutes north of the Bryant campus, Langford's house is a large, two-story Victorian. Its black slate gabled roof is adorned with a dormer on either side of a viewing terrace on the third story. Wide-eyed, Mo steps out of the car and surveys Langford's property, impressed by the sculpted bushes and manicured lawn. "Whoa! This place is amazing. Do a lot of people live here?"

"No, Mo, this is my house," Langford replies.

"How many kids do you have?"

"It's just me, at least for now."

Mouth hung open, Mo blinks repeatedly. "You live here *alone?*"

"I do." Langford pats Mo's chest, leading him to the front door. He begins his well-rehearsed presentation with a majestic sweep of his hand. "The house was built in 1901 by Alfred Vanderbilt, great-grandson of the nineteenth-century robber baron Cornelius Vanderbilt. I've spent the past eight years restoring it. The upstairs bedrooms aren't quite the way they were when the place was a vacation home; otherwise, it's back to how it looked at the turn of the century. It's been a lot of work," he sighs, "and money, but it's almost there. I maintain about two acres. The other sixty-two are overgrown. They used to be beautiful lawns and gardens, but there's no way I can keep them up. At least they give me privacy. I believe there's a cemetery on the property somewhere, but I've not been back there in years."

Mo scratches his head, finding it strange that thieves built such a beautiful house.

Langford turns on the four aligned and oversized chandeliers in the main foyer. "Just a little place I like to call home," he says with a debonair smile.

Artificial light flooding the space, Mo marvels at the heart-shaped staircase leading to upper-level catwalks fully encircling the outer edge of the room. Plaster revival artwork running the perimeter of the ceiling showcases gothic gargoyles. Amazed by their detail, he wonders if they're figures of the thieves' ancestors.

Pointing as he walks, Langford leads Mo to the far end of the foyer. "The kitchen, formal dining room, two sitting rooms, a parlor, one guest room, and the master bedroom are downstairs."

As Langford's words float by, Mo's mind drifts to when he would play hide-and-seek with Jake. He can't imagine trying to find him in this big, empty house. Looking back down Langford's foyer, littered with doors, a particularly bad recurring dream he had when Jake was four is resurrected.

In his nightmare, Mo stood at the end of a long hallway in Tinpot Alley with fluorescent ceiling lights and endless doors on either side. It was night, and the lights flickered as he played hide-and-seek with Jake, heavy rain scratching against the doors. Mo called out to his brother, but his voice, and Jake's giggles, echoed through the hall until the wind and driving rain drowned them out. Running down the corridor, he pounded his fists on each door, hollering for Jake, but the Rappahannock's quickly rising water seeped through the cracks in the doors, filling the hallway and slowing his search.

When Mo did spot his brother, the water was waist-high, Jake's arms flailing as he struggled to keep his head above water. Swimming over, Mo held onto his brother. At the far end of the corridor, he saw their father sitting in the living room, but the doors could no longer keep the river out, and the waters of the Rappahannock came flooding in. They floated down the swollen river, Jake clinging to his older brother until they saw their father at the islet near Kelly's Ford Bridge, Ken's recliner chained to a tree. Seated in his chair, their father floated with his hands held out. Mo helped Jake grip his father's hand, but his own slipped free. Continuing downstream, Mo saw carcasses of black-haired critters tossing in the rapids ahead of him. Looking back, he saw Sam tangled up in a tree. Mo always woke up at the sight of Sam hanging over his father's head.

Fingers tapping his shoulder pull Mo from the vision of Sam's swinging body, blood drained from his face.

Langford touches Mo's elbow. "You okay?"

Mo nods. "Did you ever get lost when you first moved here?"

"No, but I had to get used to it. I'm sure a lot of people would find it a little creepy living alone in an old house with so many empty rooms, but I'm not afraid of ghosts—at least not the ones that would haunt *this* house." A crooked smile crosses Langford's lips. "Maybe the ones in the old cemetery out back."

Mo shivers.

Langford stands at the base of the staircase. "There's another five bedrooms, a billiard room, and four bathrooms upstairs. It's never hard to find a bathroom. There's a total of eight to go along with seven bedrooms."

"You have seven bedrooms all to yourself?" Mo scratches his head. "There's only three at my house for all five of us."

Langford chuckles. "I don't sleep in all of them, of course. I use the master bedroom over there." He points to a large oak door under the arch to the right of the staircase. "The others are used when I have guests sleep over."

"Your guests are pretty lucky."

"You're welcome to stay over if you like."

"I *can*? *Really*? Okay. Not tonight, though, right?"

"No, not tonight." Langford puts his arm around Mo's shoulder and leads him up the grand staircase to the second floor. "But I do have a pretty impressive TV you could watch *All in the Family* on."

"My friends are going to watch it with me at home."

"I understand. Maybe you can stay over another night and watch a Red Sox game." Langford stops at the entrance to a narrow passageway. Cocking an eyebrow, he speaks in a low tone. "Want to see the *real* reason I bought this house?"

Mo nods.

"It's right up these stairs. Follow me."

As he walks up the cramped spiral staircase, Mo half expects a gargoyle to jump out and yell, "Boo!" When they reach the glass-enclosed room rising above the roof, Mo believes he can see all the way to Virginia.

"Welcome to my sanctuary," Langford says, arms outstretched. "This is called a cupola, and the railed walkway you see just outside the windows is a widow's walk." Langford tugs at his bowtie and pulls it through his collar, unbuttoning the top button of his shirt. "I come up here late afternoon sometimes to read poetry or a historical narrative as a way to get closer to nature." Langford stares out the window. "It may seem odd to connect with nature from the inside of a house, but it's why I bought the place."

Mo's attention is drawn away from the view by a brown-and-tan mackerel tabby sprawled on a low perch. Its emerald eyes stare, unflinching, though with fleeting interest.

"That's Samantha," Langford says. "Someone gave her to me so I wouldn't be alone, but she stays up here most of the time. She comes down to the kitchen when she's hungry, and her litter box is in one of the upstairs bathrooms." He tosses the cat a dismissive wave. "She's honestly the *worst* company. Whether it's because she's a female or a feline, I'm not sure, but she thinks she owns the place. Apparently likes the view up here." He starts down the stairs, waving Mo to follow. "Alright, let's go get dinner started, shall we?"

Mo sits at the island, watching Langford expertly wield a sharp knife to dice red tomatoes and yellow onions, mince fresh garlic, and crush dried basil. The soiled blade sits gleaming in the light as Langford lays out virgin olive oil, tomato sauce, and white sugar before measuring each ingredient with cups and tablespoons. He thinks back to Grandma Cleveland pouring a jar of Ragu into a saucepan.

Langford tastes the edge of a wooden spoon before mixing cooked spaghetti noodles into the sauce. "I'm sorry, Mo, if I'd known you were coming, I would've made pasta from scratch."

Mo watches the deep-red sauce boil and bubble before glancing at the four linen placements on the kitchenette table. "How come you live here all alone?"

"I like it here. I enjoy having alone time." Langford adds a pinch of salt. "Of course, it would be nice to have someone to share it with, but I haven't been so lucky."

"Did you ever get married or have kids?"

"No, I've never been married, and I've never had any kids. I work with a local foster home where I attend activities with some of the less fortunate children in our community. I've also been a scoutmaster in the past, but that's as close as I'll get to children of my own."

"Do you have any brothers or sisters?"

"No, I was an only child." Langford lays out two place settings. "As I mentioned earlier, my mother died when I was three. My father remarried when I was six, but I wasn't close to my stepmother. She had long, brown hair and was quite pretty—at least on the outside." He lights the candles on the centerpiece candelabra before plating the pasta. "But she wasn't the nicest person, sent me to a boarding school so I wouldn't be a bother." He brings warm garlic bread in foil, placing it between Mo and himself. "My father was a great deal older than my mother and quite wealthy, so when she died, and he remarried, he traveled around the world with his new wife, leaving me in the care of nannies when I wasn't in boarding school. I seldom saw my father until my stepmother left him for a younger and wealthier man. By then, I was in graduate school." Throwing a dish towel over his shoulder, he grins. "Alright, Mo, let's eat."

Mo rests his elbows on the table and interlaces his fingers. "Can we say a prayer?"

"That's okay," Langford says with a backhand wave. "You go right ahead."

Finished with his blessing, Mo scoops up spaghetti with his fork and lowers his mouth to the edge of the plate. Across the table, he sees Langford spin spaghetti onto a fork with a spoon beneath before bringing the utensils up to his mouth, each bite followed by a sip of wine.

In the absence of conversation, Mo's thoughts wander to Mike's pretty but mean stepmother and comparisons to Miss Clara, Jake's mother. She was also very attractive, though not on the day his brother was born a few weeks after Mo's thirteenth birthday.

Dr. Cross was back in the Lumen home for only the second time since Mo's mother died. The first time, Dr. Cross, Miss Clara, and Mo's father spoke in whispers at the kitchen table a few days after Miss Clara arrived. It was very late, with Grandma Cleveland asleep upstairs. Mo lay on the sofa, straining to listen, able to discern only his father's final emphatic statement, "No, Clara!" followed by the sound of the back door closing.

Dr. Cross, always careful to separate circumstance from impropriety, returned five months later, welcoming Miss Clara's baby into the world as he did with each successful delivery—a unique and joyful event. "Excellent, Clara, you're all done." Before the newborn was cleaned off, he gave the baby a firm slap on the bottom, suctioned its mouth and nostrils, and rested the baby on its mother's chest. "Congratulations, he's beautiful!"

Mo, hearing the smack and the baby's shrill cry from the kitchen, followed the sound, and his father, into the downstairs bedroom.

Miss Clara was sweaty and pale; her brown hair, damp and tangled, shone black in the dim light. He watched his father stare at Miss Clara in a way he had not seen since his mother was alive. Observing Miss Clara in his mother's bed and not liking the way she looked or his father's gaze upon her, Mo chose not to enter, standing instead near the doorway.

Unlike Dr. Cross, Grandma Cleveland was a scriptural Baptist. She did judge. But she also didn't hold the innocent accountable. Wiping the baby's back with a warm towel, she looked down at Miss Clara and spoke in a matter-of-fact tone. "Whatcha gonna name him, young lady?"

Without emotion, Miss Clara stared at Grandma Cleveland—the dark, empty stare of an inmate counting hours on death row. Unable to feel the warmth of her newborn son, she felt only the cold, sticky dankness of an unfulfilling two-hour delivery. Straining to peel the baby off her chest, she lifted it to Grandma Cleveland. "You name it. I'm tired."

Grandma Cleveland pulled the baby into her bosom. "Hello there, little lamb. Let's let your mama get some rest."

The baby's first pleas for attention subsided as he nestled into her.

His mother's eyes were already closed as Grandma Cleveland carried him out of the room.

Ken followed, sitting down at the kitchen table, shoulders slumped with a hand to his forehead.

Grandma Cleveland cradled the baby in one arm, wrapping the other around Ken's shoulders. "What's the matter? She's gonna be just fine."

Ken rubbed his temples. "It's just another mouth to feed."

She smiled and showed him the baby. "Come now, Ken, it's a beautiful baby boy."

He glanced, then stared at his mother-in-law. "Ma, I didn't need another kid."

Mo sat in a chair on the other side of his grandmother. He wasn't sure what his father meant or why he wasn't excited to have a new son. He feared his father might not keep the baby.

Before the tension in the room became too great, Grandma Cleveland broke the silence. "Ken Lumen, you took responsibility for this child when you got yourself involved with his mama and brought her into this home." She spoke sternly as only a seasoned mother could. "You're gonna do what's right and take care of your son here."

Ken shook his head. "Not sure how. Can't even make ends meet with the family I already got. Ain't getting many calls for work since she moved in." Without looking, he nodded at his new burden. "What's its name?"

"Jacob. We'll call him Jacob."

Mo touched his brother's hand, turning at the sound of the bedroom door closing.

Dr. Cross washed his hands at the kitchen sink. "Yes, sir, a healthy baby boy! Always something to celebrate!"

Ken looked up, wrinkles raised in his forehead. "How's she doing, Doc?"

Dr. Cross nodded as he wiped his hands. "She's sleeping now. She worked hard today, but mother and child are both doing well."

Ken stood, reaching for his wallet. "How much I owe you?"

Dr. Cross picked up his parched leather bag and walked to the door with a smile, patting Mo's father on the shoulder as he passed. "We don't talk about money today, Ken. Not on the day of your child's birth." Turning at the door, he looked back, his eyes twinkling. "I'll send a bill in the morning," he said, winking at Ken, "and I'll take care of the documentation." He chuckled as he stepped onto the back porch.

Ken nodded. "Yeah, uh, thanks, Doc." Hands in pockets, he avoided Grandma Cleveland's eyes before staring at the bedroom door.

Mo watched his grandmother cradle the baby as his father sat back down. Then he felt the shaking of his father's leg against the table, Ken staring at an empty cup of coffee. His father did not look at the baby.

Over the years, Mo noticed how seldom his father looked at Jake. He held him even less. And Mo often asked himself why.

When the spaghetti and garlic bread are gone, Langford wipes his mouth, rises from his chair, and brings dessert. Standing next to Mo, he scoops gelato into a side dish. "So, what happened to your father? You didn't mention much about him."

Mo's shoulders slump. "My dad, uh, father, became sick after my brother, Jake, was born. Then, he went out of business. But I saw him almost every day." He pauses. "I'm sorry you didn't get to see yours while you were growing up."

"It's alright. Family comes and goes, but with good friends, you can get through anything. I had lots of friends at school, and I have a lot of good friends now." Placing his hand on Mo's shoulder, Langford squeezes. "I hope I can include you among them." He takes his hand away. "I've never had much use for women, though. My stepmother and nannies weren't good role models, and many of the girls at school were mean." Sitting, he points his spoon at Mo. "Mean like Emily."

Mo cringes at the mention of her name, but for the first time, considers the possibility he may not be alone in his trauma. "Did they call you names and get you in trouble and hit you?"

"Sometimes." Langford looks away. "But the names they called me were different."

Mo's eyebrows scrunch. "Different how?"

"That's not important, but we do share some common experiences. I hope we can become good friends."

"I hope so, too." Mo checks his Timex. "Can we leave soon? I don't want to miss my show, and I don't want Kay or Carlton to worry."

"Okay, we can get ready to go. I just need to clean up." Langford tilts his head. "Is Carlton a student?"

"Yes. I enjoy watching TV with him and the other guys. But Kay only comes over a couple of nights a week, so I like to be there when she's over."

"Is he tall?"

"Carlton's as tall as you are. How did you know?"

"It's not a common name, and I think he may have been in my

class a couple of semesters back." Langford shrugs. "Anyway, it doesn't matter." He points to Mo's empty dish. "I guess you liked it. Would you like some more?"

"No, thank you. I'm full. That was delicious."

Langford collects the dirty dishes. "You know, you might enjoy watching your show here. I have a nice, big color TV in my room. I'm sure you'd love it."

"Thank you, but I'd rather go home so I can go to sleep after. It's been a long day, and I'm exhausted."

"Alright, I'll take you home." Langford tosses his dinner napkin on the table.

Compared to how Langford had set the table before dinner, Mo is surprised by the violent clanking of each dish the professor washes, wipes, and puts away. The silent ride home is also uncomfortable.

Arriving at the townhouse, Langford pats Mo's shoulder. "Have fun with your friends. We'll have to do this again sometime, maybe when you can stay longer." He turns on the radio before Mo is out of the car.

Hearing Langford's opera music while walking to the entrance, Mo has no desire to play poker tonight and prays Veronica's not inside.

# - 2 3 -

# AN UNDRESSED SKELETON

## SATURDAY, 30 AUGUST 1975

*P*almer's *Saturday night patrol is McEnaney's Modern on Washington.* It's convenient walking distance from his apartment, has an authentic Boston vibe, and attracts a better breed of late-night elixir. Catering to his most primitive needs, the bartender is familiar, the stools are comfortable, and the ladies are accommodating.

When it's still early, before ten, Palmer thinks about the past. Between ten and two, he thinks about the present. And after two, he doesn't think at all. In the morning, he dreams away the hangover and fleeting distraction. Sleeping, he doesn't worry about church or God, work or demons, Marilyn or the girls. Eventually, the weekend wears off. And the pain resurfaces.

On the last Saturday in August, Palmer arrives at eight, claiming a stool at the bar. The redhead in the corner's smiling through a chipped tooth, but it's not ten, and Palmer's already had that full set of teeth. Settling in, he strikes a match. Bernie slides a tumbler, starts Palmer's tab. The hunt having begun, The Beast is on the prowl.

Early in the evening, they all look different, dirty, used. Later they'll all look like Marilyn, or close enough to chat up, buy a drink or two. For now, he's content to check out the wardrobe, imagining what she'd look like in the more appealing outfits. Chipped Tooth, her back to Palmer with wine spilling from her glass, reminds him of the night Marilyn dismissed him—the first time.

Palmer arrived home to find all his personal belongings scattered across the front lawn, neighbors' drapery ruffling as he drove down the street. Leaving his briefcase in the car, he walked through the open front door. Marilyn sat at the dining room table with her back to him, face in hand, an open bottle of chardonnay angled precariously at the edge of a bread plate.

Palmer knelt next to her. "What's the matter, honey?"

She shook her head, tears wrestling free from the crevices between her cheeks and palm.

He pulled her hand away from her face, using a dinner napkin to wipe the mascara from her cheeks. "What's wrong, Marilyn?"

"I can't do it," she said, shaking her head. "I just can't do it anymore."

"Do what? What can't you do?"

"I can't pretend it didn't happen." She looked at him, the red around her eyes expanding.

Palmer had worried about this every day for weeks when he'd return from an investigation. He'd hoped it would get easier, but a year later, this one was still an undressed skeleton—one continuing to haunt his wife. "Please, Marilyn, I'm better now. I can be better. I won't let them control me."

"No, Francis." She stared at him with resolve. "You won't be better. You can't control them. It just gets worse. They consume you, and we *all* suffer."

"Marilyn, please don't do this. Think about the girls."

"I *am* thinking about the girls. Please, just leave." Her voice breaking, tears slid down her cheeks. "Go! Please! Before they come back from my sister's."

"What can I do, Marilyn? What can I do to make it better?"

"You *know* what you have to do!" She pounded her fist on the table. The bottle of chardonnay tipped over, wine spilling, seeping into the carpet.

"What, Marilyn?" The words came out, though Palmer already knew the answer. "What do you want me to do?"

"Leave that godforsaken job, Francis." She wiped her eyes. "Leave it before there's nothing left of the man I married."

Palmer stood up. He watched the last drops of chardonnay drip off the edge of the table, pooling on the carpet. He didn't worry about the stain it would leave as he turned and walked away.

It was six weeks later when Marilyn finally answered, her voice hollow. "Hello?"

He clenched the phone, struggling for the right words.

After a few seconds, she said again, "Hello." This time Palmer heard more promise.

"Honey, it's me." He waited for a click, but it didn't come. "I'm sorry, Marilyn. It's all my fault. I miss you and the girls." He could hear her tears filling the holes in the transmitter cap. "Please, honey. I need you."

He was home fifteen minutes later. She cried in his arms for an hour before they went to bed. He never left the Bureau.


Bernie comes over to check on Palmer's glass, finding two singles slid across the bar. He knows the drill. Shaking his head, he digs into his apron and drops eight quarters on a coaster. Palmer walks over to a booth in the back, closes the door, and picks up the handset. After dropping the first coin, he hesitates for a moment, tapping the receiver cap on his forehead. He hopes to hear her say the same two words tonight—*Come home*. He hasn't called in months. He's grown tired of 'hello' followed by a click. It haunts him. His fingers shake as he dials—the phone rings.

And rings.

And rings.

He holds the handle long after he hangs up. It's still early on a Saturday night. He's sure she knows it's him. He wonders what *she's* up to tonight. Has she moved on? Is she out with a stranger? Are the lights already out, and is she giggling the way only he'd known? He lifts the receiver and slams it down, runs his fingers through his hair, and heads back to his seat at the bar. It's almost ten, and Chipped Tooth is just two shots from looking exactly like her. Again.

# PEGGY'S DEPARTURE

## MONDAY, 1 SEPTEMBER 1975

P*almer stares at the return address on the envelope.* It's the only communication he gets from her, and it's not really from her; it's from the university. They had talked about her going to Wellesley during the period when Marilyn took him back. She even included it among her list of schools on the SAT. But, in the end, she chose Xavier, preferring to stay within thirty minutes' driving distance of her mother. Now all he sees is the tuition bill each semester. Still staring at the return address, he thinks back to the last time he saw Peggy.

Palmer flew out to see his oldest daughter before her freshman year, during the week between moving into her dormitory and starting classes. He took a layover flight from Houston two weeks after the Dean Corll investigation closed, showing up at her dormitory unannounced. She hadn't seen him in almost two years, though they had spoken on the phone until recently, so she was surprised to see him at her door. Likewise, he was surprised to find several young men in her room. She introduced three female roommates and her boyfriend from high school, then ushered her father out with a promise to meet him for pizza at the local Italian restaurant at six.

Palmer arrived at five thirty and stared at the menu. He sat thinking about the pizzeria in Boston where the family frequently dined on Saturday nights. Peggy looked forward to pizza at Leonardo's when she was eight. Palmer was engaged in the Boston Strangler investigation. It was Murphy, Osmond, and Palmer's first mass-murderer case after six years of hunting down fugitives. Looking back, Palmer knew the cracks in his marriage were already showing. Sitting in a different pizza joint eight hundred miles away, waiting for Peggy to arrive, the sting of a cigarette burning down to his fingers resurrected the pain of losing his daughters to a failed marriage.

Peggy showed up fifteen minutes late.

Palmer greeted her with a big hug. "Hi, sweetheart, you look beautiful, just like your mother." He didn't want to let go.

Peggy pulled herself away, sat across from him, and picked up a menu. "Why did you come here, Dad?"

"What? I'm not allowed to see my oldest daughter off to college?"

Peggy peered at him from over the menu. "I wasn't expecting you." A glower replaced the sparkle in her youthful eyes.

Palmer shrugged. "Surprise!" He beamed when the waitress came to take their drink order. "This is my daughter. She's just starting school here at Xavier."

Peggy, face red, pushed her hair in front.

The waitress offered a sympathetic smile.

Father and daughter shared a light conversation over a pizza for forty-five minutes before Peggy slid out of the seat and stood by the table. "I have to get going."

"But, why?" Palmer's face couldn't conceal the hurt he felt inside. "It's so early, and I flew here to see you."

Reaching across the bench, Peggy grabbed her purse. "I've got a date tonight. I made it with my friends before I knew you were coming."

"Can't you go out with your friends another night?" Palmer's eyebrows sagged. "I'm only here tonight."

Peggy's voice grew louder. "You can't just pop into my life whenever you want without notice."

Palmer put his finger to his mouth. "It's okay, honey, I understand. I'll make sure I talk to you ahead of time from now on, but you haven't been answering my calls the past several months." He held her arm. "Is your mother telling you not to talk to me?"

Peggy shook away his hand. "Mom doesn't tell us what to do. We were there, Dad." She spoke loud enough to drown out Al Martino trickling out of the wall speakers. "We saw and heard it all. You cared more about work than us."

"That's not true," he muttered, his eyes staring at a crack in the linoleum under the table. When he looked up, Peggy was gone.

He felt the convicting eyes of diners upon him. Watching the crack in the linoleum creep across the room, he knew it stretched eight hundred miles to the chardonnay stain in their old house. Even the menu, from its cold metal perch, stared in judgment. He estimated the amount of the bill, left an oversized apology to the waitress, and retreated with his shoulders slumped.

Peggy hasn't spoken to him since.


Alone again in his silent apartment, Palmer lays the tuition bill down. Lifting himself out of the chair, he swings by the bathroom, scooping faucet water to wash down several Valium. He looks in the mirror, wondering what he has to do to see his daughters and how to get Marilyn and the girls to forgive him. He still can't forgive himself for crossing the line. Maybe forgiving himself would be the first step, but he doesn't know how. He turns off the bathroom light before heading back to the kitchen to write a check and smoke a cigarette. Afterward, he'll lie in bed trying to forget long enough to allow the pills to kick in. And when he wakes, he'll be headed to Salt Lake City to find a monster.

# SAM'S BASEBALL CARDS

## TUESDAY, 2 SEPTEMBER 1975

M*o observes Trevor's hands, steady as a surgeon's.* The concentration on his housemate's face is evident from twenty feet away. No dinnerware, utensils, or napkins on the dining table, Mo watches Trevor inspect each piece of coated cardboard before depositing them into separate stacks. With the unaltered cadence of his movements, Mo knows Trevor doesn't hear the other boys' bickering, doesn't feel Kay's presence as she passes, and doesn't see Mo staring from the hall.

Drawn by an invisible force, Mo drifts by the other housemates unnoticed, sits across from Trevor, and remains still. The brightly colored upper and lower borders of Trevor's baseball cards fill him with a sense of need he's not experienced since Sam gave him a stack in the spring following K&E's start.

April 1960, just under a year after his mother's death, Mo's grandmother moved in permanently. The Cleveland homestead had been sold with some of the proceeds reinvested into K&E. Grandma Cleveland occupied the downstairs bedroom, her presence bringing welcome domestic comforts for nine-year-old Mo and an increasingly busy Ken.

Descending the stairs, Mo slid his hand along the banister, surprised to find dust no longer collecting in his palm, replaced instead by oil and the scent of lemon. "Good morning, Grandma," he said, rushing over to give her a big hug.

Grandma Cleveland broke from humming. "Good morning,

Little Maurice."

Mo saw the remnants of his grandmother's blond hair interlaced in an expanding sea of gray. "You look so pretty today." In her eyes, Mo saw his mother at sixty.

Smiling, Grandma Cleveland looked up from the cookstove. "My, but you keep growing so fast. You're downright bigger than I am. Now, sit down. I've made some hotcakes for your first day of work."

Mo took his tool belt—his father's old one—off the back of the chair and placed it on the floor. "I get a whole week to work with Dad and Mr. Johnson and Sam." He laid his father's new tool belt next to his.

Grandma Cleveland placed a stack of hotcakes in the center of the table before walking to the screen door. "I remember how much I enjoyed school break when I was your age. I'd work with my mama in the garden, the scent of flowers and sound of bees, mmm..." She paused, looking over the backyard. "Yes, I do understand why you'd be all excited to go to work with your daddy."

Mo heard his father fumbling in the upstairs bathroom. "Have you seen Sam yet this morning?"

"Lord, that young man's been here since the very break of day. Made a racket loading up those trucks."

"Can he come in and have some hotcakes?" Mo's eyes begged like a stray cat.

"I'm gonna have to make some fresh ones for your daddy any-way." She lifted the circular lid off the stovetop and dropped in some wood. "Alright, but hurry before your daddy gets down here." The screen door slammed behind Mo before she could finish.

Sam followed Mo into the kitchen and stood by the door. Remov-ing his baseball cap, he squeezed it against his chest. "Morning, ma'am," he said.

Mo wondered whether Sam was trying to rub the 'B' off his cap or the black off his fingers.

Grandma Cleveland flipped several hotcakes. "C'mon, Sam, set yourself down and have some breakfast. But be quick about it."

Mo recognized the concern in his grandmother's voice, usually reserved for times she felt *he* might be in trouble with his father.

She shook her spatula at Sam. "Don't be dawdling. Ken'll be down soon."

"Yes, ma'am, thank you." Sam worked his way to the table, rested his cap on his lap, and said a quiet prayer before picking up his fork.

Mo took a sip of milk. "Senators open the season against the Red Sox this afternoon."

Sam spoke through a mouthful of hotcakes. "Not gonna be any good this year, just like all the rest. Here, I got you these." He handed Mo a stack of baseball cards. "Hank Aaron's on top. He hit his second homer over the weekend." Looking at Mo, he winked. "Senators need someone like Aaron or Mays or Banks."

Mo flipped over the Aaron card and read the back. "Did he ever play in the Negro Leagues?"

"Just a short spell. About a month before the Braves scooped him up."

"How long did you play?"

"Left working Old Man Henderson's farm with my daddy when I was sixteen to play in Baltimore before the war broke out and most of us was called into service." Sam used his hat to wipe his mouth. "Mostly sat the bench cuz we was good. Always giving them Grays a run but never did catch them. Could field a lick but weren't much with the stick—too skinny and no power." He sopped up the remaining syrup with his last bite. "Not like these boys now. They done hit that ball a country mile."

"I sure hope my dad lets *me* play."

"I hope so, too." Sam slid his chair back and checked to see if he'd left any dirt on the floor. "I got to play with some of the great ones. Got a chance to play against Josh Gibson a few times. Best hitter ever. Went up against the best pitcher, too. Struck out most times against Satchel Paige, like most everyone else, but got a single off him once, just under the shortstop's glove." He smiled. "Best memory of my short career."

"Walter Johnson's the greatest pitcher in baseball history," Ken declared. He stood at the base of the stairs, tucking his work shirt into his pants. "Led the Senators to their only title. And Babe Ruth's the greatest hitter of all time." He scratched under his ear. "Hell, Ted Williams is a better hitter than any Negro. Why don't you talk to my son about Mantle or Snider instead of going on about Mays and Aaron?" Ken's voice grew louder. "And what are you doing at my breakfast table? Ain't you got work to do, boy?"

"Ken," Grandma Cleveland said, placing her hand on Sam's shoulder, "ain't no real harm done, is there? He was just talking baseball with Mo. He's been here working for over an hour."

Sam was frozen, his cap caught between his wrist and the arm of the chair.

"He shouldn't be eating at my table and filling Mo's head with all that Negro nonsense." Ken waved his finger at the door. "I told you to get a move on, boy. The men will be here any second."

"Yes sir, Mister Lumen, sir."

Mo grabbed his tool belt and followed Sam out the back door.

All that week, on subsequent Saturdays, and across the next four summers, Mo enjoyed working with his father and listening to Sam talk about baseball. Sam was careful to tailor the conversation to account for whether Ken was in earshot.

Startled by the sound of Trevor's voice, Mo shakes his head and looks up.

Trevor holds up a pack. "You want to open one?"

Mo nods, licking his lips, eyes back on the green card box with 'Baseball' and '15¢' in red.

"Here you go." Trevor places the pack on the table in front of Mo. "Open it carefully from the back."

Mo had never opened a pack with the cards Sam brought him. He peels the wax seal and unwraps the folded corners as Trevor had done. He pulls the packaging away, holding the cards gingerly, trying not to shake. But the small stack slips through his fingers, spilling the cards onto the table.

Deft as a casino dealer, Trevor reaches across and slides the cards together, resting them in his palm. "Let's see who you got."

He moves to the chair beside Mo, filtering through the cards and stopping at Harmon Killebrew. "Here's a good one."

"He used to play for the Washington Senators and was one of my father's favorite players." Mo equates the brown and orange borders to Mike's car.

"He's pretty old now, but he has the fifth-most home runs in baseball history," Trevor says, handing Mo the card. "Here, you can have it. It's a double."

"Thank you." Mo reads the statistics printed on the back, checking out 1960 and seeing all the years that have passed since the Senators left DC.

"You're welcome." Trevor points to his stacks. "I've put together a complete set every year since I was seven, going back to 1961. I usually save the doubles in the opened card boxes, but I can give you some if you want."

"Really? My friend Sam would bring me cards when I was little. I only have the White players left, though."

Trevor tilts his head, furrows his brows. "Why only the White players?"

"My father tore up the Black ones," Mo replies.

"Why would he do that?"

"Because Sam gave them to me. My father didn't like when I got Black players from him."

Trevor scratches his head. "Hmm, that's too bad, for more reasons than I care to mention."

"I thought he ripped them *all* up, but I found the White players in my father's shoebox after he died."

"I'd like to see those if it's okay with you. Too bad he trashed the Black players. Those would be some of the greatest cards from back then."

"He felt bad afterwards and took me to see Ted Williams play. That was the only time I ever left Virginia until I came here. He said Ted Williams was the greatest White player of his generation."

Trevor shakes his head. "I mostly agree with your dad. Williams probably was the greatest player, White *or* Black, from that generation. But then, I'm a Red Sox fan, so I'm biased. I'm glad you got a chance to see him play. I sure would've liked to have seen that." He gives Mo a stack of cards. "I put a Hank Aaron and Carlton Fisk in there for you. You have to take really good care of them."

"I will. I promise." Mo searches for the Aaron card, showing it to Trevor. "He was one of Sam's favorite players. He played in the Negro Leagues just like Sam did."

"Geez, Mo, I think I'd have enjoyed talking to Sam myself."

Later that evening, when the last bedroom door closes upstairs, and the townhouse falls silent, Mo lies in bed comparing his card of Harmon Killebrew from 1960 with the new one Trevor gave him. He appears much older now, just like Sam did at his father's burial. Looking at the 1975 Hank Aaron card sitting on top of the stack of new cards, he thinks of Sam's stories and how they shared food and talked baseball for several summers and many Saturdays until Sam had to leave. He hopes Trevor will one day meet Sam and listen to his baseball stories, too.

# 26

# A COUPLE OF RUNAWAYS

## WEDNESDAY, 3 SEPTEMBER 1975

*P*almer is finally in Salt Lake and ready for a nice dinner. Yesterday was a travel day with multiple connections, so meals and snacks were in the air. Tonight, he's hungry. The hotel steakhouse is quiet when he and Osmond arrive, the atmosphere mellow, the music dull. The specialty is prime rib, so two orders are in not long after the kitchen opens.

Palmer looks at photos of Bundy's tan Beetle. "Can you believe they've let him go *twice*?"

Osmond pulls one over with his finger, turns it around. "Didn't have much choice."

Palmer points to one of the pictures. "Look at that. Found the passenger seat in the backseat. That doesn't seem suspicious, right?"

"I know. Coupled with the stuff in his trunk along with the guides and brochures they found at his apartment? Really?" Osmond shakes his head. "Just haven't found the key to unlock this case."

"That's what we're here for." Palmer digs out a cigarette. "Hard to believe they confiscated the car a week ago and still haven't broken it down."

"They're following procedure, Frankie. You know that. Don't want to collect incriminating evidence just to let this son of a bitch off the hook on a technicality. At least we'll be there when they tear it apart tomorrow."

Palmer nods. Striking a match, he pulls.

Osmond tucks the photos back into the folder, places them on his bench, and opens his wallet.

Exhausting the smoke, Palmer notices Osmond staring at a photograph. "What's up?"

Osmond slides it back into his wallet. "Ah, it's my youngest daughter. She's got this boyfriend at school. Wants us to meet him."

"Doesn't seem so bad. At least she's interested in a college boy."

Osmond taps the edge of his beer glass. "That's what's eating me. I was that college boy when I met my wife. It just all goes by so fast. Seems like my daughters were little girls just a few years ago."

Palmer stares at the bowl of peanuts in front of him. "At least you got to see yours grow up. I've missed the last four years of mine. I only see the bills."

"Yeah, sorry, probably not right for me to complain. I just wonder if I've been fair to my family. It's been a long road, and looking at Dick..." Osmond hesitates, grabbing his beer glass. "Well, it just gets me wondering if it's all been worth it."

"I get it, but Dick's gonna be fine. You'll see." Palmer knows what he's saying isn't true, knows Osmond does too, but it closes a depressing discussion just as the food arrives.

The mood remains somber throughout the meal, drinks consumed at a slower-than-usual pace. Osmond heads to the bathroom after dinner, allowing Palmer to do some thinking. Had he been unfair to Marilyn, asking her to do everything for the girls, deal with his extended absences, and nurture him back to health when those absences would end? He thinks about how his mother dealt with his father's long nights and absent weekends when his cases would consume him. Between the courtroom and research, his father would always make time for golf. Was that unfair? Had his father been unfair to his mother when he was doing his job? Was his absence during the last two years of World War II unfair?

Palmer can still see the worry in his mother's eyes when they'd drive to school or church, picture the smile on her face when she'd talk about his father in his absence. Unable to recall any arguments or hostility between his parents, he knew his mother would always have his father's meal ready when he got home, his slippers and paper on the coffee table near his favorite chair. Palmer's job is just like his father's before him: bring criminals to justice. And he's exposed to the horrors lurking in society's shadows. Why didn't Marilyn understand?

Palmer has many more memories of his mother when he was young. Marilyn has had far more time with the girls. Why did she leave with them? Why had she given up? Why couldn't she see the importance of his job and take pride in his work as she had done in the early days before it became personal? Why does she keep his daughters from him? He only knows he needs them desperately. Smoking his cigarette, he appreciates her putting up with him for so long and understands her desire to get away. But he needs his girls.

Osmond returns, plopping himself on the bench with a sigh. "Sorry that took so long. I called Humphrey to get an update. Until they decide, and while he's the acting SAIC, I need to call in at the end of every day to get briefed." He clasps his hands together on the table.

Palmer taps Osmond's wrist. "It doesn't mean anything, Harry. He's acting because he's got more administrative experience and because you're out here with me."

"I understand that. He was just telling me that two young girls have been reported missing the past few days in Smithfield, Rhode Island."

"Well, two's a coincidence, right? Could just be a couple of runaways."

"I guess. State police are taking them seriously, though."

"Let's relax. See what surfaces. We've got our hands full here. Is that all that's bothering you?"

Osmond curls his lip. "Eh, it's just the uncertainty surrounding the promotion. I really don't want to disappoint my wife. I'm gonna go give her a call. I'll see you in the morning."

Palmer nods, waiting for Osmond to leave before moving to the bar. He has no wife waiting for a call, no daughter's boyfriend to meet, and no visits to plan. To his dismay, he also has no other responsibilities to his family except to pay the bills and protect them. Tapping his glass and sliding it across the counter, he settles in for a long Wednesday night. Pleased to be in Salt Lake, where he can feel the rage, he sits and waits for his chance at Ted.

# 27

# THE FIRST DEATH

## WEDNESDAY, 3 SEPTEMBER 1975

*M*o *is unnerved by Jim's repeated glances from the living room, so he changes seats at the table.* With his back to their often-temperamental housemate, Mo shows Trevor his old baseball cards.

A little after ten, Jim grabs his beer and stumbles over to the table. With no Thursday classes, he's bombed, just short of belligerent. "Aren't you guys a little old to be playing with baseball cards?"

Trevor doesn't look up. "Aren't *you* a little young to be cynical?"

"Bah!" Jim snarls, turning his attention to Mo. "Hey, big boy, the Red Sox win?"

Mo's surprised by Jim's pleasantry but doesn't look up from his cards. He knows not to engage Jim when he's been drinking, so they don't often speak, Mo keeping his words to a minimum. "Yes."

"Excellent! Come sit over here with me."

"C'mon, Jim, not tonight," Trevor says. "Leave him alone."

"What? I just want him to visit me and Carlton on the sofa."

Kay glares at Jim, "No, Mo, come sit over here."

Mo heads in the direction of Kay but is redirected by Jim. Pulled down onto the sofa between Jim and Carlton, Mo's work gloves are yanked from his back pocket.

"There we go. That's better," Jim says, demeanor still affable. "Why you always gotta wear that stupid uniform?"

"It's comfortable, and it fits me. My other clothes are too small."

Carlton inspects Mo's gloves. "Okay, but why are you always carrying these around? Is this blood?"

Mo pulls his gloves back from Carlton. "I need them to protect my hands, but I still get cut sometimes."

Jim presses a beer can against Mo's chest. "Hey, I'm dry here. Go get me another Bud. Anybody else want a beer while Dumbo's up?"

Mo wonders why Jim would refer to him as the lovable flying elephant with big ears. He wishes he could soar along the ceiling and out of his housemate's reach.

"I'll take a beer," Brian says, "since Kay *always* forgets to get me one."

Carlton pushes Mo forward from the shoulder. "Yeah, get me one, too."

Jim trips Mo as he shuffles by, causing Mo to stumble toward Kay.

"Hey, watch what you're doing there, Moby." Carlton winks at Brian. "That's my girlfriend."

Mo straightens himself up, apologizes to Kay, and heads to the kitchen. He's unsure if Carlton's referring to the character in his father's favorite book—the paperback sitting in the shoebox under his bed—the one Mo's never read.

Jim's brows bury against his lashes. "What's the last grade you finished anyway? Kindergarten?"

Trevor walks over, stands behind Kay's chair. "Cool it, Jim."

Mo reenters the living room carrying three cold cans. He places one on the table in front of Jim. "I was in eighth grade, and then I was done with school."

Jim grabs Mo's head, shaking it between his hands. "So, you retarded or something? Or are you like the big dummy from that stupid-ass Steinbeck book we had to read in high school?"

Trevor steps to the side of Kay's chair. "Seriously, Jim, knock it off."

Mo hands Brian a beer, then heads back to the sofa, giving Carlton the last can as he sits.

Carlton points his unopened can in Brian's direction. "Maybe B's skirt the other night was on to something."

"Carl! Don't you say that!" Kay stands, extending her hand. "Come on, Mo, you should get to bed."

Trevor nods. "Go ahead, Mo, go with Kay. These guys are drunk. They don't know what they're saying."

Mo pushes himself up but is pulled down by Jim.

"Where are *you* going?" Jim scowls. "Sit back down." He looks past Mo to the opposite end of the sofa. "Looks like this bastard's trying to steal your girlfriend."

"Jim, let him up right now! Carl, stop him!" Kay's restrained by Carlton. "For crying out loud, Carl, stop it!"

Mo overpowers Jim and rises to his feet. "Let her go!" He liberates Kay from Carlton's grip and pushes him back onto the sofa, leading Kay into the hallway.

Jim sneers as Carlton follows them. "You better get your bitch under control!"

"Don't you touch me!" Kay pushes Carlton away, closing the door to Mo's bedroom.

The noise in the other room subsides.

Kay holds Mo's hands. "Don't listen to them. They're drunk. They don't mean anything."

Mo slumps at the edge of the bed. "I'm sorry, Kay, I didn't mean to do anything wrong."

"You didn't do anything wrong. *They're* the ones that need to apologize. They just act like idiots when they've had too much to drink." She runs her fingers through his hair. "Why don't you lie down and go to sleep? I'll see you Friday night. I'm gonna talk to Carlton for a few minutes before I leave."

Mo hears Kay and Carlton's faint voices talking outside his room, Kay insisting she will leave Carlton if he doesn't stop this behavior and get control of the others. Mo lies in bed, not understanding why his housemates would be so mean. He's heard the same hurtful words—*retard* and *dummy*—many times before. And he knows how it all began: his father's own anger, bitterness, and hateful words on the day Mo got hurt...two weeks before his twelfth birthday.

His father's words were the last he heard before the silence and the darkness.

By the fall of 1962, K&E's success had resulted in permanent six-day workweeks. On the first Saturday in October, Ken set himself down on a boulder under the sprawling canopy of a Southern live oak while Earl sat on a patch of grass planted between the tree's above-ground root system. Most of the crew joined them, devouring lunch and talking shop in the cooling shade. Mo and Sam sat just beyond the tree's reach.

Mo pulled out a package of Twinkies from his lunch pail. "Sam, how come you don't eat lunch with my dad and the others?"

"Let me see," Sam said. Lifting his cap, he scratched just below his receding hairline. "I already got a tan, so the sun don't do me no harm like it does your daddy and those other White folks." He laughed, nudging Mo's shoulder. "I'm just messing around, Mo." He pointed to the other men, his face turning serious. "Over there, they all talk about the war and hunting and stuff I don't much care about." His smile returned as he looked back at Mo. "Besides, I prefer sitting here, talking baseball with you."

"But didn't you fight in the war, too?"

"I don't much like talking about that." Sam tilted the open end of his bag of chips toward Mo. "My time in the war was different than your daddy."

"How was it different?" Mo rested two Twinkies on a napkin between them before reaching into Sam's bag of chips.

"They all carried guns and got involved in the fighting. I was in a Black regiment that dug ditches and unloaded supplies." Taking a bite of a Twinkie, Sam swallowed hard, looked down at his feet. "We all fought for freedom in some way, I suppose."

"None of them want to talk to me either," Mo said, smiling. "I like talking with you about baseball, too." He bit into his sandwich.

From under the tree, just yards away, Ken preached to a captive audience, his voice loud enough for Mo and Sam to hear. "See all that rioting on account of that Meredith boy wanting to go to school at Ole Miss? They got their own colleges, don't they?" He shook his head. "Supreme Court taking away our rights and Kennedy letting us down on this one, men." He waggled a finger at the crew. "'No appreciable harm,' my ass! Tell that to those two dead White boys." He stared over at Sam. "Ain't no need for no educated niggers."

As the other men cheered his father on, Mo glanced at Sam and whispered, "I'm sorry."

Sam shrugged as he continued to eat.

Taking a deep breath, Mo laid back. Elbows by his side, hands resting on his chest, he felt the steady rise and fall with every passage of air through his lungs. The sun's rays penetrated his eyelids, creating a wondrous pinkish-red tint only his concealed eyes could enjoy. The smell of nearby lavender filled his nostrils, bringing back memories of when he was very young. With God's grace draped over him, Mo thought about his mother and how she would've liked Sam. Conversation in the background was replaced with the melodic swishes of branches swaying. Coupled with natural light and floral essence, the environment transported him. He drifted. The enveloping aromas grew acrid. Struggling to open his eyes, Mo was unable to discern dark from light. Shadows loomed over him. There was commotion.

Then silence.

And darkness.

Mo's first death passed into memory.

He woke up three days later to the faint glow of a solitary nightlight above his hospital bed, registering how sterile and unnatural the room smelled. Mo strained to raise his arms. Resting them again, he brushed the cold steel of the bed rail, a shiver running through his body as he called out in a soft voice, "Daddy?" He couldn't see his father on the far edge of the room but recognized his breathing. "Daddy?" he called again, followed by the sounds of his father untangling himself from the hospital chair and shuffling over to the bed.

"I'm here, Mo," Ken said in a reassuring voice. "I'm here." Leaning over the bed, he hugged his son.

Shaking, Mo let his fear drain into his father's shirt.

By the end of that week, Mo was sitting up and alert.

Sitting in a chair by the bed, Dr. Cross placed a hand on Mo's shoulder. "Good morning, young man! Great to see you looking a little better. How are you feeling today?"

"Tired," Mo said. "I hurt all over."

Dr. Cross leaned closer. "That's to be expected. Do you know what happened to you?"

"My dad says I had an accident." Mo looked to where Ken was nodding. "But all I remember was laying down on the grass. And then I woke up here."

"You had what's called a grand mal seizure," Dr. Cross said. "You see, your brain works by sending out messages to the rest of your body like a telephone call. These messages tell your body how to move and do normal activities. During a seizure, your brain makes too many calls at once, and your body can't keep up. This causes your muscles to tighten." He checked to see if Ken was following before turning back to Mo. "Then, you lose control of your body and start to shake all over. After a bit, the shaking stops, and your body relaxes again. You're sore because of how much work your muscles did during your seizure. Does that make sense?"

Mo examined his hands as he tightened and released his fingers. "But why don't I remember it?"

"When you have a seizure, you aren't awake. You don't know anything's happening. To you, it just feels like a few moments lost." Dr. Cross squeezed Mo's shoulder as he stood. "Not to worry, you're a healthy young man, and we've been giving you medication to keep it from happening again. For the time being, just get some rest. You'll be able to go home soon. Now, if you'll excuse us, Mo, I need to talk to your father for a minute." Dr. Cross patted Mo on the hand, closed the curtain, and walked over to his father.

Mo's father spoke before Dr. Cross could turn to face him. "Doc, why'd this happen? I almost lost my son!" With a trembling hand, he rubbed his heavily stubbled chin.

"Ken, we don't know what caused this. Mo's an otherwise healthy boy. There's no reason he should've had a seizure, especially one of this magnitude. There's no family history of epilepsy near as we can tell. We'll need to monitor his progress here another week, run more tests." Dr. Cross looked at the curtain surrounding Mo. "His seizure lasted almost ten minutes, you said. Is that right?"

"Yeah, longest ten minutes of my life," Ken muttered.

"Hmph," Dr. Cross sighed. "A seizure lasting *five* minutes is considered a medical emergency. Mo's episode lasted almost *twice* as long." He shook his head. "It's a miracle he survived. But no one comes out of something like this unscathed."

"What are you saying, Doc?"

"I'm not sure, Ken, but a seizure of this magnitude will very often do irreversible damage to a person's brain. Mo seems himself right now, but I feel we need to monitor him."

"What kinda damage?"

"Well, in an extensive event such as Mo suffered, it's very likely a person would experience memory loss, headaches, and impaired motor functions. These will normally improve or go away with time. I'm more concerned about Mo's intellectual development." Dr. Cross paused, assessing Ken's consternation. "It may turn out Mo's intellect is limited to what it is now, that of an eleven-year-old. If that's the case, it will become apparent over the coming months and years."

"Are you saying my son may be retarded?" Ken clasped his hands behind his head. After a few breaths, he folded them across his chest. "Is there anything we can do?"

"Unfortunately, all we can do is wait and see."

Mo kept his eyes closed but listened to every word.

Ken ran his hands down his face. "Ugh, thanks, Doc, I guess." Pulling the curtain back, he stared at his son.

Mo pretended to be asleep, waiting several minutes for both he and his father to ponder the doctor's words before propping himself into a seated position. "Dad, why did Mom have to die?"

The question shook Ken from his trance. He looked up at the ceiling as though the right words were printed in the plaster. After a moment's pause, his father answered. "God determines when we all gonna die."

"I wish she were here to help me. The nurses are nice, but I want Mom."

Watching his father nod, Mo knew their grief wouldn't go away. But at least it was something they shared.

Mo lies in his bed in Rhode Island, struggling to understand why people use hurtful words. He's heard those words—*retarded, dummy,* and *idiot*—often since his seizure, only ever understanding they meant he was different somehow, and the people saying them were often mean or afraid.

When the townhouse falls silent, Mo's thoughts turn to his baseball cards still sitting on the table. He exits the safety of his room to retrieve them, placing them on his nightstand when he returns. He looks at the stack of old cards, glad Sam was by his side when he had his seizure.

He falls asleep thinking about Sam's house in Tinpot Alley—Sam's house that Mo never saw. Did Sam even have a house? Or an apartment? Or just a strip of grass with the rain and cold surrounding him? He wonders if Sam could've been one of the black-haired critters his father spoke about in Tinpot Alley. He wonders if Sam's body will one day get tangled up in the trees after a big flood and float down the Rappahannock. And he wonders if his own body will float alongside Sam's when *he* dies.

# BUNDY'S BEETLE

**THURSDAY, 4 SEPTEMBER 1975**

*P*almer *can't tear his eyes away from Ted's Beetle.* Standing behind a wall of glass that separates him from the state police barracks garage, he watches the forensics team scour Bundy's car with the fervor of sugar-crazed children on an Easter egg hunt. Through the thick, tempered window, he listens to the muffled, industrious sound of exploration: ratcheting nuts and bolts, scraping along sheet metal, and ripping mats from floorboard. Inside his head, competing with the noise, he hears a familiar hum, low and menacing, growing louder. The Beast knows The Monster's handiwork is present.

Two hours in, arms crossed with a cigarette resting between his fingers, Palmer's still grinding his teeth. He doesn't blink. Encroaching red shadows distort his vision until all he sees is the Beetle, the hum now a deep growl rising from his abdomen.

"Frankie!" Osmond's voice channels through as if he's speaking underwater. "Frankie!"

Palmer snaps his head around, dropping his cigarette before lighting another. He closes his eyes, takes a drag. "He's here, Harry. I know it."

"Relax. We'll get him." Osmond releases a sardonic chuckle. "That poor kid. Gets herself a new car, and the cops swoop in. Take it before she can even warm up the engine."

Palmer stares at the passenger door. "Yeah, well, she should be thankful Bundy sold her his ride instead of taking her for one."

Osmond nods.

Shaking his head, Palmer points his cigarette. "Fucking car's a rolling crime scene. No doubt about that."

Lead State Forensics Investigator Bachman waves Palmer and Osmond into the garage. Standing by the vehicle, he holds out a handful of evidence bags. "Investigator Palmer, here's what we got."

Osmond takes the bags from the air in front of Palmer. "Hairs. That's something."

"They're all brown, so they could just be Bundy's," Bachman says, walking them around the car. "Found them wedged into the back seat."

"Hairs?" Palmer snarls. "That's it? No blood?"

"Sir, the interior's all vinyl. The suspect did an excellent job of scrubbing the car. We were getting concerned we'd find nothing at all."

"At least we got hairs," Osmond says. "At first glance, they don't belong to the same person. They appear to be different shades and lengths."

"That's true, Investigator Osmond," Bachman says. "However, it's quite common for hair of different lengths and shades to come from the same person's head. It's my understanding that the suspect's hair length varied a great deal over time."

"But the suspect would've had little reason to be in the back seat, right? It's quite a cramped space for a full-grown man."

"Still, young adults find a way to use the back seat of any vehicle, so it's possible some real nightmares occurred in the back seat of this vehicle."

Palmer holds his arms out, scanning the surrounding floor. "Hold on. The lab will confirm any of these theories. I'm still trying to wrap my head around your team taking all this shit out, examining every square inch of the interior, and finding just a few strands of hair. Unfucking believable!" The growling returns.

Bachman squares his shoulders. "You can see as well as I can, Investigator Palmer, they've checked everything. There's no trace of anything else on the seats, the floor, the door panels, the dash, or inside the trunk." He nods at Palmer. "My men have done their job."

Half-opened eyes locked on Bachman's, Palmer's breathing slow and even, he doesn't hear him.

Osmond pats Bachman on the shoulder. "We appreciate your efforts. This is a good haul. Will the specimens be sent to our local field office?"

Bachman nods. "We'll be analyzing them against the Utah victims' database before sending them over to Bob at the FBI Salt Lake Field Office for a national check."

Osmond turns back to Palmer. "With any luck, we'll get a match or two."

Palmer catches his own eyes glaring back at him off the rear window of the car. "I've gotta get him, Harry. I've gotta stare this bastard down, beat him with his own tongue."

"Well, this is a step in the right direction. You've said it before: he's gonna make a mistake if he hasn't already."

Palmer places his hands on the hood, whispers to himself, "Come on, what did you leave me, you prick?" He pauses, feeling the chill of hollow metal slither up his arms and down his spine like a snake. Stepping back, he kicks the tire. "Fuck you!"

At the sound of Palmer's voice yelling louder than the clanging of mechanic tools, a dozen heads pop up.

Osmond grabs Palmer's arms and pulls him back. "Jesus, Frankie!" Stepping in front of Palmer, he puts his hands on his colleague's shoulders. "We all want to get him. We *will* get him." He turns Palmer away from the car. "Go get some rest. They're wrapping it up here anyway. I'll check in with you a little later."

As Palmer moves farther away, his muscles relax, feeling the worst of the rage melt off and cling to the Beetle. Without a word, he walks to the other end of the garage toward the exit, rubbing his face and running his fingers through his hair. There's something they're missing. He knows it. And the only way he can find it is to confront The Monster.

-29-

# ANIMALS

## FRIDAY, 5 SEPTEMBER 1975

M o reads the photocopied invitation on the wall in the library. They've been hanging all over campus the past two weeks. He'd been looking forward to the 'Legendary Four Horsemen's Back to School Party' until Tuesday night. Since then, he's been avoiding his housemates, knowing Kay wouldn't return until tonight. So, he's spent the past two nights eating in the dining hall, reading the newspaper in the library, and listening to night games in the laundry room. Now, nearing eight, with the party about to begin, he leans against the card catalog cabinet watching the final seconds tick away on his Timex, looking forward to Kay's presence, and dreading Jim's.

A little before midnight, an intoxicated mass of raging hormones compete for attention. Over the noise, Kay hears Jim and several others engaged in some kind of disturbance. Forty eager young men, entertaining themselves with alcohol and an equal number of unattached, nubile girls, are congregated downstairs, spilling out onto the patio deck.

Unable to discern where the commotion is coming from, Kay excuses herself from a vapid conversation near the refrigerator, navigating several beer kegs and an ice bucket of bug juice—a hostile mix of vodka, whiskey, gin, and tequila—strewn across the kitchen floor. Weaving her way through narrow cracks in an otherwise impenetrable wall of bodies, she makes her way through the living room and slides along the hallway wall before knocking on

Mo's bedroom door. Hearing no response, she peeks in to find the room empty before forcing her way toward the back deck, grabbing Trevor along the way.

Jim's voice rises above the commotion. "Bark, you fucking dog!"

Mo, down on all fours, obeys Jim's command. A dozen partygoers surround him, including Jim, Carlton, and Brian, laughing, red Solo cups in hand.

Jim pours bug juice from his cup onto Mo's head. "Louder, you son of a bitch! And growl! What grade did you get kicked out of school, you stupid bastard?"

A girl with long, brown hair is cackling in Mo's ear. She tugs at his hair, pulling Mo's face up in an attempt to capture Jim's stream into his mouth.

Mo lifts his hand off the deck and blindly searches for the girl's ponytail.

Carlton pulls Mo's hand away and holds it against his back. "Louder!"

Mo howls in pain, struggling to stay balanced.

"C'mon, you can do better than *that!*" Brian kicks Mo from behind.

Kay elbows her way through the spectators while Trevor holds back the growing crowd.

"C'mon, get out of the way!" Kay says. When she arrives at the disturbance, her heart sinks. "What are you *doing?!*" She shoves Jim, causing him to stumble down the deck's two steps and onto the lawn.

"What the hell's wrong with you, Kay?" Jim growls. "Carl, you better teach your bitch some goddamned respect!"

Carlton jumps on Jim, holding him down. Trevor assists Carlton from the opposite side.

Jim resists, throwing and landing several punches. "Stop it! Get the fuck off me!"

Feeling Kay's glare, Brian sighs before releasing the two girls in his arms to assist Carlton and Trevor.

Kay crouches next to Mo. "Come on, let's get you out of here."

Carlton stands, leaving Jim to his housemates. "*Kay!*" He rushes through the thinning crowd, catching up with his girlfriend as she walks Mo to his room. "Kay, I'm sorry. I didn't—"

"Please!" Kay puts her hand up to Carlton's face. "Don't say anything. Just keep your mouth shut. Help him get cleaned up and into bed. I'll wait in the hall." Placing Carlton's arm around Mo's back, she says in a soothing voice, "Goodnight, Mo. I'll see you tomorrow morning." She points at her boyfriend, her eyes locked on him, her words filled with disgust. "And I'll see *you* in a few minutes."

By the time Carlton steps into the hall, the townhouse is quiet, Jim safely tucked in bed. Mo listens to the conversation seeping through his closed door, holding the sepia-toned photograph to his chest.

"What is *wrong* with you, Carl?" Kay says. "I can't believe you would do something like that!"

Carlton leans in to hug her. "Kay, I'm sorry."

She pulls away. "Be quiet! I'm tired of your apologies. You and your friends should be ashamed. He wants so badly to be accepted by you. The way you all treat him in return is disgusting. Trevor's the only one that doesn't treat him like an animal."

"I know. I'm sorry. I'll talk to them."

"You *will*. I'm going to talk to my parents in the morning about having Mo move in with us. This is unacceptable. Jim's uncontrollable, and you know it. And Brian's a dog. The girls he brings here are disrespectful to Mo *and* me. It's not okay. If I have to bring Mo home with me, I will. And I *won't* be back."

"Come on, Kay, don't say that."

"I mean it! I won't be with someone who can't understand when a person needs help and friendship. And *you*, of all people!" She points her hand at him. "You treat me with the utmost respect, showing remarkable self-control, but you can't do the same for *him*? You should feel horrible about tonight. If Mo gets hurt again, we're through."

"Okay, I'll make it right. I promise."

"You *better*. I'm going home now. When I come back tomorrow, we're going to take Mo someplace nice. Do you understand me?"

"Yes, Kay. I'm sorry."

"Let me think about where I want to go tonight. I'll be here before noon. Make sure you're ready to go. And you better apologize to him in the morning—you and all your so-called friends. I won't stand by and watch any more abuse in this house."

Mo hears the front door close and Carlton climb the stairs. The boys in their rooms and the guests gone, along with the brown-haired girl and her ponytail, Mo still feels the sting of their actions and words. They did treat him like an animal, just as Kay said. This was something his father worried about on his last day of school, several hours after Ken and Earl decided to close K&E for good.


Crowded, the principal's office at Sumerduck Elementary was hot and stagnant as the outside air threatened to sneak through his open window, the tension in the room making it feel hotter. Ken sat across from Principal Bailey, between Mrs. Harrington and Mo's eighth-grade teacher, Mrs. Wilson.

Mo sat on a chair in the corner of the office, bouncing Jake on his knee and picking his younger brother's toy off the floor whenever he dropped it. He listened carefully, trying hard to understand his father's concern.

"What d'ya mean you've been lenient in advancing my boy?" Ken's eyes glared at Principal Bailey. "He's done the work, hasn't he? Passed the tests?"

Mrs. Wilson cleared her throat. "Ken, being his teacher this past year, I'm the one to blame."

"You're not the one throwing my boy outta school," Ken snarled. "It's John here who's deciding to limit my son's future!"

Mrs. Harrington placed her hand on Ken's shoulder. "Please just listen to what they have to say. Everyone's on Mo's side."

Mo knew his father would listen to Mrs. Harrington, recognizing she'd been so important the previous two years in helping Mo get through his studies. He saw how they all stared at his father, Ken looking like a trapped opossum.

Ken sighed, slumping back into his seat. "Fine. Go ahead. Say your piece."

Fidgeting with the pencil holding her bun in place, Mrs. Wilson continued. "This last year hasn't been easy. Mo isn't grasping much of the material. He's falling further and further behind the rest of the class, which requires a great deal of my time. It's unfair to the other students. Mrs. Harrington has been kind enough to help when she can, but she has her own classroom responsibilities. Despite the extra attention, he's unable to pass his tests. Of course, we've been encouraging him, but his absolute best is a fifth or early sixth-grade level." She shook her head. "It's not his fault. We aren't saying that."

"We bent the rules sufficient to get Mo through seventh grade," Principal Bailey said, "but we can't continue to overlook state-enforced standards. Mo will find it impossible to keep up in high school. His progress has stalled. This will have to be the end of the road for his schooling."

Ken slumped in his chair, pleading in a way Mo hadn't seen since his mother lay silent in her bed six years earlier. "Isn't there anything we can do for my son?" He waved the back of his hand at Principal Bailey. "What about that educational funding legislation I been reading about in the papers?"

Principal Bailey straightened the papers in front of him. "I think you're referring to the Elementary and Secondary Education Act. Yes, it's expected to be signed into law by President Johnson in the coming weeks. While it targets low-income families, I'm quite certain it does not address children with special needs like Mo. In any event, I'm afraid it will be too little too late as it will take years for those funds to filter through the education system or have any real impact. There are clearly still segments of the population not benefitting from President Johnson's Great Society."

Leaning into Mr. Bailey's desk, Ken's spine stiffened, his nostrils flared. "So you're saying there's nothing can be done about my son?" Ken's voice grew louder. "You're saying my boy won't even be treated like some poor folks' kids? On your authority, he's condemned to a life in the shadows like some kinda second-class citizen? An animal?" He pounded his fist on the table. "I pay my taxes! My son's got rights! My boy ain't no second-class citizen. And he sure as hell ain't no animal." He threw his hands in the air.

"What do I have to do to get my son the same rights as every other American?"

"I'm sorry, Mr. Lumen. We don't make the laws." Principal Bailey motioned with his hands. "They're tied, Mr. Lumen. You may not see it, but the government's got them tied."

Ken shoved his chair back, rising to his feet. "That's a bunch of crap, and you know it! You just didn't try hard enough! You don't care that he'll work as a farmhand or dig ditches, working alongside Coloreds and uneducated White trash. You'd condemn my son to a life of slave wages and prejudice—people treating him different just because he don't look or talk like they do."

Jake began crying. Mo shook his knee faster.

Mrs. Harrington reached out to touch his father's arm. "Ken, we've all done the best—"

Ken whirled around to address Mrs. Harrington, his face all red and tangled. "No, Janice! *You* failed him! *Wilson* failed him! *John* here failed him! This damn school failed him! Hell, the United States of America failed him!" He looked back at Mr. Bailey. "And what d'ya suppose I do now, huh? I work nights! Sleep days! I have that baby to take care of! I'm just supposed to be Mo's teacher now, too?" Ken stomped over to the door. "To hell with you!" He threw up his hands. "To hell with all of you!" He slammed the door behind him.

Red-faced, Mo took Jake's hand and guided him across the room. Grabbing the doorknob to exit Principal Bailey's office, he could feel the heat of his father's rage still radiating. Approaching the pickup, he saw his father slumped forward and hanging over the steering wheel, head shaking and tears running down his cheeks.

Sitting in his townhouse bedroom, Mo examines a photograph of his father, holding his red-hearted medallion and wondering why it didn't protect him against Jim and the others. He misses the shelter of his parents' home in Virginia. He wishes his father were still alive to shield him from the harsh words and abuse. And he wonders how he might have contributed to his father's sickness.

Recalling his father's grief, Mo contemplates the cause. Was it his mother's death? Was it *his* seizure? Was it Jake's birth? Was it his father's own sins or the sins of others? Poor judgment or prejudice? Had all his father's battles for freedom and justice taken their toll? Or had he been fighting on the wrong side all along? In the end, all that lingers is the agony on his father's face as Ken fought for his sons' futures—their rights, recognition, and self-respect.

Kneeling beside his bed, Mo asks God to heal his father's wounds and cleanse his father's sins. He prays his own suffering—suffering rooted in history, resurrected by ongoing hate and fear—will not have to be endured alone. Climbing under the sheets and resting his head on the pillow, Mo realizes that time and distance will not allow him to escape his past. Even as the roar of injustice fades, the echo of whispers persists.

# -30-

# SCARLET

## SATURDAY, 6 SEPTEMBER 1975

*Palmer hasn't been bowling in over a decade.* He'd been in a league for years before the constant travel caused considerable absence, but it takes only a few frames for his form to return. It's 'win with color pins' night at Northwest Shoshone Bowl, and by the fifth game, they've earned enough free drinks to make Osmond's lane approaches a little wayward. Palmer has always held his liquor better.

Knowing Osmond's goal is to distract him from his normal Saturday night routine, Palmer's plan is a developing one. By eleven, he's dropped Osmond off at his hotel room and headed to the nearest thing to a dive in the city—the Salt Lake Shake 'n Stir. If the city's a dry town, it's not apparent on this night. Palmer stands by the jukebox for thirty minutes before securing a seat at the bar. Next to him, a frolicking tongue dressed in scarlet makes for tedious conversation and endless possibilities. She'll do.

Palmer's midnight walk back to the hotel room is a silent one, disturbed only by occasional passing vehicles and the stumbling of Scarlet's heels on the sidewalk. While he walks, he thinks. He thinks about Ted. He thinks about Dick. And he thinks about Harry. He thinks back to when they were a team. He cycles every investigation through his memory as he walks the four blocks. One sticks out in particular, as it has since that day in late fall 1957.

Their team was new but showed promise. Murphy had already earned office cred for his work on the Brink's Robbery. Osmond's several years on the street proved he was fearless. Palmer was green. He was sharper than anyone else in the office, there was no debate about that, but he was also reckless. Murphy liked the kid and saw promise.

They were on a stakeout down in Dorchester near Franklin Park. Albert Cantoria was wanted for armed robbery, aggravated assault, and first-degree murder in a string of bank heists around Kansas City, sitting on the FBI's Most Wanted for eighteen months along with one of his partners, Ferguson. Lowrey, the third in their gang, had been arrested in the last holdup, spilling *his* guts like a pig on a butcher's table. Witnesses at the robberies said Cantoria was the ringleader. All said he didn't carry a weapon. Ferguson, on the other hand, was considered armed and dangerous. Through his squealing, Lowrey confirmed their testimony.

Cantoria and Ferguson were spotted in the Buffalo area several months earlier, after which, they were believed to have split up, both heading east. Though the whereabouts of Ferguson remained a mystery, Cantoria was recognized by residents in a brownstone apartment building south of Boston, where he had been holed up for the past eight weeks. Now, with the sun shining off the apartment building windows, three FBI agents sat in Murphy's sedan waiting for Cantoria to exit onto Talbot.

Murphy held his coffee up to Osmond's face. "My son played with Heinie at Holy Cross."

Osmond blew on his coffee. "Invite him over for a couple of beers then."

The seven months following the Celtics NBA Championship, Palmer had heard Murphy tell his Tommy Heinsohn stories a dozen times, enjoying Osmond's reactions. He preferred to play instigator. "Cooz is the playmaker on that team."

Murphy pushed his chest out. "He went to Holy Cross, too. I went there. So did both my boys."

Osmond cracked his window to let out the oppressive mix of smoke and hot air. "Let's invite *him* to your house party too." He flicked his cigarette butt to the pavement before turning to Palmer in the back seat. "Russell's the dominant player on that team. He'll have a handful of rings before he's—"

"Shh!" Murphy placed his hand on Osmond's shoulder. "Here he comes."

Cantoria descended the granite stairs, then walked toward a taxi parked at the corner of Talbot and Wales. Palmer tugged at the door handle.

Murphy raised his hand. "Stop! He's not going to the taxi. Both lights are on. Neighbor says he walks to Maldonado's for breakfast in the morning." He rested his hand on the seatback. "Relax. We'll be able to pick him up easier at the restaurant."

The taxi lights shut off as Cantoria stepped from the curb, reaching for the door. Palmer sprang out, shifting sideways along the sidewalk to get around Osmond's door, which had flown open.

Two hands on his pistol, Palmer put his left foot forward, staring down the barrel, "Hands up, Cantoria!"

The shot came from a second-floor window. Osmond spotted Ferguson just before he pulled the trigger, leaped out, and pushed Palmer into the side of the building. Murphy fired two shots, lodging the second in the side of Ferguson's head. Cantoria jumped in the taxi, disappearing, along with the sun, into the shadows. Osmond lay on the ground, bleeding from his chest. Murphy radioed for assistance. Palmer sat on his ass, held the back of his head, and watched Osmond struggle to breathe.

An ambulance arrived minutes later. Paramedics placed an oxygen mask over Osmond's mouth, wheeling him away on a stretcher. Murphy drove Palmer back to the field office in silence. Palmer was Catholic, at best nonpracticing, but he sat praying in Murphy's car on that day.

Arriving back at the Peery, Palmer summons the desk clerk, exchanging a ten for a brown bag, Scarlet hanging on his shoulder. In the elevator, she unwraps the package, protesting his preference for Jack. The disagreement ends when the door lock clicks behind them. With Osmond asleep in the next room, The Beast will do no more talking tonight.

# EMILY

## SATURDAY, 6 SEPTEMBER 1975

M*o reaches down to retrieve a curlycup gumweed and feels a dull pain in his shoulder.* Rubbing it as he walks, he wonders why Carlton bent his arm back last night. Was Carlton worried about him pulling the brown-haired girl's ponytail? *She* was the one pulling *his* hair last night. Would he have pulled her hair if given the opportunity? Was he trying to pull her hair? Unsure, he wonders if he had ever wanted to pull *Emily's* hair. She said he had. But did he? He didn't remember then. He still doesn't. Was she lying? Riddled with questions, seeking resolution, he ventures deeper into the woods. Though he returns without answers, he is no longer burdened. When he gets back to the townhouse, Mo stops at his bedroom before heading to the living room.

Kay's sitting on the sofa reading *Cosmopolitan*. She puts her magazine down when he enters. "How are you this morning?"

After tucking his shirt into his pants, Mo runs his hand through his hair. "I'm okay."

"Looks like you went for a walk. Did it help you forget about last night?"

Mo looks at his hands before feeling for his gloves. "Yes, I feel much better now."

"Where did you go?"

"I walked around campus, then to the store to buy some baseball cards. They're in my room if you want to open them with me."

Kay laughs, motioning for him to sit down. "That's okay, I'm not into baseball cards. My father would be, he loves everything baseball."

"Trevor says he needs some cards to finish his set, so we're trading later."

"That's nice. Trevor's a good friend." Kay curls several loose strands of hair around her ear. "Carl's your friend, too. He's made a few mistakes, but he promises he'll be much better. Did he apologize to you last night?"

Mo nods. He feels a tickle in his tailbone as he watches Kay play with her hair.

"Good. We're taking you to Stillwater Trail. I packed lunch, and my mother made an apple pie." Kay winks. "So I snuck a slice for you."

Mo responds with an appreciative smile—a smile he had once reserved for his mother, grandmother, and Mrs. Harrington. But this smile's somehow more. This one threatens to expose the rapid and rhythmic pounding in his chest.

Kay smiles back. "Would you like to go to church with my family? I've noticed you give thanks before you eat. You do it quickly, I think, because you don't want the boys to see, but I've caught you a few times."

Mo blushes. "My mother told me to always thank God for sharing His bounty."

"I agree. My family's Catholic, but you're welcome to join us for services tomorrow morning if that's alright with you. I can pick you up and drop you off."

Mo nods. "I've always been a Baptist, but my mother said God's present in all churches."

"Alright, then, I'll pick you up at nine thirty." Kay extends her pinky toward him.

Mo stares at her finger. "Okay."

Kay giggles. "Wrap your finger around mine like this." She interlaces her two pinkies. "It's to make a promise."

Mo's pinky is larger than Kay's middle finger. He holds it out, letting her do the wrapping. When their fingers touch, a tingle races up his arm and into his chest. Startled by the phone ringing, he disengages just as he's about to bend his pinky to clasp hers.

Kay springs from the sofa. "I'll get it," she says, rushing to the phone. "Hello. Yes, he's here. Can I tell him who's calling?" She lays the receiver down on the counter, walking back to the sofa. "It's Professor Langford," she tilts her head with a look of surprise, "for *you*."

Staring at the dial, Mo holds the receiver to his ear. "Hello?"

"Hi, Mo, this is Mike. How've you been?" Langford's voice sounds much less dignified over the phone.

"I'm good, Mike. How are you?"

"I'm good, too. Hey, I'm thinking about heading up to Boston this afternoon. Was wondering if you'd like to come along. Don't know if you've been yet, but there's some nice stuff to do there. We could go to Boston Common, maybe take a ride in a swan boat. Thought you might like to join me."

Mo twists the coil cord around his finger. "I'm sorry, Mike, I'm already going somewhere today."

"Oh, okay, no problem. So, where are you going?"

"I'm going to Stillwater Trail with Kay and Carlton."

"Carlton, you say. Hmm, well, sounds like fun."

After an uncomfortable silence, Mo shakes the receiver, "Hello? Mike? You still there?"

"Oh, I-I'm sorry, yeah, well, w-we'll go another time. You kids have fun. Alright, well, bye."

Mo says goodbye. Holding the receiver after he hangs up, Mo tries to recall the last time he'd spoken on the phone. He wasn't allowed at the Branch home, and the phone at his father's house had been shut off soon after Grandma Cleveland's passing. He answered the phone when he was younger, but only to hand it off to his father or grandmother.

He likes the feel of the grooved plastic receiver in his hand, enjoys listening and talking into it, and appreciates having a friend call him at home. He knows Mr. and Mrs. Branch won't let Jake call him. Does Sam have a phone? How nice it would be for Sam to call from Virginia. How good it would be for him to be able to call Sam and tell him everything he's learned about baseball. Are there phones in heaven? How wonderful it would be to hear his mother, father, and Grandma Cleveland's voices again. Releasing the receiver, he pours himself a glass of water before heading back to sit by Kay. He hopes she will one day call him on the phone though he prefers being with her.

Kay waits for Mo to sit down. "What did Professor Langford want?"

"He asked if I wanted to go to Boston with him today."

"Oh, fun. Would you prefer to go with him today? We can always go another day."

"No, I'd rather go with you."

"How do you know Professor Langford?"

"I went fishing with him and Mr. Griffin last Saturday. Do you know him?"

"I had him for humanities my freshman year."

"You went to school here?"

"I did," Kay pulls a hair from her sweater, "freshman year, but then I went to help my father at the hardware store."

"Is that when you met Carlton? Did he take the class with you?"

Kay leans back. "No, I met him last year at a party on campus. It will be a year next month. Carlton's never taken a class with Professor Langford. In fact, last year, Carlton had Langford on his schedule but dropped it because he said everyone told him they didn't like Langford's classes. I thought the class I had with him was interesting."

"Why did you leave school?"

"I didn't actually leave. I just took some time off. I'm thinking about coming back next year." Kay wraps a hand around her wrist. "I made a mistake and needed some time away from school to gain perspective." She picks her magazine up from the coffee table, muttering, "Just wish I could get away from the mistake." She shakes her head. "You should go get ready. Carlton will be down soon."

Back in his room, Mo opens the packs of baseball cards he purchased earlier. Separating them, he stacks the Red Sox cards on his nightstand before placing the rest in his father's shoebox. By the time Mo rinses his face and brushes his teeth, Kay and Carlton are waiting in the hall by the entrance door. He grabs his transistor radio as they head out.

Just northwest of Georgiaville Pond, Stillwater Scenic Area is a short drive from Bryant College. The primary trail's a nearly five-mile loop running along the banks of Stillwater Pond and Capron Pond. Most weekends, the footpath's quiet, with most visitors walking only the quarter-mile to a picnic area where the scenic trail begins on the northwest bank of Stillwater Pond.

They arrive with the heat and humidity at peak, temperatures in the high nineties. At the picnic area, Mo sits on the edge of a blanket, enjoying the warbles of native songbirds while watching a kaleidoscope of monarchs settle onto some late-season milkweed nearby. After eating, he lies on his side, looking across the pond when a butterfly lands near his name patch. Its orange-and-black pattern, a stark contrast to the serene blend of blue and green in the background.

With the start of the baseball game, Mo brings his radio to the water's edge, affording his friends time to themselves. Listening to the game, he takes off his boots and socks to dip his feet into the water, tossing twigs and small stones into the lake while trying to identify distinct ring patterns from the disruptions. Returning to the picnic blanket with the game half over, he sits next to Kay.

She offers him a Sprite. "How are the Sox doing?"

Reaching for the can, Mo nods. "They're winning in a blowout."

"My father must be happy." Kay nudges her boyfriend. "Carl has something he wants to say to you."

Staring down, Carlton rubs his hand along the edge of the blanket. "I'm really sorry, Mo. What the guys and I did was wrong. I'm not gonna let it happen again. I'll keep the other guys from doing anything to hurt you. You're a wicked nice guy and a good housemate." He flicks a few small crumbs off the blanket before looking up. "Kay and I want to start taking you on outings like this on weekends. You're new to the area, and we like doing stuff away from the other guys sometimes, so we'd like you to join us."

"I'd like that, too." Mo hopes Carlton will be different but relishes the thought of spending more time with Kay.

Carlton looks at Kay. "Unfortunately, we can't go next Saturday because I'm going home to see my mother. But we can go some-where the following week."

Choked up, Kay says, "Okay, we'll work out the details later." She puts her arms around Carlton and Mo. "For now, let's just try to be nice to each other and have some fun on the weekends, okay?"

Looking at each other, the boys nod.

Kay collects their trash. "Alright, let's go for a walk."

The trail is almost empty. Following most visitors' departures, there's a gentle, cooling breeze off the lake. Mo stays ahead of Carl-ton and Kay. Gloves on, he stops periodically to take a closer look at wildflowers or waterfowl, allowing his friends to catch up.

About halfway to the southern end of Stillwater Pond, Carlton waves Mo to continue without them. They sit side by side at the water's edge, the unfortunate events of last night a distant memory.

A jogger dodges Mo as he looks back to check on his friends. Apologizing as she pulls away, her long, brown ponytail falls against a white tank top.

Walking the full length of both ponds, Mo absorbs the beauty around him. He sees a baby bird chirping frantically on the ground, its small brown-and-black feathers still soft and furry. His interest in a foraging raccoon draws him close enough to watch it eat a grasshopper. Though he can't see the pain in the grasshopper's face or hear the agony in its cries, he knows it must be suffering. Unable to do anything, feeling as helpless as he did at last night's party, Mo reflects on an incident fourteen weeks earlier, the final Friday in May, when he was similarly vulnerable.

Mo leaned against the schoolyard's chain-link fence, talking to Paul and a few of his friends while he waited for Jake and the other Branch children. He heard loud voices behind the school, and looking up saw a group of older girls running in his direction. "Stay away from those little kids, you freak!" they said. "We don't want no village idiots here!" Their hurtful words stung as Emily led the way.

A girl from Emily's class screamed louder than the others. "What's it like to have a big, dumb retard living with you?"

Emily didn't respond. Instead, she directed her anger at Mo. "I hate you! Everybody hates you!"

Turning away from the approaching brood, Mo began to walk home, Paul following a few steps behind. Moments later, he was overcome by the angry mob of teenage girls as they pushed, shoved, and shouted at him, pulling at his clothes until, overwhelmed, he fell to the ground.

"Go home! Don't come back! Stay away from the little kids!" The girls kicked and hit Mo while he endured their verbal abuse amid his physical agony. Aware he couldn't fight back, he sat on the ground, rolling into a ball to make himself as small as possible. As the girls continued their assault, Mo pulled his arms out, using his hands to shield his face.

Two minutes after the riot began, it was over. With the help of some older boys, Jake and Peter started pulling the girls off. In the process of derailing the ruckus, Emily's hair was pulled with aggression. When the teachers arrived, they found Mo huddled and rocking on the ground, his head in his hands. Emily lay next to him, howling in pain.

Peeking through his fingers, Mo saw Mrs. Harrington standing above him. "I'm sorry," he said through tears. "I'm sorry!"

Mrs. Harrington helped him up. "Let's clean you up, so we can get you home."

The cool of a small chrome strip on the inside panel of Mrs. Harrington's car door felt good on that warm Friday afternoon, and the air smelled of freshly cut grass and dandelions. It was one of those perfect spring afternoons when Mo should have been exploring the woods or sitting on a rock at the edge of the river. Instead, arriving home bruised, he worried about what Mr. and Mrs. Branch would say. While Mrs. Harrington conversed with Mrs. Branch in the driveway, he walked to his favorite boulder along the Rappahannock.

Mo felt Paul's tiny hand on his shoulder a short while later, the youngest Branch boy sitting on the ground next to him.

Paul's squeaky voice sounded hopeful. "You wanna play hide-and-seek?"

Mo didn't take his eyes off the river. "No, not right now."

Paul tugged at Mo's shirtsleeve. "C'mon, let's play. It'll be fun."

Mo kept silent, skipping stones along the water.

"Please, Mo?" Paul hugged him around the waist. "Forget about my dumb sister. You'll feel better if we play a game."

Mo hung his head. "Go in the house. I don't feel like playing right now." He picked up a stick, poking several clustered leaves floating by.

Paul stayed. Dion joined them. They sat there without speaking until it was time to eat.

Mrs. Branch's hands shook as she set the table that night. Her compressed lips, though silent, spoke volumes. Of average height with modest features and medium-length, brown hair, Mrs. Branch is no delicate woman. Her hands calloused, neck tanned from countless hours tending the gardens, she's not one to complain and has little sympathy for those so inclined. She doesn't tolerate tattling or instigating, both capable of testing her patience. The children are well aware when their mother is irritated.

*That* night, she was irritated.

She began dinner with a provoking comment to her husband. "Emily and Mo were in a fight today in the schoolyard."

Mr. Branch looked up from his fork, a piece of well-gravied turkey dangling from the tines. "How's that?"

"Well," Mrs. Branch explained with a huff, "Emily says she and some of the other girls went over to confront Mo. He grabbed her hair when they started fighting. Pulled it hard—almost off her head. She came home complaining of a headache."

He looked at Emily. "Is this true?"

Emily nodded, rubbing the back of her head.

"No, it's not!" Paul looked to Peter for support. "The older girls were yelling at Mo, and then they jumped on him. Somebody else pulled Emily's hair."

"Are you finished, young man?" Mr. Branch said before turning to Mo. The piece of turkey fell to his plate, splattering brown dressing onto Mr. Branch's white collared shirt. "Explain yourself, Mo." He smudged the gravy into his shirt with a dinner napkin. "Did you

169

pull Emily's hair?"

Mo, hands shaking, put down his fork. "I don't know, sir. I don't remember."

"What do you mean you don't remember?!" Mr. Branch threw down his dinner napkin. "What don't you remember?"

Mo's whole body shook. "I don't know what happened."

Mr. Branch's face turned red as a beefsteak tomato from his wife's garden. "What's that supposed to mean? You don't remember pulling Emily's hair? You don't remember fighting? What don't you remember?"

Mo stared at his plate. "I was just standing at the fence when the girls started yelling at me." He rubbed his eyes. "Then they jumped on me and hurt me, and I went to the nurse's office with Mrs. Harrington."

"Janice drove Mo home," Mrs. Branch said. "She says some of the older girls had to be pulled off him but doesn't know how the fuss began." She took a sip of chardonnay. "Emily says he was playing with a second-grader. Looked like Mo was trying to hurt him." She raised her eyebrows.

Emily nodded. "It's true, Dad! My friends saw it, too!"

Paul pointed at his older sister. "She's lying!"

Mo kept silent, his jaw clenched. He could feel his heart beating in his ears.

Pushing his chair back, Mr. Branch rose to his feet. "Silence!" He glowered at Mo. "Is this true?"

Mo looked up at Mr. Branch, struggling to keep his voice steady. "No, sir, I was waiting at the fence like always."

Mr. Branch slammed his fist on the table. "Mo, tell me what happened!"

Mo focused on Dion, sitting next to Mr. Branch. "I don't remember," he said, the pounding in his ears racing the beating in his chest. "I'm sorry, I don't remember."

"*How?*" Mr. Branch roared. "How can you not remember? It just happened today. It's just not possible." He shook his head.

Mo rose from the chair, his face red and wet. "I'm sorry." Turning, he hurried upstairs.

Later that evening, Mr. Branch entered Mo's bedroom. Sitting at the edge of the bed, he placed a hand on Mo's shoulder. "I've been talking to Paul and Emily. Paul swears you didn't do anything, and Emily admits she and her friends were pretty far away. I'm going to take Paul's word and pretend this didn't happen, but you need to understand fighting or anything else with children isn't going to be tolerated."

Surprised by Mr. Branch's comforting tone, Mo lifted his head from the pillow. "Yes, sir."

"You have to remember you're much bigger than they are. You could accidentally hurt them easier than they can hurt you." Mr. Branch patted him on the back twice before departing.

Mo heard Mr. Branch's footsteps descend the stairs, replaced by lighter footsteps coming up. He reached over to turn off the lamp.

Emily poked her head in, whispering loud enough for him to hear, "Freak."

Light evaporated as Mo pulled the sheet up over his head.

Paul entered and shook Mo's shoulder. "Are you okay?"

Mo pretended he was asleep.

Kneeling along the edge of the water, Mo gets up from the ground with dusk approaching. Checking his wrist, noticing his Timex is wet, he realizes he's been gone a long time. He sprints back to where he left Carlton and Kay, only to find they're gone. By the time he rejoins his friends at the picnic area, Mo's disheveled.

Running up to Mo, Kay holds out her hands, placing them on his shoulders when she draws near. "Are you okay? Did you get lost? Why's your uniform dirty and your neck all red? Did you fall?"

Dizzy from Kay's flurry of questions, Mo looks down at his knees. "I was looking at some flowers and saw a dead baby bird on the ground, so I buried it and said a little prayer. Then I watched a raccoon for a while. I guess I lost track of time. I'm sorry. I came back as fast as I could."

"Weren't you scared it was gonna get dark? We were just heading out to look for you."

"No, I was okay. There's a waterfall near the end of the path. I stopped there for a while to enjoy the sound."

Whatever light remains now seems concentrated on Kay as they head back to the car. A welcome drizzle dots the windshield on the ride home. Kay and Carlton lower their windows a few inches to take advantage of the evening breeze. Having purged himself of the pain he felt earlier in the day, Mo sits silently in the back seat, his mind swirling from a tumultuous twenty-four hours while his body revels in the cool air engulfing him. Sports news on the radio highlights the home team's lopsided victory. After a difficult start, it has been an almost perfect day.

# WILD KINGDOM

## MONDAY, 8 SEPTEMBER 1975

Palmer's vantage point affords him an unobstructed view of the diners at the trattoria, though there aren't many at five on a Monday afternoon. He watches with mild interest as a couple is seated. The woman appears much older, possibly twice the man's age. Though she offers her date a demure smile, Palmer reads much into the way she flicks her napkin out with force before smoothing it across her lap. Her gem-laden fingers and diamond-clad ears are misplaced in this mid-scale restaurant, exposing her intentions. In the grip of a cougar, without a spade sharp enough, her date's eyes glimmer with fear—the kind of fear a male black widow knows when the post-event feast begins. Unnoticed, his curiosity piqued, Palmer observes their predator-prey dance like an episode of *Wild Kingdom*.

He motions to Osmond when he sees him walk in.

"Hey, Frankie. Sorry, Humphrey dumped a pile of shit today." Osmond glances around before pulling his chair out. "Geez, this place is dead."

"I ordered you a scotch." Palmer nods to the glass parked in front of Osmond.

Osmond eyes the glass with suspicion.

"Don't worry. It only cost me a fraction of my paycheck."

Taking a sip, Osmond nods, an approving smile crosses his face. "Didn't want to order me any of that bottom-shelf compost you seem to like?"

"The problem with living the high life is going back to the low-rent district." Palmer points his glass toward Osmond. "Better to just nestle into the bottom shelf. Besides, they don't have Jack, and

I figured you wouldn't be interested in his Kentucky cousin, Jim."

While Osmond scans the menu, Palmer eavesdrops on Wild Kingdom's conversation—a terse exchange over whose watch holds time better: her Rolex or his Timex.

Closing the menu with finality, Osmond breaks the silence. "Well, at least Bachman says the hairs matched one of the victims in Utah. FBI Lab here in Salt Lake says another matches a victim in Colorado."

Seeing the waitress approaching through the swinging kitchen doors, Palmer glances at the menu. "Yeah, but it's not enough to hang him—not even enough to show him the gallows. I'm missing something. There's more to that Beetle."

The waitress circles their table several times before descending on them like a vulture swooping down for fresh roadkill. With her rehearsed charm, Palmer can feel The Vulture's talons scratching at his wallet. He regrets ordering Osmond's scotch.

When The Vulture departs, Palmer lets Osmond control the dialogue while he watches the body language over in the Wild Kingdom.

The Cougar licks her lips with zest between a flurry of words.

Her date tugs at his two-dollar tie in exhaustion.

When Osmond's diatribe on the benefits of daily fiber is complete, and Palmer's observed enough nonverbal carnage at the nearby table, he points his tumbler at his partner. "Alright, Harry, I know you've got something. Your conversation's even more insipid than usual. What is it?"

Osmond grabs his tumbler. "I'm heading back to Boston."

"What? Why?"

"There was a body found in Smithfield, Rhode Island. A girl. Teenager." Osmond holds up his free hand. "I know what you're thinking, Frankie, but hold on. They're treating it as an accident."

Palmer pulls out a cigarette. "One of the two missing girls you told me about last week from that area?"

Osmond finishes off his scotch. "No, it happened sometime this weekend. They've already identified the body. It's not one of the missing girls. For the time being, they're just keeping us informed.

With all the mass murderers in the news, every barracks is on high alert. Right now, though, this one's just speculation."

Palmer exhales smoke to the side. "Sounds like heavy speculating. But not enough for you to be called back. What else you got?"

"Humphrey didn't have much. They just discovered the body this morning. He's supposed to get more background information on all three this evening." Osmond stares into his empty glass. "Oh yeah, and Murphy's back in the hospital."

Palmer raises his eyebrows, says nothing.

"I guess they found some stuff on the tests they did last weekend. He went in last night."

Palmer waves him off. "Dick will be fine. I'll bet he's pulling some theatrics to get sympathy from his wife; make sure none of us forget about him in retirement." He takes another drag. "When you flying back?"

"I'm headed out tomorrow morning. I assume you're coming with me?"

"Not a chance. I'll head out Friday." Seeing their food carried over by The Vulture, he stubs out his cigarette. With a couple of shots of cheap bourbon in the tank, her blond curls and pillowy lips look appetizing. Palmer's no longer sure what he ordered from the menu. Wishing it were a Saturday, he takes a bite of saltimbocca, placing his hopes on *this* meat satisfying him tonight.

After slicing his meatballs into quarters, Osmond looks up. "I can't direct you, Frankie, but you're authorized to come home earlier than Friday. Why don't you fly back with me tomorrow?"

Palmer sits back, looks past Osmond. "Thanks, Harry, but I still got some sightseeing to do here in Salt Lake." He smiles. "Never know who you'll run into."

"I know what you've got your eye on, but I think your time would be better spent coming home. Murphy would appreciate the visit."

"I'll phone him tomorrow. Be back before you know it."

Studying Palmer, Osmond sighs. "You do what you need to do. Just know sometimes the sights ain't worth seeing in place of friends."

Palmer nods, knowing he's dodged a disagreement.

Plates cleared, drinks drained, and belts loosened, Osmond

drops enough cash to cover the bill. "Give me a ride to the airport?" Palmer nods.

"Stay out of trouble, Frankie. I'll see you in the morning."

Lurking just above, The Vulture lunges over Palmer's shoulder and clutches Osmond's cash, releasing a soft, raspy hiss as she departs. Osmond's never been a great tipper.

Watching Osmond walk away, Palmer lights another smoke, wallet unscathed. He hears the conversation escalating in the Wild Kingdom, listening to how it clashes with the lounge music playing in the background. He cycles through Osmond's words to drown it all out: Murphy's in a Boston hospital, a young girl's had an apparent fatal accident in Smithfield, and Ted's got a tail eight hundred miles long, stretching from Salt Lake to Seattle. Murphy and the girl are back home. Not much he can do about them. But Ted's right here—here in Salt Lake City. Palmer's here, too. And he's not ready to go home.

Wild Kingdom rises to leave. The Cougar dusts her dress and slides into the arms of a fur coat, held in hopeful anticipation by a willing partner. Palmer smells her Chanel Number Five and her companion's Aqua Velva, sees her lavish Italian heels and his worn dress shoes, and knows they're both hunting tonight. Sometimes, he thinks, predator and prey become indistinguishable, and the harm they do is self-inflicted. When Wild Kingdom departs, and the show is over, Palmer's focus shifts. He's on the prowl for a different kind of predator—an indiscriminate monster.

# MRS. HARRINGTON'S OBITUARY

## TUESDAY, 9 SEPTEMBER 1975

M*o enjoys raking, the smell of fresh bark, and Tuesdays.* This morning is perfect bliss. Under cloudy skies, with the promise of an early autumn whispering in the breeze and rustling through the first layer of leaves, Mo spreads mulch, listens to his coworkers' excited voices, and inhales the aromatic bounty of late summer in New England. It's Tuesday morning, and all the Bryant groundskeepers look forward to lunch.

Even when Mo works alone, he never grows tired of raking leaves, enjoying all the uneven shapes and vibrant colors. It reminds him of the Southern live oaks strung along the Rappahannock behind the Branch home; how they dropped their leaves even in early summer. Working alongside Jake and Peter, he'd rake them into a pile before tossing handfuls into the river to watch them float, bright and tangled, atop the rushing water. From a book Grandma Cleveland had him read, he'd think about Huck and Jim traveling down the Mississippi, wondering what it would be like to float on a leaf raft with Sam on the Rappahannock and what adventures they'd have.

Mo looks to the wrought-iron archway on the other side of the pond. As he stares at the black oracle, his thoughts wander. Would walking through the archway bring him back to the shore of the Rappahannock? Back to raking leaves with Jake and Peter? Or back to sitting on a rock with Dion? Would it bring him back to fishing with his father under Kelly's Ford Bridge near Tinpot Alley? Back to sharing lunch with Sam separate from his father and the other workers? Or back to the smell of rotting carcasses floating downstream after a flood? He wonders if he could graduate from school here so that he could see his future. For now, he rakes and wonders but does not think he wants to pass through that archway. Not without knowing what he would see from his past.

When lunchtime arrives, King rides to Tony's Pizza in Griffin's pickup. There's nothing Mo can do about that. He peers back, not understanding why Juanito, Theo, and Sprinkles get enough room to line dance in the rear seat of the crew cab while he's wedged between Flatbush's biceps and Sarge's barrel belly up front. Despite the cramped space, driving with the team has its advantages: getting closer to his coworkers; its rituals: the radio loud enough to drown out Sprinkles and his endless chatter; and its challenges: being jostled around while Sarge and Flatbush alternate between jazz and flamenco stations before settling on pop as the truck pulls into the restaurant parking lot.

Once inside, Mo's surprised to see Langford sitting with Griffin.

Looking up, Langford smiles. "Hello, Mo! Derek invited me to join you guys for lunch. How was your weekend?"

Mo takes a seat next to his friend. "Hi, Mike! It was good. I went on a picnic with Kay and Carlton on Saturday. Then, I went to church with Kay's family on Sunday." Mo's eyes bulge. "Their church is *huge*. It's all made of stone. They could probably fit all the wooden churches in Fauquier County inside. Afterwards, I got to watch the game on the giant TV at Kay's parents' house. Mr. Thompson really loves the Red Sox."

"Sounds like you had a wonderful time. Red Sox holding up pretty well?"

Mo taps his fingers on the table. "They're doing okay. They've got a six-game lead, but it was eight last week."

"It's great how much baseball you've picked up in just a few weeks. You're such an enthusiastic fan now." Langford slides a napkin back and forth on the table. "So, are you doing anything Friday night?"

"Not really. I'll eat at the dining hall while I do my laundry. It's also payday, so I'll walk to the store if it's not raining and buy some baseball cards so I can trade with Trevor."

Langford's eyes follow his napkin. "Fun. I'm having a small party with some friends for dinner on Friday night. I was wondering if you'd like to join us. I can pick you up after work, say five thirty, and we can stop by the store on the way so you can buy your baseball cards. Interested?"

Mo rubs his chin. "I'll have to wash my uniforms Thursday night, but that's okay. I'd like to meet your friends."

"I'd like for them to meet you, too." Scrunching the napkin into a ball, Langford tosses it in the direction of a nearby trash can. "Alright then, I'll see you Friday." He doesn't stay for pizza, apologizing to Griffin for having to leave. Picking up his wayward napkin from the floor, he drops it in the trash, waving to Mo as he exits.

Mo sits undisturbed, watching his fellow workers drink their beer and converse. He's thankful for his new job, new home, and, most of all, new friends. And he's curious about Langford's friends. Will they be like his coworkers? Will they be like his housemates? Will they be like his father's workers? Will he eat with them or at a different table in a separate room? Will he eat alone, or will Mike eat with him? When the pizza comes, he waits for everyone else to take a slice before he grabs one for himself, hoping Mike's party isn't like his housemate's party last Friday.

Returning home from the Shed at the end of the workday, Mo swings by the Unistructure and collects the mail, finding a letter from Jake. In his bedroom, he tears the envelope open. Once again, there are two documents inside: a letter from Jake and a cutout from the newspaper. He unfolds the letter first:

*Big Brother,*
 *Sorry I haven't written sooner. I started school on Tuesday and sixth grade's going to be way harder than fifth. There's already a ton of homework. Ms. Tuttle's strict. Mrs. Harrington died on Labor Day. That's*

*why we have a new teacher. She didn't last as long as the doctors said she would. We had an assembly for her and all the teachers said nice things. Then they had the funeral today. Everyone in town was there and people were crying. It sure seems like everybody liked her. I saw Dion sitting on your rock by the river yesterday when I came home from school. He misses you. Emily's being a brat to me and Peter now that your gone. She thinks she's so special because she's in high school. We put a whoopie cushion down before she sat on the couch and everyone laughed including dad but we got in trouble for it. I'll write again in a few days. I love and miss you. Jake*

*P.S. I included Mrs. Harrington's obituary from yesterday's paper. Sorry you couldn't be here for the funeral.*

Teary-eyed, Mo reads the newspaper clipping. Only a half-dozen words—*brief illness, five children*, and *sixth grade*—stand out. He's thankful he had the chance to stay with Mrs. Harrington's family for a few weeks at the beginning of the year. Gratitude turns to fear as he considers where the Harrington children would go if anything happened to Mr. Harrington. Would any family want their thirteen-year-old son who can't go to school? Would he be separated from his brothers and sisters? Would he have to stay at the Fauquier Motor Lodge and be raised by The Woman Leaning Against the Door? Tears, falling all the harder, collect on the newspaper clipping and blur the print into a gray stain.

Mo lies back on his pillow, thinking about all the things Mrs. Harrington did to help his family over the years. He's sure she was his mom's best friend. Even after his mother died, Jake was born, and his father went out of business, Mrs. Harrington was always there. After his father got sick, Grandma Cleveland died, and the Branches didn't want him anymore, Mrs. Harrington was still there.

Mo remembers Mrs. Harrington's devotion to him and his brother when there was nowhere else for them to go at the beginning of the year. How she sat there, the second Friday in January, in her own house, pleading for more time to place them together in the same home.

Unnoticed and pretending to read a book, Mo listened with a view from the next room. He saw Aunt Elizabeth seated at the table, wringing her hands and staring at the doily under the centerpiece.

A gloomy-looking man with poor posture extended his hand toward her. "Mrs. Cleveland?"

She didn't look up. "*Ms.* Cleveland, but please, call me Liz."

The gloomy man pushed his badge into her face. "Good morning, Ms. Cleveland. My name is Arthur Forrester. I'm with the Children's Bureau, a division of the Administration for Children and Families under the Department of Health and Human Services."

"Good morning, Mr. Forrester." Aunt Elizabeth glanced at his badge, placing her limp hand in his.

Mo, seated just beyond the dining room entrance, wondered whether Forrester's work title fit on his tiny badge while noting the smoothness of his hands and well-trimmed nails.

Forrester gestured toward a chair. "May I sit down?"

Aunt Elizabeth shook off her blank stare, responding, "Oh, yes, of course. Where are my manners? Please. Sit down."

"Thank you." Forrester grabbed a pen from his white vinyl pocket protector and clicked it three times, as though the first protrusion of the tip was somehow less worthy. "Mrs. Harrington, will you join us?"

"Of course," Mrs. Harrington said, relieved to escape the glare of the table's pendant lighting off Forrester's balding forehead, his last several strands of black hair offering little reprieve.

Forrester peered through his round, metal-framed glasses. "Now, Mrs. Harrington, I understand Jacob Lumen has been living with you for the past week?"

Mrs. Harrington put her elbows on the table, clasping her hands. "Yes, sir. He and Mo came here last Friday. They had nowhere else to go."

Leaning back, Aunt Elizabeth folded her arms. "I stayed with them in their father's house until last week," she said, "but they were evicted on the second. I live with my sister, Mary, in Arlington.

We're their only local relatives. There's nobody on the father's side, and our other sister lives in California. We've not heard from her since our mother died." Her lips quivering, she rubbed her palms against the table. "Mary can't take them in. She has five children already, which means there are eight of us living in the house. If I had my own place, well…" She placed her head in her hands.

"Mm-hmm." Clicking his pen twice, Forrester began scrawling. "It's interesting, ma'am, I couldn't find any records for Jacob Lumen. Not altogether unusual for home births more than a decade ago, things being much less rigorous and country folk not following up with the state, but it will require a bit more work now."

Mrs. Harrington looked at Aunt Elizabeth with confusion before turning to Forrester. "What does *that* mean, Mr. Forrester?"

He waved his pen. "Nothing, I'm sure. Just a formality at this point. Where is the boy now?"

"Jake's probably upstairs playing with the others. It's too cold for them to stay outside." Mrs. Harrington glanced around the room. "I thought I saw Mo just before you came in."

Forrester's head hung over his pen. "That won't be necessary, Mrs. Harrington. I'm here to see Jacob."

Mrs. Harrington rose to her feet. "Would you like something to drink?"

Forrester brushed lint from his pants. "No, thank you, ma'am. I'll only be here a short while." He removed his glasses.

Mo watched Forrester's unmagnified, deep-brown pupils turn to black raisins.

"Ms. Cleveland will need to come down to the district office and fill out some documentation." Forrester laid his pen with his notepad. "I'm just here for an initial assessment of Jacob's living circumstances. Can I see the boy, please?"

"Sure, I'll go get him. I'll be right back." Mrs. Harrington left the room momentarily, returning with Jake in tow.

Approaching Forrester, hands in pockets and face down, Jake dragged his feet like a horse to the slaughter.

Forrester peeked over his shoulder, the few remaining strands of his hair curling upward like smoke from a cauldron. "Good morning, young man. How are you today?"

Jake dusted his shoe across the floor. "Good."

Swinging around, Forrester motioned to Jake. "Come closer so I can see you."

Jake inched forward, head still down.

"How do you like it here with the Harrington family?" Forrester tucked his smooth forefinger under Jake's chin and pushed up.

Mo understood now why his nails were well-trimmed.

"Good," Jake replied, his eyes still focused on the floor.

Forrester leaned closer to Jake. "Would you prefer to stay here?"

Jake's eyes opened wide. Stepping away from Forrester's hand, he nodded. "Yes, sir. Mo and I like it here with Mrs. Harrington and her family. She's gonna be my teacher at school next year."

Double-clicking his pen, Forrester grabbed his pad. "Are you eating enough?"

"Yes, sir. We eat much better here than when we were at home."

"Mm-hmm, and do you get in trouble? Do you ever get scolded or hit for getting in trouble here?"

Mrs. Harrington placed her hand on Jake's shoulder. "Oh, no, Mr. Forrester, my husband and I don't believe in hitting the children."

Forrester sneered at her. "I'm talking to the boy at the moment, Mrs. Harrington."

Noticing Forrester's shoelace tie, Jake placed his hand over his mouth to keep from giggling. "No, sir. We haven't gotten into any trouble. Haven't been hit or nothing."

Forrester eyed Jake down his long, sloped nose. "What's so funny, Master Jacob?"

"Nothing, sir, we just have so much fun here."

Forrester dismissed Jake with a wave. "Okay, thank you. You're free to go." He cleared his throat, adjusted the silver ornamental clasp on his bolo tie, and resumed taking notes. When Jake was back upstairs, he turned to Aunt Elizabeth. "Was the child's mother Black?"

"No, sir. She was southeast Asian if I'm not mistaken." Aunt Elizabeth furrowed her brows. "Why would that matter?"

Forrester shrugged, his head twitching. "Well, why do you *think* it would matter? Obviously, the pool of potential families for placement is much smaller for Black children, much as it is for the physically handicapped and mentally retarded, Ms. Cleveland, as I'm sure you'd understand."

Aunt Elizabeth straightened herself up in her chair, "*Well*, I'm not sure *I'd* understand *anything* about the adoption process or the prejudice that lies therein, but I am certain Jake's father would never have raised a Black child."

"Mm-hmm." Forrester placed his glasses at the tip of his nose. "Tell me, Mrs. Harrington, why can't Jake stay here with you and your husband?"

Mo watched as Mrs. Harrington folded her hands out in front of her. He thought she might start praying, but she spoke instead. "Well, sir, we'd love to have the boys with us, but we've talked it over, and our house is too small. Although we both work, we barely make ends meet as it is. We also have our thirteen-year-old son, Lyndon, who has muscular dystrophy and requires a great deal of attention."

"I see." Forrester fingered his spectacles up the slope of his nose. "That's unfortunate." With his jagged teeth and narrow eyes, Mo thought Forrester looked like an opossum.

Aunt Elizabeth tilted her head. "Why is that?"

Forrester opened his hands. "Because now Jake will be placed into the foster care system. Children respond better to homes where there's familiarity. We know this."

Mrs. Harrington lunged across the table, brushing Forrester's hand. "What about Mo?"

Forrester stared at Mrs. Harrington's hand, eyebrows raised, nostrils flared. "Mo is not our concern at the Children's Bureau. As I understand it, he's twenty-four with mild mental retardation."

Mrs. Harrington pulled her hand back. "Yes, he had a seizure when he was eleven, and it stunted his intellectual growth."

Forrester straightened up. His voice became colder. "Well, he's recognized as an adult by the State of Virginia; therefore, he does not qualify for the foster care program. If he cannot find someone to live with or willing to help, there are community mental health centers in Fredericksburg and Alexandria to assist him. Otherwise, he will need to be institutionalized. Based on what I understand, he's capable of holding a job. Recent changes to the Social Security system can provide him with financial subsidies and medical help once he is deemed eligible."

"But he's never been on his own. He's never held a job."

"There are jobs that don't require more than a grade-school education." Forrester's lifeless eyes returned to his pad. "Plenty of Black folks get by with less."

"Oh, but Mo and Jake have always been together. They must stay together." Mrs. Harrington latched onto Forrester's hand. "Please."

Mo imagined Forrester's hand feeling like an old catfish being hauled out of the Rappahannock.

Forrester yanked his hand away. "Mrs. Harrington! That is not our concern." Pulling a napkin from his shirt pocket, he began wiping his fingers. "We are interested in the successful placement of Jacob into a suitable home with responsible foster parents." Clicking his pen, he slid it back into his pocket protector. "Unless you can find a compliant home for Jacob, also willing to accommodate his older brother, he will be placed into the foster program, and his brother will be evaluated by the state."

Mrs. Harrington sat back in her chair. "How long do we have to find a family?"

"Ms. Cleveland will be scheduled to go down to the district office no later than ten business days from today. Once the paperwork is complete, Jacob will be placed in the foster program as a ward of the state. It takes five to ten days, on average, to process a child. He can't stay in this home for more than thirty days without formal documentation, so you have until the end of the month, at the latest." Forrester stood, sliding his chair back in.

Mo entered the dining room, face red, hands wrapped around his book. "I want to stay with Jake!"

Forrester shook his head. "Mm-hmm." He turned to Aunt Elizabeth and Mrs. Harrington. "Mr. Lumen here looks like he has a strong back and able body." Stepping away from the chair, Forrester bowed his head. "Thank you, ladies. I'll show myself out."

Mrs. Harrington walked over and held Mo's hands. "It's okay, we have three weeks, and I've got some ideas."

Mo feels the dampness of the pillowcase on his neck as he retrieves the sepia-toned photograph from his nightstand. Sitting up, he clutches it to his chest, wishing it had the power to heal the ache of his loss. A single tear falls onto the photo. In his pain, Mo doesn't notice. When he looks again, there is a stain marring the image of his mother. Panicking, he wipes it away. He wipes repeatedly, but the smudge won't disappear. Dropping his head onto the pillow, he pulls his knees to his chest, knowing photographs, like loved ones, fade away.

# A DISFIGURED CORPSE

## WEDNESDAY, 10 SEPTEMBER 1975

M*o sleeps straight through to Wednesday morning.* Still in his previous day's work clothes, he doesn't shower. Instead, he splashes his face and brushes his teeth. Missing last night's baseball game doesn't even cross his mind. Like a ghost, he walks aimlessly in the pre-dawn gray, drifting along familiar pathways, unable to feel the crisp air or numbing drizzle on his skin.

With first light, Mo notices an unusual number of whitetails among the trees. He imagines all God's creatures staring at him, expressionless, waiting to see how he responds in the wake of another death. Rubbing Mrs. Harrington's medal as he arrives at the Shed, Mo enters Griffin's office, head down and without his customary wave.

Griffin pushes Mo back through the door. "Morning, son, you're a few minutes late. Let's not make it a habit. Get in the truck. We've got to remove a carcass along the road."

Mo's voice croaks. "A carcass?"

"Yup, a deer got hit by a food supply truck last night. Now it's all mangled from the cars driving in. With the wind and hard rain last night, it's caused a buildup of branches and debris. Now, rainwater's running across the road. It's a mess."

Looking out the window, Mo stares into the woods, wondering if deer feel the way people do when they lose someone close to them.

Griffin shakes his head. "So many deer out here; I'm surprised it doesn't happen more often."

When they arrive on the scene, it's more gruesome than Mo expects. He tries to look anywhere but at the disfigured corpse, but a glimpse of its eyes makes him shudder. He can feel the spirit of the deceased in the eyes he knows are watching from the woods. Eyes once bearing testament to his youthful innocence now stand in judgment. Of what, Mo is uncertain.

He lifts the hundred-pound doe, placing it in the bed of the pickup. His uniform, gloves, and work boots suffer mud splatter that will wash off and bloodstains that will not. Holding the lifeless animal, he prays for both their souls.

Later, in the woods away from the road's edge, Juanito joins Mo to dig a shallow grave in the moist soil. The doe's body is folded up and laid to rest while dozens of speechless witnesses gaze from a safe distance. Without formal prayer, Mo uses his gloved hands to compress the mud before spreading fallen leaves, placing several large stones to ensure heavy rains and scavengers won't resurrect the carcass. A life lived with little regret. A death curated with little emotion.

After returning his shovel to the Shed, Mo removes his gloves and feels for the medals on his necklace, a practice he repeats each time he takes them off. He panics when he discovers one is missing. Feeling the otherwise-empty chain around his neck, he looks down to see his father's medallion.

Mo races to Griffin's office. "Mr. Griffin! I-I-I lost my Saint Christopher medal! Mrs. Harrington gave it to me. I-I-It's all I have left a-a-and—"

"Whoa there," Griffin says, placing a hand behind Mo's neck, the other on his chest. "Take a breath. It's alright. When was the last time you had it?"

"I had it on this morning. Then me and Juanito buried the deer. When we got back, I felt for it here in the garage. It's gone!"

Griffin pats his back. "Okay, okay. Don't worry. We'll find it. Let's retrace your steps."

Enlisting Juanito, they form a hunting party, searching from burial site to cleanup location over thirty minutes. For Mo, it's an eternity.

Griffin holds up his hand, metal shimmering in the dull daylight. "Is this it?"

Mo rushes over. "Yes, that's it! Thank God."

"It was right here in the truck bed. Must've fallen off when you loaded the deer. Lucky it didn't fall out. Might not want to wear it to work, just to be safe."

Mo sits on the tailgate. "I know. I'm sorry, Mr. Griffin. It's just…" He swallows a lump rising in his throat. "I found out last night Mrs. Harrington died. This is all I have left of her."

"Oh, no. I'm sorry, son." Griffin pats his back. "Let's head back to the Shed." He notices Mo's boots are spotted with bloodstains. "That deer sure made a mess of your boots."

That evening, Mo's reading in his room when he hears shouting upstairs. Heavy footsteps and arguing continue as two housemates make their way down. He waits until the disturbance has moved to the back of the house before leaving his room.

Carlton stands over Brian. "Are you even gonna see her again?"

Brian sits at an angle, one leg on the sofa armrest. "Probably not."

Making his way to the kitchen, Mo stands beside Trevor. They watch the scene unfold with little concern.

Carlton shakes his head, his hands waving. "Why would you let her go through my notebook?"

"I didn't *let* her." Brian pushes Carlton away. "I went to the bathroom. I didn't know she moved it."

"I left it closed in the drawer of my dresser last night. When I went upstairs just now, it was lying open on top of the dresser. Who does that?"

Brian shrugs. "Some bimbo with no ethics? I can't babysit every chick I bring into the bedroom."

Mo turns to Trevor, his eyebrows furrowed. "No wonder I couldn't find the chickens."

Rolling his eyes, Trevor whispers, "C'mon, Mo. 'Chick' is just another word for girl."

Eyes lighting up, Mo nods, mouthing, "*Oh.*" Blushing, he releases an awkward chuckle.

Carlton lunges at Brian. "B, this is no joke! I have personal stuff in that notebook!" He grabs Brian's head, holding it against the sofa cushion.

"You mean *diary,* don't you?" Brian says, his voice muffled. "If you don't want anyone to see it, leave it at your mom's house."

"*Nobody's* allowed to look through my notebooks! Not even Kay! And then you just let your...your...trash go through my private stuff?"

"Dude, would you relax? I doubt anyone cares what you have to write about anyway."

They continue scuffling on the sofa until Carlton sits up and folds his arms. Fixing his shirt, Brian settles at the opposite end. They sit without looking at each other for several minutes before Carlton stomps upstairs, slamming the door behind him.

Trevor approaches Brian. "You do need to be more careful about who you bring into the house. Some of those girls are borderline homeless."

Brian grunts before exiting out the front door.

Trevor turns back to Mo with a shrug. "Did you say you picked up some new packs?"

"Yeah," Mo says. "You want to trade?"

"Sure. I'll go get my doubles."

At bedtime, Mo rests his new cards on the nightstand and leans the Saint Christopher medal against the sepia-toned photograph. Looking at the smudge in the photo, he's disappointed it rubbed out his mother's face but glad it didn't erase his only image of Mrs. Harrington. He rests his head on his pillow, staring at the photograph, medal, and stack of baseball cards. Still grieving, he realizes how important it is to have friends. He falls asleep with life and hope seeping back into his body.

# DINNER WITH TED

## WEDNESDAY, 10 SEPTEMBER 1975

*The Beast is in full control by Wednesday evening.* Palmer drove Osmond to the airport at dawn on Tuesday, picked up five gallons of water, two six-packs of Miller, and a carton of Marlboros. He emptied one gallon outside the store and headed straight to 565 First Avenue. For thirty-six hours, he's surveilled The Monster, never leaving his car to eat or sleep, all the while keeping track of which gallon containers are for drinking and which are not.

Even without Palmer's presence, Ted wouldn't be alone. In front of the boarding house he lives in, with a perfect view of the fire escape on the right side, an unmarked Ford LTD Brougham with two state detectives makes itself obvious. Though less conspicuous, Ted knows Palmer's there. While Ted frequently peeks out his window, the detectives occasionally bring Palmer a coffee.

Palmer's eyes stay fixed on the side-by-side, double-hung dormer windows of Ted's room, except for quick glances in the rearview mirror to make sure *he's* still there. When Ted emerges at six on Wednesday evening, they're both hungry and out of patience.

Palmer watches Ted approach the LTD, talk through the passenger window, and hop in the back seat. He follows to a local diner seven blocks away. Ted closes the car door, waving to the detectives while entering the restaurant. Sitting at a window booth, he smiles at the waitress when she hands him a menu. Palmer believes The Monster wants company. The Beast is interested.

Palmer sits in the adjacent booth facing Ted. He also smiles at the waitress when she drops off a menu. Ted stares at his coffee mug, tapping his finger on the side and deep in thought. Palmer stares at Ted, noting their similarities and wondering what's running through Ted's mind. Both are good-looking and fit, though Palmer's rugged and tall where Ted's pretty and slight. Both have wavy, dark-brown hair, steel-blue eyes, and five-o'clock shadows. And both harbor demons.

Ted looks up from his coffee, notices Palmer staring, and nods with his eyebrows raised. His eyes fall back to his mug for an instant before looking up with a smile—a knowing smile. "You wanna keep me company?"

Palmer grabs his menu and slides into the bench opposite Ted. The rage he's felt staring at Ted's dormer the past day and a half—rage that elevated tenfold when he sat in the adjacent booth—is sufficient to ignite the pack of cigarettes in his pocket as they sit face-to-face. The Beast is close enough to swallow The Monster. But Palmer orders a coffee, hamburger, and fries.

Ted's smile grows wider as he looks up at the waitress and orders the same. Readdressing Palmer, his smile does not dim. "What a coincidence. I didn't expect to have dinner with the distinguished Investigator Palmer this evening. For that matter, I didn't expect to have dinner with *anyone* tonight. Except for the two detectives outside, I don't seem to have many friends at the moment." His smile twists into a devilish grin.

Palmer pulls out his pack of Marlboros and points, his eyebrows raised.

Ted lifts his hand off the mug with a subtle wave. "Sure, sure, go right ahead."

Palmer raps the pack against his finger, pulls a cigarette out with his lips, and slides an ashtray to the center of the table.

Ted massages the handle of his mug, crow's feet stepping out from the edges of his eyes. "So, what brings the FBI's biggest star to Salt Lake City?"

Continuing to stare, Palmer strikes a match, pulls, and blows a cloud of smoke toward the window.

"It can't be for something as small as suspicion of burglary, right?" An abbreviated chuckle escapes Ted's mouth. His grin grows more twisted.

Palmer raps out another cigarette butt from the pack, points it at Ted.

"Thanks," Ted pulls out the peace offering, "I prefer Camels, but a Marlboro will do. I'm sure you already knew that, though."

Striking another match, Palmer holds it over the center of the table. When Ted leans in, Palmer can see the flame reflected in Ted's eyes and the fires of hell radiating from the black holes at their center. Ted settles back. Palmer shakes the match and drops it in the ashtray, a trace of smoke all that separates their mutual curiosity.

The one-sided conversation falls silent for several minutes. Ted gazes out the window. Palmer studies Ted. Each puffs on their cigarette. Each wonders what the other has to say. And each believing he can outwit the other. One is right. When their burgers are delivered, and their coffees refreshed, Ted meets Palmer's glare. The Monster's ready to talk again.

"I'm innocent," Ted says as he flicks his cigarette over the ashtray and rests it on the edge, "of everything."

Palmer nods, taking a final long drag before stubbing out his cigarette and biting into his burger.

Ted moves the ashtray aside, unfolds a half-dozen napkins, and piles them up in its place. Holding a Heinz jar upside down, he shakes until his patience runs dry, digging the ketchup out with a butter knife. Eyebrows raised, and using both hands, he points to the mound of red on the stack of white as his own peace offering. "There, we can share."

Palmer offers an appreciative nod before dipping a french fry into the ketchup.

Ted swipes several fries across and holds them just below his mouth. The fries bleed ketchup onto his plate. "Why are you here, Investigator Palmer?"

Palmer takes a sip of coffee, staring at the mutilated potatoes under Ted's chin. "I was hungry."

"No, I mean, why are you here in Salt Lake?" Ted tosses the soggy mess into his mouth.

"I'm looking for a killer, Mr. Bundy."

Ted talks with his mouth full, red paste leaking down the sides of his mouth. "Weren't you just hunting down a killer in Seattle?"

Palmer nods and continues to eat.

"I didn't see where you caught him." Ted wipes the sides of his mouth before licking his finger clean. "What happened?"

"These things take time. It's like becoming a lawyer. It can take years, especially when you're juggling work and other hobbies. Isn't that right, Mr. Bundy?"

The smile that's been with Ted since Palmer sat down fades. "So, you have any leads on the killer in Seattle or the one here?"

Finished eating, Palmer raises his elbows to the table and grips his fist. "As it turns out, we're tracking a pretty good lead right now."

"You got a suspect?"

"We might."

"Here or in Seattle?"

"Not sure, maybe both."

"Well, I hope you catch him soon before someone starts thinking it's me with all the attention I'm getting from the police."

"Why would you say that, Mr. Bundy?"

"A guy named Ted driving a light-colored Beetle? I watch the news." Ted tosses his napkin onto his plate, rests back in his seat. "Can I get another cigarette, please?"

"No, sir, I don't think so. They'll kill you, you know." Palmer taps one out for himself.

Ted jerks forward. "Is that supposed to be some kind of sick joke?"

Palmer looks at his cigarette and smiles. He knows Ted's right where he wants him. "The harmful effects of smoking are no joke, Mr. Bundy. Just read the Surgeon General's warning on the pack here."

Ted, red-faced, waves off Palmer's mockery. "What do you want, Palmer?"

Watching the fiery red creep from the corners of Ted's eyes, Palmer strikes a match. "At this point, nothing at all. You invited me over to eat with you."

"You're looking up the wrong skirt. You'll find no satisfaction here."

"That may be, Mr. Bundy." Palmer lights his cigarette and blows out the match.

"The police have nothing, not on the burglary or anything else." Ted waves his hands over his head. "Why would I want to steal anything or, God forbid, rape and kill some girls? I'm a recently baptized Mormon in good standing, working my way through law school, who has no problem with the ladies."

"That's true. It does seem odd that a reasonably attractive young man filled with religious fervor, who's served on a crime prevention advisory commission, worked in emergency services and crisis centers, and is pursuing a law degree, would either have the time or the inclination to commit heinous crimes against young women. I agree with that. Unless..."

Ted's brows furrow. "Unless what?"

Palmer takes a long, slow drag, waiting several excruciating seconds to release. "Unless the killer wanted to create a facade and understand how the system works so he could use those to his advantage."

"I didn't do any of it. And if I did, you'd have nothing."

Palmer can see Ted's veneer cracking—The Monster exposed. "But, Mr. Bundy, you just said we've got nothing."

"I mean that if *I* were raping and murdering those girls—which I am not—none of them would've gotten away. Not like the one that climbed out of the killer's passenger window in Murray last November. The killer's sloppy. I'm not sloppy. And you have nothing because *you're* sloppy."

Palmer glares at Ted, takes another long drag.

Sliding out from the bench, Ted stands by the table. "Well, I don't mean to be rude, Investigator Palmer, but my ride is waiting, and we're out of things to discuss." He taps his knuckles on the table. "Thanks for dinner. I don't expect we'll be doing this again. You're not good company."

Palmer nods as Ted walks away. Watching Bundy climb back into the LTD and the vehicle drive off, The Beast is nourished.

Palmer sits for another forty-five minutes while he thinks over Ted's words. Looking at the windows, the paint, and the pictures on the walls in the diner, he notes how they observe silently, just as he does. Diners eat, argue, drink, and laugh. The windows, walls, and pictures don't flinch. They just observe. Like Palmer. And like the windows and vinyl interior of Ted's Beetle. They offer no comfort while witnessing the drama and the horror.

He knows if the seats, flooring, and door panels in Ted's Beetle could speak, and the windows could provide testimony, their stories would be damning; fear and pain soaked deep, bled down into the crevices and seeped into the seams. Bundy's mobile killing machine, on the surface, looks like any other cute Bug. And The Monster that was its previous owner passes for just another charming guy.

Palmer rubs his forehead with greater aggression as he tries to comprehend how so many lives could be taken in that car without a shred of evidence to speak for them, like a crossword with no clues. And yet, he always completes his puzzles. Always solves to the final word. Always.

Ashes drop to the table. As he looks at the scattered cinders, Palmer's thoughts wander to Hampton Beach in New Hampshire and a particularly sandy trip with Marilyn and the girls. Everyone shook out their towels, rinsed off their feet, and brushed off their folding chairs. Still, sand invaded the car. When they got home, Palmer wiped every surface, vacuumed all the carpeting, and used the crevice tool to suction out everything else. The sand remained, embedded in the grooves of the seat, nestled in the fibers of the carpet, and rooted in the seat hardware. The sand never left, sold with the car several years later.

Focus returning to Ted's Beetle, he wonders how dozens of women with long hair, sharp nails, and pints of blood could be transported and murdered in that vehicle without leaving a trace behind. He considers the plight of the teen who escaped by propelling herself through the half-open passenger window in Ted's Beetle. Imagining a handful of sand thrown out the same window, he knows it would end up in so many unreachable places: in the air vents, behind the dashboard, even down in the base of the stick shift.

Palmer jerks his head up, drops a twenty, and hustles to his rental. Searching several blocks, he locates a parked VW Beetle, inspecting it before driving back to Bundy's apartment. There, he walks over to the LTD, knocks on the driver's window, and slides in the back seat.

The driver looks at Palmer through the rearview mirror. "Evening, Chief Investigator Palmer. How was your dinner?"

"The food was good." Palmer hands him a note. "Here, give this to your captain as soon as possible."

"You really think we may find something in there?"

"The girl who got away climbed out the passenger window. It had to be a hell of a struggle. If we're lucky, we may find some physical evidence: hair, nail polish, something linking the victim to Bundy—and maybe she'll be able to pick him out of a lineup. That would give us physical evidence *and* a surviving victim's visual testimony."

"But they went through the entire car."

Stepping out of the car, Palmer lights a cigarette by the driver's door. When the window descends, he peers inside. "They didn't take the door panels off to check the window mechanism."

Gripping the steering wheel as he drives to his hotel, Palmer screams—one loud, primal scream. Back in his room, he takes a shower, two Valium, and three shots of Jack. He turns on the television for the light and noise before getting into bed, Jack keeping him warm. He slides the sheets over his head, using the Valium and a thin layer of cotton to shield himself from the demons all around.

# - 36 -

# EMERALD

## FRIDAY, 12 SEPTEMBER 1975

P *almer relishes an empty flight.* It eliminates the nearby passenger crapshoot, and stewardesses are more attentive. There's just one other passenger in first class, a middle-aged European with a handlebar mustache and bowler hat, seated on the opposite side of the aisle. The comely flight attendant they share lavishes greater attention on Palmer. She does not hide the interest evident in her emerald eyes. Palmer accepts her hospitality, and several mini bottles, with a genuine smile before evaluating her assets during the pre-flight safety demonstration.

After the interior lights dim and Handlebar with a Bowler falls asleep, the plane backs away from the gate. Palmer stares at other planes waiting at their gates, wondering where they might be traveling. Are they headed to vacation destinations like Hawaii, Orlando, or Cabo? Are they flying to dream destinations like Rome, Paris, or London? Or are they shuttling passengers back home to see family in cities like Chicago, Saint Louis, or Saint Paul? Is there one bound for Cincinnati?

Palmer might be on that plane tonight, had he always listened to Osmond in the past. Instead, he's going back to Boston to visit Dick in the hospital and see Harry at the office. Back to his lonely apartment and the demons that torment him. Palmer latches his seatbelt, takes a sip, and stares at the flight magazine, thinking back to the day he was happiest to be back in the office.

It had been four months since Osmond was shot. Palmer visited every day he was out: the first five weeks in the hospital, after Osmond's punctured lung became infected, and the balance with Osmond rehabilitating at home.

Murphy downplayed the incident in his report, and when he was well enough, Osmond signed off without objection. Ross stepped in while Osmond was down and became an extended member of the team. When Osmond did return, the celebration began midday, spilling over to the following daylight.

After the office cake had been mutilated, they carried their empty coffee mugs back to the pool of desks. Ross cycled between them with fifths of enlightenment, courtesy of Southern inspiration in popular Kentucky distilleries and Scottish creativity in secluded narrow valleys. By mid-afternoon, they were convened at Osmond's desk, Murphy telling stories about the war, family, pets, anything crossing his mind. Palmer watched Osmond smile and laugh.

"Here you go, Harry," Palmer held a pack in front of Osmond, a single butt sticking out, "back on the horse."

Osmond waved him off. "No thanks, I can't for a long time. I've decided to quit altogether."

Palmer nodded. "Okay. I can respect that, under the circumstances." In a show of solidarity, Palmer quit cold turkey. Still, the lure of nicotine, security of a butt between his fingers, and Marilyn's pleading ended the ill-fated attempt within a month. Peggy was almost two, and Marilyn was struggling with her husband's long days. When she *did* get his attention, he became irritated without smoke saturating his lungs. She left packs and matchbooks all over the house, begging him to resume. He'd never make another attempt to quit.

When the office ran dry, Palmer, Murphy, Osmond, and Ross collected their parched throats and moved the celebration to Amrheins down on Broadway in Southie. In that part of town, an early-evening glow and jagged footsteps were just part of the scenery.

At the bar, Osmond raised a glass. "To the wives, may they never grow tired of our sorry asses coming home late and sodden."

"Hear, hear!" Palmer cheered as bourbon sprayed over their heads.

The bartender shuffled them to the back of the bar well after midnight—when the stools were filled with intoxicating foxes and inebriated pigeons—before the boys started winding down.

"Sometimes," Murphy's speech slurred, "I think I should have become a mailman. A lot less stress and every night at home with the family." He pushed away the coffee cup the bartender placed in front of him.

The bartender pushed it back.

Ross poured a third packet of sugar in his hangover stew. "I would've liked to be a football player." He stumbled over the words. "I was a pretty good halfback in high school."

Osmond turned back on his way to the bathroom. "I wanted to be a cowboy in the movies, like John Wayne in those old Westerns."

Palmer thought to himself, the effect of the alcohol wearing off, *I'm doing exactly what I always wanted to do: solving puzzles and getting the bad guys.* He hailed the taxi, ensuring each of his friends got back to their families before getting off last and paying the fare. Marilyn was awake with a pot of coffee on the stove, a carton of eggs on the counter, and a forgiving smile on her face. Though it was the beginning, she knew who she married.

Palmer looks up when Emerald taps his shoulder, her smile a welcome return to the present. Handlebar with a Bowler two rows back is trying to get her attention, whacking the back of the seat in front of him with his cane, but she remains focused on her favorite passenger. Palmer hands her his empties, her fingers brushing his with purpose as she hands him back a couple of fresh ones and a slip of paper. He knows he'll be back in ten days, and Saturday nights in Salt Lake just got more promising.

# SCAVENGERS

## FRIDAY, 12 SEPTEMBER 1975

M*o stares out his window, waiting for daylight and looking forward to dinner at Langford's house.* Three days removed from news of Mrs. Harrington's death, he's excited to be visiting the professor but anxious about meeting his friends. When morning light does come, it brings cloud cover and the promise of rain. Eager to get the day started, he sets off for work.

Arriving at the Shed with time to kill, Mo visits the deer burial site from Wednesday. With his head down in prayer, he notices a hole near one of the stones. He wonders if that's where the deer's soul escaped and rose to heaven. Peering down, he sees torn skin and chewed muscle. Realizing a scavenger, maybe an opossum or raccoon, has tunneled for food, he fills the hole with dirt before rolling a large stone over it.

Staring down at his work boots as he walks to the Shed, Mo considers how the deer's bloodstains connect them. He also considers the role of scavengers once we, as prey, have fallen victim to the predators. Do we feel anything when they feed off our bodies? Are they able to get into our coffins underground? Do we become skeletons because they eat everything but the bones? He thinks about his parents, Grandma Cleveland, and Mrs. Harrington, all buried in the earth. He hopes they felt no pain when the scavengers came. He hopes God had already recovered their souls before the feasting began. And he hopes his body floats down the Rappahannock when he dies.

Emerging from the woods, Mo spots Griffin's pickup truck in the parking lot. He watches his boss kicking the office door to jar it open. Following Griffin into the office, he sees a familiar-looking shoebox resting on the edge of the desk. When Griffin points to the box, Mo expresses gratitude and laces his new work boots, feeling further removed from the deer and the morbid thoughts that shadowed him from the gravesite.

Langford's house is lively when Mo arrives. A handful of Langford's close friends are gathered in a sitting room off the main foyer. Oversized glass windows offer a view of heavy rain against early evening gray. Despite the artificial lighting and blithe conversation, the forest-green plastered walls, brown oak trim, and sky-blue ceiling—design elements intended to mimic the natural beauty outside on bright, sunny days—are drab on this bleak night. Mo stands next to the professor and observes his guests.

Like a domesticated feline, Rose Hathaway stretches across a chaise lounge, wrapped in fur. Cigarette smoke from her opera-length holder drifts by the others like an afterthought. She exudes a life of luxury and leisure, fitting in well with the furniture.

Tom Collingsworth and his close friend Todd Delancey are glued to each other's side on the love seat. Both are wearing snug, Paris green sweaters, the former sporting a red necktie and black, thick-rimmed glasses, while the latter dons untarnished and untied work boots with tight-fitting Levi's. With their shaggy haircuts and matching sweaters, they look to Mo like Thing One and Thing Two from a Dr. Seuss book his mother read to him numerous times when he was very young.

Jared Phillips, the youngest member of Langford's circle of friends, talks about his upcoming graduation from Harvard Law School while disparaging his unrefined classmates. Although living in Boston, he's Langford's closest companion, visiting the professor—a friend *and* generous benefactor—on most weekends. Mo watches the young man hold a hot chai tea close to his mouth, gripping the sides of the mug like a squirrel eating an acorn.

The final member of Langford's assembled guests, George Bentley Stanford, is seated on one of the paired baron wingback chairs.

He's wearing blue jeans and a wide-collar dress shirt unbuttoned to his navel, with a thick gold chain strung across his hairy chest. Crossing one leg over the other, he extols the virtues of his successful floral arrangement business. Because of Stanford's obsession with flowers and his golden-dyed perm, Mo equates him to the marigolds in Mr. Ford's Garden.

Gazing upon the extravagant setting and eclectic gathering, Mo's intimidated and bewildered, but not unwilling or unwanted. With a few steps forward, Mo will place himself at the center of scrutiny, the professor's guests eager to meet the young man about whom they've heard so much. For now, he's content to observe, by Mike's side, just outside the room, as yet undetected by the professor's guests.

"I can't *fathom* living in a dorm room. You might as well call it what it is—a litterbox," Rose says with the expression of a disgusted cat sniffing old food.

"Indeed, it's quite appalling," The Squirrel says. "You would think the living quarters would be more suited to the offspring of the privileged families Harvard attracts." He blows on his latte. "That's why I spend much of my free time here." He grins. "Michael's a *much* better teacher anyway."

Fascinated by The Squirrel's flamboyant gestures and drawn-out manner of speaking, a giggle escapes through the hand covering Mo's mouth.

"Well, well, well, look what the cat dragged in," Marigold says, glancing at his host. "I say, you look like a drowned rat, Michael Langford."

Their host raises his hand as he walks into the room. "Yes, indeed. It's raining cats and dogs out there. I see you've all made yourself quite comfortable." Langford bends into an arms-open bow as a royal gesture, his hand pointing in Mo's direction. "Everyone, I would like you to meet Maurice Lumen."

Thing One points. "Is this the famous Mo we've heard so much about?"

Mo gives a small, uncomfortable wave.

"Please. Come join us," Thing Two says.

"We don't bite," Rose assures Mo, smiling like the Cheshire Cat. Looking at her tobacco-stained teeth, Mo isn't sure he believes her.

After being introduced, Mo settles next to Marigold, fascinated that their chair backs almost touch the ceiling. The conversation continues between Langford and his friends for some time.

Witnessing their animated gestures, Mo attempts to visualize the distinct fluctuations and nuances in their voices to see if they align. He finds it peculiar that Thing One and Thing Two both hold their pinkies out as they sip sherry. Thinking of Jim crushing beer cans with his fist, he finds the distinction curious. The Cheshire Cat speaks as though there were marbles in her mouth, her words mashed together. He envisions her speaking in cursive or sketching pictures, illustrating her distaste for many things by mumbling large words between puffs of her cigarette. He notices that even when Mike's friends express dissatisfaction, they remain courteous in doing so. He doubts any of his housemates would fit in with this crowd. *Maybe Carlton*, he thinks, *on a good day*. Despite all the chatter, Mo's disappointed there's no mention of baseball.

After several hours of superficial gab, a portion accomplished in the dining room while enjoying a feast prepared by a local chef-for-hire, the guests arrive on the topic of Langford's newest friend.

Once again resting on her chaise lounge, The Cheshire Cat begins the examination. "Mo, how do you know our dear friend, Michael?"

"I work with the groundskeepers at the college, and Professor Langford is friends with Mr. Griffin." Mo uses Mike's title, thinking it might fit better into the conversation.

"Mr. Griffin is Mo's boss," Langford clarifies.

The Cheshire Cat blows a smoke ring into the air. "Do you attend classes at the school?"

"No, ma'am," Mo says. "I left school in the eighth grade."

Thing One furrows his brows, angling his head in an exaggerated fashion. "Why is that, Mo? Did you grow up on a farm? Where *did* you grow up?"

"No, sir, I grew up in Virginia. There were lots of farms around, but I didn't grow up on one. My dad owned a business." Mo ignores his father's last job, deciding it sounds better this way.

Thing Two leans forward, placing his glass of sherry on the coffee table. "Do your parents still live there?"

"No, sir. My mom died when I was eight, and my dad died earlier this year."

"I'm sure we're all sorry to hear that." Thing Two pulls a microscopic fuzzball off his sweater, drops it to the floor. "How did your mother die?"

Mo fidgets with a cloth napkin, kneading it into textile dough. "She was sick when she was young, and it got worse after I was born. She stayed in bed the last few years before she died."

"I see." Thing Two tosses an imaginary ball to Thing One.

Straightening up, Things One pretends to place the imaginary ball in his pocket. "How is it you came to *our* little neck of the woods?"

"After my dad died, me and my brother went to live with the Branch family, but they only wanted to adopt Jake, so Mrs. Harrington helped me come here and get a job with Mr. Griffin."

The Squirrel stops sipping. "Do you like your job at the school?"

More animated, Mo nods. "Yes, Mr. Griffin's great, and I get to work with flowers and trees and all kinds of stuff outside. I like the other workers, too."

The Cheshire Cat looks at Mo as if she's gotten a whiff of Limburger. "Do you *always* wear your uniform?"

"Yes, ma'am," Mo replies. "I like the way it feels when I wear it. I haven't had a lot of clothes that fit me."

She leans forward. "Do you know why your education ended in the eighth grade?"

"Careful, Mo," Langford says with a nervous smile, "this rose has thorns."

"Michael," The Squirrel reaches out and taps the professor's hand, "let Maurice speak. We're all adults here." He winks at Mo.

Mo scans the faces of his inquisitors. "I got hurt pretty bad after my mom died, and I couldn't go to high school."

As he feels their condemning glances, Langford's eyes dart from guest to guest. "Mo lives with four male students in a senior residence at the school. He's adjusting well and works very hard, according to his boss, Derek Griffin."

A dab of vanilla custard falls from the spoon The Cheshire Cat uses to eat her crème brûlée. She licks it off the back of her hand. "So, how often do you come to Michael's house?"

"I came here once for spaghetti," Mo says, "after me and Mike, uh, I mean, Professor Langford went fishing with Mr. Griffin." He looks at her, expecting another question, but she settles back with a self-satisfied smile.

Thing Two rubs his hands together. "Did you happen to sleep over when you had dinner here?"

Mo notices Mike's leg shaking. "No, sir, I went home to watch TV."

Langford speaks through clenched teeth. "Mo's become a very dear friend. Derek Griffin and I, among others, are helping Mo acclimate to his new surroundings."

The Squirrel yawns before turning his attention back to Mo. "We're all sleeping over this evening. Will you be joining us?" He offers Langford a knowing grin.

Receiving surprising assistance from his convicting company, Langford turns to Mo. "Yes, you are more than welcome to stay. I can bring you back tomorrow morning as early as you like."

"I guess so," Mo says, "but I should let Carlton know, so he doesn't get worried. Can I use your phone?"

"Of course. Follow me." Ushering Mo out of the room, Langford's relieved to get the lamb out of the lion's den.

Marigold, up to this point content to sip his chamomile and listen to the interrogation, contributes, "Hmm..." in an inquisitive tone as Langford and Mo exit.

Langford leads Mo to an upstairs bedroom, providing clean towels and a new toothbrush. When Langford has left, Mo stares at the window, watching raindrops weave their way down the pane. Turning his attention to the guests' cars in the driveway, he reflects on how Mike's friends seemed curious but not cruel—unlike the Branches or his current housemates. It's a victory for the malcontents below, albeit a morally hollow one.

# AFTER THE WITCH HUNT

## SATURDAY, 13 SEPTEMBER 1975

Mo watches Langford perform napkin origami the following morning. Folding each in the same precise manner, Langford positions a linen swan at the center of every place setting on the formal dining room table. Noticing Mo standing in the doorway and not wanting to wake his other guests, Langford holds a finger to his mouth. When finished, he wheels his service cart past Mo, motioning his guest to follow. In the kitchen, they sit at a swanless island, talking over a breakfast of breads, fruits, tea, and juice.

Langford fills Mo's glass with orange juice. "My friends will be up soon. I'd rather we're gone when they come down."

Mo looks at him with surprise. "Don't you want to have breakfast with your friends?"

"Normally I would, but last night went far too long. I'd rather have a quiet morning than engage in tiresome chatter." Langford butters a crumpet before handing it to Mo. "Here, try one of these."

Mo takes the odd-looking muffin. "I thought they were nice."

"That's because they understand how to be condescending with a smile." Langford sighs. "Trust me; they were all on a witch hunt last night with their tedium and pretense."

Mo doesn't understand Mike's big words but does notice he's holding his pinky out like Thing One and Thing Two last night.

Langford watches Mo chomp on his crumpet. "I thought it might be much more fun to seek solace in a quiet, natural setting. We can go fishing this morning if you'd like."

Mo nods. Not wanting to disappoint his host, he shoves more of the dense muffin into his mouth, though still unable to swallow the first bite. Alarmed, he thinks there should be even more odd-looking holes drilled along the surface. His cheeks swell like a chipmunk storing food for winter.

Langford looks down to keep from laughing. "I think we should leave. I hear some movement upstairs."

With a hand to his mouth, terrified the doughy mass will self-propel, Mo mumbles through his food, "Don't you want to say goodbye to your friends?"

Staring at his teacup, Langford mutters to himself, "More than you know," before shaking his head. "No, it's fine. They know how to take care of themselves, and I'm not worried about the house being unlocked. It's quiet out here." He tosses his napkin on the table. "Okay, why don't you wash that crumpet down with some juice and get ready to go. I'll clean up our mess. Meet me in the car when you're done."

Mo stares into the mirror as he brushes his teeth, surprised Mike didn't want to see his friends this morning. Does it mean Mike's not friends with them anymore? Will he see Mike's friends again? Would they want to see him again? What if Mike one day stops being *his* friend? He rinses and spits, wiping his mouth on the towel before creeping down the stairs and over to the front door. He sees Langford nestled behind the driver's seat of his car with the window down, tapping his fingers to opera music on the radio and oblivious Mo's watching. Feeling the crumpet come up, Mo gags.

Langford takes Mo to Olney Pond in Lincoln Woods State Park to catch a break from the self-righteous and possibly some largemouth bass, rainbow trout, or chain pickerel. Sitting under the shade of a large chestnut oak, they fish and discuss baseball. Mo's anxious, knowing the home team's lead has dwindled. Langford's relaxed being away from his guests. Mo does most of the talking. Langford asks superficial questions, and Mo provides detailed answers.

Eventually, Langford steers the conversation to Mo's past. "Mo, you mentioned Emily last time we went fishing. Can you tell me why she bothers you so much?"

Mo tosses a rock into the water. "I don't like talking about Emily."

"I know, but sometimes it's good to get troubling things out." Langford leans toward Mo. "Helps release the anger."

Mo's contented smile fades. He shrugs.

Langford scratches his chin. "What made you so mad?"

"It was a bunch of stuff, and it made her parents not want me."

"Can you tell me what some of those things were?"

"She said mean things to me in the upstairs hallway." Mo rests his chin on his chest. "Then she said I did something bad to one of Paul's friends, so then a bunch of her friends hurt me."

"Did she lie about what happened?"

"Yes, I was outside the chain-link fence, but she said I was inside. Paul tried to tell his parents, but they wouldn't listen." Mo clenches his hands. "Then I couldn't go to the schoolyard anymore or walk home with them."

"That must've been torture."

Mo pushes his knuckles into the ground. "Then I had to go away, but Jake's getting adopted." He pulls out his gloves. "Jake doesn't write much, either. I've written five letters in the past two weeks but gotten only one in return." He slaps his gloves on his leg.

"I'm sure he's just busy. School must've started, and he's probably got a lot going on."

"That's what he said in the letter. He also told me Mrs. Harrington died." Mo rubs his eyes.

Langford massages Mo's shoulder. "And she was very important to you, I know. Well, I'm here, and I hope you can see I care very much about you." He picks up Mo's hand, holding it in his own.

Mo pulls his hand away. "Thanks, Mike. I'd like to go for a walk if that's okay."

Noticing Mo shaking, his body rigid, Langford backs off. "Sure, I'll stay here and watch the poles. It's about eleven thirty now, so let's plan on leaving by one."

Mo follows a path by the water on the eastern edge, along a peninsula jutting into the pond from the northeast. He enjoys the breadth and beauty of the park, the canopy just beginning its annual transition. He stops to inhale the scent of aster, stonecrop, and black-eyed Susans dotting the landscape. In all, he walks a little over three miles before rejoining Langford a little late, mud stains on the knees and ankles of his uniform, his shirtsleeves damp. Seeing Mo peevish, Langford asks no questions.

On the ride home, Mo rolls his window down, letting his hand cut through the wind. Having cleared his negative thoughts, he avoids discussion, focusing instead on the upcoming afternoon game. Watching his friend, he thinks Langford looks more relaxed driving his fresh-smelling car and listening to classical music than sitting among his friends the previous evening.

With the Bryant entrance in sight, Langford lowers the radio. "Did you sleep well last night?"

Mo nods.

"Did you find the room comfortable?"

Another nod, this one more enthusiastic.

"Did you like my friends?"

Mo nods again, this time turning to look out the passenger window.

"They can be tiresome. I won't invite them the next time you sleep over." Langford says. "You do want to sleep over again, don't you?"

Looking back at Langford, Mo smiles. "If it's okay with you."

Langford releases a relieved sigh. "Excellent! So, would you like to get together for lunch Wednesday at the dining hall?"

"Sure! Can I ask Mr. Griffin if he wants to come?"

"Uh, sure." Langford stares straight ahead, brows raised, lips pressed together. "You can ask him if you want." He looks at Mo sideways, leveling his brows. "But it might not look good to the other workers if he's having lunch with you all the time. You wouldn't want the guys thinking you're his favorite." He shakes his head. "Could hold it against you."

"Yeah, I think you're right," Mo says, nodding, "I already spend a lot of time with Mr. Griffin driving around in the truck."

"Alright, then, that's settled." Langford raises the volume.

Mo doesn't like Mike's music but is happy his friend doesn't ask any questions about Emily or the Branch family when the radio's on.

Langford pulls his car in front of Mo's townhouse. "Are you going anywhere tomorrow?"

Mo unbuckles his seatbelt. "No, I don't think so. I hope Kay asks me to go to church again." He steps out of the car. "I'll see you Wednesday. Thanks for letting me sleep over." He can hear Langford's music playing louder as he approaches the townhouse door. It drowns out any lingering anxiety as he arrives home.

# 39

# MURPHY'S GAS CHAMBER

## SATURDAY, 13 SEPTEMBER 1975

*almer has two enduring memories of Mass General from his youth.*
Neither pleasant. Stepping out of the elevator to the oncology
ward corridor, he's immediately reintroduced to the bitter smell of
mortality accompanied by vivid images of his mother's final battle.
Each step, a painful flashback to childhood loss, Palmer reminds
himself he's here for a very dear friend—one that would be here
for him.

Palmer stops at the nurses' station. The perm with a temporary
smile points him in the right direction before resting her lips. Further down, Murphy's wife is sitting outside her husband's hospital
room. Palmer places a hand on her shoulder. She looks up, her eyes
puffy and nose chafed, offering Palmer a slight nod.

In his bed, Murphy's sitting up and smiling but looks weary and
gaunt. It's hard for Palmer to believe this is the same man who
poured shots in his office just two weeks earlier. But his smile's still
the same—infectious.

Palmer puts his hand on Murphy's arm. "Hey, Dick," he says.
"Giving your wife a scare?"

Though it doesn't seem possible given the circumstances, Murphy's smile broadens. He motions behind Palmer. "Close the door,
Francis."

Palmer obliges before pulling up a chair. "Getting ready to tell
me where the money's buried?"

Murphy laughs—an abbreviated laugh raising the gunk in his
chest up through his throat, deposited into several tissues clutched
in his emaciated hand. "She puts on a good show, doesn't she?"

His words wheeze out like they're dodging a piece of lung caught in his trachea. "Those are tears of joy." He motions Palmer to lean in. "I paid the life insurance policy back in May." He laughs louder, coughs harder.

Murphy's sense of humor always bordered morbid, but this afternoon it's laudable in its intimacy, humorous in its audacity, and gut-wrenching in its candor. Palmer laughs along, squeezing Murphy's arm a little tighter. He imagines what it would have been like to hold his father's arm as he lay on the thirteenth green, maybe listening to some final words he could use right now.

Murphy grazes Palmer's ribs with the back of his hand. "Osmond was here this morning. Told me you set them up in Salt Lake. Hairs they found inside the passenger door matched the girl who got away last year. Bundy's—" Murphy stops, unable to catch his breath.

Palmer reaches for a nearby water glass. "Not gonna be enough to hold him for long; maybe an aggravated assault with a few years to piece together a stronger murder conviction if she identifies him."

After taking a few sips, Murphy's coughing subsides. "Better than the burglary charge they had."

"That's true, but you know it's not enough for this bastard."

"So, when you headed back?"

"Week after next. But let's not talk about that right now. I'm here to see you. Why did you have me close the door? What did you want to tell me?"

Murphy's eyes stare at Palmer like a rabid fan seeking playoff tickets from a scalper. "Got a cigarette, Francis?"

"C'mon, Dick, you know I can't do that."

"Francis," Murphy says, "have one more cigarette with me for old times' sake."

In Murphy's request, Palmer hears himself asking his father for one more beer, wishing he'd had the opportunity to share a thousand more. Reaching into his pocket, he digs out two cigarettes, lighting them with a single flame and pulling on both. He hands one to Murphy and watches his old friend take a hesitant drag followed by a satisfied exhale. They sit together in Murphy's gas chamber, enjoying the toxins. Neither say a word. Neither cough. Not until Dick's final puff.

Murphy's wife walks in and yanks the cigarette from her husband's mouth. Tossing it on the floor, she turns to Palmer. "Are you crazy? Take your cigarettes and go."

Standing, Palmer takes a final look at Murphy, his partner, boss, and friend. He knows it may be the last time. Murphy's still smiling that infectious smile—the smile Palmer will remember. Murphy's wife shoos Palmer away, dismissing him for a second time.

Standing in the elevator, Palmer considers Murphy's wife protecting her husband, her dismissals preserving him, even if just for a few extra moments. Marilyn's second dismissal, the final one, was also an act of preservation—self-preservation for her and the girls.


Palmer spent the final two months of summer conducting a post-investigative analysis in the Juan Corona case. The discovery of twenty-five tortured bodies dumped in a peach orchard outside Yuba City, California, had caught the authorities by surprise. All but one of the victims were slaughtered with a machete. The outlier was shot in the head with a 9mm pistol. Unable to generate the same public interest as those where the killer focuses on middle-class White girls, the story was late to break and scarcely merited a byline. The victims, all middle-aged or older, were undocumented male immigrants or illegal workers.

When Palmer returned home, he surprised the family with tickets to Disney World. Marilyn chose not to go. She was planning her own getaway with the girls. She had tried to make it work for a year, smiling in front of the girls, gritting her teeth when she and her husband were at parties, but the veneer was worn.

Two weeks after Palmer and his daughters returned from Orlando, Marilyn was gone. She took the girls and fled to Ohio. Palmer walked into their cold, empty house and found an envelope on the kitchen table. The chardonnay stain on the rug bore silent witness as his trembling fingers pulled out a folded paper. The letter was brief—too brief after nineteen years together. And it was blunt. He read it out loud. He read it a second time. And he read it with an ache similar to the one he'd had in the first-floor dormitory restroom at Harvard twenty-one years earlier.

*Francis,*
*I've taken the girls to my parents'. We won't be back. I can't watch them suffer the way I've suffered. I will always love the man I married. I wish I knew where he went. I've already forgiven you, but I must escape you. I can't live with your demons, and I won't allow the girls to continue watching you descend. We'll pray for you.*

*Marilyn*

Palmer sold the house in the spring. The divorce was finalized later that fall. The phone calls ended the summer after that. Pauline would still talk to him if she answered, whispering across the miles that she missed him and asking if she could visit. Palmer reassured her that he loved her while explaining it would be better if she stayed with her mother. But it tore him apart.

Palmer stops at the gift shop before leaving. Purchasing a bereavement bouquet, he writes 'Helen' on the envelope and leaves them for delivery to Murphy's room. He drives out of the parking garage, picturing Murphy's infectious smile as his wife smells the flowers.

Later, Palmer drives by his family's old house. He sees Peggy at ten and Pauline at five running out the front door to jump on him in the driveway. He feels Marilyn's hug as he places his briefcase inside the front door. And he smells dinner waiting in the dining room. He's certain the chardonnay stain is still there—some damage can't be undone.

# 40

# NANCY

**SATURDAY, 13 SEPTEMBER 1975**

M*o ignores the mess around him, his housemates now picking up after themselves.* He opens packs of baseball cards at the table, separating the Red Sox players and placing the rest aside for Trevor to look through. Taking a midafternoon break, he hears a mass of trudging footfalls make its way downstairs. Through the bathroom door, he can smell the stench of stale beer on their collective breath as they pass through the hallway.

"Where's the idiot?" Jim growls. "This place stinks. Someone slide the doors open."

Mo cracks the bathroom door a sliver and peeks into the living room.

"Do it yourself! And for the love of Christmas, stop shouting," Trevor says, staggering to the kitchen. "Anybody else need aspirin?"

"Yeah, just bring the whole bottle," Brian says.

Jim brushes trash from the chair before falling into it. "Where's the dumbass? This place is a fucking shithole!"

Carlton's head rests back on the sofa, eyes closed. "Don't talk that way about Mo."

"I don't care! It's his job to pick up after us, remember? Where the hell's that stupid bastard? And where was he last night?"

Carlton rubs his temples. "It's none of your business, Nancy. What are you, his mom? He can go wherever he wants."

Mo tiptoes into his bedroom.

Jim pulls himself up with some difficulty. "Fine, *I'll* open the goddamn doors." He kicks several red Solo cups, their color matching the rage creeping onto his face. "He needs to get his ass out here and clean up this mess."

Trevor glares at Jim. "Clean it yourself. You made most of it anyway."

Jim's foot lands on the edge of a can. "Goddamnit! I'm gonna teach that fucking moron a lesson!" He rushes to the hallway, tripping on beverage containers.

Carlton hurries after him, followed by Brian and Trevor. "Jim, stop! *Jim!*"

Mo's bedroom door is thrust open, Jim lunging toward the bed.

Grabbing the front of Mo's uniform, Jim's unable to lift him. "Get out there and clean up that mess!" His face is inches from Mo's. "Get out there, you piece of shit!"

Mo can see the unleashed rage in Jim's eyes as he pushes him away.

Grabbing Jim around the waist, Carlton pulls him back, but not before Jim lands several glancing blows to Mo's face.

"Let go of me! I'll kill him!" Jim kicks and screams like a giant toddler. "Let go of me, you son of a bitch!"

Brian yanks Jim back, causing him to stumble.

Trevor helps Brian hold down Jim's arms.

Carlton sits on his stomach.

"Get off me!" Jim thrusts his hips, trying to buck Carlton off. "I'm gonna fucking kill you all when I get up."

Unable to free himself, Jim eventually settles down.

Carlton stands, allowing Trevor and Brian to grab Jim under the arms and haul him out of the room.

Stunned, Mo rubs his face, curling up in the spot furthest from the door. Moments later, hearing the front door slam, the shouting subsides.

Carlton returns. "Hey M, you alright?" He speaks as if approaching a wounded animal.

Mo rubs the side of his face. "Yeah, I'm okay, I think."

"Sorry about Jim. We got him out of the house." Carlton mutters as he stares out the window, "Crazy drunk bastard."

Mo looks up, eyes peeking through his hands. "Is Kay coming over?"

"I'll give her a call in a few minutes. Let her know what happened." Crouching near him, Carlton pulls Mo's hands down. "You want any ice for your face?"

"No, thank you. I just want to see Kay."

"Okay, buddy, I'll see if she's able to come over."

Early evening, Mo emerges from his bedroom, face still stinging from Jim's wrath. Kay and Carlton are on the sofa watching a movie.

Mo holds his hand over the left side of his face. "Hi, Kay. When did you get here?"

"Just a little while ago," she says. "I heard you listening to the game in your room. Thought it best not to disturb you. How are you feeling?"

Mo sits down on the chair closest to her. "I'm alright, I guess."

"Carl told me what happened today. Jim won't be coming back."

"Will Trevor have a new roommate?"

"Brian has agreed to move in with Trevor and allow Carl more privacy. Carl will talk to his mother about whether he needs a roommate next semester. Brian feels bad about what happened. He realizes he needs to focus more on his studies and less on all the distractions. I think you'll find the house a lot better now."

"Yeah, M," Carlton says. "I talked with the guys this afternoon. There won't be any more parties here."

Mo smiles, noting Carlton's unexpected use of a single letter to address him.

"Also, no girls are allowed unless they're like Kay—someone significant—and we'll limit our drinking to ensure we behave better." Looking down, Carlton twiddles his thumbs. "It's gonna get better, I promise. We all like you a lot, and we're sorry we've treated you poorly."

"I'm sorry," Mo says, "I'll be better, too."

"No, you just have to be yourself. We're all learning so much about ourselves because of you. It's important for us to see who we are before we get out into the real world." Putting his arm around Kay, Carlton gives her a squeeze. "Kay saw it first, which is something

I love about her. You just be yourself, and we'll all be better for it."

Kay looks closer at Mo's face. "Do you want some ice for the swelling?"

Mo nods. "If you think it will help."

"Let me get you set up with some ice in a towel. Looks like you got a little cut up, too."

"Probably Jim's stupid high school ring," Carlton says. Watching how calm Mo is with Kay tending to him, Carlton's thoughts wander to childhood memories of his mother and a time an amber bottle was used to cut him up. How calm he became as she stopped the bleeding. His mom's hands were so gentle as she cleaned his cuts, promising she would never let it happen again. Carlton shudders. "I'm sure Kay will make it feel better."

Kay dabs at a small cut by Mo's eyebrow. "Did you enjoy going to church with my family last Sunday?"

Mo nods, enduring the iciness of the towel to enjoy the warmth of her hand.

"Would you like to go to church with us again tomorrow morning? Carl's coming, too."

"Yes, please."

"We don't have family lunches every Sunday like we did last week, but Carl and I are going to head over to Hunt's Mill for a picnic afterwards if you want to join us."

"That sounds like fun."

"Alright, I'll be here at nine thirty to pick you up." She points at Carlton. "Make sure *you're* ready, too."

When Kay leaves, Mo heads to bed. After slipping under the covers with the side table lamp still on, he hears a knock on the bedroom door.

Carlton peeks inside. "Sorry again about today. It's gonna get better now, I promise. Plus, we'll make sure we have some fun on the weekends."

Seconds after Carlton shuts the bedroom door, Mo turns off the light and is asleep before his bruised head hits the pillow.

- 41 -

# A GATHERING STORM

SUNDAY, 14 SEPTEMBER 1975

M o sits in the back seat, indulging his senses—twenty minutes of bliss. After mass, on the drive to Hunt's Mill, the loose curls of Kay's long blond hair spill over the seatback, resting gently on his knees. Several strands float inches from his face, courtesy of the vehicle's in-dash air conditioning, carrying the scent of vanilla and jasmine with the promise of a budding friendship. When they reach the popular picnic destination, Mo takes his eyes off of Kay just long enough to catch the sign at the entrance to the parking lot.

The picnic area overlooks a waterfall on the Ten Mile River. The trail itself is an easy hike along the river and through the woods back to the park entrance. On this late summer afternoon, a few families occupy tables, children playing hide-and-seek while parents grill hot dogs and hamburgers. Kay places a tablecloth over a picnic table, laying out lunch while Mo and Carlton chat.

Digging a Sprite out of the cooler, Carlton offers it to Mo. "How you feeling this morning? How's your face?"

Mo rubs the welt on his cheekbone. "It's fine."

"You must be glad Jim's gone. He was fine last year but has been bitter and angry since he got back."

Mo shrugs. "Maybe something happened over the summer. Maybe someone's sick or dying in his family. Grandma Cleveland used to say people aren't born mean; they get that way because bad things happen to them. Maybe something bad happened to him."

"Geez, Mo," Kay says, placing her hand on his back, "it's so sweet you're concerned about Jim after how he treated you."

"Yeah," Carlton says, "seems like a lot of folks are mean to you, like Jim and Brian's dumb girlfriends and that Emily girl before you got here, when all you do is try to be nice. Heck, even Brian and I didn't treat you well. Honestly, you're a wicked good guy."

Mo doesn't like hearing Emily's name, or the other mean girls mentioned, even if he understands Carlton's point. He grips the picnic table bench.

Kay, noticing Mo's discomfort, changes the subject.

When they're finished eating, Carlton packs the picnic stuff in the car. They head to the trail, Kay and Carlton walking arm-in-arm ahead of Mo as they pass several old buildings along the way, Kay pointing out their significance.

Head down, his mind occupied with the hope his friends will stop bringing up Emily, Mo remains distracted until they arrive at an area called Terrace Garden just after entering the trail.

"This area's lined with beautiful flowers called mountain laurel from late May through most of June," Kay says.

Mo scans the flowerless field. "What do they look like?"

"Let me see; they have five white petals connected in the shape of a saucer with pink edges and red near the stem when they bloom. They're everywhere in late spring."

Mo pictures a blizzard—individual snowflakes being chased down by drops of blood. He imagines red seeping into the petals, a pinkish hue forming along the outline of each delicate and harmless contributor to a gathering storm. Holding onto this vision and noting his friends' tracks as they follow the path, Mo recalls a trail of upsetting footprints in a fresh blanket of winter white seven-and-a-half years earlier.

A late-February storm dumped more than a foot of overnight snow across the region. Mo woke up to a winter scene straight out of his favorite Christmas book, yards and roads buried, trees ready for lights and garland. With snowflakes the size of postage stamps whetting his appetite, the smell of Grandma Cleveland's breakfast wafting upstairs drew him to the kitchen for sweet-milk waffles fresh off the stovetop.

Sitting at the table, Mo dug his finger into the homemade preserve jar and received a smack to the back of his hand as he attempted a second poke.

"Rest of us gonna be eating that," Ken said, "and we don't need to be tasting the filth under your fingernails."

Jake giggled as he handed Mo a butter knife.

Ken flicked Mo's arm with the back of his hand. "Grab me a beer outta the fridge." His voice sounded like sandpaper across stone.

Mo knew this beer would be the first of many across the upcoming weekend. Buried under all that snow, Sumerduck Road, not a main artery, would remain unplowed and impassable for days, an opportunity for their father to spend time with the boys. But Mo understood that snow, like a sick day, meant his father missed work, drank beer, and slept. He also knew his father's sick days were becoming more frequent. *Still*, he thought, *there was hope. His father had made it to the breakfast table, after all.* With ill-advised optimism, he turned to his father. "Can you build a snowman with us, Dad?"

Ken grunted. "Think I got time to play? I work every night to provide food for the table." Hanging his head over his empty plate, he rubbed the back of his neck. "I'll tell you what I'm gonna do." He pointed to the living room with his thumb. "I'm gonna sit on that recliner in there, get some rest, maybe watch some TV, and take advantage of this snow."

Listening to his father's words, Mo heard the tragic resonance of misplaced resolve. Looking into his father's eyes, he saw the grim reflection of imminent surrender. Not understanding the nature of all his father's battles, Mo witnessed only the physical consequences: the gnarled mash of brown and gray on Ken's face signifying months of disinterest; the twisted threads of blue on his nose representing years of bitterness. Though the war was not yet lost, the struggle was consuming Ken. Mo knew his father would not help them build a snowman.

Jake was first to grab a waffle, dropping it on his plate and poking his older brother with a fork. While Mo sliced his waffle into bite-sized pieces and poured syrup, Jake bounced up and down. "Please, Daddy, can you help us make a snowman?"

Ken stabbed several waffles with a fork, shook them onto his plate. "I'm not building any goddamned snowman. Mo, you're gonna get your ass out there and shovel the driveway after you eat. And take your brother with you so I can relax."

Grandma Cleveland laid a plate of cornbread in the center of the table. "Mind your father, boys." She sat down, holding out her hands.

Mo and Jake joined their grandmother in blessing the food. Ken stuffed a forkful of syrup-drenched waffle into his mouth.

After breakfast, Grandma Cleveland wrapped a scarf around Jake's ears, nose, and mouth, then tightened the hood of his coat. Jake followed Mo onto the back porch and into a four-foot snowdrift. Mo rescued Jake, throwing his little brother on his shoulders.

It took two hours to reach the end of the driveway, with Mo shoveling, and Jake making snow angels. By that time, several hearty neighborhood families had ventured out. Looking up and down the road, Mo spotted footprints in the snow. They stayed in the center except where they hugged the far side in front of his home.

Looking back, Mo saw his father coming down the driveway. He watched Jake run up to greet him, his little brother smiling as he wrapped his arms around Ken's legs. Mo held his breath, hoping his father had changed his mind about building a snowman.

Ken peeled Jake off and continued walking toward Mo. "Your grandmother says it's time for lunch."

A family approached with three children following the imprints of earlier passersby. Drawing closer, Mo saw the parents place their arms around the children and whisper in their ears.

Ken stood by Mo's side, following the path of the family. "Morning," he said, a rare smile crossing his lips.

Their whispers growing a little louder, the family's pace quickened along the opposite side of the road.

The smile drifted from Ken's face and dissolved into the snow. "I said morning, Henry!"

Scooping up the youngest, the father hustled his family down the center of the road. When there was sufficient distance, he shouted back, "Go have another drink, Ken. And take the retard and the brownie with you."

Mo felt his father choke the handle of the shovel and heard him grunt before Ken retreated to the house. Icicles on his upper lip, Mo watched the family disappear into the distant snow, taking their footprints and their hypocrisy with them. He threw his brother on one shoulder, the shovel on the other, and walked up the driveway. Having heard those words before, and knowing they were unkind, he was glad Jake had a scarf and hood to cover his ears.

Following his friends along the trail, Mo wishes there had been something to cover his ears and shield his face when Jim attacked him last night. He walks, feeling the bruises on his face and the accumulated weight of every insult endured since his seizure and Jake's birth.

Kay and Carlton pass Sunset Rock, stopping at Otter Rock instead. As Kay explains, both locations offer attractive views of Ten Mile River, but inscriptions from the turn of the century appear on Otter Rock when the water level's down. Kay and Carlton sit side by side, facing the water and holding hands.

Arms folded, Mo reads inscriptions while waiting.

"Mo, you can keep walking if you want," Carlton says. "The trail leads back to the parking lot. We'll meet you near the waterfall."

Mo nods before continuing along the nearly empty path. Farther down, searching for unique flowers, native trees, and woodland animals—possibly an otter or beaver—he puts on his gloves. Noticing one other late afternoon hiker, he waves to her as he crouches to check out a praying mantis. She stops to investigate with him.

When Mo arrives back at the waterfall, his friends rush over to greet him.

Kay's hand is on her forehead. "Where were you?"

Checking his Timex, Mo realizes he's been gone for almost two hours. "I'm sorry. I lost track of time."

"We were so worried," Carlton says. "We were getting ready to start searching from opposite ends of the trail."

Kay places her hand on Mo's shoulder. "Why are you out of

breath?"

"I ran as fast as I could when I saw it was getting dark." Pulling the gloves from his pants pocket, Mo wrings them out.

"And why are you all wet?"

"When I rinsed my face in the water, my gloves fell in. I got my shirt all wet when I reached in to grab them." Mo lifts his hand. "I was afraid my watch stopped in the water, but it's still working."

"That's good," Kay says. "Why don't we get going?"

Mo nods, his anxiety laid to rest on Hunt's Mill trail.

# 42

# GRAPHIC CONTENT

## TUESDAY, 16 SEPTEMBER 1975

*Palmer enjoys guest lecturing at Harvard.* This morning, he parks near Christ Church, hiking the fifteen minutes through the Old Burial Ground, Harvard Yard, and across Cambridge before heading east on Kirkland to the psychology building. A short distance from Massachusetts Hall, William James Hall is far removed architecturally. Aside from their strict classical symmetry, James Hall's new formalist, white-cement veneer bears little resemblance to the Georgian-influenced red brick facade of Harvard's oldest building. Palmer may have little use for nature walks, but he appreciates a leisurely stroll through the city's historic districts, admiring the architecture.

When he arrives at the lecture hall, Palmer stands by the podium, waiting for students to file in. He hears the anticipation in their whispers, recognizes the drowsiness in their body language, and smells the mask of their morning deodorant. Because his lectures often involve graphic content, attendance is restricted to graduate students, with preference given to students attending the schools of psychology and criminology. Despite receiving annual invitations for more than a decade, Palmer does not believe students are familiar with his investigative background beforehand. But they are. The lecture hall is filled, as always, to capacity.

Palmer never deviates from his customary workweek attire: a polyester brown sportscoat over a white oxford shirt with beige slacks, black dress socks, and Florsheim wingtips. However, his neckties do vary, alternating between shades of burgundy and gold in traditional patterns. Today, he sports a crimson silk with gold fleur-de-lis.

His lecture is two hours and seventy-five slides long, highlighting suspect profiling advances made the previous dozen years and their application to thirteen high-profile FBI investigations. At its conclusion, Palmer answers predictable questions, receiving an enthusiastic round of applause as he slips into the welcome anonymity Harvard's famed campus provides.

Palmer walks to Anderson Memorial Bridge. Watching the sculling crews on the Charles River, he pictures his mother in her rowing days and his father watching from the far bank. His parents met while students in Cambridge. His father, attending Harvard Law after serving in the army during the First World War, was ten years older than his mother, an undergraduate at Radcliffe. Both came from distinguished Boston families.

His mother never used her business degree for financial gain, a fortune already secured when her parents sank with the Titanic. His father's ascent through the ranks of one of Boston's most prestigious law firms was swift. Their only son was doted on by intelligent, nurturing parents.

Palmer spent many weekends with his father but saw his mother every day. At bedtime, she would read to him, showering him with kisses that made him giggle while she tucked the covers around him. Whether he struggled with grammar in elementary school or geometry later, she always encouraged him, showing remarkable patience. After his father was called upon to assist with legal matters in advance of the European landings during World War II, Sunday services became everyday devotions.

Palmer's mother would read the front pages with her son, comparing the evils of the enemy with the righteousness of the US war effort. In the second half of April 1942, headlines focused on the fall of the Philippines. As the horror stories coming out of Bataan intensified, she reassured her little boy the tide would turn.

"The war isn't over, Francis," she said. "Our navy's rebuilding while the draft's strengthening our ground forces."

Palmer rubbed his eyes. "But the Nazi submarines are sinking our ships in the Atlantic, and the Japs are all over the Pacific."

"Oh, come now, it's only been a few months since we got involved. It's going to take some time to beat back the enemy. They had a big head start. Wait and see; they'll be running scared by the end of this year or next."

"You really think so?" Palmer's squeaky voice cracked.

She placed her hand over his. "Absolutely. The darkest hour is always before dawn."

"What can I do to help?"

Smiling, she hugged her son. "We can plant a victory garden in the backyard. You can come with me to the scrap metal drives. We can also help by making care packages for the soldiers or supporting organizations like the Red Cross. There are lots of ways to do our part."

Palmer stood on his bed, saluting to the war poster that hung over his pillow. "I'm gonna help win the war!"

"That's good, but remember, Francis, even when this war ends, there will always be those who need our help. We can always assist those dealing with poverty and economic inequality, racism and social injustice. Every day, your father works hard to protect individual rights, ensuring freedom from oppression in any form. I'm sure you will, too."

"Does he make money while he does those things?"

"He earns a paycheck, yes, but we also donate to charity and engage in civic duties." She ran her hand through Palmer's hair. "Just remember that money's not the most important thing. You'll always have your intellect and your ethics. Money's quite easy to come by if you have those. Never focus on dollars and cents, Francis, but rather what you do for others. Use your talents in appreciation of your good fortune to take care of those most in need while promoting the things you most believe in."

"I will," Palmer made an 'X' across his chest, "I promise."

"You'll do the right thing when you get older." His mother kissed him on the forehead. "I know you will."

Palmer pushes himself from the sidewall of the bridge, taking a last look at the reflection of the boathouse in the undulating waters of the Charles before walking away. He thinks about the day his father's attorney read the will. The inheritance meant little compared to the love and encouragement his parents had given him—things accountants couldn't measure. Three months later, after the house was sold, with all his parents' financial wealth deposited, he calculated the amount he would need to finish school and donated the rest. He's never regretted his decision.

# 43

# THE LADY BEHIND
# THE LUNCH COUNTER

## WEDNESDAY, 17 SEPTEMBER 1975

*M*o *doesn't wave to the lady behind the lunch counter as he passes by.* She is never amused, nor is she cordial. He tried greeting her each day for several weeks when he first arrived, but she never smiled, didn't say a word, and made no attempt at eye contact. So, he stopped trying. Today, as with every other day, he watches her transfer plates of food from stainless-steel racks to the stainless-steel lunch counter, her mood matching the temperature of the metal. He wonders, as he often does, why a woman about his age, working at the same school he does, would be so cold. Does she have a family? Do they live in a bad area? Has she been banished? Is she angry because she's the only worker wearing a hairnet? Do her coworkers treat her the way his father and the K&E workers treated Sam because she's the only Black worker in the dining hall?

Mo slides his tray in front of the cashier. She raises a finger and walks away while he waits, cash in hand. His eyes follow her progress as she makes her way toward the stainless-steel racks, tapping The Lady Behind the Lunch Counter's shoulder when she draws near. The Lady Behind the Lunch Counter looks up and observes the cashier flashing her fingers in different directions and patterns. Mo watches a smile cross The Lady Behind the Lunch Counter's face as she moves her fingers in a similar fashion. He considers Louie the swan and his grandmother's words about understanding someone when we learn to communicate with them. And he understands a little about The Lady Behind the Lunch Counter for the first time.

The cashier returns, offering Mo an appreciative nod. He smiles. She smiles back. Turning, he sees Langford flagging him down. Sitting across from him, Mo observes Langford's use of hand gestures to accompany his disparaging comments about the food. When the professor's verbal and nonverbal assaults are complete, he steers the conversation in an unexpected direction.

"I got to thinking the past few days," Langford says, "and maybe the people I thought were my friends aren't what's best for me." He looks up from a french fry just dipped in ketchup. "I didn't like the way my friends treated you the other night. I suspect they would have been disrespectful to Derek as well if he were there. So, I've decided I would prefer to surround myself with friends like you." A dollop of ketchup falls onto Langford's lap.

Mo watches as Langford's distressed eyes follow the wayward condiment. "I liked your friends. I didn't understand much of what they said, but I'm not that smart, and they're really smart."

Using a napkin, Langford dabs at the ketchup on his pants. "They are intelligent, but they're also callous and shallow. Their questions were intended to belittle you and antagonize me." He reaches for another napkin, dips it into Mo's water glass, and resumes wiping. "I've known them for a long time. Frankly, they're not very nice. It took you coming over for me to realize I don't need friends like that." He lifts the napkin, shocked to find his rubbing has stretched the blotch to his zipper.

"I'm sorry. I didn't mean to make you not like your friends." Mo peeks under the table to check on Langford's expanding stain, recalling his father's words—*A hotdog is to ketchup as life is to relish.* He's curious whether that applies here as he reaches for a pickle.

"It's okay. You're my friend now, as are a few other common, decent folks like Derek." Langford shrugs, rolls his eyes, and flings the wet napkins on his tray. "So, did you go anywhere on Sunday?"

"I went to church with Kay's family. Carlton came, too. Then we went to a place called Hunt's Mill."

"Hunt's Mill is a lovely place for a picnic. In fact, I went there recently. It's beautiful along the trail this time of year. The waterfall's really flowing. Uh, I mean, uh, it must really be flowing, with all the rain we've had." Langford clears his throat. "Are you doing anything this weekend?"

"I'm going with everyone to a place called Lincoln Park on Saturday. It's an amusement park. I guess it's pretty far away." Mo spears a cherry tomato with his fork. "I told Trevor I've never been to one. He said it's like a permanent carnival. I've been to the carnival before."

"Sounds fun. I went there many years ago with friends." Palm open, Langford gestures to Mo. "You could come to my house for dinner Friday night. Maybe stay over, watch the Red Sox game on my big TV."

"I think I should sleep at home because we're supposed to leave early. It's an afternoon game on Friday anyway."

"Alright, we can wait." Langford taps his fork on the table. "How about next week?"

"Sure, I think next week will be good. The Red Sox play a night game against Cleveland."

"Sounds like a plan." Langford places the fork on top of his untouched and cold panini. "Anything special you'd like for dinner?"

"I like pizza, but anything's good."

"Okay then, it's a date. I'll pick you up Friday at six." Langford stands, looking dejectedly at his pants. "Boy, have I got some explaining to do to my students." He walks away, hiding his shame with a textbook.

Mo chuckles, deciding not to tell his friend the stain has bled to the seat of his pants. Emptying his tray, Mo wishes he were a fly so he could cling to the wall in Mike's classroom, listening to him explain the stain to his students.

On his way out, Mo walks by The Lady Behind the Lunch Counter and waves, knowing she won't look up but realizing it's the only way he can communicate with her. So, he'll keep trying. He wishes he could move his fingers the way she does. And he wishes Mike liked the food in the dining hall and had more interest in baseball.

# HARDCORE FUGITIVE

**FRIDAY, 19 SEPTEMBER 1975**

P*almer places the last of the folders into a file box, marking the side* *'Campus Killer' along with his name and the date.* Staring at the box, he lights a cigarette, fighting the urge to cross out 'Campus Killer' and write above it 'Ted Bundy.' Though the slaughter abruptly ended in Washington State more than a year ago, the case is still active. Palmer's connection is now indirect, stretching southeast to help Utah State Police get Ted off the streets for good. Palmer will not rest until he sees Bundy held accountable for his actions in every state where he's committed at least one crime. The Beast will not be satisfied until The Monster burns in hell.

Palmer grips his coffee, taking several long sips while staring at the stack of newspapers piled on the side of his desk. He considers tossing them but decides to take the file box to Records instead. Getting off the elevator on the second floor, he walks to an over-sized, gray metal desk, placing the box at the edge.

The head of Records Management, Ernie Shore, is a former field agent in his late sixties. Though his disability isn't apparent, he was reassigned to this desk job more than fifteen years ago. Ernie knows everyone in the building and everything that goes on inside. Palmer avoids him like he would a mad dog approaching in a crooked line.

Sliding the box across the desk, Palmer gives a quick nod before walking away.

"Too bad about Murphy, huh?" Ernie says, his white, crew-cut hair standing at attention.

"Yeah," Palmer says, taking three steps toward the door, "hope he gets out soon."

"*Oh*," Ernie says, "you don't know yet."

Palmer stops, turns to face Ernie, his eyebrows raised. "Know what?"

"Murphy died in his sleep last night at the hospital."

Ernie's words hit Palmer like a shell finding his foxhole. After the initial disorientation, his brows relax. As he exits, his head hangs and his pace slows. Palmer stands in the elevator, slack-jawed and shoulders slumped, and recalls his last meaningful discussion with Murphy seven months earlier. He was being assigned to the Campus Killer investigation and remembers the gravity in Murphy's tone as he sat at his office desk.

Murphy asked Palmer to hold up while Osmond and Ross left his office. "I'm not gonna be in this job much longer, Francis," he said, his eyes moist, cigarettes conspicuously absent from his desk and fingers. "You need to think about getting away from the noise before it swallows you up." He pointed his thumb at the wall. "You don't want to end up like Ernie down in Records."

At first, Palmer dismissed Murphy's words as the usual office bullshit. "I hear you, Dick, but I know where I belong."

"You're the best there is, Francis, no doubt about it, but these investigations take a toll. Ross is almost done. Osmond doesn't let things get to him. But you bring every one of these back with you."

"I'm fine," Palmer said. "I just can't stop thinking about the bastards until they're off the street."

Rubbing a finger along the inside of his ear, Murphy looked down at a folder on his desk. "When you get back from Seattle, I'll either be leaving or gone. You need to give some serious thought to submitting." Palmer started to speak, but Murphy raised a hand. "You can make all the excuses you want, but you come back from each one of these a little more broken. You can't deny it. Hell, you've already lost your family."

Palmer realized it wasn't an ordinary discussion. He nodded, staring back at Murphy with an attentiveness he normally reserved for forensics and subject matter experts.

"Your father was a friend of mine. I promised him I'd take care of you." Murphy got up, sat on the corner of his desk. "I saw a bright young kid looking to change the world when you got here, Francis. Now I see a hardcore fugitive from joy." Starting to cough, he walked over to the window.

Palmer lit a cigarette, not realizing then how thoughtless it was. He didn't speak. Everyone knew not to speak when Murphy was telling stories or imparting wisdom. Palmer knew this wasn't story time.

Murphy turned from the window. "I can't make you do it," he said, his face gray, eyes soggy, "but I pray to God you do before you lose anything else." He tapped the desk. "And, Francis?"

Palmer looked up from where he had been staring at the tip of his cigarette. "Yeah?"

"For your own good, give up the smokes before they bury you." Murphy sat back in his chair and waved Palmer, and his cigarette smoke, out of the room. "Now get out to Seattle and help them find this son of a bitch."

Palmer nodded, walking toward the door.

"Francis," Murphy said.

Palmer looked back.

"Think about what I said. Harry's ready and able, but he doesn't need this job as much as you do. You can take care of him when you're sitting in this chair." He choked out the last few words. "Promise me you'll think about it."

Along with a grateful smile, Palmer offered a half-hearted nod. He knew he didn't need to think it over. This was one time he wouldn't listen.


Stepping out of the elevator, Palmer walks over to Osmond's desk. Before he can ask, Osmond looks up, eyes glazed. Palmer compresses his lips, nodding while walking away. The newspapers by Palmer's desk tell him the world will go on without Murphy. Reaching into his pocket for a Marlboro, he finds no solace. He crushes the empty pack, tossing it on his desk. He pulls out one drawer after another, searching for a cigarette, slamming each with greater force before pounding his fist on the desk. "Fuck!"

Osmond walks over, stands in front of Palmer's desk. "Let's take a walk, Frankie."

Palmer nods. Nicotine-deprived, he coerces Osmond to follow him down to the vending machines on the first floor. In the break room, they share stories about their fallen comrade. After some coffee and a few cigarettes, his mood improves.

Osmond pulls a piece of paper from his inside coat pocket. "I got the promotion, heard yesterday afternoon."

Nodding, Palmer smiles and pats Osmond on the shoulder. "You deserve it." He stares without listening as Osmond explains the benefits of his new position. Instead, his thoughts drift back to that day seven months earlier in Murphy's office. Lighting another cigarette, he realizes he didn't take Murphy's advice twice that day.

# MISS CLARA

M o sits in the backseat of Carlton's 1971 Chevrolet Caprice Sport Sedan, trying to make himself as thin as possible. Squeezed between Trevor and Brian on the long drive to Lincoln Park, he keeps his legs together, his arms folded, and his breaths as short as possible. When a Captain and Tennille song plays on the radio, the other boys beg Carlton to change the station, but Kay slaps his hand away from the dial while singing along. Amid their whining, Mo's heart races when she looks back at him while singing the chorus to *Love Will Keep Us Together*.

Driving across the Braga Bridge along I-195, Trevor gives a brief historical account of Fall River, Massachusetts. "At the end of the nineteenth century, Spindle City, as Fall River was known then, became the textile manufacturing capital of the country. It was also one of the most populous cities in the United States, greater than Los Angeles at the time." Placing his forearm over his mouth, he talks like Dracula. "It's also home to the most notorious murder mystery of the nineteenth century."

Carlton lowers the radio. "Mo, you ever heard of Lizzie Borden?"

Mo shakes his head, intrigued by a discussion involving murder on their way to an amusement park.

Carlton glances at Mo in the rearview mirror. "She's probably the one they coined the phrase 'getting away with murder' after."

"Let me see how much I remember," Trevor says. "I had to do a report in high school, so it's been a while. I think she killed her parents in August 1892. Andrew Borden, her father, was a rich businessman in the city. His second wife was Lizzie's stepmom."

Considering people he doesn't like, Mo can't imagine killing them, much less his own parents. "Why did she kill her parents?"

"Most people think she didn't like her stepmom; thought her stepmother married her dad for his money. There were other tensions, like her father being a miser and her stepmom angling for Lizzie's inheritance. I can't remember everything."

Brian cuts in, eager to get to the juicy part. "The story goes she hacked them both up with an ax. Apparently, she didn't hold back."

Carlton points to the back seat. "How's that rhyme go?"

Brian recites the words:

*Lizzie Borden took an ax,*
*And gave her mother forty whacks.*
*When she saw what she had done,*
*She gave her father forty-one.*

"Anyway," Trevor says, "despite there being ample evidence she did it, she went free."

"Yeah, it was the crime of the century," Carlton says.

Mo lets the information sink in before shaking his head. "I never could've killed my mom or dad. I loved them. I wouldn't kill my stepmom either if I had one."

Kay looks back at Mo. "I'm sure you wouldn't."

Unable to get the rhyme out of in his head, Mo's thoughts grow morbid. Did Langford want to kill his pretty but mean stepmother? How many people *do* kill their stepmothers? How many *wish* they could kill them? Alarmed by his thoughts, Mo shifts his focus to Jake's mom and the time he came closest to having a stepmother.


When Miss Clara moved into the downstairs bedroom, Grandma Cleveland took Mo's bedroom, and Mo slept in the living room on the old sofa. Sleep was difficult on the sofa's hard, wool cushions. Tossing and turning, years of unabated pilling along the cushion welts would scratch any exposed area on his body.

Two weeks after Jake's birth, Mo's eyes fluttered open when

headlights flooded the living room at one in the morning. Blinking away the fog of sleep, he heard light footsteps. He made his way to the base of the stairs to investigate. "Miss Clara?" He whispered.

Working her arm into her coat, Miss Clara jumped at his voice. "Go back to bed, Mo," she said, her voice hollow. "Please."

Mo stepped toward her, shivering as his bare feet hit the cold tile floor. "Where are you going?"

Unwrapping her scarf from the back of a chair and draping it around her neck, she avoided Mo's gaze. "I have to go out. I haven't been out of this house in five months."

"But—"

Miss Clara placed her trembling hand to Mo's mouth before bending down to pick up her suitcase. A soft whimper from the bedroom caused her to freeze. She held her breath. After a few silent moments, she exhaled, straightened up, and looked toward the kitchen door. "I need to get away for a little while." Tears shielded under a veil of darkness, she turned away from Mo, walking to the rear door. "I know you don't understand. But I have to go."

Imagining her lifeless words hanging like icicles off the front porch, Mo felt a chill run through his body as Miss Clara, like a ghost, drifted away, her footsteps fading into the early morning's cool breeze. Cloaked under a moonless night, she walked down the driveway, reappearing for a moment as she stepped into an unfamiliar car waiting at the bottom. She never looked back. The car pulled away, and she was gone, leaving unanswered questions and a bundle of responsibilities.

Mo lingered at the window until a loud cry shook him from his thoughts. He turned and headed into the downstairs bedroom, where a motherless Baby Jacob laid restless on his back. Mo reached into the crib and caressed his tiny hand.

Mo's father stood at the bedroom entrance. "What are you doing in here? Where's Clara?"

Spooked, Mo gasped, "Baby Jacob was crying...She left, Dad."

"She left? What d'ya mean she left?" Ken's eyes widened as he searched the room for answers, picking up an open book from the dresser.

Mo struggled for words. "There was a light outside. I woke up. She had a suitcase and said she had to go. Then she left in a car."

Ken sat on the end of the bed, staring at the inside cover of his paperback. Laying the novel on the bed, he rested his face in his hands. "Dammit," he sighed. "Shoulda known."

"She just said she needed to get away for a little while," Mo said, looking at the spine of the paperback, recognizing it as the one his father was reading to Miss Clara.

Ken cleared his throat. "Time will tell, I guess." Hanging his head, he stood and placed the book back on the dresser.

When his father looked up, Mo could see his eyes were glistening. "I'm sorry, Dad," he said.

Ken shook his head. "Nothing you coulda done, Son. Go wake your grandma so she can take care of this baby. Then, get yourself back to bed."

Mo stopped in the doorway. Turning back, he saw his father pick up Jacob, Ken's eyes fixed in deep contemplation.

"Shshshshsh, c'mon now, don't cry." Ken held the baby away from his body. "It's okay. Grandma will be right here." He looked up at Mo, his brows arched. "Hurry up, get going!"

Staring out the window of Carlton's car, Mo wonders if Langford's stepmother was like Ms. Clara. Did his stepmother come to live with him the same way? Does Langford have a half brother or sister he doesn't talk about? He wonders if all stepmothers are mean and uncaring. Will Mrs. Branch be Jake's stepmother? Is Jake happy living with Mrs. Branch? Wondering about these things, Mo's glad he had his grandmother instead of a stepmother.

Carlton drives his Caprice into the parking lot at ten, just as the gates open. Named Midway Park when it was introduced in 1894, Lincoln Park sits on forty-two acres along Route 6 in North Dartmouth. Even before he can see the park itself, Mo notices its most intimidating attraction, The Comet, looming high above and welcoming guests as a harbinger of impending doom. The Comet's twisting layout has all the features of a thrilling wooden rollercoaster: height, speed, sharp turns, and a head-chopping effect.

As they walk through the entrance gate, Brian rubs his hands together. "Who wants to go on The Comet first?"

Trevor raises his hand. "I'm in. Mo, you gonna join us?"

Mo looks up at the coaster, his heart racing. "No, I don't think so." He remembers the last thrill ride he went on when he was young. His father took him on the Tilt-A-Whirl at the carnival and became angry when Mo threw up during the ride. They left the carnival immediately after, driving home with all the windows down. Afraid of ruining their trip, Mo turns to Trevor. "It looks too scary."

Brian nudges Mo. "Too scary? For a big guy like you?"

"Ignore Brian," Trevor says. "I'm sure that ride's more thrilling than any occurring in his bed."

"Ooh!" Carlton high fives Trevor.

Brian shrugs. "Whatever, man, at least I *have* something occurring in my bed."

"Guys!" Kay motions toward Mo. "Not right now." She puts her hand through Mo's arm. "It's okay. You can go on some of the other rides with us. I don't like the coaster either. Besides," she says, glaring at Brian, "not all thrill rides are good ones."

Brian shakes his head. "Touché."

The park's crowded on this last day of summer. While Brian and Trevor spend most of the morning testing their patience in line and flaunting their masculinity on the featured attraction, Mo enjoys several of the less perilous rides with Kay and Carlton. Afterward, they try their luck at the ring toss, balloon dart throw, and milk bottle games.

Having played catch with Sam and practiced pitching against the brick sidewall of Sumerduck Elementary when he was younger, Mo's good at throwing a baseball. He wins a giant teddy bear, holding the prize in front of Kay. "Here, you can have this."

Kay places her hands over her heart. "Aww, for me?"

"You can hug it anytime you get scared." Recalling a Winnie the Pooh bear he gave Jake years ago, a surge of nostalgia hits Mo. But it's swept away by an ocean of warm rising in his chest when Kay gives him an appreciative peck on the cheek.

"Thanks, Mo. You're the sweetest." Kay squeezes the bear before pushing it into Carlton's chest. "Will you carry this?"

"Ugh, why do *I* have to carry it?" Carlton says. "It's *your* bear."

"Because," Brian smirks, "that's what boyfriends do."

Carlton shakes his head. "Why did you have to go there, B?"

"*What?* You don't see any toy bears sucking on my nipple."

Carlton grumbles as he takes Kay's bear.

They play miniature golf as a group before agreeing to go on The Comet. Once in line, Mo has second thoughts. Opting to go for a walk instead, he offers to take the stuffed bear to the car. Carlton can't get the keys out of his pocket fast enough.

The woods behind Lincoln Park are dense, running nearly a half-mile thick to insulate the expanding suburban developments from the noise and lights. Behind the parking lot, several footpaths carved through the trees provide pedestrian access to the park.

It's dusk when Mo, already gloved, enters one of the primary paths. Midway through his walk, he finds a giant swallowtail perched on a large stone, its black, six-inch wingspan showcasing bright yellow flourishes. Leaning over to observe, he knows the butterfly is late for its southerly migration, too weak to make the trip. He uses Carlton's key to lure it from the stone.

Several steps into the brush, Mo notices a young girl walking by. When she slows down, he holds the butterfly out for her to see.

She steps closer, reaching for one of its wings, but the butterfly folds it away.

Kneeling, Mo sets the butterfly on several leaves, using the key to hold it down by its thorax. He retrieves a small twig near his feet to hold one of the wings in place so the girl can feel it. Her brown ponytail hangs near his face as she stands beside him.

"It's okay," Mo says, "you can touch it."

"No, thank you," the girl says. "Please don't do that. I think you're hurting it."

Mo shakes his head. "It can't feel anything."

She sees the unrestrained wing flapping against the ground, struggling to break free. "Mister, please stop doing that. You're pulling its wing." She takes a step backward toward the path.

Mo stands, leaving the butterfly on the ground. Shushing her, he reaches out to place his hand over her mouth. "You're going to scare it away."

"It can't fly. You pulled its wing!" She backs further away before stumbling over a root.

Mo leans over to help her. Looking back at the butterfly and watching it struggle, he recalls a day along the water behind Earl's house, the spring after his seizure.

Each year, on the last weekend of May, when purple milkweed, at full maturity, stood erect and red creeping thyme stained the landscape, Grandma Cleveland visited her sister in Charlottesville. That year, 1963, being no different, Mo looked forward to spending a rare Saturday night with his father.

Throughout the previous year, except for Sundays, Mo seldom saw his father in the evening. Mr. Johnson's second marriage had all but eliminated Earl's nighttime visits while Ken kept himself busy with sales appointments, often long after Mo's bedtime. So, Mo spent many nights alone with Grandma Cleveland, finishing homework, reading, or watching television.

Saturday nights, in particular, had become quite busy for Ken. Arriving home from work, he'd devour dinner, clean himself up, and kiss Mo goodnight before departing, the smell of Old Spice lingering long after he left.

On the morning of Grandma Cleveland's departure, Mo investigated the woods behind Earl's new house while the men fixed one of the work trucks. He followed a path to Rock Run, one of many streams feeding the Rappahannock in that area. He finished a popsicle, courtesy of Mrs. Johnson, before setting himself down on a boulder by the water. Building a makeshift fishing pole by attaching a hook on some string tied to a small branch, he dropped the line in the water, wedging the branch between several rocks.

After a few minutes, Mo noticed a wolf spider camouflaged on a nearby tree. Intrigued by its size, stretching the length of his index finger, and knowing wolf spiders aren't poisonous, he decided to take a closer look. Using two pieces of bark to coax the spider to settle on one, he inspected its intimidating fangs, impressive array of eyes, and the two parallel black lines on its back. He pressed the popsicle stick on its abdomen harder than intended. Hearing a squishing sound, he imagined the spider's tiny but gruff voice howling in pain. Easing up on the popsicle stick, he felt the hair on the spider's legs as it struggled to get away. When he did release, the spider pounced on his hand, sinking his fangs between Mo's thumb and forefinger before jumping off and hobbling away. Letting out a faint wail, Mo stomped his foot before sticking his hand into the stream's cold water to relieve the pain.

Mo spent several hours relaxing on the bank and watching the line. He used the popsicle stick to disrupt the flow of the water while listening to the birds above.

Early afternoon, his father, still wiping grease and oil from his hands, came down the path to retrieve him. He pointed at Mo's hand. "What happened there?"

Mo looked at his wound. "I got bit by a spider."

"That looks nasty. Did you see it bite you?"

"Yeah, I was trying to pet it."

Ken's brows furrowed. "What color was it?"

"It was brown," Mo replied. "Pretty sure it was a wolf spider."

"Wasn't a black widow then, so that's good." Ken leaned over, pulling Mo's crude fishing pole from the water. "Let's head back to the house. Let Mrs. Johnson get a bandage on that." As he straightened up, Ken pointed to a patch of dirt next to Mo's leg. "That the spider that bit you?"

Looking at the ground, Mo could see spider legs and drying guts. "No, sir."

"You sure? Looks like a big old wolf spider to me, and one that wasn't killed too long ago."

"No, sir. The spider that bit me ran off."

Ken's voice grew stern. "Mo, that *must* be the spider that bit you."

Mo's eyes teared up. "No, Dad. Honest, I didn't kill the spider."

Ken rose to his feet. "Alright then, show me the bottom of your boots." He pointed to a detached hairy leg with sticky spider guts in the sole of Mo's boot. "Son, why would you lie to me?"

"I didn't, Dad, I don't remember."

Ken sighed. "C'mon, let's go get you bandaged up."

Twenty minutes later, Mo climbed into the pickup. Like an ominous passenger, the hole in the dashboard stared at Mo as his father checked out his bandage.

Starting the truck, Ken turned to Mo with a smile. "Let's grab some lunch. We gotta get home so I can take a nap and get changed. You're gonna come with me tonight. We're headed to a friend's house."

Mo waved to Earl before turning back to his father. "Where are we going?"

"We're going to see Mrs. Willoughby. You know her from church, right?"

Mo thought for a moment before answering. "Uh-huh." In truth, he only remembered her husband had toys. He hoped he might be able to play with them. "Will Mr. Willoughby be there?"

"No, Son, not tonight."

"Is Mrs. Willoughby nice?" Mo thought of 'nice' in the context of his mother, grandmother, and Mrs. Harrington.

"I think you'll like her alright."

His father smiled as he stared down Sumerduck Road, Ken's mind elsewhere and their talking done.

Mo looks down at the girl, releases her hands, and apologizes before walking away. Silent, she stares back. Still wearing his gloves, Mo checks for the medals hanging from his chain as he heads back to the path, unable to feel the warmth and protection they provide. Hearing a scuffle and thinking it may be a deer, he turns back to look. He no longer sees the girl.

Ten minutes later, Mo crosses the rear parking lot before reentering the main gate. Marveling at the giant, white coaster while appreciating the squeals and screeches of its enthusiasts, he understands how the serenity of a nature walk can be upset by even a single scream. He waits for his friends at the exit of The Comet.

Kay greets Mo from behind. "Did you have fun today?"

"I had a great time," Mo says. "I've never been any place like this before. Did you enjoy the roller coaster?"

"I couldn't do it. Carlton took me for some cotton candy instead. We ended up playing the nickel-pusher game." Kay points. "Here comes Trevor and Brian."

They head out to Carlton's car. The evening sky shifting from dark gray to black, the parking lot's lit by pole lights and a million distant stars. Mo imagines the stars falling like fireworks.

"Kay, do you remember where we parked?" Carlton searches for the keys in his pockets before remembering where they are. "Hey, M, toss me the keys."

Mo throws them harder than intended.

"Whoa, buddy," Carlton says, laughing as he catches them with his hands and stomach, "I don't have a glove on." He looks down. "Hey, what did you do with these?" He looks closer. "They're all, ew, sticky."

Mo shrugs. "Sorry, I used them to hold down a big butterfly, but I accidentally poked it too hard."

"Oh, gross." Carlton shakes off his hand, wiping it across his pant leg.

Kay points two rows over. "There's the car."

Approaching, Carlton notices the rear driver's side is sloped down. "Come on! *Seriously?*" He unlocks the door before tossing the keychain over to Trevor. "T, can you help B get the jack and spare out of the trunk?" He sets the parking brake, pointing Kay in the direction of picnic tables several yards away. "Why don't you wait over there with Mo. This shouldn't take long."

Trevor pushes the plush animal aside. "Hey, Carlton, I get the wrench set, floodlamp, oil, transmission fluid, fan belts, jumper cables, and jack, but why's there an old fold-up shovel in here?"

"I have it in case I get stuck in mud or need to bury a body." Carlton chuckles. "Nah, my mother gave me that old relic just in case I ever need it. My dad brought it back with him from the war."

Trevor unfolds the shovel while Brian struggles with the spare. "Sure looks like your dad used it a lot."

Yanking the shovel from Trevor's hands, Brian drops it to the ground. "Hey, man, can you please give me a hand getting this tire out? I wanna get home tonight."

"I'm not kidding; it looks like it's been used recently—more recent than thirty years ago." Trevor pulls the center hole of the spare, freeing it and causing Brian to get a tire smudge on his white tee. "Oops, sorry."

Brian brushes the smudge with his hand. "Come on! This is a new shirt."

Carlton tosses his hand at Brian. "Relax, it'll wash out. Roll the tire over here."

Trevor leans the spare against the side panel. "So, what did your dad do in the war?"

"He was in the Battle of the Bulge. His company got hunkered down in foxholes for like a week in freezing cold and snow. My dad told me the story about a dozen times when I was little, but he didn't focus on any of the guys who died over there. I'm sure he used the shovel a bunch of times to dig in from France to Germany. Got shot twice, neither hurt him much, but he definitely went through some wicked crazy stuff over there he wouldn't talk about."

"Wow, I didn't know that. Your dad's like a legit war hero. My uncle died in Italy during the war. It would've been nice to ask him about it." Trevor pauses, staring at the shovel. "Hey, how do Germans tie their shoes?" He doesn't wait for a response. "In little Nazis."

The three boys laugh while Carlton tightens the final bolts, Brian waving Kay and Mo back. The drive home's filled with laughter as each tells their parents' jokes, hoping the others haven't heard them before.

Mo listens in silence, his head filled with the sights and sounds, smells and flavors, joy and thrills of an unforgettable day. When a sports update recaps a Red Sox loss to the lowly Tigers, he's unconcerned. He'll worry about that tomorrow. Tonight, he revels in what he controls.

- 46 -

# HUNTING WITH CLOSE FRIENDS

## TUESDAY, 23 SEPTEMBER 1975

*Palmer grips the cold, hard steel of the handlebar.* He follows Osmond and Ross along the cemetery path in his only suit—black for all occasions, black for today. Along with three family members, they rest Murphy's casket on the bier next to the grave. Huddled under a temporary canopy, he watches mourners struggle through the short memorial, raindrops beating like solemn drums on the canvas above. When the time comes for him to toss dirt on the coffin, he pulls loose tobacco out of his pocket, mixing it with soil before dropping it in.

After the service, Palmer follows the parade of vehicles making their way to Murphy's wake. Family, friends, and former coworkers listen to clicks of Murphy's life spin through a projector, each slide offering a stationary point in the arc of a man's measure. For Palmer, the images blur as he reflects on the past twenty-five years, wondering who will attend *his* funeral.

Osmond would be there. Ross, too, along with a few others from the office. Maybe Otis. Would Marilyn fly in with the girls? Palmer has no parents, no brothers or sisters, and just a few aging aunts, uncles, and cousins he hasn't seen since his father's funeral a quarter of a century earlier. Outside of work, he has no friends, no drinking or hunting buddies, and just a few neighbors with whom he's barely acquainted.

Refocusing on the projected 35mm images, Palmer knows Murphy had many friends, part of a colorful life. He also knows his own life is gray—gray like the newspaper print reporting the monsters he's hunted down. And he knows he's increasingly surrounded by darkness, allowing the color to seep out and turn black—black like the headlines he's tried to avoid. His obituary will be unavoidable. He wonders how it will read and how many people will remember his name for his professional accomplishments rather than his personal life. The alcohol in his glass turns bitter.

When the celebration's over, Palmer walks with Osmond and Ross to the parking lot. Standing near Osmond's car, they chat for several minutes under ominous but temporarily dry skies.

Ross pats Osmond on the shoulder. "When's the date, Harry?"

"Friday. It was supposed to be next Wednesday, but Humphrey's leaving for a trip with his family Friday morning. I think he had enough of filling the acting role. Wanted a break before returning to his old job."

Ross nudges Palmer's elbow. "Probably a little pissed off he didn't get the promotion, too. Right?"

Osmond opens his driver's door. "I don't think so. Jack seemed pretty upbeat during the turnover this past week. I'm not sure he liked the hours or the stress."

Palmer and Osmond exchange a few knowing glances while Ross shares some information about his upcoming weekend getaway.

Osmond settles in the driver's seat. "What about you, Frankie? When you headed back to Salt Lake?"

Palmer lights his first cigarette in over two hours. "Next Monday. I want to be there for the lineup late next week, maybe stand in it myself right next to the smug bastard." He holds the top of Osmond's door and raises his eyebrows. "Didn't get approval to fly this week from Humphrey. Know anything about that, Harry? Anything on the table?"

A tiny smile crosses Osmond's face. "Might be." He nods. "Just might be."

Palmer takes a long, satisfying drag. "You hear about the girl's body they found in North Dartmouth? Lincoln Park?"

"Looks like the boyfriend, Frankie."

"Maybe," Palmer says, releasing a billow of smoke, "but I hear there's a growing number of missing girls being reported in Rhode Island and Southeastern Mass."

"All I know is there's been what's being called an accident in Smithfield and this one that looks to be the boyfriend in North Dartmouth."

Palmer pulls away from the car door. "I know, Harry, I've been reading the papers, too. Usually starts with an accident, though. Right?"

Osmond closes the door, staring at Palmer through the driver's side window. He shakes his head as he pulls away. Ross tips his cap before walking a few rows over to his own car. Palmer waits for Ross to exit the parking lot before walking behind the restaurant where a row of trees lines the pond.

Looking across the water to a well-manicured patch of lawn behind a suburban home, he pictures the thirteenth green at Brookline. He remembers standing on that green in the middle of a particularly bad round, his father offering advice to live and play by: *Sometimes you'll take advantage, Francis. Other times you'll minimize the damage. But always remember to play the course. Don't worry about anyone else's score. How you play the course is what matters most.*

Standing there, looking across the pond, Palmer laments the advice his father didn't have time to share with him—advice about friendship, family, and work. Maybe his mistakes could have been avoided by listening to his father's voice as a compass and not the voices in his head. Murphy dead, Osmond moving up, and Ross nearing retirement, he wonders whether the monsters he hunts down are his closest friends.

Dark clouds all around, and mocked by the rain's resumption, Palmer flicks his finished cigarette into the pond, shaking his head as he walks away.

# WICKED MUDDY

## WEDNESDAY, 24 SEPTEMBER 1975

Mo lies on his bed, listening to the rain dance on his windowsill. Wednesday evening—the midpoint of a rain-drenched week—he relaxes, thinking back to an evening with his parents when he was almost five. After more than a week of heavy rain, severe flooding made all roads around Sumerduck impassable. He laid next to his mother, listening to her read about Noah and the Great Flood. There was never any frustration in his mother's voice as she turned the pages back numerous times to a picture of the paired animals marching onto the ark.

On the opposite side of his parents' bed, his father slept, temporary relief from the anxiety of a lost paycheck.

After finishing the story of Noah, Mo knelt at the side of the bed and said prayers. That evening, he was allowed to sleep in their bed. Nestled between his parents' warm bodies, he listened to the windswept rain hammer the roof shingles, his mother running her fingers through his hair until her breathing aligned with his father's light snoring. Soon he was focused on the warmth and his parents' breaths, not the windswept rain. He fell asleep dreaming about being on Noah's Ark, floating with all the animals downstream in a great flood.

A knock at Mo's bedroom door jolts him awake.

Carlton pops his head inside. "Hey, M, it's me. Can I come in?"

Mo slides up, resting against the headboard. "Sure."

Carlton sits at the foot of the bed. "Hey, I gotta head home tonight. The water behind my mother's house is pouring into the basement. She wants me to come clean it out, uh, tomorrow."

Carlton looks down at the floor. "I'm gonna, uh, stay at my mom's tonight and tomorrow night, so I won't be around until Friday sometime." He taps the toe of Mo's boots. "You should take these off before you lay in bed. You're getting the bedspread dirty."

"Oh, right." Mo sits up and slides his legs off the bed.

Carlton stands. "You need anything before I head out?"

"No, I'm okay." Mo starts unlacing his boots. "Oh, yeah, I almost forgot. Can you give me a ride to Mike's house on Friday afternoon? If you're home in time, I mean. He wrote directions down."

Carlton tilts his head. "Mike?"

"Oops, I mean Professor Langford."

"Professor...Mike," Carlton mutters to himself. "Professor Langford? Oh, from here at school?"

"Yeah. Do you know him?"

"No, uh, I mean, um, I have friends who've taken his classes. Sure, I've heard his name."

Mo reclines on the bed. "So, can you give me a ride?"

"Yeah, yeah. Sure." Carlton puts his hands in his pockets, stares down at the carpet. "Uh, well, let me check with Kay. You said Friday afternoon, right?"

"Yes, Friday." Mo pulls his legs back on the bed. "Are you okay?"

"Me? Yeah, I'm fine," Carlton's face is flushed. "It's just Friday night's date night. Kay and I are going to see a movie. I was trying to remember which movie." Carlton taps Mo's foot. "So, you're friends with Professor Langford, huh?"

"I went fishing with him and Mr. Griffin. Now, he's a friend of mine, I guess. He has a huge house and lets his friends sleep over. That's where I was when I called that night."

"Oh, okay. Trevor said something about you calling, but I was several beers deep that night, so I didn't put two and two together." Carlton smacks the bedspread. "Well, I better get going."

Heading to the door, Carlton notices Mo's blood-stained work boots on the floor of the closet. "Hey, are you going to do anything with those?"

Mo follows the path of Carlton's eyes, "No, I got a new pair from Mr. Griffin. I keep those just in case." He looks over to his housemate.

"Why, do you need them?"

"Yeah, I mean, I, um...I guess I could use them. That is, if you don't need them. I know it's gonna be wicked muddy in the backyard and my mother's basement. I don't wanna mess up my boots. I was afraid I'd have to do it in my penny loafers."

"No, sure, you can have them."

Carlton picks up the boots. "Sears Craftsman! I wonder what size." He lifts the tongue, inspecting the inside of the boot. "Look at that! Exactly my size and the same boots I wear. Hey, thanks!"

"You're welcome. Mr. Griffin gives everybody the same size boots. You're about the same height he is."

Carlton reaches deeper into the boots. "Can I have these, too?"

"Sure, I've been meaning to throw them out."

Carlton looks back, holding the boots and the gloves up as he exits. "Thanks again, buddy."

- 48 -

# SAMANTHA

FRIDAY, 26 SEPTEMBER 1975

*M*o *follows another day of working in the rain with a nice hot shower before staring out his bedroom window, hoping his friend hasn't forgotten.* A little after six, he hears a car horn and hustles out the front door.

Carlton snaps his fingers. "Hurry up, M. Kay and I are going to the movies, remember? She hates it when I'm late."

Mo struggles with the seatbelt. "What are you going to see?"

Carlton grins. "*Dog Day Afternoon.* I'm sure Kay won't like it, but I've sat through more of her romance movies than I can count." He revs his engine. "Now it's time for some intense drama with Al Pacino."

After snapping his seatbelt, Mo hands Carlton a piece of paper. "Here's the directions."

Carlton takes a casual glance without touching the sheet. "Got it."

Mo hesitates before pulling it back. "You sure? You didn't even look at it."

Carlton turns up the radio, yelling over the music, "It's like three turns, Mo, I got it," before putting the car in gear and hitting the gas.

Concerned about Carlton's speed and the wet roads, Mo stares at the windshield, trying to tell whether the raindrops are getting smaller. When they pull into the driveway, Mo notices Langford standing on the front porch. Carlton, too absorbed in his music, does not. With the rain a fine mist, the early-evening shadows make Langford's house look like a lit Halloween pumpkin.

Dressed in gray, Langford's an apparition as he descends the porch stairs and approaches the car, rapping on the driver-side window. Carlton jumps.

Mo and Langford share a laugh at his expense.

"I'm sorry," Langford says, chuckling. "I didn't mean to spook you."

"It's okay," Carlton says through a nervous laugh, "just didn't see you there."

"Did you have any trouble finding the place?"

"Nope. Piece of cake."

Mo walks around the car. "Mike, this is my housemate and friend, Carlton."

"Ah, yes," Langford reaches toward Carlton, "Mo has mentioned you a few times. I've seen you on campus. It's nice to finally meet you."

Carlton gives Mo a sideways glance as he leans forward and takes Langford's outstretched hand. "Yeah, uh, you, too."

Langford wraps his other hand over Carlton's in a warm handshake. "Would you like a quick tour of the house?"

Carlton pulls his hand out from between Langford's, arching sideways to look at Mo's Timex. "Oh, uh, well, I'm running kind of late."

"I'll make it a quick tour." Langford grins. "I promise."

"You need to see it." Mo's eyes light up. "It's enormous!"

"Okay, but it's gotta be fast. I don't want to get in trouble with my lady." Carlton stares at Langford with a contemptuous smirk.

Langford places his arms around Mo and Carlton's shoulders, guiding them into the house. "Excellent."

True to his word, Langford's tour is brief. Within minutes, they are standing in the cupola where Langford's cat is curled up on a cushion. As is her custom, Samantha troubles herself with only the slightest interest, eyes squinting, ears perked.

Langford points to Samantha. "Would you like a cat? She's not much company, but she'll let you feed her and change her litter box."

"I'm not sure the guys would like that," Carlton replies.

"I understand. Samantha and I have a game we play: she ignores me, and I sometimes forget about her. If I don't fill her dish for a couple days, then she lets me know she's around."

"Sounds about right," Carlton says as he pets her head. A purr emerges. "She's sure pretty, though."

"Aren't they all?" Langford nudges Mo.

Carlton, whipping his head around, stops petting.

Unfazed, Samantha turns away from the discourteous onlookers. Langford chuckles. "Next time, maybe I'll get a goldfish."

Lifting Mo's wrist, Carlton checks his watch. "I hate to be rude, but I need to get going."

"Of course," Langford says, arching an eyebrow. "Maybe I'll see you in one of my classes sometime."

With a smug smile, Carlton says, "Don't think so. Got a full load next semester, and then I'm done."

"I'm sure you do. Either way, it was a pleasure to meet you." Langford offers Carlton his limp hand.

Carlton ignores the professor's hand, choosing to nod instead. "You, too." He squeezes Mo's shoulder. "Call me if you need anything at all. Okay, M?"

"I will. Thanks."

Carlton hurries out, with Mo and Langford following close behind. He hops into his car and waves before driving away, his car's azure finish blending, then disappearing, into the dusk.

Langford turns to Mo, forming a bridge with his hands and tapping his fingers. "So, ready for a night of fun?"

Once in the kitchen, Mo listens to the pregame. Langford prepares homemade pizza. After enjoying their meal, Langford does the dishes while Mo explains how he would approach handling the Red Sox lineup with their star left fielder lost for the season.

Langford hangs the dishtowel on the rack. "Wow! You could manage the Red Sox." He clamps his hands together. "You must be dying to get out of that uniform. Let's go see your room where you can get into something more comfortable before the second game starts." He escorts Mo to the downstairs guest bedroom, handing him some fresh towels while showing him the adjoining bathroom. "There's nightclothes hanging right here behind the bathroom door. Just come over when you're done. The TV in my room's the biggest in the house. You know where my room is, right?"

Mo nods, staring with concern at the robe and pajamas. Despite Mike's height, the pajama bottoms are well short, and the pajama top won't close, his belly peeking through strained buttons. Standing in Langford's bedroom, he keeps his arms by his side, afraid of tearing the robe at the shoulders.

Langford steps out of the master bathroom and sees Mo admiring his twenty-five-inch console. "Is it not the biggest you've ever seen?" Hands on his hips, he smiles.

Mo shakes his head. "It's big alright, but I think Mr. Thompson's is bigger."

Langford's smile disappears. "Oh, I guess he has the twenty-seven-inch." He points toward Mo. "Looks like the TV isn't the only thing of mine that isn't big enough."

Tugging at the pajama top, Mo tries to stretch the material. "Most clothes don't fit me. That's why I like wearing my uniform."

"Hmm, I think I'll have to shop around for bigger nightclothes for you. Come on in. The game's about to start. Take a seat wherever you like."

Mo sits down on a wooden bench at the foot of the bed.

Langford lays a pillow against the headboard. "That may not be the most comfortable place to sit for an extended period. There's not a lot of cushioning and no support for your back."

The bench moans as Mo lifts himself. He then nestles into a reading chair, his hips getting stuck between the polished armrests. After Mo wiggles his way out, Langford gestures for him to come over.

Langford pats the bedding. "Mo, it's okay to sit on the bed. There's plenty of room."

Mo is relieved by Langford's suggestion.

Reaching across the bed, Langford fluffs a pillow, holding it at the headboard for Mo to rest against. "There, is that better?"

"Yes, thank you."

When the second game of the doubleheader ends, Langford turns to Mo with an irresistible offer. "Let's get a late-night snack."

"That sounds good." Mo follows his host to the kitchen, where Langford spreads Oreos onto a plate and warms milk on the stove.

For several minutes Langford smiles in amusement, Mo repeatedly dropping several Oreos into his milk and subsequently struggling to locate the ripest one. When the plate is empty, Langford breaks the silence. "Have you ever had a girlfriend?"

Fishing an Oreo out of his glass, Mo inspects it before looking up. "I haven't had many friends that were girls." He drops it back in the milk to finish marinating.

"Not friends that were girls. I mean a girl you felt special feelings toward, maybe a girl you thought you loved."

"I loved my mom and Grandma Cleveland and Mrs. Harrington." Mo checks the saturation of another before adding, "And I love Kay, too."

"Kay is Carlton's girlfriend." Langford points to the empty plate. "Will you be wanting more?"

Mouth full and eyes wide, Mo nods.

Langford spreads the remaining cookies on the plate. "Have you ever wanted a girlfriend of your *own*?"

"No, I don't think so." Mo points the head of his spoon at Langford. "Do *you* have a girlfriend?"

"I was never interested in girls. They were always looking to impress the other guys and were often mean to my friends and me. I've always had more fun doing stuff with my guy friends: traveling together, fishing, or hanging out at the pub. In fact, I have some other friends I'd like you to meet who are more like Mr. Griffin and yourself."

"I like Mr. Griffin. He's always good to me. I guess Kay's my only friend that's a girl, kind of like Miss Hathaway is for you."

"Rose isn't my only female friend. But, yes, I see your point." Langford rests his elbows on the table and leans toward Mo. "Do you find girls pretty?"

"My mom was really pretty." Mo rubs the back of his head. "Kay's pretty."

"What about other girls? Did you find other girls pretty when you were growing up? Do you find them pretty now?"

Mo furrows his brows. "What other girls?"

"Oh, I don't know, just the girls you went to school with, or the ones you were friends with."

"I never was friends with any girls." Mo holds the glass over his mouth, shaking out the last bit of Oreo paste.

"How about the ones you said were mean to you? Were any of them pretty? Is Emily pretty?"

"No!" Mo slams the glass down on the table. "No! She's not nice. She's not pretty. I don't like talking about her." After several seconds of silence, he sits back. "I'm sorry, I'd rather not talk anymore."

"I understand, Mo." Langford's smile is laced with success. "I guess we just aren't enslaved to the whims and wiles of the opposite sex."

Mo doesn't attempt to follow this last comment and, with the warm milk kicking in, begins to rub his eyes. "I'm tired. Is it okay if I go to bed?"

"Sure, you know where it is. I have to help a friend clear tree branches in the morning, so feel free to sleep in. If you want to go for a walk, just leave the front door unlocked. It's fine. I should be back around ten. Then, we can go for an early lunch before I take you home."

Mo nods, tugging at the front of his robe. "Goodnight."

# STIRRING THE CAULDRON

## SATURDAY, 27 SEPTEMBER 1975

*P*almer's *been going to the same barber for over thirty years.* The black leather chairs are worn, the orange neon sign is faded, and the red, white, and blue pole no longer rotates, but the barber is always current. Anything happening in the neighborhood gets discussed there, and Palmer gets updated once a month, travel permitting.

The first time his mother took him to Bennie's Barbershop, Palmer's father was in England. Otis worked there, catering to a few tolerant, White customers along with the Black clients, until Bennie retired, surprising everyone by leaving the store to Otis. Most of the White customers never returned, and the Black clients were too few, so Otis moved his shop, and Bennie's became a fixture in the south end of the city.

In its original location, Palmer's mother found the barbershop convenient, and she wasn't concerned with a Black man cutting her son's hair, working alongside her husband, or eating at the family dinner table, for that matter. When Bennie's moved, Palmer's mother followed and retained a friendship.

Despite limited schooling, Otis is an astute student of history and has a keen sense of moral obligation, educating his younger customers through experience and acquired wisdom. As a small business owner in segregated Boston for many years, his path has been challenging. Still, he understands his contribution to the much larger movement, choosing to share rather than preach.

The barbershop opens at nine, so Palmer arrives at eight the last Saturday of each month, departing before any neighborhood regulars arrive. It's an understanding suiting the circumstances: passive in its acceptance of the way things are, conscious of the way they have to be. Palmer's never late.

Otis smiles through his overgrown white mustache as he secures the neck strip. "Sure been awhile, Mr. Palmer, hasn't it?"

"It certainly has," Palmer says. "Been out of town the past six months."

Otis flings the barber cape around Palmer and ties it around his neck. "Big business stuff going on? Mergers and acquisitions and all that high finance stuff?"

"Yup, business has been booming."

"I wish I'd gone to school for business or something like that. Maybe I'd have been able to help the community more."

"Maybe, but I think you're better off right where you are. You provide a genuine service to folks here in the neighborhood. I have to deal with some real dangerous men in my business. They'd just as soon tear your head off as listen."

Otis checks the length of Palmer's hair between his fingers. "I hear what you're saying. There's a lot of vipers and vultures in corporate America."

"Absolutely. And a lot of animals running wild in the streets."

"Say, how's that family of yours doing?"

"They're doing well, thanks for asking," Palmer checks himself in the mirror, "but my hair isn't. Couldn't find a decent barber in Seattle. Stopped trying a couple months ago."

"I can tell." Otis combs Palmer's hair down in front, covering Palmer's eyes. "But at least you've got hair to worry about. All I got is this ring above my ears and around back." He laughs. "Wife says she's gonna trade me in for a full head of hair one of these days."

Palmer enjoys laughing with Otis—a very good barber and an excellent conversationalist. He shares just enough half-truths to move the early dialogue along. When the superficial discussion ends, they often switch to a topic of local significance. Today is no different.

Otis lathers the back of Palmer's neck. "What do you think about this busing situation?"

Palmer clears his throat. "It's a tough one. Don't you think?"

"Sure is." Otis swishes the straight blade along the razor strap. "I'm not sure I much blame the Irish folk here in Southie. I've been living in Roxbury my whole life. Many of the folks there would rather send their kids to local schools, too. I sure hope the violence settles down. Police escort the buses in motorcades right by the store here. The government's got to do a better job of funding schools in poorer communities; help these kids get a better education near their homes."

Palmer nods. "I agree with you, Otis. For what it's worth, I think it might make sense to look at reallocating citywide educational funding to improve the schools in historically underprivileged and underserved communities like Roxbury. That might eliminate the requirement to bus children while improving the financial prospects of students from traditionally low-income neighborhoods."

Otis stares at Palmer in the mirror. "Amen. That's a mouthful of common sense right there. You should think about running for governor. I know I'd vote for you."

"I wouldn't know the first thing about politics, but I'm not sure forcing folks to confront endemic problems when those forced to bear the brunt are the ones with the least means is a practical approach. The wealthy deal with it by taking their kids out of the public school system, while the poor and working class become embittered. There's an air of hypocrisy about it."

Otis puts his hands on his hips. "I couldn't agree more. Until folks of every race, creed, and color can accept others as equals, mixing up the bottom of the cauldron amounts to stirring up a lot of muck."

Palmer checks the length of his bangs. "Suffice it to say, we live in a complicated society. We aren't gonna figure it out until everyone's given the same opportunity to sit at the table. We aren't there yet. Maybe sometime in our lifetimes, the table will be large enough for everyone."

"Don't know about my lifetime," Otis says, "but maybe yours. I sure hope so. I'm not sure this is what Dr. King had in mind. Good people still dying for no reason and violence in the streets. Whites and Blacks still fighting over segregation, and politicians still wringing their hands. We all breathe the same air but seems like some folks wanna make it so others can't breathe it just cause they're different." He removes the cape, brushes Palmer off. "I guess some change is just gonna take longer, right, Mr. Palmer?"

Nodding, Palmer hands him a ten. "I'll see you next month, Otis. I sure hope things settle down here."

"Me, too." Otis rings up the register. "Better days are a-coming."

Palmer continues to nod as he slips out. He looks up and down the street before lighting a cigarette and hopping in his car. Turning right on New Dudley towards Columbus, he sees graffiti on an abandoned building, swears mixed with racial slurs spray-painted in bright colors. He shakes his head, knowing the answers won't be black or white either.

# LANGFORD'S PROMISE

## SATURDAY, 27 SEPTEMBER 1975

M o wakes up in Langford's downstairs guest bedroom, tired and restless. After a night of tossing and turning, he heads over to the
kitchen, where Langford has placed carafes of milk and juice along
with an assortment of fruit, muffins, and cereal on the island. As
it was during the night, he dwells on Emily. Did he think she was
pretty when he lived with the Branch family? Did he try to get her
to like him? Did he make an effort to be friends with her? Would
he still be with Jake at the Branch home if he'd tried harder to be
friends with her?

His questions extend to his brother and the Branch parents. Why
did Jake move to Peter's room? Why did Jake like Peter more than
him? Why did Mr. and Mrs. Branch like Jake more? Why didn't
they believe him? Why did they believe Emily instead? Why was he
banished? Cycling through questions he cannot answer, he's filled
with disappointment, betrayal, and anger.

After breakfast and five days of rain, Mo, like many of the locals,
is eager to enjoy a cloudless morning. Walking along the access
road, he passes a few individuals enjoying the early autumn foliage.
Several hundred yards down, he notices a small opening between
trees leading into the back of Langford's property, an old path hidden under groundcover.

Mo gets distracted in the woods behind Langford's house for
over an hour. When he emerges, his boots are muddied, as are his
gloves and the lower part of his uniform around the ankles. He's
sweat-stained from the humidity hanging under the canopy and
has scratches all over his hands, arms, and face from fighting his

way through the undergrowth.

Back at Langford's house, he sits on the porch swing. Taking his boots off, he places them next to Langford's equally muddy pair. Mo notices the professor's boots are identical to his but more worn, the side stitching lifting from the sole.

Langford steps onto the front porch. "Wow, did you roll around in the mud?"

Mo moves his boots and gloves into the sun to dry. "It's soaking wet way in the back of your yard. It was fun, though, because everything's so green...except the ground. It's brown."

"It's been so long since I've ventured back there. Did you find anything interesting?"

"It's hard to walk around, but there's a lot of beautiful trees and some flowers still blooming in one nice open area."

"I'm glad you enjoyed it." Langford holds the door open for Mo. "I'm also glad you took your boots off. You can go take a shower if you'd like. We'll head out for an early lunch before I take you home."


Riding in Langford's car, Mo's exhausted but glad the rain and his overnight distress have passed. He looks forward to going to church with Kay's family tomorrow. Mrs. Harrington, herself a Catholic, had helped arrange for Mo's family to attend church with the Branches. After Jake's mother came to the house, Ken would never again step foot in a church until he was carried in on the day of his funeral.

When they first went to church with the Branch family, Paul and Mary hadn't been born, and Peter and Jake were just babies. Mrs. Branch and Grandma Cleveland would hold them during service while three-year-old Emily sat by Mo, sometimes in his lap, playing with her dolls and stuffed animals. For those few years, until even a new Branch station wagon couldn't transport them all, he loved little Emily and thought she loved him. At the time, Mo *did* think Emily was pretty.

Langford pulls his car to the curb in front of Mo's townhouse and lowers the radio.

Mo steps out and rests his arms on the sill of the open passenger window. Looking in, he says, "I had a nice time and liked walking around your property this morning." He hesitates while pulling away before leaning back in. "Mike?"

"Yes, Mo?"

"Can we please not talk about Emily anymore?"

"Yes, I promise not to talk about her in the future."

Mo turns and walks to the townhouse, hoping Mike will keep his word.

# Part III

# THIRTEEN CIGARETTES

# OSMOND'S SERMON

**SUNDAY, 28 SEPTEMBER 1975**

*Palmer has no need for an alarm clock.* This morning, the first light hit One Boston Place at six thirty-seven. It didn't creep into the windows on the thirty-second floor until two minutes later, and it crossed the path of Palmer's eyelids at six forty. That is, it *would've* crossed the path of Palmer's eyelids at six forty if it weren't Sunday. Today, the drapes stayed closed.

Palmer's fingers fumble along the nightstand, knocking over a half-full bottle of Jack, a pack of Marlboros, and a box of Trojans. He coughs into the phone. "Yeah?" His toes feel under the blanket for wayward boxers. "This is Frank." Sitting up, his feet land in a puddle. "It's Sunday." He turns on the light, rubs his eyes, and checks his watch. "Yeah, I can see it's almost eleven thirty." He lifts an empty envelope with the words, *Thanks, Steve. – Vickie*, scribbled on the face, the 'V' made into a heart using lipstick. He crumples the note, tossing it in the wastebasket. "I understand." Reaching down, he picks up the pack of cigarettes, whiskey dripping off the cellophane. "Yeah, I'll be there in twenty minutes." He smacks the pack against his finger, pulls out the driest one, lights, and takes a long drag.

Faces on aligned photos stare at Palmer as he walks through the entrance hall of the field office. He doesn't look back. He also doesn't read the bold lettering on the office door as he pushes against the glass. Once inside, he checks his palm. "Didn't expect the paint to be dry."

Osmond stares out the window. "Chipper mood, I see." He turns to face Palmer. "Damn, Frankie, you look like shit."

"Thank you, *sir.*"

"Knock it off." Osmond points to the other side of the desk. "Take a seat. And, put out the damn cigarette."

"Yes, *sir.*"

"Cut the shit. This isn't a joke."

Palmer sits, takes a final drag, crushing his cigarette on the desk in front of Osmond's nameplate. "Better than a badge and gun, huh, Harry?"

Osmond leans across the desk, waits for Palmer's eyes to meet his. "It's been four years, Frankie. She's not coming back."

"What are you talking about?" Palmer looks away. "They give you a title, and now you're a goddamned shrink?"

Osmond straightens up. "C'mon, I know it hurt when she took the girls. But look at you. You call this coping? Saturday night parties? Reckless behavior? Hell, it would get you thrown out of the Bureau if anyone else knew." He shakes his head. "Did you even get a name?"

"Veronica, Valerie, something with a 'V,' I think." Palmer yawns. "This how you get a nameplate?"

"Everyone in this office looks up to you. The younger agents want to be you when they grow up. You're the closest thing we have to a rock star." Osmond's voice softens. "We've been friends a long time, Frankie." He crosses his arms. "You're well into your forties. It's time to get your personal life in order. And, for God's sake, give up the cigarettes. You don't want to end up like Murphy."

"Did you call me down here on a Sunday for a sermon?"

"Alright," Osmond sits down, "as I'm sure you've figured out, there's growing suspicion there may be a mass murderer around Providence. The Rhode Island State Police have put together a task force with local authorities. They've requested FBI investigative resources. Captain Monroe asked if you were available." Osmond slides a folder across the desk. "These are the files on the first two girls: the one found along the water in Smithfield and the other down in North Dartmouth."

"So I take it I'm not headed back to Utah?"

Osmond shakes his head. "Utah State detectives and Salt Lake investigators have it under control for now."

"I understand, but from what you said last week, didn't sound like the two girls here were connected," Palmer says. "What changed?"

"They didn't think so until they found a third body in Lincoln, north of Providence, this morning. Hasn't hit the papers yet, but I'm sure it will soon. I told Monroe you'd be there tomorrow. I'll send Ross to assist when he gets back from vacation. He's out of the country until Tuesday. I've been having him mentor a young agent, so they'll both be there Wednesday morning. Let me know what else you need."

Palmer peels a small piece of tobacco from his lip. He inspects it before dropping it to the floor. "I'm not gonna be able to handle long meetings in here, you know, not without smoking."

Osmond laughs. "It's for your own good, Frankie; you smoke a shitload more than Murphy ever did."

Over the course of several silent seconds, Palmer brushes the ashes from Osmond's desk. "I do get it, Harry, I understand." He pushes his chair back. "I feel it, too. We get one of these assholes, and there's another right behind him. Sometimes it feels like swatting the flies in your house during summer. You don't know where they come from, and you can't always figure out what they're looking for, but they just keep coming, and you keep going after them. Murphy died swatting. I understand, and I appreciate the concern." He stands, sliding his hand across Osmond's freshly polished desk.

"There's younger guys to work the field," Osmond says.

Rubbing his fingers with his thumb, Palmer walks to the door. "I know, but I can't keep from thinking about the parents who've lost their daughters. It feels like it goes from bad to worse."

"Before you go."

Palmer turns. "Yeah?"

"They've got a number of missing persons reports in addition to the three dead girls." Osmond stares at Palmer, his brows furrowed. "This one looks like it could get *much* worse."

Palmer brushes his hair across his forehead. "Let me dive into the files this afternoon. I'll head down to Providence in the morning and let you know if I need anything."

Osmond nods, rotating his chair to look out the window. "Oh, and Frankie?"

"Yeah?"

"Go easy on the new kid. He's green, but he shows promise. Kinda reminds me of you years ago. I don't need you scaring him away."

"Better tell him not to get too close then. Everything about what I do is scary." Palmer walks out at a quickened pace, leaving his fingerprints on Osmond's door and knowing The Beast has a new hunting ground.

# GRANDMA'S WORRIES

## SUNDAY, 28 SEPTEMBER 1975

*Mo drops to a knee, angles forward, and levels his eyes with the top of the waterfall.* Despite a drop of just three feet, water cascades over a broad, flat, and gracefully arcing ledge that stretches across the river, creating a curtain-like appearance during peak season. Stepstone Falls along the Wood River in West Greenwich is charming and picturesque. With all the recent rain, the rush of water is deafening at the often-overlooked recreational site. After a few minutes of watching and listening, Mo rejoins Kay and Carlton at a picnic table far enough from the falls to converse.

Carlton taps his fingers on the table. "How was Langford's house, M?"

"It was good. I got to watch the game." Mo looks over at Kay. "But his TV isn't as big as your dad's."

Kay smiles. "My dad will be pleased to hear his TV is bigger than a prominent professor's."

Carlton winks at Kay before turning back to Mo. "So, you had fun?"

Mo nods. "He has a lot of land, so I can walk around and explore."

"Where did you sleep?" With a leg resting on his knee, Carlton's foot taps in time with his fingers.

"I slept downstairs. It's an even nicer room than last time." Mo nods. "It has its own bathroom. Mike says it's mine whenever I sleep over."

"Did you watch the game in there?"

"No, we watched on the big TV in his bedroom."

Carlton stops tapping, raises his eyebrows, and leans forward. "Does he have chairs set up in his bedroom? Where did you sit?"

"We sat up on the bed. It's a *big* bed."

"Didn't it make you feel uncomfortable to be on his bed alone with him?"

"Not really. We just watched TV. After the game, we had cookies and milk."

Kay looks at her boyfriend with a sideways glance. "Carl, what are you doing?"

Carlton shows her the palm of his hand. "Relax, I'm just making sure Mo's okay going over there. Doesn't it worry you this guy would have Mo sleep over alone?"

"Seems awfully cynical," Kay says.

"Maybe, but I'm just looking out for M." Carlton returns his attention to Mo. "Does it ever seem weird when you're there? Does he say or do anything that makes you feel uncomfortable?"

Mo considers how uncomfortable Carlton looked at Langford's house Friday night. Now, Carlton's questions remind him of Dr. Winchester's. "No, it makes me feel special. I feel like I'm a little kid again, and he's an older brother."

Carlton exchanges a glance with Kay before clearing his throat. "I used to play with my mother's friend when I was little. Sometimes, I would run out of my house and hide in the trees for hours." He looks down, swiping his hand along the edge of the bench. "If I hid well enough, I felt like I was safe from the bad guys."

Kay studies Carlton. "Your poor mom must've been worried sick."

Carlton digs his shoe into the dirt. "Most times, I felt safer in the trees."

Kay begins to ask why, but Mo interrupts. "That's how I felt at the Branch house." He clenches and unclenches his fist. "Is it okay if I go for a short walk now?"

"Of course," Kay says, "but, this time, please keep track of the time. That's what the watch on your wrist is for, you know. And please don't be gone more than an hour. I promised my mother I'd be home in time to make dinner."

"Yeah, M, and try to stay on the trail," Carlton says, "I don't understand how you get so dirty."

Walking along the river, Mo thinks about Carlton's questions and his evening with Mike. He wonders why Carlton asked if he felt uncomfortable or anything seemed weird when he slept over. Why would Carlton worry? Should *he* be worried? Are Carlton's worries similar to Grandma Cleveland's worries twelve years earlier?

The afternoon after Miss Clara left, Mo's grandmother held Jake on her lap as she fed him with a bottle.

Mo played with Jake's toes. "Grandma, why did Baby Jacob's mom leave?"

"Because she had done all she could. May God be with her."

"Did she *have* to leave?"

His grandmother took a moment to consider Mo's question before answering. "She chose to leave." She held Jake closer. "Sometimes God chooses when it's time for us to leave. Your mama, she had to leave. God decided it was her time. Baby Jacob's mother? That was her choice, and her reasons are between her and God."

Jake looked at Mo, flashing a toothless grin.

Mo made a goofy face back at his brother. "Can I hold him, Grandma?"

"Not right now. You need to read a chapter in your book first."

Mo grabbed *The Adventures of Huckleberry Finn* off the dry sink on his way to the living room. "Okay, *then* can I hold Baby Jake?"

"I'm putting him down to sleep now, so we'll see how he is after he wakes up. You know how fussy he gets." Grandma Cleveland carried Jake to the downstairs bedroom and laid him in his crib. Peering through the doorway, she said, "Alright, baby's sleeping, so keep it down."

"Okay, Grandma." Mo sprawled across the sofa and opened the book, reminding himself that Jim and Huck were on a raft making their way down the Mississippi, Jim had been sold for forty dirty dollars, and Huck was scheming to steal him back out of slavery. Mo wondered if the money was physically dirty or dirty because it was used to buy a Black man.

Grandma Cleveland turned on the radio, keeping the volume low while she washed dishes.

Before long, Mrs. Harrington appeared at the rear screen door. "Hello, Anne," she said. "Can I come in?"

"Hi, Janice. Of course. You know you're always welcome."

Mrs. Harrington gave her a hug. "Finally got a spare minute to drop by to see the baby."

"I just put him down for a nap." Grandma Cleveland motioned to the downstairs bedroom. "He's right in there. You can wake him, and I'll put him back down afterwards."

Mrs. Harrington gave Mo a little wave as she walked by, returning to the kitchen holding Jake. "Oh, he's adorable. Where's his mother?"

Grandma Cleveland raised her hand in front of Mrs. Harrington, increasing the radio volume with the other. "Hold on a second, Janice," she said. "Let me hear this." The color drained from her face. "Mo, turn on the television. President Kennedy's been shot."

Mrs. Harrington took a seat on the sofa next to Mo. Grandma Cleveland laid Jake back in his crib before collapsing into Ken's recliner. They watched Walter Cronkite put on his familiar thick-rimmed glasses to report:

FROM DALLAS, TEXAS, THE FLASH APPARENTLY OFFICIAL, PRESIDENT KENNEDY DIED AT 1:00 P.M. CENTRAL STANDARD TIME—TWO O'CLOCK EASTERN STANDARD TIME—SOME THIRTY-EIGHT MINUTES AGO.

Grandma Cleveland and Mrs. Harrington looked at each other and began sobbing.

Mo knew his father voted for Kennedy, and though Ken had both praised and criticized the young president, he believed his father admired him. He thought back to hunting in the cold, damp woods, his father firing in the darkness at the innocent deer.

"I don't understand," Mrs. Harrington said through sniffles, "why would someone want to assassinate that nice, young man?"

Grandma Cleveland wiped away tears. "I just don't know. I know that nice, young *Black* man, Martin Luther King, said recently he has dreams, but I think maybe all we got is worries. I worry about the world our grandchildren are inheriting. We been through so much in our lives: hardships of The Great Depression, losing our fathers and brothers to war, and then sacrificing our sons all over again. But we fought the good fight; always had hope and promise." She paused, reaching for a handkerchief in her apron. "I worry about these kids. I worry about Mo and little Jake. Ain't no hope. Ain't no promise. Just cynicism and violence. And those wars will just keep coming. And, for what? Can't make no sense of it." She looked over to where Mo was sitting, quiet and face blank. "I want these boys to stay safe, but I don't know what's gonna happen." Jake started crying. "I gotta take care of that baby. Somebody's gotta take care of these kids, or they'll lose their way. Now, someone's gone and killed the president. Who's next? When will we stop hating and fighting and killing? I worry about the changes coming. Will they come fast enough? Will they be big enough? Will they come before our dreams turn into nightmares? I just got worries."

Teary-eyed, Mrs. Harrington nodded, hugged Grandma Cleveland, and trudged out of the room.

Mo heard the screen door close and Mrs. Harrington's steps on the porch stairs. He watched Grandma Cleveland dry her eyes and slowly rise from the recliner to quiet Jake. Opening his book and sprawling across the sofa, he exchanged his grandmother's worries for Huck's dilemmas, though he didn't understand anything about slavery, prejudice, or societal norms—not any more than he did about assassination, hate, or war.


Wet and muddied, standing alone by the Wood River, Mo removes his gloves and places them in his pocket. His anxiety, stripped away, masked by falling leaves, now rests at his feet. The independence he's gained over the eighteen months since Grandma Cleveland died has come at the cost of greater unease. What did she think of his treatment by the Branches and his banishment to Rhode Island? And how he's handled the adversity—Emily, Veronica, Jim? And the resulting trauma?

Would Grandma Cleveland still have worries?

# A STAIN ON THE LANDSCAPE

## MONDAY, 29 SEPTEMBER 1975

*P almer pulls his car into the Providence Police and Fire Headquarters parking lot a little before eight.* When Palmer arrives at his office on the third floor, Police Chief Steven Metcalf is sitting behind his desk talking to State Police Captain of Homicide Jefferson Monroe. Flipping through a file as they talk, Monroe is seated on the opposite side of Metcalf's desk.

Metcalf made his mark investigating organized crime in the city, working with state and federal authorities to bring the head of the New England Crime Family to justice. When it came time to appoint a new chief four years earlier, his experience and relationship-building skills earned him the promotion. He's not afraid to use his position, influence, and resources to enlist the support of his friends at the state police and FBI when things get messy. He knows the current mess is spreading.

Metcalf motions Palmer to take a seat. "Investigator Palmer, good morning, come on in. Good to see you again. I believe you know Detective Monroe from the state police."

Palmer winks at Monroe. "We've worked together in the past."

"This one's escalating, Frank," Monroe says. "In addition to the three dead girls, we've got a handful of new missing persons reports here in Providence, North Smithfield, Slatersville, and across the line in Rehoboth. We thought the first one, Carr, was an accident, maybe fell into some rocks while walking across the dam at Stillwater. We figured the bruise on her left temple might've been from hitting a rock when she fell."

Palmer takes a seat next to Monroe. "Do we have an estimated date on that one?"

Monroe runs his fingers across morning stubble. "She was reported missing on the seventh and last seen by her parents the previous afternoon, so we believe she was killed the afternoon or evening of the sixth. Didn't seem to be any connection to the Nadeau girl—the one whose body was found in the woods near Lincoln Park in North Dartmouth. That one looked to be the boyfriend. It didn't initially match the M.O. because the victim's eye had been pierced with a sharp, jagged object. But the guy has an airtight alibi, and forensics later identified blunt force trauma just above the girl's left eye."

Palmer pulls out a cigarette. "You mind?"

Monroe shakes his head.

"Fine by me." Metcalf walks around the desk, sits on the edge. "I might need one myself if this continues."

Palmer strikes a match. "Tell me about the third girl."

Monroe's eyes shift between Palmer and Metcalf. "Name's Meagan Beth Hooper. Another young brunette. Out jogging. Found her body along Olney Pond in Lincoln Woods just north of the city. Non-lethal head trauma around the left temple. Asphyxiation by drowning. Looks to be about two weeks ago." He drops a folder in Palmer's lap. "Here's everything we've got so far."

Palmer flips through the photos. "Any connection between the girls? Did they go to school together? Common friends? Related in any way?"

"Not from what we can tell. Only connections so far are age, physical similarities, and trauma to the left temple." Monroe glances at Metcalf before looking back at Palmer. "Frank..." he pauses, staring at Palmer. "They found another body just before you got here. Another young girl. My guys are securing the scene."

Palmer stands. "What's the location?"

Metcalf lifts himself from the desk. "I'll have a car escort you to the scene." He massages his forehead. "We gotta get this guy, Frank. I've got three teenage daughters..." he pauses, "and they've all got my wife's brown hair."

Sandra Lynn Grafiano—nineteen, five foot five, a buck fifteen, brown hair, blue eyes, healthy, fit, pretty, daughter, sister, part-time waitress. Maybe a notch in a belt or two; otherwise, too young to have left a permanent mark. She'll be remembered by family, friends, and schoolmates; neighbors, parishioners, and old boyfriends. And now, apart from being probable victim number four, soon to be forgettable. But not today. Today she's news. Another tragic story. A stain on the landscape. Evidence.

The trail's closed off in this part of Arcadia Management Area, with cruisers parked between trees and a handful of blue uniforms strung along the path. A cluster of blue and black stand down near the pond, and a news chopper hovers over the water. Twenty-five yards down, two young men are sitting on a log beside the trail.

Without breaking stride, Palmer flashes his badge and descends the embankment. Pressing his fully smoked cigarette into the dirt and pulling out another, he hears the whispers.

Dean Stricker, a horseshoe-mustached walrus with spectacles, comes strutting over. "Chief Investigator Palmer, what a pleasant surprise."

Palmer continues his descent. "Morning, State Trooper Stricker."

Stricker stomps his foot. "It's *Detective* Stricker, and we got this, Frank."

Palmer's eyes stare straight ahead. "I know you do, Lieutenant. I'm just an interested observer today."

Stricker walks alongside Palmer. "Who called you in? Was it Monroe?"

Palmer doesn't respond. Reaching the officers by the water, he holds up an unlit cigarette. "Anybody got a light?" Several matchbooks are thrust in his face. After pulling, he shakes the match and tosses it without looking up, releasing the first surge of smoke in silence, focused on the girl's lifeless body several yards away, her Nikes resting in the water. "What do you think, fellas?"

Bright-eyed and grinning, a young blue with no neck and sideburns down to his shoulders steps forward. "We were talking about how she looks like she's dreaming, Chief Investigator Palmer."

Palmer nods. "Yeah, I always wonder whether it's easier or harder this way." He checks the officer's name patch. "Well, Officer Rullo, would you prefer a gruesome murder scene or one like this? Which do you think the victim prefers?" He looks over at the other officers. "Maybe her parents will be thankful for an open casket? Or maybe they'll be disappointed to discover there's less evidence."

Rullo pulls back, mouth open, head down.

Palmer, lowering his shoulders, looks up into Rullo's downcast eyes. "Yeah, I guess it doesn't matter. It's all a nightmare for them, right?"

Stricker pushes the stunned officer back. "Alright, Frank, enough with the theatrics. Leave the kid alone."

Palmer glares at the assembled blue and black. "I thought this was an investigation of a crime scene."

Stricker puts his hand on Palmer's shoulder. "Calm down. Crime Scene Management just left. We're just waiting for the coroner."

Palmer pulls away. "If they're done investigating, then get them the hell out of here."

Stricker waves the officers off. Turning back to Palmer, he lowers his voice. "It doesn't look like sexual assault. No signs of a struggle, so she was either drugged or subdued before being held underwater."

Palmer leans over the body, his face inches from the victim's face, her ponytail still in a hair tie. "There's a bruise above her left temple." He straightens up. "It's barely visible below the hairline, but it's there. I believe it's how the killer subdued her."

"That?" Stricker looks from the dead girl's feet. "That could be a pimple."

"But it's not."

"The coroner's office will be here shortly." Stricker sucks in his gut, tugs on his belt. "We'll know more after they take a look."

"When was the body discovered?"

"About seven this morning." Stricker points to the two young men sitting on a log. "Those fellas found her lying there. Called it in about twenty minutes later."

Palmer scans the nearby waterline. "Any physical evidence

around the scene? Footprints? Anything left behind?"

"Nothing worthwhile. We recovered a hat, but it's probably the girl's. Took a few photos of the soil around the body, a few light indentations, but nothing conclusive." Stricker looks up at the coroner's station wagon backing down the slope. "Hold on. I gotta take care of this."

Palmer bends down to look at two rocks protruding from the dirt, a foot from the victim's head. Standing up, he heads over to the two young men. "Good morning, gentlemen. I'm Chief Investigator Palmer with the FBI. Can I ask you a few questions?"

The shorter one, with neck-length hair and tight-fitting cutoff jeans, answers. "Yes, sir, but we already gave our information to the heavy officer over there a little while ago."

"I understand," Palmer says, offering them each a cigarette, "but I just got here, and I'd like to talk to you for a few moments if you don't mind. I apologize if the questions are redundant."

"Okay," the beard in Bermuda shorts, thin as construction paper, says, shielding his eyes from the sun.

Palmer crouches in front of them. "What time was it when you discovered the body?"

Cutoffs answers first. "A little before seven this morning."

"What were you doing in the park so early?"

"We just decided to go for a walk."

"Do you walk here often?"

"Sometimes. We have some friends that live near here, so when we visit overnight, we might take a walk around Ben Utter Trail here."

"How did you discover the body?"

"We were walking," Bermuda says, searching his bag, "and we stopped to rest on this log."

Cutoffs raises a finger. "I saw her yellow top first."

Frustrated, Bermuda pulls his hands from the bag. "Anyway, we could see it was a girl, just like you can now, because of the clothes and her ponytail, but we thought she was asleep by the water. Obviously, she wasn't asleep, so I went back to the car and drove to our friend's house to call the police."

"Did either of you touch the body?"

Cutoffs bridges his fingers, raising them to his chin. "When we got down to her, she didn't look dead. We thought she was sleeping, so I tapped her shoulder." He looks at Palmer, eyes watery. "She didn't move; just stayed sleeping." Pushing up on the log, he straightens his back. "Geez, we jumped when we realized she was dead. She doesn't look dead. We thought she was sleeping." He shakes his head.

"So, you walked around the girl's body?"

Bermuda nods. "We thought she was sleeping."

"So I've heard. Did either of you step between the rocks near her head?"

Cutoffs raises his hand.

Palmer's knees crack as he stands. "You left your names and addresses with the fat trooper?"

They nod.

"Okay. Thank you, fellas." Palmer takes a few steps before turning back. "Oh, one last question. Did either of you know the girl?"

"No, sir." Bermuda leans back, withdrawing into the shadow of a tree. "We don't live here."

"Yes, you did say that, didn't you?"

Palmer walks back to where the corpse is being loaded into the coroner's station wagon, stopping behind Stricker. "All four have mild trauma to the left side of the head, near or above the temple."

Stricker faces Palmer. "We don't know that about this one."

Palmer motions in the direction of Cutoffs and Bermuda. "Get someone out to their friend's house. Find out where they were late yesterday afternoon and last night." Palmer drops his cigarette. "Probably nothing, but you need to check them out."

"I already talked to them. Got their statements before you arrived. I know what I'm doing."

"Well, then, you can have your officer up there give the one in Bermuda shorts his denim bucket hat back."

Stricker's face turns red. "I know how to do my job, Frank."

Palmer starts up the hill. "Never said you didn't," he says, his voice growing louder, "but Monroe called me in for a reason."

# 54

# FLATBUSH'S SILENCE

## TUESDAY, 30 SEPTEMBER 1975

Mo sits against the wall of Tito's Taco Shop with Jake's most recent letter unfolded on his lap. Holding it under the table, hidden from view, he rereads his brother's words, hoping they've somehow changed overnight. But they still bring misery. In addition to being upset with Jake's new letter-writing cadence, he doesn't believe his brother's suggestion that Mr. and Mrs. Branch will welcome him back for Thanksgiving. He's sure it's just another lie. His anger palpable, he crushes the letter and shoves it back into his pocket, silently stewing as he waits for his burrito.

Today is the first time Mo's working alongside Flatbush. Aside from the shortest of greetings and minimal instruction, Flatbush doesn't speak. Flatbush never speaks. So Mo spent a quiet morning edging lawns, thinking about Jake's letter, and becoming increasingly bitter. Now, having revisited his brother's words, and with Flatbush sitting across from him reading the paper undisturbed, Mo resigns himself to his fate. He resolves to focus on his life in Rhode Island going forward. Here, among housemates, work family, and friends, he feels appreciated. He'll continue to write his brother, but only once a month, and only in response to receiving a letter. He will no longer allow himself to be disappointed by Jake's correspondence, news of the Branch family, or anything else that remains from his past in Virginia.

When the food arrives, Mo hands Flatbush several napkins.

Flatbush nods. The rustling of the newspaper is the only sound he makes.

Sitting next to Mo, Griffin nudges him with his elbow. "Why so glum today, son? Thought you'd be talking up a storm about the playoffs with the guys."

"I know," Mo says. "I am excited about the playoffs. Saturday's going to be a great day. After the game, Kay and Carlton are taking me to Roger Williams Zoo." Mo's eyes display a sliver of their normal wonder. "I've never been to a zoo before."

"Sounds exciting. So why do you seem down?"

Mo rolls the saltshaker between his hands. "I got a letter from my brother yesterday. Mr. and Mrs. Branch will only let him write one letter a month from now on."

Griffin smiles. "Doesn't seem so bad, does it? I mean, he must be very busy with school and chores, right?"

"I guess, but that's not what's bothering me the most."

"So, what is it then?"

Mo stares at the saltshaker. "Emily's lying to her parents, saying Jake isn't doing his homework and isn't keeping up at school. Jake says he's doing fine, but they believe Emily."

Griffin places his hand on Mo's shoulder. "Why would you let it bother you? They'll find out the truth when they meet with his teacher or when grades come out, right?"

Mo, head hung down, sets the saltshaker on the table. "I'm afraid Emily's lying will make Jake have to leave like I did."

Griffin pats Mo's back. "That's not gonna happen. You said the Branches are adopting your brother. It sounds like she's just doing typical teenage girl stuff like playing pranks on her brothers, teasing them, even lying to get them in trouble. I'm sure she does the same things to her other brothers."

Mo looks at Griffin. "I guess you're right. Jake did say she's mean to Peter, too." Running his finger along his nose, he wipes a tear on his shirt. "Jake's really smart. Mr. and Mrs. Branch will see he's not falling behind at school. Then, they'll know Emily's lying. And if Jake can only write one letter a month, then I'll only write one letter a month, so they don't get mad at him for getting too many letters. I'll show them I'm busy, too. I have lots of friends here."

"That's the spirit," Griffin gives Mo one final pat on the back. "You do have a lot of friends, and some are right here at the table.

I'm sure they'd be interested in hearing your thoughts on the Red Sox's chances. I know I am."

Heeding Griffin's words, Mo contributes to the group's conversation with a wealth of statistics. When the discussion migrates from baseball to the discovery of a fourth girl's body, Mo withdraws with little interest and nothing to offer.

Nearing lunch's end, Griffin gives Mo a friendly punch to the arm. "Feeling better?"

"Yes, sir."

"Have you spoken with Professor Langford recently?"

Mo nods. "I slept over his house Friday night."

Griffin's eyebrows raise, his tone an octave higher. "*Really?*"

Mo notices Flatbush fold his paper and look over. "We meet for lunch every Wednesday, and I've slept over his house twice. The first time, I met a bunch of his friends. Then, we went fishing the next day."

"It sounds like you two are becoming fast friends." Griffin's eyebrows furrow. "What were his friends like?"

Mo scratches behind his ear. "They seemed okay. They use a lot of big words. Mike says he's not going to be friends with them anymore. He says he wants more friends like you and me—normal friends, I guess."

Griffin laughs. "Sounds like you met some of his high-society pals. I'm sure that must've been interesting. Not sure they'd appreciate our kind."

Observing Flatbush as Griffin talks, Mo witnesses no emotion. As usual, Flatbush doesn't say a word. Instead, he listens, stone-faced, staring at their boss.

"Listen, Mo," Griffin says, "always remember there's good in everyone, even in Professor Langford's friends. Sometimes, you just have to get past the muck."

Mo nods.

"So, what do you do when you sleep over?"

"We watch TV and talk. Oh yeah, and we eat dinner and have snacks at night."

"Do other people sleep over?"

"His friends slept over the first time, but it was just me and Mike this past Friday night."

Griffin leans a little closer to Mo. "And where do you sleep?"

"I sleep in one of the other bedrooms." Mo's eyes fill with excitement. "He has seven bedrooms in his house, but he lives there alone. Have you been there?"

"No, I haven't. Are you sleeping over his house again anytime soon?"

"I don't know, but I hope so. I have a lot of fun there, and he has a big TV."

Griffin leans back. "Sounds like you will." He rubs his chin. "Maybe the three of us should go fishing again. I'll have to ask him next time I see him."

Flatbush unfolds his paper and resumes reading.

Several minutes later, after pulling on his Red Sox cap, Griffin claps his hands. "Let's go."

Mo goes back to work with Flatbush. And silence.

# 55

# ELVIS & COSTELLO

**WEDNESDAY, 1 OCTOBER 1975**

*P* *almer sits at a window booth, working on a third morning coffee and fifth cigarette.* He waits for Agent Ross and his sidekick at the Downtown Providence Howard Johnson's near the corner of Weybosset and Dorrance, a short and equidistant walk from Palmer's hotel and the Providence Police and Fire Headquarters. A little after eight thirty, he spots Ross and his new protege crossing the parking lot. The younger agent struts, taking long, confident steps—yellow-tint Ray-Bans scanning from side to side. Ross shuffles, struggling to keep pace—a beige balloon in a trench coat floating alongside. Despite his humorless mood, Palmer is reminded of Abbott and Costello.

Ross tosses his coat on the seat opposite Palmer. "Morning, Frank. How you been?"

Palmer surveys Ross's tie, suffocating as Ross squeezes into the booth and slides to the window.

"This is Agent Lowe," Ross says, out of breath. "Not sure if you've met him."

Looking out the window, Palmer ignores the introduction.

Lowe hangs off the edge of Ross's bench. He reaches his hand across the table. "Hello, Agent Palmer. We met once at the lab. I'm Nelson Lowe."

From the side, Palmer glances at Lowe's hand, blowing a cloud of smoke at the window. He slides the ashtray away from the center of the table. "It's eight forty-five, gentlemen. This isn't a nine-to-five job."

"Sorry, Frank," Ross says, nudging Lowe. "The kid here was late to the office."

Lowe brushes the arm of his sport coat. "Yeah, it's my fault. Wife asked me to drop the kids off at school."

Ross rolls his eyes, muttering, "Oh, shit, here we go."

Palmer turns to face them, glaring at the metal frames of Lowe's sunglasses. "Let me give you some advice, Agent Lowe: family and career don't mix. Pick one or the other, but not both. You wanna play daddy? Doting husband? Be late for work? Get a construction job." He looks out the window. "You wanna be an FBI agent, either leave raising the kids to their mother or leave the wife."

Ross loosens his tie knot. "Geez, Frank, you're subtle as shit. I thought *I* was jaded after twenty-nine years of this job."

"Gerry, I'm not gonna take lessons on friendliness from you." Palmer frowns, focusing on Ross's pursed lips and the twin bowling pins on his forehead—a permanent seven-ten split separating arched eyebrows. "You wake up an ornery bastard, and it's the best part of your day."

A middle-aged waitress with cyclone hair and thick, layered lipstick stands over them, chomping her Wrigley spearmint. "Can I get you boys anything?"

Taking off his FBI cap, Ross hands it to Lowe. "Morning, sugar. I'll have coffee and a stack of pancakes."

"Put your hat back on, Gerry, before you blind Agent Lowe." Palmer turns to The Cyclone. "Ignore him, please."

"C'mon, Frank. We haven't eaten this morning."

"You can skip a few meals." Palmer nods toward Lowe. "And Elvis here doesn't look like he eats pancakes or anything else that might damage muscle tissue. You want a coffee, Lowe?"

Lowe nods.

"Just three coffees to go, please. Thank you, ma'am."

"Damn, Frank. You never change." Ross's stomach grumbles, sending a shiver across the table.

"Neither do you, Gerry." Palmer grabs several folders. "Okay, let's get you two caught up. Here's what's been collected on the four girls." He hands the folders to Ross. "I need you to circle back around to statements collected on the victims; talk to the families and friends. I know the police have already talked to most of them, but I need your perspective on this. Let's see if there are any connections between the girls, the individuals who discovered the bodies, or any common friends or acquaintances. Doesn't seem to be on the surface, but let's run those to ground. Collect all the names, including neighbors. You know the drill."

Palmer turns to Lowe. "You need to talk to forensics. From what I've been able to gather, there's no wet evidence. It's clear the killer doesn't have a sexual motive. Maybe he's got mommy issues, I don't know, but we need to start profiling this son of a bitch. Frankly, there's almost no evidence to work with. Several footprints were photographed and cast at the crime scenes, but there was significant contamination by the individuals who discovered the bodies. It appears there are at least two unique footprints at each location, possibly a consistent larger one, but the size and type of footwear are indeterminable at this point. Just not a whole helluva lot to go on."

Palmer places his cigarette on his lower lip. He spins a stack of photos on the table, starts flipping through them. "What we do know is all were found fully clothed with no evidence of a struggle. All the victims are young females—mid-teens to early twenties—and have brown hair. They all went out to wooded locations—recreational areas to walk or jog—and all ended up with a contusion on the left side of their head above the temple. In every case, the cause of death was either asphyxiation by apparent chokehold or drowning."

Palmer takes a quick drag and exhales. "Gut instinct tells me the killer's tall and powerful. Given the location of the blunt force trauma and larger footprints, I'd put him at a couple of inches taller than I am, possibly six-four or six-five, maybe taller. It's not much to work with, so I need you to follow up with state forensics. Have soil samples and clothing, along with anything collected from the victim's skin and hair, sent back to the lab in Boston. Let's see if there's anything else in trace evidence—foreign hair, fibers, soil, plant material—anything we can start building from."

Palmer takes his coffee from The Cyclone, hands her a ten, and slides out of the booth. "I'm gonna talk to Metcalf and take a walk around the crime scenes. I'll also give Osmond a call to request some research support. I need to see if there have been any similar crimes along the East Coast; have them check the database of known felons in Rhode Island and southeastern Massachusetts. We're grasping at straws, but it's all we've got at this point." He steps away.

Ross motions Lowe to slide out of the seat. "We're on it, Frank."

Several steps from the table, Palmer stops, turns back. "Oh, and Agent Lowe?" He digs in his shirt pocket for a Marlboro. "Lose the shades. This isn't Hollywood, and we're not chasing tail."

- 56 -

# PREYING ON A
# WILLING VICTIM

## FRIDAY, 3 OCTOBER 1975

**P**almer has never been interested in what sprouts from the ground. He's never been inclined to tinker in a garden, places no symbolic value on flowers, and never forgave his father for not hiring a lawn service when he was young. So, the prospect of spending a Friday morning with Dr. Daniel Ryan, listening to the FBI forensic expert list off scientific names of flowers, shrubs, and trees, is, to Palmer, the investigative equivalent of water torture.

Located in the basement laboratory of the FBI Boston Field Office, Ryan's office is windowless and claustrophobic. Surrounded by gray, mason block walls, Palmer and Lowe sit in orange plastic chairs squeezed between stacks of research documents and scientific journals.

Walking through his office door, Ryan tilts his head, offering an abbreviated wave. "Good morning." He nods at Palmer. "Frank."

Palmer knows Ryan's monotone presentation will test his endurance. Before long, lost in scientific names, he watches Ryan's hands flip through sheets of green bar computer paper while he waits for a point. Ryan's hands are extraordinary—very large with thick fingers, hair creeping from under his shirtsleeve, crawling across the back of his hand, and running down to his knuckles. Along with his pronounced buck teeth, Palmer thinks Ryan more lab beaver than rat.

Palmer clears his throat. "Dan, is all this ancient Greek heading somewhere?"

Ryan sighs. Closing his eyes, he rubs his temples. "I thought *you*, of all people, would be interested in what we were able to retrieve from the soil samples."

Palmer waves his hand. "Continue."

Ryan straightens up. "Alright then, I'll summarize. And I'll try to use as many simple words in plain English as possible." His eyes transfer from Palmer to Lowe. "It's Agent Lowe, correct?"

Lowe looks up from his notepad. "That's right."

"Agent Palmer, here, is beloved by us lab folks for reasons I'm sure you're already aware." Ryan nods in Lowe's direction. "Maybe *you* will understand why what I'm saying is important."

Unfazed, Palmer reaches for his shirt pocket.

Ryan points at Palmer. "Don't you dare."

Pulling his hand back, Palmer slouches, settling in for more tedium.

Ryan's eyes stay on Palmer as he turns back to Lowe. "The dirt samples from the clothing and neck tissue of two of the victims show significant plant matter in addition to processed products like mulch, bark, and fertilizer. Silt loam, consistent with Rhode Island's glacial till landscape, is present as well. The plant matter is largely consistent with Rhode Island native species, but the variety, when compared to the localized plant profile of the crime scenes, implies you may be looking for someone—"

Lowe points his pen at Ryan. "Who works in a greenhouse or on a farm!"

Swallowing hard, Ryan glances at Palmer before returning his attention to Lowe. "Let me continue, please. When taken independently, the variety *may* imply the killer works on a farm or in a greenhouse. But I suspect they are more apt to be found in botanical gardens or large institutions like hospitals, schools, or state and county buildings. It's also possible for some bigger corporate compounds to have large, complex plant networks. Therefore, I believe it's quite possible the killer works for the government or another large-scale employer with substantial and diverse landscaping, maybe a floral supply wholesaler."

Palmer rises from his chair. "This is helpful, Dan. It leaves a lot of ground to cover, but points us in the right direction."

Lowe closes his notepad.

Ryan motions them to remain seated. "Hold on. I think you may find this next bit of information interesting." He slides a folder to the center of his desk. "We found plant matter in the samples that did not match any native Rhode Island species. It also did not match any of our data records within the Bureau, so we had to do a bit more digging." He pulls a photo from the folder and holds it up. "Do either of you know what this is?"

Palmer and Lowe lean forward to investigate the image on the photo—a vertical string of flowers along a green shaft with pink and lavender petals forming what appear to be lips around a crystalline white tongue. They shake their heads.

Ryan glares at Palmer. "I'll apologize in advance for the big words. It's a *Spiranthes sinensis* or Chinese spiranthes. Part of the orchid family, spiranthes are commonly known as ladies' tresses. We have them all over Rhode Island and across the United States. They're effectively wildflowers, or weeds, growing almost anywhere: gardens, large open fields, roadsides. Because they have twelve to twenty-four seeds on each plant, they spread, well, like wildflowers."

Lowe shifts in his chair. "If it's a wildflower and it grows anywhere, why's it important?"

Palmer motions Lowe to stop talking.

Ryan turns to Palmer. "I'm glad I finally have your attention. Most American spiranthes are white, or a mix of faint yellow and white, as they are here in Rhode Island, but these are quite colorful, as you can see." He taps his finger on the photo. "The *Spiranthes sinensis,* like the one shown here, is a scientifically significant species, with plant matter used in medicines to treat fatigue, inflammation, and kidney diseases."

Lowe scratches his head. "I'm sorry, Dr. Ryan. Can you spell that, please?"

"I've prepared some documentation for you to take with you. It's courtesy of the Harvard University School of Botany, from their research work with Wuhan University in China, and should provide everything you need." Ryan slides the folder in front of Lowe and places the photo on top of it. "Despite being widespread, the *Spiranthes sinensis* does have several sub-species considered rare, including this colorful variant which botanists believe may only be found in the Chinese Himalayas. They're still working on a classification for this particular one as either a subspecies or variety. Therefore this designated, but still-unnamed, variant isn't exported from China. So it would be difficult to near impossible to bring into the United States other than by exception from Chinese and US Customs for use in medicinal or botanical research."

Lowe slides to the edge of his chair. "So, you're saying we need to look at research labs?"

Palmer snaps his fingers. "Agent Lowe! Let Dr. Ryan finish."

"You might start at research facilities in the pharmaceutical industry or with universities having medical programs or offering botany as a graduate program. However, you may want to talk to US Customs first. See if they can pull up a list of individuals or programs having been granted permission from Chinese authorities to bring this specific *Spiranthes sinensis* into the country. Given its status as a potential variant, it has a preliminary classification designator that I've provided in the documentation package. That would be how Customs would have tracked any possible imports into the US."

Palmer tugs at the pack of Marlboros burning against his chest. "And if Customs has no record of these orchids coming into the country?"

"If Customs is unable to help, I suppose you could visually inspect the grounds of major institutions in the general area you believe the killer might be located. There would be an abundance of these clustered if they do exist. This variant appears to only grow in a boreal climate, so they typically flower in very late spring and early summer. However, they might flower later, possibly into very early fall, in a temperate climate. Even so, it's unlikely they would bloom this late in the year. As a result, I suspect you would be looking for the rosette of leaves forming the base. It remains green all year. If you do find any intact, and they have retained their stems, you will see the remains of glandular hairs near the base that distinguish this variant. I've provided pictures of the base and stems as well. We also have the means to verify this particular plant here at the lab now."

Palmer checks the clock above Ryan's head, still with his hand over his shirt pocket. "Is that everything?"

"Just one last thing. If you must conduct visual inspections, I believe you may want to start your search at the highest elevations in the area, as this variant of *Spiranthes sinensis* only grows in the upper foothills of the Himalayas."

Palmer smiles and motions with his head for Lowe to follow him. "Thanks, Dan," he says, lifting a cigarette from his pocket. "Riveting as always."

Ryan's hand engulfs Palmer's. "You're welcome, Frank. Good luck finding this killer, and thank you for not smoking."


Apart from its trademark chrome vertically split grille, Pontiac's 1968 Bonneville doesn't attract much attention. Palmer's metallic-blue hardtop is pristine with low mileage. Most days, he walks to work. On rainy days, he takes a taxi. Everything he needs—groceries, newspapers, clothing, and nighttime diversions—is a short walk from his apartment. As a result, he passed on the factory eight-track option for an FBI-installed phone and under-dash gun mount. When not on the phone, he listens to the news on AM radio.

Phone ringing as he merges onto 95 South, Palmer pulls the receiver from the slip. "Yeah?"

An excited voice responds. "Frank?"

"Hey, Gerry. Finished up with forensics a few minutes ago. What do you got?"

"I'm here at the Providence police station. Metcalf received a call about ten minutes ago. Another body's been discovered at Hunt's Mill in East Providence. I'm getting ready to head there now."

"I wonder if that's the missing girl from Rehoboth. It's just over the state line."

Ross hesitates for a moment. "That's the Billington girl, right?"

"Yeah. Do you have a photo from the file?"

"I've got all the files with me."

Palmer registers an upcoming exit sign. "I'm about forty-five minutes out. Check the left side of the head for a bruise."

"Of course."

"Anything from the interviews?"

"No, nothing. I've talked to almost everyone. Background checks are clean, and there are no apparent connections. I've got a few left, but it appears the killings are completely random."

"Thanks, Gerry. Sounds like a textbook disorganized mass murderer. I'll be there as fast as I can." Palmer hangs up the phone, turns up the radio, and accelerates.

Southern New England's autumn foliage peaks in early October, but the natural beauty of the resultant colors is wasted on Palmer as he makes his way along the trail at Hunt's Mill. His eyes are focused on the riverbank and maze of footpaths crossing the primary trail, his ears on voices deeper in the woods. He catches up with Ross a little way down the trail.

Ross rests against a large boulder. "Hey, Frank, you made good time."

Palmer stands next to Ross, his foot on the boulder. "What's going on down there?"

"They're still working the scene. The body's in second-stage decomposition, starting to bloat a bit, but it's her—the Billington girl."

"Contusion near the temple?"

"Hard to tell with the discoloration."

"Who found the body?"

"A young couple from Pawtucket. They're sitting in the lot." Ross removes his trench coat, sweat stretching from his armpits to below his belt. "You want me to question them?"

Palmer pats Ross on the shoulder. "That's alright. We'll go talk with them in a few minutes. Let me take a look at the crime scene first. Just rest here."

Palmer approaches from the bank, his shoes teasing the water.

The victim's body lies face down in the mud, the back of the neck and sides of the face marbled gray. Crouching, Palmer checks along the left hairline, finding a darker brown area from a likely blood deposit. Several fist-sized rocks lie a few inches from her feet, sediment depressed between them. Palmer uses a twig to clear some leaves, revealing two distinct parallel depressions in the dirt moving away from the river. He clears several feet before Stricker approaches.

"Whatcha doing, Frank?"

Palmer rests the twig on his knees. "I'm enjoying a beautiful day on the river, Dean. What about you?"

Stricker crouches next to Palmer. "C'mon, whatcha looking at?"

Palmer points with the twig. "Look closely. These are the drag marks of her jogging shoes in the dirt. Have your men clear the leaves and debris to the path. With any luck, we may find a viable imprint or two of the killer's shoes."

"Been quite a bit of rain the past two weeks."

"That's true, but the leaf cover may have hardened the soil."

Stricker whistles, motioning to several officers. "Could end up being the footprints of the couple that found her."

"They're not." Palmer lights a cigarette, tossing the match into the river. "These tracks are covered with leaves. The couple that discovered the body has a dog, good-sized, and approached along the bank from the same direction I did." He points to the other side of the body. "You can see their depressions just above mine, with paw prints near her head. Those are the ones your boys have been taking photos of, but they're clearly fresh and go in both directions. So, the couple approached and retreated along the same path. They're also much smaller than my shoe prints, which, I believe, makes them too small to be the killer's." He points to the fist-sized rocks. "I believe the killer knelt here as he drowned her, then retreated along the water, in the opposite direction from where we approached, before rejoining the trail farther down. Those tracks will be impossible to locate after two weeks, but he dragged her along these lines from the trail after he subdued her. These leaves have been layering for a couple of weeks, so I believe we may be able to get a good imprint somewhere along here."

Three troopers approach.

Palmer takes a step to the other side of the drag marks. "Easy, fellas. Hold there for a second."

Stricker steps alongside Palmer. "We'll take it from here, Frank."

"Alright, Dean, but stay to the right of the drag marks."

Stricker lifts the bill of his cap, scratching his head. "Why? Which right?"

Palmer takes a few steps up the embankment before turning back to the troopers. "The drag marks will be through the killer's shoe prints unless he redirected. The killer's right-handed, so his corrections most likely would have been to his right with his back to the river. As you clear, stay to the right with your backs to the river. We may get lucky, find an undisturbed left shoeprint to the left of the drag marks."

Eyes wide and bracing themselves, the young couple watch with concern as Ross adjusts himself to the unnatural configuration of a picnic table. The fury of water cascading over Hunt's Mill Dam isn't sufficient to drown out the strain of carriage bolts and moaning of bench crosspieces against threads. Palmer watches the drama unfold from behind Ross.

"Good morning. I'm FBI Agent Ross, and this is Chief Investigator Palmer. We'd like to ask you a few questions." Picking his coat off the ground, Ross places it on the end of the table. Reddish-brown dirt rises in a flurry. "Are you okay with that?"

"It's fine," the young man says. "We've already talked to the police, but we'll answer any questions you have."

Ross opens his notepad. "Can we get your names, please?"

"Sebastian and Anita Hoffman."

"Do you live nearby?"

"We live in Pawtucket." Sebastian pets their German shepherd. "We like to let Schultz run around while we walk the trail."

"Is that what you were doing this morning?"

"Yes, sir."

Sebastian's Adam's apple skates along his neck like the slide of a trombone, and his left arm rests on the table in front of his wife. Hands clenched, his leg shakes feverishly outside the bench.

Anita taps her fingers—nails jagged, raw skin just beneath. She has a bald patch in her hairline, symptomatic of the trauma evident on her body—ligature marks on her wrists and a bruised right eye.

Ross continues. "What time did you get to the park?"

"About seven thirty," Sebastian says. "Maybe a little later."

"How long after you arrived did you discover the body?"

"We'd been walking about ten minutes when Schultz started sniffing around the water." Sebastian rubs the dog's ear. "He wouldn't come back when we called, so we went down to get him."

"What was the location of the body when you discovered it?"

"We walked along the water toward Schultz. When we got closer, we could see clothing through the leaves, then a hand almost touching the water."

"Did you touch or move the body?"

Sebastian shakes his head. "I just grabbed Schultzie's collar, and we came back up to the trail."

Looking down, Anita begins sobbing.

Palmer places his hand on Ross's shoulder. "Mrs. Hoffman, you and your husband were married quite recently, is that correct?"

Face still down, Anita nods.

"When was that?" Palmer lights a smoke.

Wiping her eyes, Anita looks at her husband. "Last month."

"Congratulations. And when is the baby due?"

Anita's eyes fix on Palmer, her mouth open.

Sebastian puts his hand on hers, voice trembling. "I don't see how this is relevant."

"Relax, Mr. Hoffman," Palmer says. "I'm not here to render judgment; just some friendly advice."

Anita pushes her husband's arm away at the wrist, frowning at Palmer. "The baby's due in March."

"Best wishes on the birth of your baby." Palmer points his cigarette at her hands. "I recommend you get some bacitracin on those fingers; maybe have a professional take a look before they get infected." He turns his attention to Sebastian with a glare that peers straight into the young man's soul. "You and your wife are free to go. I sincerely hope we won't need to speak with you again, Mr. Hoffman." He leans forward, placing his hand on the table. "You can be certain we'll contact you if that becomes necessary."

Walking back to the parking lot, Ross shakes the remaining dirt off his coat. "You talk to Osmond this morning?"

Palmer nods. "Swung by his office before heading to the lab."

"He tell you the survivor picked Bundy out of a lineup yesterday?"

"Bob in Seattle and Jerry in Salt Lake both gave me a call last night. I let Harry know this morning."

Ross pats Palmer on the shoulder. "They got him now."

"We'll see. The bastard's cagey."

Ross furrows his brows. "Hey, Frank, why'd you have to go there with these kids?"

Palmer opens his car door. "Go where?"

"Why investigate their relationship?" Ross says, putting his coat on.

"Because, Gerry, they have bigger problems." Flicking his cigarette onto the gravel, Palmer slides into the driver's seat, looking up at Ross. "So, maybe my words get Mrs. Hoffman to show a nurse her fingers, and maybe the nurse will notice Mrs. Hoffman's bruises and the bald spot in her hairline while documenting she's pregnant. Maybe the nurse will encourage Mrs. Hoffman to make an appointment to see a therapist along with an obstetrician. Then, maybe, Mrs. Hoffman will go; maybe work up the courage to tell somebody. And, maybe, just maybe, she'll get away from her piece-of-shit husband and raise that kid with her parents."

"Geez, Frank, I didn't think you cared."

Palmer looks up from the driver's seat. "I don't, Gerry. If I did, I'd talk to her parents and not leave it to a bunch of maybes."

Ross leans into the driver's window and taps on the chrome. "I saw the bruises. Why not bring the kid in for more questioning?"

Palmer stares straight ahead. "If he were a foot taller and right-handed, I'd have more interest. As it is, he's just another monster-in-waiting preying on a willing victim."

# 57

# FATHER'S BLACK-HAIRED CRITTERS

## SATURDAY, 4 OCTOBER 1975

Mo's baseball cards are spread out on the dining table; assembled so each Red Sox player in the starting lineup is placed in his defensive position. Only the first baseman is missing—the one card Mo still doesn't have. In a playful gesture, Trevor has placed the Oakland equivalents on the opposite side of the table. During commercial breaks of the pregame, Mo lurches over the cards before returning to the living room, where he stands by the sofa, stares at the television, checking his Timex intermittently.

When the first playoff game begins, he coils on the far end of the sofa, his hands gripped together, leaning on the armrest. He doesn't make a sound, his only movement involuntary shaking. Focusing on the screen, he does not blink. And he doesn't feel the four pairs of eyes monitoring his breathing pattern, his every facial expression. The tension in the townhouse is thicker than a bowl of his grandmother's cornbread batter.

What had been angst during the regular season is now agony in the playoffs. Watching her friend suffer, Kay suggests to Carlton that they head to Rogers Williams Park a little early. Mo's surprised when Carlton shakes him midway through the game, asking if he still wants to go to the zoo. Torn, Mo agrees under the condition they listen along the way. The anxiety in the house transfers to Carlton's car before arriving at the park midafternoon.

Despite resistance, Kay persuades Mo to leave his transistor radio in the car. "There are a lot of different things to do here," she says. "It's a pretty special place, according to my dad."

Strolling alongside her, Mo looks in Kay's direction as often as he can, careful not to walk into anyone. While helping take his mind off the game, it also makes him feel more buoyant.

"My father would tell me all about the park when I was young. Let's see how much I remember." Looking at the ground, she begins reciting. "Roger Williams Park is a Providence landmark located on 435 acres. It has eight lakes and borders Cranston to the south."

Her hand gestures and the cadence of her voice make Mo think of the waitress at McGuinn's reading the daily specials.

"Founded in 1871," Kay continues, "the park represents the last of the original land granted in 1638 to Providence Plantation by Chief Canonicus of the Narragansett tribe. Along with a museum of natural history, Victorian rose garden, and zoo, the park has a boathouse and an abundance of walking paths." She looks up at Mo. "How did I do?"

Mo smiles, hoping she won't quiz him.

Kay laughs. "That's good because I memorized the brochure while we were driving here. It took me years to figure out my dad would do the same thing to me."

Carlton walks behind them. "She does it all the time. I watched her preparing in the car while you were listening to the game."

Kay playfully elbows Mo. "Let's go to the rose garden first. I think you'll enjoy that, right?"

Mo nods, Kay's nudge leaving a warm tingle in his side.

The rose garden is beyond what even Mo could imagine. As he walks through a flurry of red, yellow, pink, and white, Mo's only comparison is Mr. Ford's Garden—equally colorful but significantly smaller. From a distance, a sea of tightly clustered white roses appears as the homemade sail of a fisherman's skiff, his mother's bedsheet tied to the mast, billowing in the breeze. The visual surges through him, carrying him back to one of the last times his mother was able to leave the house.

Not quite five, with red popsicle staining his shirt, Mo and his mother were drifting three property lines over in a light breeze and drowning heat to Jimmy Pierson's house, having been invited to watch the grand opening of Disneyland on their brand-new television. Their progress was slow, young Mo navigating as he held his mother's hand. They docked for a time in front of Mr. Ford's Garden, so his mother could inhale the sweet aroma of lilies, lavender, and gardenia.

When they finally arrived, Mo sat on the floor alongside Jimmy and his sister. Awestruck by their black-and-white television, Mo wondered what colors the flowers were in the floral arrangement of Mickey Mouse's face in front of the Disneyland train station. Looking back to the sofa behind him, he was touched by his mother's warm smile, her wooden cane by her side.

Mo bumps into a park bench, snapping him back from the past. He sees Kay walking with Carlton up ahead. His mother wasn't much older than Kay when she died. He wonders what Kay will be like when she becomes a mother. Will they still be his friends? Will they go to Disneyland together? Does Kay look forward to seeing him as much as Mo looks forward to seeing her? Having had similar questions about Emily when she was little, he shakes his head before catching up with his friends, letting them know he's had enough of the rose garden.

During the ten-minute walk to the zoo, the status of the game hangs over Mo like one of Old Man Southerland's prize-winning hogs at the Fauquier County Fair. However, working his way through the exhibits, his thoughts return to the past, and his parents, as he gazes upon animals he had previously seen only on television, in pictures, or as drawings in books his mother would read to him.

Stopping longest at the black bear and panther exhibits, Mo looks at the chain-link fence surrounding their enclosures. The fences make him feel safe—safe the way he does within the chain-link fence surrounding Mr. Griffin's home when he visits. When he was young, his father would tell him about the black bears and panthers that roamed the woods of southern Fauquier, though he never saw one. He recalls asking his father if they were the black-haired critters that got hung up in the trees and floated down the Rappahannock. But his father told him they weren't. His father's black-haired critters walked upright and spoke nonsense.

One night, when he was twelve, lying awake in bed and worried he might be one of those black-haired critters, Mo decided he would never again ask his father about them.

The afternoon sails by as Kay and Carlton wait patiently at each exhibit until Mo moves on to the next. Often, they seek cover from the late afternoon sun on a nearby park bench. When the zoo closes at six, their journey ends. His friends head out for a quiet dinner, leaving Mo to explore the park grounds. They agree to meet at Betsey Williams Cottage by eight. Park attendance thins out in the early evening, attractions closing, and most people switching their interests to Saturday night activities.

Mo walks to the more wooded southern end of the park, along some quieter trails around the ponds. Still unaware of the outcome of the game, Mo struggles to focus on other things. He thinks about the animals in the zoo, wishing Jake had come along. He wonders if Jake has gone to the zoo with the Branches, curious whether his brother wishes he were there with him. Thinking about his brother's letter, he wonders how Jake has been impacted by Emily's lies and her parent's resultant anger. Fearing what would happen if Jake were discarded by the Branches the way he was, Mo shudders at the thought of his brother being sent to the Fauquier Motor Lodge with The Woman Leaning Against the Door watching over him.

Trying to keep his mind on the zoo and the animals and Jake while he walks, his thoughts keep circling back to his banishment, to Emily and Mr. Branch and how it all ended—the day his path out of the Branch home was decided.

Mr. Branch looked haggard, his five o'clock shadow a tad longer, his white collared shirt a bit more wrinkled. "Mo will sleep in my home office until I figure out what to do."

"But, Daddy—" Paul cried.

"I cannot allow Mo to put our family at risk, and I will not listen to any more arguments. It won't happen again."

Nodding, Mrs. Branch stood next to her husband, her face like an overboiled egg.

"We'll set up the cot," Mr. Branch said.

Peter leaned forward from the sofa where he was sitting. "Dad, you can't make Mo stay in there all alone."

Next to his older brother, Paul's head hung low as he nodded.

Jake sat on the opposite end of the sofa with his fingers interlaced. "Please, Mr. Branch. Please don't make him sleep in there all alone. He'll be good. I promise."

Mr. Branch closed his eyes, shaking his head. "Boys, I've made up my mind, and that's it."

Paul raised his hand. "Can I sleep with him?"

Mr. Branch shook his head with greater vigor. "There's only one cot in there. A sleeping bag will be too cold on the floor."

"I don't mind," Paul said.

Mr. Branch glared at him. "No, young man, you're not sleeping with Mo. You have your own bed." His head fell to one side, his shoulders slumped, looking at Paul through the top of his lenses. "Besides, the storage boxes are in there."

The room went quiet. Paul walked over and sat beside Mo, hugging him as he sobbed.

Mr. Branch massaged his forehead. "Dion can sleep with Mo."

Paul looked up at his father, drying his eyes, brows furrowed. "How come *Dion* gets to sleep with him?"

"Because Dion's older, and he's not afraid of spiders."

Dion stared at Mo. In his mute gaze, Mo knew this Branch needed him as much as he needed Dion.

Paul shivered, his head resting on Mo's side. "How long do they have to sleep in there?"

Mr. Branch's voice was hoarse. "Mo will stay there until Virginia Social Services determines where he goes next. There will be no further discussion tonight. Everyone go to bed." He swept his hand. "Mo, come with me and bring Dion with you."

Head down, Mo followed Mr. Branch. Later that night, lying in his cot and not knowing who or what to pray for, he stayed up with Dion for hours before falling asleep.

When Mo's thoughts return to the present, he's clenching and unclenching his gloved hands. Having dragged himself, and his burden, through the trees and down to the lake, solace is present on the bank of Deep Spring Lake. When Mo arrives back at Betsey Williams Cottage a few minutes late, he's relieved to see Carlton approaching from the opposite direction. He follows Carlton back to the car, where Kay informs him that the Red Sox won. Laying across the back seat, his anxiety's lessened on several fronts.

# 58

# MOLESTATION

## MONDAY, 6 OCTOBER 1975

*P almer collects remnants of cool morning air in his palm.* Leaning against the cold cement of a portico column at the entrance to Boston Customs Tower, standing on the granite landing in a field of discarded cigarette butts, his eyes strain to read the words of a nearby billboard—*Come to where the flavor is.* He takes a puff, savoring the mythical flavor of his cigarette. He wonders if the taste is better somewhere else. Maybe in the tobacco fields of North Carolina or the wine region of Napa Valley outside San Francisco? In the mountains west of Denver or the steel mills in the Ohio River Valley? Pulling his hand from the portico column, he shakes off the cold, wondering what the weather's like in Middleton, Ohio, this morning.

Seeing Lowe climb the stairs, Palmer adds his unfinished cigarette to the collection at his feet, compressing the unobjectionable litter into grooves of rock slab with each step. He rereads the eye-level sign stating there's no smoking in the building, knowing their meeting will brief.

Lowe's wavy black hair bounces like the mane of a loping stallion as he ascends. He gives Palmer an abbreviated wave at the top. "Morning, boss."

"Agent Lowe," Palmer says, tipping his head. "Drop the kids off early this morning?" He snickers.

Lowe sighs. The two continue to the fourteenth floor in silence.

Herman Oglethorpe holds his office door open, waving his guests in. "Good morning, gentlemen. I apologize for the mess. We don't get many visitors here at the Animal and Plant Health Inspection

Service. As you might expect, they like to keep us cooped up." He chuckles.

Palmer checks the office view of the city. "Good morning, Mr. Oglethorpe. Thank you for agreeing to meet with us. I'm Chief Investigator Palmer with the Federal Bureau of Investigation. I believe you've already spoken with Agent Lowe."

"Yes, we talked on the phone." Oglethorpe motions for them to have a seat. "So, I understand you're interested in recent import history for a designated variant of *Spiranthes sinensis*." He rests his elbows on the desk, rubbing his hands together. "Does this have anything to do with the murders in the Providence area?"

Lowe scoots his chair forward. "It does. Please continue."

Oglethorpe points to a bowl on the desk. "Would you like some jellybeans, gentlemen? I apologize if there aren't any red ones. I always eat those first. I find they relieve stress."

Palmer, noticing the grime under Oglethorpe's fingernails, forces a smile. "Thank you, but I wouldn't want to spoil my breakfast."

"It normally takes weeks to research all the documentation for restricted plants or plant matter," Oglethorpe says, his eyes filled with childlike awe. "But, given it was at the request of the FBI, I instructed the team to research the matter over the weekend so we could provide some preliminary results." Oglethorpe pokes around the bowl with his finger. "We can do more extensive research, if required, but it would take weeks to sift through physical documents as opposed to microfiche." He leans back with several jellybeans in his palm. "Orange is okay when there's no more red." He tips the bowl away from himself. "Sure you're not interested?"

Palmer shakes his head, holding down the pulp that was his morning bagel.

Lowe winces as Oglethorpe tosses the jellybeans into his mouth before wiping his hand across his white collared shirt. "We appreciate your taking this matter seriously, Mr. Oglethorpe."

"We went through nine years of import data from China. There are codes to mark restricted species, subspecies, varieties, and designated variants you know." Oglethorpe chews while talking, spit collecting at the edges of his lips. "We were able to determine three unique instances of your designated variant coming into Logan on an approved waiver." He eases into his chair, placing his feet at the end of the desk.

Palmer witnesses the stress on Oglethorpe's shirt above his belt. "Would there be any other avenues for this flower to get into the area?"

Oglethorpe pats his belly. "There's always illegal transit, but I don't think anybody's trying to bring these flowers into the country as a form of illicit drug." Nodding, he smirks. "It's no *Cannabis sativa* if you know what I mean." He laughs, waiting for his guests to join in.

They do not.

Oglethorpe's smile fades. Taking his feet off the desk, he sits up. "No, I don't think so, Agent Palmer."

"Were you able to identify where this plant matter, or these flowers, went after they arrived at Logan?"

"Yes." Oglethorpe pulls a document from his desk drawer. "In two of the three instances, the material was delivered to a biologist at Pfizer in Cambridge. One shipment was in late 1973, the other in early 1974, both care of Dr. Charles Roeper." He points to Lowe's notepad. "It's a weird spelling, has an 'e' after the 'o.'"

Lowe nods, scribbling the biologist's name on his pad.

"Those arrived as plant matter, so they wouldn't have been usable for replanting. But..." Oglethorpe's eyebrows rise, "the instance from 1971 involved full flower stems brought into the country. They were carried in aircraft stowage by Professor Gan Hsu at Brown University Medical School on a research waiver." Oglethorpe reaches again for the jellybean bowl.

Unable to witness another candy molestation, and ready for a smoke, Palmer stands, tapping his knuckles on the desk. "Excellent, Mr. Oglethorpe. I really must be going. Please provide any relevant documentation to Agent Lowe. I can show myself out."

"Uh, thank you, Agent Palmer." Oglethorpe stands, cradling the bowl. "I-I have homemade saltwater taffy if you'd like to take some with you."

The door closes behind Palmer with a gentle click.

# GERMINATION

*Palmer can't help but compare laboratories.* The well-organized space and natural light of the Brown University Medical Research Laboratory are far superior to the congested and windowless basement lab at the Boston FBI Field Office. A transom window between Dr. Hsu's office and the large, open laboratory is angled open, as are the windows on the opposite wall. And though Hsu's office is well ventilated, all Palmer can smell is tuna fish.

Hsu takes a bite of his sandwich. "I'm sorry, Investigator Palmer, but I only have forty-five minutes to eat between classes."

Palmer runs his fingers across his nostrils. "That's fine, Doctor." He hands Hsu a photo of the orchid in question with its preliminary classification designator. "Can you tell me the reason you brought this variant of *Spiranthes sinensis* into the US in the summer of 1971?"

"Ah, yes. We were conducting a joint research project with the Beijing Medical School to evaluate its potential dietary benefits." Hsu bites into a bok choy stalk, crunching and swallowing before continuing. "We were researching it for similar properties to a critically endangered subspecies of *Dactylorhiza hatagirea* from the same alpine region of the northwest Himalayas."

Palmer avoids eye contact with the sizeable leaf waving at him from Hsu's front teeth. "What part of the plant were you testing?"

"We evaluated the petals and the heart, or the lips and tongue as some would call the flower. We ground the petals to observe the matter under a microscope, using heating and cooling procedures to analyze the chemical makeup. Afterward, we provided our data to the researchers in Beijing." He bites into another stalk.

Palmer shudders at Hsu's chomping, wishing he had visited between meals. "How were the remnants of the plant disposed of when your research concluded?"

"The ground petals had been boiled into liquid form. Being nonhazardous, they were disposed of in the laboratory sink. The stems were sent to composting here on campus. The seeds were planted in the laboratory to see if they would grow in a controlled environment."

"What happened with the planted seeds?"

Taking off his glasses, Hsu rubs his earlobe. "My team was unable to get any of the samples beyond the germination stage."

"I'm sorry, Doctor, my knowledge of botany's very limited. Can you describe the germination stage?"

"It's when a tiny root breaks through the seed and into the soil, sending up a shoot called a seedling that works its way above ground."

"So, the plants did not flower?"

"No."

"How many seeds were planted?"

"Five."

"And these seedlings grew in a pot?"

Hsu reaches for his napkin. "Five seeds were placed in separate pots."

Noting the sweat beads along Hsu's forehead, Palmer feels for the pack in his shirt pocket. "How did you determine the seedlings wouldn't flower?"

Hsu wipes his mouth. "The approximate time from seed to flower is shorter than most perennials because it grows in a cooler climate. When the seedlings didn't produce leaves after a month, we knew their development had ceased, so we disposed of them."

Lifting the pack from his shirt pocket, Palmer points to it. "You mind if I smoke, Doctor?"

"There's no smoking allowed in the laboratory." Hsu wipes his forehead with his shirtsleeve.

Palmer shoves the pack down. "Were all five plants disposed of properly?"

"Yes."

"And how was that accomplished?"

"The seedling remnants were crushed and sent for composting."

"Now, as I understand it, Doctor, each of these flowering plants produces one to two dozen seeds. If you had three, and my math is correct, there should have been somewhere between thirty-six and seventy-two seeds. Is that correct?"

"Yes." Hsu scratches the back of his hand. "I don't remember the exact number, but it would've been in that range."

"So, Dr. Hsu, I'm curious about all the other seeds. Do you remember what happened to those?"

Dr. Hsu sighs. "A friend here at the school was leaving at summer's end for another opportunity. His new job was in a rural area with an elevation about five hundred feet higher than Providence. I felt the elevation and chemical makeup of the soil might support growth there, so I gave him the remaining seeds."

"Do you know if the plants flowered?"

"I do not. I haven't spoken with him since the seeds were given as a parting present."

"Then I guess he wasn't a very close friend?"

Hsu tosses his hand up and shrugs. "He was a groundskeeper, Agent Palmer. I only knew him because he would pick up the compost material. I'd sometimes see him on the campus grounds. He was more of an acquaintance."

"Do you remember this groundskeeper's name and where he went?"

"Derek Griffin became head groundskeeper at Bryant College in North Smithfield."

Early evening, Palmer stares at a hunk of plaster on Metcalf's desk. Picking it up to take a closer look, he sees lettering but can't make out the words. He sets the plaster cast back on the desk when Monroe walks into the room. "Which crime scene was this recovered from?"

Monroe sits on the edge of Metcalf's desk. "Dean Stricker

retrieved this from the Hunt's Mill scene. We had some inconclusive partials from two previous crime scenes, but this one's complete, provides some valuable information."

Palmer feigns a smile while lighting a cigarette. "Stricker, huh? Interesting."

Monroe rolls his eyes, handing Palmer and Metcalf each a document. "The first page is a picture of our latest imprint. Along the breast of the sole, there's a series of horizontal, wavelike grips with three dots in between each. There's also a discernible crown on the three-eighths-inch raised heel. Based on these attributes, we reached out to manufacturers, matching it to the Sears Craftsman model shown on page two. We requested production and distribution information from Sears, and they responded with what you see on the third and fourth pages."

Bluish-black sky seeps through Metcalf's office windows as Palmer walks to the door and flips the light switch. "Why's there no production data after the middle of 1973?"

"Unfortunately, the imprint matches a retired line phased out about two years ago."

"Will they be able to provide sales data?"

"The problem is many of the later production units were sold as part of clearance sales where size-specific data's not recorded. Though regional distribution information would have been available through the end of production, sales data would be inaccurate after that date. Sears did tell us many of the size twelve and a half boots matching this imprint were consolidated and sold out of the Midland Mall in Warwick to a single buyer. Unfortunately, it appears to have been a cash sale, so no credit account information's available."

"About how tall would that boot size make our killer?"

"They stated their work boots tend to run about a half size larger to accommodate additional toe space for steel or hardened leather tips, so, unless our killer's a hobbit, we expect he'd be about six-three or six-four, give or take an inch."

Metcalf hands Monroe back the document. "Okay, so we're looking for a very tall man wearing Craftsman steel-toe work boots.

While a man that size could use these boots for hunting—and he evidently is, in a perverse way—it more likely suggests a construction worker or mechanic, maybe a sanitation—"

"Or landscaper." Palmer leans against the back of his chair.

Monroe and Metcalf glance at each other before staring at Palmer.

The ash cylinder of Palmer's cigarette dangles over the seat. "We've been following up on a lead our forensics team found in the trace evidence collected from the neck and clothing of the victims."

Metcalf slides an ashtray along the desk in the direction of Palmer. "Landscaper seems pretty specific, Frank. What do you have?"

"It wasn't much to go on before today, but I need to visit Bryant College tomorrow to follow up."

Monroe inches closer to Palmer. "What *did* they find?"

"They found a wide variety of plant matter."

"So did our guys down at the state lab."

"They also collected environmental samples from the crime scenes and determined many of the plants and flowers, in addition to the soil, didn't match the surrounding areas. In addition, mulch was present that had clearly not been at the locations of the murders." Palmer grinds his cigarette into the ashtray, grabs a fresh one.

"So, the killer works on a farm or in a greenhouse, but why jump right to landscaper?"

Palmer strikes a match. "They discovered something else." He pulls, takes a drag, and lets the smoke cool down before exhaling. "They found traces of a rare orchid—one that's native to China and not available in the US—among the plant matter. I received confirmation this afternoon the same species was found in the trace evidence collected from under the arms of the most recent body discovered at Hunt's Mill. Agent Lowe and I met with Customs yesterday. Earlier today, each of us visited one of the two locations where the only legal imports were transported."

"This sounds promising," Metcalf says. "Let's hope it leads somewhere."

"Agent Lowe met with the scientist at Pfizer in Cambridge. There was nothing to learn there." Palmer eyes Monroe and Metcalf as he flicks his cigarette ashes into the ashtray. "I met with Dr. Hsu at Brown University Medical School earlier this afternoon. He told me the seeds of this orchid were handed over to the head groundskeeper at Bryant College. We're gonna follow this lead, but I also think we need to conduct a news conference to share what we know and make a public appeal."

"What do you want to share?"

Looking outside, Palmer sees unforgiving dark pressed against Metcalf's office windows. "Public's getting more concerned. We need to inform them we're making progress. We should provide general descriptive information concerning what we think we know about the killer. Keep it simple, generic; try to calm their fears about the safety of their daughters and girlfriends when they're home at night."

"How much detail do you want to release about the crime scenes and the nature of the murders?"

"I would recommend providing the estimated dates along with the location of each murder, asking for any information about suspicious activity, unusual behavior, or strange individuals and vehicles that might have stood out. I wouldn't offer any details about the crime scenes beyond physical similarities of the victims and method. But I *definitely wouldn't* mention anything about the trace evidence or the work boots. We don't want the killer to know what we've got."

"I can put something together tonight," Monroe says.

Metcalf reaches for the phone. "I'll announce a news conference for tomorrow morning."

Stubbing out his cigarette, Palmer heads for the door. "Okay, let's set it up for ten and meet here at eight to review. Let's make sure the public knows we're actively pursuing the perpetrator. Let's request their help. But we don't want to alert the killer. We don't want this bastard on the run."

- 60 -

# INFESTATION

**WEDNESDAY, 8 OCTOBER 1975**

P*almer understands the nature of mischief.* Vans and mounted cameras form a backdrop for the growing number of reporters and television crews assembling on the lower steps of the Police and Fire Headquarters. He has no beef with their kind, no ongoing grudges. They do a job and pay bills just like detectives and investigators. They scamper under the bright lights of celebrity, nestled in layers of hypocrisy, and find absolution under a veil of ignorance. Investigators and detectives crawl in the shadows of doubt, clinging to fragile truths, and seek solace upon the scales of justice. He knows society would prefer to live without them but understands their garbage feeds the rats.

Lowe runs his fingers through his hair. "I'll bet there are more reporters here than when the Red Sox arrived back from Oakland last night. Can you believe we're headed to the World Series?"

"Alright, Agent Lowe, let's focus on what we're doing here." Palmer winks. "That will be an entirely different heartbreak."

Chief Metcalf opens the press conference. "Good morning. After discovering the remains of five female victims in Rhode Island and southeastern Massachusetts; the Providence and Fall River police departments, along with Rhode Island State Police and the Federal Bureau of Investigation, have created a joint task force to centralize evidence collection and coordinate investigative efforts as we work to bring the perpetrator of these crimes to justice. The task force is officially considering the five homicides to be connected—the actions of a single mass murderer. We have here Chief Investigator Francis Palmer from the FBI to provide a preliminary profile and identifiable patterns of the offender."

Palmer raises the microphone. "Based on the Bureau's initial psychological profiling, including mental, emotional, and personality characteristics associated with the killer's actions, and physical evidence left at the crime scenes, we believe the perpetrator's a disorganized, or opportunistic, killer. That is, the victims just happen to be in the wrong place at the wrong time. With few, if any, precautions taken to cover up the criminal actions, the crime scenes do not suggest the murders were premeditated. Based on what we know, the responsible individual may have a low IQ and be antisocial. He likely has no close friends and is isolated from his family.

"We are highly certain the killer's male. We expect he's either regularly unemployed, repeatedly fired, or frequently reprimanded at work. He may be laboring in a highly systematized, low-skill job. We don't believe the culprit's married or in a serious relationship unless it is, or has been, a homosexual relationship. Mass murderers of this type often live alone."

Palmer watches the journalists' frantic scribbling and wonders what embellishments he'll read in the papers tomorrow. Continuing, he describes the consistencies in the attributes of the victims, method of immobilization, and cause of death before turning the microphone over to Monroe.

Monroe greets the audience with a nod and unfolds his papers. "Ladies and gentlemen, in addition to the five known victims, police in North Smithfield and East Providence have several recently opened missing persons reports fitting the killer's victim profile. Over the past several days, two additional missing persons reports filed in the town of Slatersville are being evaluated for possible connections. The task force has identified each as a potential homicide to elevate priority, allowing for possible inclusion in the broader investigation. We're asking the public for any information concerning suspicious activities, individuals, or vehicles at the murder scenes around specific dates." Monroe concludes his remarks by detailing the locations and approximate dates for each murder.

After providing the phone hotline number and a final appeal for the public's help, Chief Metcalf closes the press conference without taking questions.

Palmer turns to Ross and Lowe. "Let's get out of here. I hate these scripted dog-and-pony shows. It's like an infestation, and I need a cigarette."

Palmer arrives at Bryant shortly before two. He walks around the central campus, taking an unusual interest in the landscape, before arriving at the president's office and giving his name to the secretary at two fifteen. Moments later, President Archer opens his office door and welcomes Palmer. At two thirty, Archer's secretary shows the head groundskeeper in.

Archer directs Griffin to take a seat. "Good afternoon, Derek. This is Chief Investigator Palmer from the FBI. He's working the case of the murdered girls in the area, and he'd like to ask you a few questions."

Griffin removes his Red Sox cap. "Hello, Investigator Palmer." He brushes his right hand on his shirt and offers it to Palmer. "Not sure how I might be able to help, but I'll definitely try."

Palmer's grip is equal to Griffin's. "I believe you may be just the man to help us."

Griffin shares a concerned look with Archer before sitting down. "What would you like to know?"

"Are you the head groundskeeper here at Bryant College?"

"Yes, sir."

"How long have you been working as head grounds–keeper?"

Griffin's hands rest on his knees, his cap in between. "I came onboard when the school moved from Providence four years ago."

"Where did you work before that?"

"I spent almost a decade working at Brown University."

"Then it would be correct for me to assume you are a profession-al with a great deal of landscaping experience. Your knowledge of trees, flowers, and other plants would be significantly greater than the average person. Is that correct?"

"Yes, sir, I guess it's an accurate assumption."

"Thank you. Were you good friends with Dr. Hsu from Brown

University?"

Griffin shrugs. "I knew him, but I wouldn't say we were *good* friends."

"Did you ever do anything socially? See him anywhere other than on campus? Exchange presents on birthdays or at Christmas?"

"No, sir. I just picked up the compost from the lab, sometimes saw him around campus."

"So, it's fair to say you were acquaintances?"

"Yes, that would be a fair description."

Palmer holds up a picture. "Mr. Griffin, do you know what kind of plant this is?"

"Those are nodding ladies' tresses. You can tell by the vertical row of small flowers along the stem. Some people think they're a weed the way they spread in fields and pastures. They're all over Rhode Island. Mostly white, though, not as colorful as that one."

"Have you seen any with these pink or purple flowers?"

Griffin rubs the back of his neck. "Yes. We have them in several locations here on campus, with a large collection in the open area behind the front sign as you come in from the turnpike. There's also some around the pond here in the center of campus. Not blooming now, though. They bloom between June and August."

"Have you seen them anywhere else besides here on campus?"

Griffin's right knee begins shaking, the vibration causing his cap to fall. "No, sir, I don't believe so."

Palmer picks up Griffin's cap. "Don't wanna lose this. Might be good luck for the Series." He smiles at Archer while reaching for his shirt pocket before noticing a 'No smoking, please' placard on the president's desk. Disappointed, he continues questioning Griffin. "Is there any reason you believe you've not seen this orchid anywhere else?"

Hands wringing his cap, Griffin looks down. "Yes, Investigator Palmer. Dr. Hsu gave me the seeds just before I came here in 1971." Looking up, Griffin's eyes meet Palmer's gaze. "He thought they might grow better here."

Unable to smoke, Palmer drums his fingers on the desk. "I thought you and Dr. Hsu didn't exchange presents?"

Griffin runs his hand down his face. "We didn't. He felt giving them to me was better than destroying them." He looks at Archer. "I'm sorry, have I done something wrong?"

Archer smiles. "Relax, Derek. Investigator Palmer and I spoke a short while before you arrived. He just needs some information about the orchid and our groundskeepers here at the college."

"Yes, Mr. Griffin," Palmer says. "You're not considered a suspect. I don't understand the laws concerning planting endangered or restricted species, but I don't believe any harm's been done. I suspect it could prove beneficial to researchers. I'm only interested in who has access to these orchids."

Griffin nods. "I'll be as helpful as I can."

"That's good, Mr. Griffin. All we need at this point is for President Archer to provide us with the personnel folders of all your current groundskeepers. I would ask that you not let anyone know we've spoken and make yourself available for any follow-up questions I, or any one of my agents, may have."

Griffin rounds the bill of his cap. "I understand."

Palmer rises to his feet, his voice chirpy. "Who's pitching game one?"

"They're going with Tiant."

Palmer smiles. "Then we've got a chance, don't we?" He walks toward the door. "Thank you, President Archer. I'll send one of my investigators for those files at five." Reaching for the door handle, he stops. "Mr. Griffin, if I may, one last question?" He turns, stepping toward Griffin, who's now standing. "Those look like nice work boots. What brand are they?"

Griffin follows the path of Palmer's eyes. "These are Sears Craftsman steel-toe. Really good for what we do."

"I'm gonna have to check those out. Gonna be a smaller size than you're wearing, though, right? What are those, elevens?"

"Twelve and a half. I got them on clearance," Griffin says. "Got a whole batch of them. I give a pair to each of our groundskeepers. Unfortunately, they don't sell this style anymore."

"Shame," Palmer says as he turns and heads out the door.

# FRANKENSTEIN

## WEDNESDAY, 8 OCTOBER 1975

M*o's focus shifts to the Big Red Machine.* The Red Sox having swept the mighty Oakland A's, Mo is obsessed with anything involving the World Series, the home team, or the Cincinnati Reds. So, sitting on the couch, watching the evening news with his housemates and Kay, he endures twenty minutes of boring reports before sports. Leading with the press conference at police headquarters, the first ten minutes of tonight's broadcast keeps everyone silently glued to the television. With the commercial break, discussion begins.

Brian shakes his head. "Holy crap! Five!"

"One of them was at Lincoln Park," Trevor says. "We were just there."

Kay nods. "We were there the same weekend that girl went missing."

"Yeah, we were," Carlton says. "In fact, we've been to most of the places where the bodies were found."

Kay uses her fingers to count. "Let's see, we went to Stepstone Falls, Hunt's Mill, Lincoln Park, and Stillwater Pond, but we didn't go to Capron Pond." She puts her hand on Carlton's elbow. "What was the other one?"

Carlton runs his fingers around his mouth. "One was at Olney Pond, but we didn't go there. So, we've been to three of the five locations."

Kay rests her chin on her hand. "Four, if you count Stillwater."

"Yeah, but her body was found below the waterfall. We never went anywhere near there."

"The killer clearly likes wooded areas," Brian says.

Carlton shrugs. "Isn't that true of most mass murderers, though? They usually dump the bodies in remote locations, often in the woods."

A shiver runs through Kay's body. "The police said the murders occur close to where the bodies are discovered. It's creepy, even if it's just a coincidence."

Carlton puts his arm around Kay. "We've been going to picnic areas with trails and ponds almost every weekend, so we're bound to hit some of the places the murders are occurring."

Kay stares at the floor. "Maybe we should stop going to those places for a while."

"That might be a good idea," Trevor says. "You guys have quite a trend developing."

Carlton frowns. "What are you implying?"

"I'm not implying anything. I'm just stating facts. We all went to Lincoln Park, and you guys went to Stepstone Falls, Hunt's Mill, and Stillwater Pond." Trevor nods. "Sure sounds like a trend to me."

Carlton rises from his chair. "I'm sure we could figure out which weekends we were at those locations. I've got a couple of weeks' newspapers upstairs that might spark our memory."

Kay grabs Carlton's wrist. "Oh, no, Carl, please don't. It's bad enough thinking about being at the same places as the killer. I don't want to think about it being at the same time. I'll have nightmares."

"Okay." Carlton walks to the kitchen to grab a beer.

Trevor's eyes transfer between Carlton and Kay. "Does anybody remember anything strange, or anyone acting weird?"

Kay shakes her head. "I don't."

"I don't either," Carlton shouts from the kitchen. "I'm not good at remembering things like that. A guy would have to look like Frankenstein for *me* to remember."

Kay sighs. "Mo, it was late when you went walking around the trail at Hunt's Mill. Did you see or hear anything strange?"

Mo hasn't been paying attention to the conversation, his mind fast-forwarding to Saturday's first series game and the pitching matchup. Surprised to hear his name, he turns his head in the direction of Kay with a vacant stare.

She repeats the question.

Mo scratches his head. "No. I saw one girl go by, but I didn't pay attention to what she looked like. I don't remember seeing anyone else."

Carlton, walking back into the living room, stares at Mo, one eyebrow curled. "How can you possibly remember that?"

"I make a memory for every place we go, and I only pay attention to the flowers, trees, and animals I see."

Carlton shakes his head. "I don't get it. If you're paying attention to those things, how do you remember a girl going by?"

"Because I was looking at a praying mantis, and she stopped to see."

"It's crazy you can remember something like that from weeks ago." Carlton does a doubletake. "Hey, what if she was the girl that got murdered? You may have been the last person to see her alive."

"And...on that note," Kay says, "we're done."

Carlton looks at Trevor. "Maybe we can quiz Mo on everyone who walked by him Sunday while he was viewing the animals in the zoo."

Mo joins in the laughter, though he doesn't understand what's so funny. He doesn't want to think about dead girls. He just wants to enjoy the sound of laughter at home after so many sobering years.

# GROUND ZERO

## THURSDAY, 9 OCTOBER 1975

*P*almer's *least favorite meal is breakfast.* He likes it even less when he's working with Ross. He wakes up to coffee and doesn't like babysitting. This morning, at half past seven, he and Ross are sitting on opposite sides of a booth at Friendly's on Mineral Spring Avenue. Ahead of Lowe's arrival, he's drinking his morning brew, watching Ross mutilate a stack of pancakes with a fork, and guarding the syrup dispenser. This morning feels like babysitting.

Ross mumbles through batter. "C'mon, Frank, you're not even eating anything."

"Stop the whining, Gerry. I can't stand sitting here while you smother each piece into a coffee cup of liquid sugar. The sound of you slurping syrup makes my skin crawl."

With Lowe's arrival, Ross slides closer to the window. "Any worse than you sipping caffeine and sucking nicotine all day? I feel like I smoke half your cigarettes."

With a dismissive wave, Palmer turns his attention to Lowe. "Glad to see you could make it, Agent Lowe. Leave the kids in daycare?"

Lowe, fighting the urge to give Palmer the finger, mumbles unintelligibly.

Palmer cups his ear. "What's that?"

Lowe shakes his head. "Nothing, Chief."

Reaching for the glass syrup dispenser without success, Ross sighs. "Give the kid a break, Frank. He's not late." He nudges Lowe, pointing to a nearly full syrup dispenser on an empty table.

Palmer's glare tells Lowe, *Don't you dare.*

Lowe forces Ross deeper into the booth with his hips.

Palmer wipes a splotch of Ross's pancake-infused spittle off the table before pointing to Lowe. "Alright, let's see what you've got."

Lowe unfolds several pages. "We got identity history summary checks on all eight, including Griffin. They also did criminal cross-checks and pulled court records. Griffin's clean. He's forty-two, stands six-four, has a wife, five kids, and owns a house in a working-class Black neighborhood on the west end of the city. He's held a steady job for more than twenty years.

"Two had misdemeanors for simple assault. Thomas Clayton Moore's also Black, thirty-eight years old, and lives down on the South Side. Looks like he punched a kid last year, daughter's boyfriend, apparently. Charges were dropped. Otherwise, he's got a clean slate with twelve years in the military, a wife, and three teenage daughters. License says he's five-eleven."

Ross shakes his fork. "Gotta be a bitch raising teenager daughters on the South Side."

Lowe nods before continuing. "Lucious Spencer Branch also has a couple of misdemeanors for simple assault from about twenty years ago. Grew up in the Chad Brown projects, so could've been gang-related or self-defense. He's Black, five-nine, and has a house in Olneyville with a wife and four kids. He's thirty-nine years old.

"One has minor drug convictions; no time served. Juan Ortiz Diaz is thirty-two, Latino, and divorced with two young sons. Doesn't appear to have any legal issues since he started working at the school about seven months ago. Lives in Central Falls and only lists as five-five.

"Three others are young with no court records. Stephon Elroy Johnson's twenty-four, Black, five-eight, not married, and lives in Woodlawn. Theodore William Harris is twenty-one, Black, five-ten, not married but has a four-year-old daughter. He lives on the east side in the Mount Hope area.

"There's not much on Maurice Leroy Lumen. He's twenty-four, the only Caucasian on the crew, born in Sumerduck, Virginia, and has no previous jobs listed." Lowe's eyebrows rise. "He's been working at the school for under two months and lives on campus in student housing. No marriage records, no kids, both parents dead.

Doesn't appear to have any family here in Rhode Island. But he also has no criminal record, according to the State of Virginia. Oh, and he's six-eight."

Ross stabs his last piece of pancake. "*That's* a big farm boy."

Palmer slides the syrup dispenser over to Ross. "Tell me about the last one."

"Jericho Simon Gonzalez is a veteran of WWII and Korea and served hard time in New York for, get this, voluntary manslaughter of a young woman. He got arrested in 1955 and was convicted. He was paroled in 1964. He's held a series of outdoor manual labor positions, from construction to masonry and landscaping, and he hasn't held a job for more than a year while moving from state to state across New England over the past decade. There are also several periods where he's collected unemployment. He's been at the school for about eight months, working part-time. He's Latino, from Brooklyn, forty-nine, never married, and no kids. He lives in the Hartford Park Project on the west side. Only the one felony offense, but he did almost nine years in maximum security. Also had some misdemeanors for disorderly conduct and drug charges before the felony arrest, but didn't serve any time for those." Lowe emphasizes his final words. "He's also six-three."

"Sounds like Mr. Gonzalez deserves some attention," Ross says.

Palmer waves the waitress over. "Can you get this young man a coffee to go?"

Ross tosses his napkin on the table. "Can I get a Jim Dandy to go, sugar?"

Shaking his head, Palmer puts his hand in front of Ross. "Please don't listen to him. Just make that three coffees to go and the bill, please."

"We got a long drive, Frank."

Palmer checks his watch. "It's not even eight," he says, closing his eyes, "and I don't want to hear you lapping up hot fudge and caramel in the car."

Ross rests his head against his bridged hands, looks down at his empty plate, and grumbles.

Palmer returns his attention to Lowe. "Alright, I need you to get up to Bryant College. Talk to Griffin and find out everything he knows about his employees. I want to know what they drive, what they do on weekends and evenings. We need to know about their personalities, who they hang out with, anything you can get." He checks the tab, drops fifteen dollars on the table, and slides Ross and Lowe their coffees before picking up his own. "Ross and I are going up to Slatersville. Monroe has a couple dozen men searching around the reservoir."

Ross licks the last remnants of syrup off his fork. "You think Gonzalez may be the killer, Frank?"

"I'm not thinking about that right now, but I suspect he may be a key to the puzzle."

Lowe slides out of the booth. "I'm on it, Chief."

"Hey, Lowe," Palmer says, his eyebrows raised. "I wanna know what time this Gonzalez fella shits in the morning."


Dean Stricker stands, hands on hips, watching his troopers comb the field down to Slatersville Reservoir. Most find Detective Stricker useless at best, obstructionist at worst. But nobody in the State or Providence Police makes the mistake of underestimating his influence in the politics of public safety. Born into a powerful family—one uncle a former governor of Rhode Island, and his father a seated US senator—Stricker's entitled and inept. Therefore, Monroe keeps a watchful eye, allowing him to work in the field with more qualified personnel above and below.

Palmer neither appeases nor allows himself to be distracted by Stricker. After all, the Bureau has its own politics, and he sees the inadequate lieutenant as nothing more than a minor nuisance, accepting that if it weren't him, it would be someone else in his place. This morning, Palmer observes Stricker from a distance. Seated in the driver's seat of his Bonneville, he and Ross share a laugh as Stricker frantically waves at invisible, flying insects, each time readjusting his belt and feeling the holster for his gun.

Palmer pops his door open. "Let's go see Dean."

"What the hell's happening to the police force, Frank?" Ross grunts as he uncorks himself from the passenger seat.

"Be nice, Gerry." Palmer slams his door shut. "Must be tough for someone like him to grow up in a highly successful family."

Pushing his door closed, Ross nods. "Must be even tougher on his family."

Stricker turns at the sound of car doors, scurries over to Palmer and Ross. "Morning, boys. Monroe told me to expect you." He smiles, raising his eyebrows. "Little late for you, Frank, isn't it?"

"Sure is, Dean. I had trouble crawling out of bed this morning. All those hotel lice kept me up most of the night." Palmer scratches his head before offering Stricker his hand.

"Uh, yeah." Stricker winces as he clasps Palmer's hand, each strand of his black, slicked-back hair combed in perfect rows, forehead to collar. "Let me explain what we're doing here."

Stricker's lips move, but Palmer doesn't listen. Leaving Ross to digest the monologue, Palmer backs away. He enjoys a smoke near the water's edge, scanning up, down, and across the reservoir. Hearing his name, he turns to find Ross stumbling down the slope, waving him to come back.

Palmer stops where Ross is bent over, arms on knees, looking like an oversized pill bug. "And you wanted a Jim Dandy." He waits for Ross's panting to subside. "What's up?"

"Stricker just heard on the radio..." Ross catches his breath. "They've found another body—North Smithfield." Straightening up, he takes off his cap and wipes his forehead, eyes wide. "Bryant College."

"Holy shit." Palmer pulls out his cigarettes. "Get Lowe on the radio. Have him give me a call right away. I'll let Stricker know we're leaving without sharing anything."

"Alright." Ross puts his cap back on and lets out a deep breath. "I guess they want Stricker to keep searching up here."

"Sounds about right, sending him on a fool's errand. They won't find a body here," Palmer says, patting his pants pockets with an unlit cigarette hanging from his lips. "There's no trails."

Palmer's Bonneville pulls into the gymnasium parking lot at the rear of the Bryant campus just before eleven. Several police vehicles block the access road, with several more sitting in the lot. Officers on foot form a perimeter, blocking pedestrian entry from the campus. The gym has been evacuated and locked tight.

Palmer walks alongside Ross and Lowe in the direction of Monroe, the smell of sulfur hanging in the air. He knows this one's not fresh, even if it is ripe. Dropping his cigarette on the gravel, he flattens it with his shoe. "Who found the body?"

"Two of the groundskeepers here, Branch and Harris," Lowe replies.

"Where are they now?"

"Over at the building where they keep the trucks and equipment. Where Griffin's office is."

"Take Ross over. Talk to Branch and Harris." Palmer waves them off as he approaches Monroe. "What's it look like, Jeff?"

Monroe looks over his shoulder. "This one's been here a while, well into stage three decay, maybe two weeks exposed. Forensics and photography won't be here for another twenty minutes, so we're just preserving the scene."

Palmer nods. "Mind if I take a look before they get here?"

"Of course not." Monroe waves him past. "Just be careful. There was some rain overnight, and this is a naturally swampy area."

Ducking under the barricade tape, Palmer enters the woods. Accustomed to the smell and knowing to approach upwind, he descends into the mud, plodding as he works his way around the perimeter to avoid contaminating the probable path of the killer. By the time he reaches the remains, his shoes are caked. The victim's skin has dissolved into the marsh, a cloud of insects and a mass of larvae feasting on the last shards of tissue. He doesn't linger, inspecting the layout of the remains and the skeletal formation of the skull, face up and visible through brown leaves and a collection of maggots.

Finished, Palmer pulls the barricade tape over his head and tamps a pack against his palm as he reengages with Monroe. "They'll be using dental records on this one." He stomps his shoes on the gravel. "Wonder what the students thought the smell was the past few days."

"This one's pungent, that's for sure." Monroe wrinkles his nose. "Were you able to determine anything?"

"Her feet are facing the campus, so she was immobilized on the footpath here, dragged into the woods, and asphyxiated in the swamp. Killer would've been a muddy mess coming out of there. I wonder if anyone noticed him." Palmer looks down at his shoes. "I gotta go get a towel out of the car. I'll be right back."

As Palmer scrubs his shoes, Monroe walks over. "You're not gonna believe it, Frank." He shakes his head. "Bunch of kids found another body down at Roger Williams Park. Headed there now. This guy's busy." He turns, heading to his car.

Palmer tosses the soiled towel in his trunk. "I'll be right behind you." He takes a long drag and releases a surge of smoke before calling out to Monroe. "Might want to think about reassigning Stricker's team to the campus here."

Monroe looks back, shouting. "Think there might be more?"

Palmer gazes across the rear lot to the pond fountain in the center of campus. "Maybe. This is beginning to feel like ground zero."

# 63

# AN INTIMATE ENCOUNTER

## FRIDAY, 10 OCTOBER 1975

M*o looks forward to his overnight visit with Langford, but baseball occupies his thoughts.* The last two days of the workweek stall as he grows anxious waiting for the World Series to start. By Friday afternoon, with his obsession uncontained, Mo talks over the radio as he rides in Langford's car.

Smiling, Langford raises the volume in small increments until Mo is entirely drowned out. Arriving home, he steps out of the car, speaking to Mo over the top. "I have a surprise for you." Leading Mo into the kitchen, he points to a bag on the island. "Go ahead. Open it."

Mo peeks inside. "New pajamas and a robe!"

"They're **XXXL**, and the robe's terry cloth. Unfold it. Let's take a look."

Mo stares at his monogrammed initials. "Thank you, Mike." He works his arms into the sleeves. "It's so soft."

"Looks good on you. Bring it home with you, so you have it at the townhouse."

"Thanks, Mike. I like the baseball pajamas, too. Can I go put them on?"

"Sure, use the same bedroom as last week."

Mo enjoys the feel of Pima cotton and the softness of a new pair of slippers he finds on the bathroom counter. Returning to the kitchen, he shucks corn on the patio table.

Langford lights a handful of mosquito coils. "It's a beautiful night, but the mosquitos might be a bit pesky because of all the rain. If it gets intolerable, we can bring the food inside."

After dinner, they retire to Langford's bedroom to watch the ABC Friday Night Movie and evening news before making their way to the kitchen for a late-night dessert. Langford warms cinnamon rolls and pours two glasses of milk before pulling his island stool closer to Mo. "I enjoy your visits, Mo."

"Me too."

"You could sleep over more often. I go to the campus every day, and I always have early classes."

"I appreciate that, but I like to walk to work."

"Don't you like your bedroom here better?"

"It's a lot nicer, but I like living with Carlton, Trevor, and Brian, too."

"But you could sleep over almost any night. You know that, right?"

"I know."

"I want to be *best* friends with you." Langford places his hand on Mo's knee. "You don't have to sleep in your bedroom tonight. You could sleep in my bed." He rubs Mo's upper thigh, staring into his eyes, now wide with concern.

Mo's body freezes. He holds his breath. After a few frightening moments, he says, "I-I-I'd rather sleep in my own bed." His lips curl, voice uneven. "I-I-I'm really tired, and I should get to bed. It's late." Trembling from head to toe, Mo recalls his father's talks about inappropriate touching.

Langford removes his hand, face flushed. "Oh, no! I only meant like sleeping in a tent." He eases away from his guest. "Like, we could make a tent in the bed and grab a couple of sleeping bags I have in the garage."

Mo stands, still shaking, and slides away from Langford. "That's okay. Goodnight, Professor Langford." He retreats to his bedroom, locking the door behind him. Lying in bed, he considers his mother's old downstairs bedroom. It was a special place when he was young before his mother died. After her death, it became a place of great sorrow until his grandmother moved in. Then Miss Clara came, and it was an unhappy place. But it became a special place again when his grandmother reoccupied the room after Jake's mother left. He resolves not to sleep over again, though he will continue meeting with Langford on Wednesdays in the event he's wrong about his friend's intentions. Maybe, he thinks, Langford's downstairs guest bedroom will become a special place again.

Light scratching at his bedroom door concerns Mo at first, then provokes his curiosity. He opens the door with trepidation, and Samantha enters, seeking attention. He pets her while she sprawls on the bed before exiting. He again locks the door, turns off the lamp, and pulls the covers over his head. Darkness embraces him on this final night in the professor's house. Outside, Mo hears the tremolo of an eastern screech owl, its cries offering little solace on this grayest of evenings.

# 64

# LANGFORD'S GARDEN

## SATURDAY, 11 OCTOBER 1975

*Mo wakes early, finding Langford already working in his flower garden beside the garage.* Unlike Mr. Ford's much larger garden in spring and summer—an unruly sea of color sprawling the length of his front yard—Langford's modest, autumn garden is brown and tidy, chicken wire stapled to lattice preventing overhang into the walkway. Still, there are weeds in his garden, and Langford, head down and on his knees, works this morning to remove them. Mo observes for several minutes without alerting the professor to his presence.

When he was young, Mo would bring his mother escaped flowers from Mr. Ford's Garden—the ones that peeked through the rails. Then, he'd listen to her explain how gardens are a place of perennial hope and renewal where old and dying plants are replaced with new and budding ones. She would talk of tending to the soil, planting seeds, and nurturing the plants, describing how it takes one to a place of promise and purpose. Watching Langford, Mo wonders if the professor understands the significance of a garden or if he's only interested in harvesting its beauty for himself.

Sitting back on his boots, Langford looks up. "Good morning," he says with a smile. "You're up early. I trust you slept well."

"Good morning, Professor Langford," Mo says. "I'm going to go for a walk."

"Okay. I'm just clearing out the garden." Langford taps the ground with his hand trowel. "Have to be careful not to damage the base of these, or they won't come back next summer. I'll be here a while, so go have some fun." Leaning forward, he resumes stabbing.

Mo points at Langford's new boots. "Did Mr. Griffin give you those?"

Langford stands up to stretch. "Derek dropped them off at my office this past week. I was disappointed I missed him." He points the trowel at Mo. "Thanks for reminding me; I still need to drop by the Shed. He left a note saying he wanted to talk about something."

"Mr. Griffin gives everybody at work the same size boots."

"Hmm, I wasn't aware. I figured this was an extra pair he had. Did you happen to mention I needed a new pair?"

Mo squints. "I think so."

"Well, thank you. I was wondering how he knew." He waves the trowel at the main road. "It's going to take me a while, so go ahead, have some fun exploring. I'll be here when you get back."

Mo heads straight for the back of Langford's property. The outer edge is lined with cedar, spruce, and pine trees. Among these evergreens, Mo belongs to a family of natural conspirators, the struggle for survival ever-present, predator and prey equipped with natural and adaptive tools to advantage themselves in the hunt. Treading deeper, Mo hears the gentle rustling of mature leaves clinging to life, suckling on maternal oaks and maples amid a pleasant, yet perilous, breeze. This, along with the indiscriminate scurrying of woodland creatures across the dead and discharged foliage, serves to nourish the forest soil and perform an arboreal symphony sufficient to vanquish his anxiety.

Focused on the World Series and not wanting to be late, Mo strides back to Langford's home with purpose. After a shower, he folds the pajamas and robe, leaving them on the bed, uncertain he will visit the professor's home again. He sits on the front porch and waits. With Langford's return, Mo leads him to the car. He's ready to go home. And he has been since last night.

Mo follows the same routine for the World Series as he had with the three playoff games, Red Sox cards laid out on the table. Trevor aligned the Cincinnati player cards before Mo arrived home. Mo's already sitting on the sofa when everyone else joins him in the living room for the start of the game.

Kay places her hand on Mo's shoulder. "How are you doing? You okay?"

Breathing heavier than normal, Mo angles his knees up to his stomach with his toes tucked between two sofa cushions. "Yeah, just a little nervous."

"That's obvious. You should have a beer," Brian says, getting up to get himself one.

"No, thank you."

Carlton sits at the other end of the sofa. "How was Langford's house last night?"

"Oh, uh, it was okay."

"I'm sure his fancy home beats the townhouse, huh?"

Mo's focus stays on the television. "It's nice, but I think I prefer to sleep at home from now on."

Poised to ask a follow-up question, Carlton stops, his attention drawn to the television for a news update on the body found at Bryant. "Anybody notice the police on campus Thursday afternoon?"

"I didn't see anything," Trevor says. "Mo, you must've seen something, right?"

Waiting on the first pitch, Mo's fixated on the screen.

Carlton snaps his fingers near Mo's face. "Hey, M, you see anything Thursday when the cops were here?"

Mo blinks. "Uh, yeah, King and Theo found a body in the woods behind the gymnasium. I went with Mr. Griffin back there, but he didn't let me get close. It was really stinky."

"Were there a lot of cops?"

"Uh-huh." Mo gives Carlton a dismissive wave. "Please let me watch the game."

"That's way too close to home," Brian says. "How many now? Seven?"

"Yeah," Carlton replies. "Seven and counting."

Brian scratches his chin. "Leslie Marie Delaney? I wonder if I knew her. Sounds familiar, but so hard to keep track."

"Right," Carlton sneers. "Well, if the number keeps climbing, maybe they'll get to one of your female friends, and *you'll* be interviewed on the news."

Kay shakes her head. "Carl! Please be sensitive to those poor girls' families. We went to Roger Williams Park last weekend, and the other one was right here on campus."

Trevor looks away from the game. "Hold on. You guys went to Roger Williams Park last weekend?"

"Yeah," Kay says, "I know what you're thinking."

Trevor curls his lips and furrows his brows. "Uh, yeah. Don't have to be Sherlock Holmes to know bodies are popping up everywhere you guys go. Now they found one right here on campus."

"It's getting wicked scary," Carlton says. "Like the killer's following us."

"Anybody consider it could be one of us, or more accurately," Trevor points to Mo, Carlton, and Kay in succession, "one of you three?" He rubs his chin. "I doubt it's Kay."

"Gee, thanks." Kay hits Trevor with a throw pillow.

Trevor speaks as if narrating. "Carlton and Mo, however, make good suspects: Carlton, the conflicted mama's boy, and Mo, the unassuming drifter."

Brian nudges Mo's shoulder. "Yeah, Mo. Haven't you had issues with girls? How old was that girl in Virginia?"

Turning his attention from the television, Mo answers through clenched teeth. "Fourteen."

"Hmm, a little young, but who knows, maybe you're the tormented victim who takes out his rage on young girls."

Kay throws up her hands in disgust. "Brian! Seriously?! You sound like Jim now. Have you been drinking?"

"Nah, sorry. I was just playing along with Trevor's film noir detective." Brian gets up, scratching the back of his head. "I know it's not you guys, but others might have questions if they knew you've been to all these places. It gets crazy when there's a maniac on the loose."

Carlton nods. "That's true. Let's hope they catch him before it gets to that point."

Trevor rubs his hands together. "You know, it's surprising they haven't come up with a catchy name for this guy."

"Yeah, I wonder what they'll call him," Brian says.

"What about Countryside Killer?" Kay blurts out.

"Not bad," Carlton says. "How about the Suburban Slayer?" Brian points at Trevor. "Or maybe, the Arboreal Annihilator?"

"Guys," Trevor says, "he doesn't annihilate his victims; he drowns or strangles them. It's not so gory. He also doesn't violate them. I believe something using the word 'assassin' would be more applicable, like the Woodland Assassin, or, better yet, the Arboreal Assassin."

Carlton shakes his head. "You've got it all wrong. The key is he punches them or gives them some kind of blow to the head before he kills them." His eyes brighten. "How about the Bucolic Blower?"

All but Mo break out in laughter.

Brian struggles to get the words out. "Or, Foliage Flogger?"

His housemates laughing louder, Mo shushes them.

Trevor whispers, "Swimsuit Slayer?"

Returning his attention to the game, Mo's curious how Trevor knows the killer wears a bathing suit or the victims are clad in bikinis.

After a Red Sox victory, Mo walks to the off-campus variety store to buy a few packs of baseball cards. Along the way, he marches into a wooded roadside path under a cloudless, late-afternoon sky. Deviating from the path to explore the woods, a place few walkers or joggers venture, he finds some resilient orchids still in bloom that remind him of Langford's Garden and the uncomfortable events of the previous evening.

Up ahead, Mo spots a small collection of deer and finds himself, likewise, a subject of interest. Considering the bodies discovered by the police, he wonders whether any deer found them first or even watched them die. He wishes deer could talk but decides it's better they don't; otherwise, they too might ask painful questions. When he's done walking, Mo heads back to the townhouse, only knowing it has become dark quickly.

# 65

# STRICKER'S STRANGLER

## MONDAY, 13 OCTOBER 1975

*P*almer *taps his coffee mug, The Beast and his belly grumbling.* Gazing out the restaurant window at the few vehicles visible in the early morning darkness, he mulls over the loss of Emma Lee Powell, her body discovered on the embankment of Deep Spring Lake in Roger Williams Park. Did her parents get any more sleep than he did last night? Are they sitting up drinking coffee at four thirty, just as he is? And are they tormenting themselves over how they might have better protected their daughter, just as he worries what he's overlooked that might leave his and others' daughters vulnerable?

Staring out at the vehicles, one stands out. An off-white VW Beetle sits alone under a light post at the far end of the lot. His focus shifts to the teenage girl who recently identified Officer Roseland out of a police lineup in Utah. Why had she been fortunate enough to escape Bundy's Beetle where Powell had fallen prey in the woods? What had her parents done differently? Was it luck? Or was it time for the mistake that must come? When will The Monster nearby make his mistake?

Observing the Beetle, he considers how cars, like people, are sometimes unreliable, often indistinguishable. But when a vehicle is an accomplice to heinous acts, it gains notoriety. Attention can, in a perverse way, promote interest. While fame may be fleeting, infamy tends to linger. He taps and stares and thinks. Light sweeps over the vehicles.

Ross removes his coat, hanging it on the booth hook. "Morning, Frank. Get any sleep?"

Palmer, still looking outside, shakes his head.

Ross waits for Lowe to reach the table. "Go ahead, Nellie. You get in first today." He slides in after Lowe. "Strange day Thursday, huh?"

Lowe grabs two menus and hands one to Ross. "Two bodies discovered fifteen miles apart on the same day," he says. "Bet *that* doesn't happen very often."

Palmer, eyelids heavy, looks across the table. "No, Agent Lowe, this doesn't happen…ever." He looks back at the Beetle. "Not two bodies discovered in separate locations, forty-five minutes apart."

Lowe reaches for the sleeve of Palmer's coat. "You okay, Chief?"

Palmer pulls his arm away, says nothing.

Ross peers into Palmer's ashtray, finding a full-length cylinder of cindered tobacco resting on a dozen discarded cigarette butts. "Frank doesn't sleep," he says. "Not when he's trying to crack a case. Some of the guys think he's a vampire. Others think he gets into the mind of the killer, unable to sleep until he exorcises the demons." He looks at Lowe and smiles. "Me? I'm on the fence."

Palmer's voice is hoarse. "You guys get something to eat. Then we'll talk about what we have from yesterday."

Ross glances at Palmer over his menu. "Alright, Frank."


Thirty minutes later, the smell of peppermint clings to the wet table as The Cyclone walks away with their dirty dishes. Palmer keeps an eye on the Beetle, interested who will drive away in it.

"I think she likes you." Ross winks at Palmer while lifting the ice cream menu.

Palmer's stare is stoic. "What did you get from the kids who discovered the Powell girl's body at Roger Williams?"

"You nailed it." Ross scrolls the menu. "Damn kids were poking the body with sticks before the police arrived. Got the little bastards to admit it when I threatened them with time for disturbing evidence and lying about it." He snickers.

"How many were there?"

"Five. Just a bunch of kids from the South Side." Hailing The Cyclone a few booths away, Ross points to the menu. "Probably gang material in a few years."

Palmer runs his hands down his face. "Seems like they did a good job of contaminating the scene. What about the two groundskeepers who discovered the Delaney girl's body at Bryant?"

The head of Ross's spoon points straight up from his fist on the table. "I spoke with Branch and Harris for about twenty minutes. Some students complained about the smell, so Griffin sent them to find the source."

Palmer looks at Ross through the steam rising from his coffee. "Did they tamper with the crime scene? How close did they get?"

"Branch said they thought it was a deer carcass at first, but as the kid, Harris, got closer, he could see sneakers. Says they didn't get any closer than fifteen or twenty feet. Never touched the body."

"Guessing the kid's the one who threw up in the parking lot?"

"Yeah. Said the smell really got to him."

Lowe uses a butter knife to slide Ross's sundae over to him, caramel oozing over the side of the glass goblet.

Looking at Ross's morning dessert, Palmer shakes his head. He points at Lowe. "What did you get from Derek Griffin yesterday?"

Lowe pulls a sheet of paper from his shirt pocket and hands it to Palmer. "I got the make and model of every car they drive. The Lumen kid doesn't own a car. He walks to work from campus housing."

Palmer unfolds the sheet. "What does Gonzalez drive?"

"An orange 1968 Datsun 510. He was working yesterday, so I had a chance to take a look at it. Car's pretty beat up. High mileage, from what I could tell."

"They call him Flatbush, huh?"

"Yeah, he's originally from Brooklyn, right?"

"I know. It's a perfect nickname."

"For a killer?"

Palmer rolls his eyes. "For anyone from that part of Brooklyn." He slides the folded papers behind his pack of Marlboros. "I wanna focus on this Flatbush character and the Lumen kid."

"You think one of them could be the killer, Frank?" Ross scrapes his spoon along the outside of the glass.

"I wouldn't know, but they're both big enough. Gonzalez has a conspicuous past, and Lumen has none, far as we can tell." Palmer finishes his coffee. "I want to know everywhere they've lived. I want you to crosscheck those dates and locations against any similar homicides having occurred. Get the names of anyone who lives with them. Let's see how comfortable they are in Rhode Island and how long they intend to stay."

"I saw them both Thursday while I was talking to Branch and Harris." Ross wipes his mouth, missing a spot of caramel on his chin. "Gonzalez seems to fit the bill. Lumen kid seems pretty tame."

"I agree," Lowe says. "According to Griffin, he's a really nice kid, but he's got a mental deficiency of some kind; makes him like an eleven-year-old or something." He stretches his hands apart. "He's huge, too. Seems even bigger than six-eight."

"I read that in your notes."

"Did you see the last line?"

"Yeah, they all have the same work boots, and they all look like they're the same size." Palmer taps the handle of his coffee cup.

"Apparently, Griffin gives them all a pair of boots when they start, but they're all his size." Lowe smiles. "Little guys still wear them, even though they must be huge on them." His smile disappears. "What makes you think it could be the Lumen kid?"

"I don't know whether it's him or not," Palmer says. "But I do know he arrived in Rhode Island just before the killing started."

Ross pushes the empty and spotless goblet to the center of the table. "He's big enough, too."

Palmer looks out the window. The Beetle's vanished, and any potential monster is gone with it. But he knows his focus must remain on the current monster, and his immediate automotive interest must be on Gonzalez's Datsun. The Beast is occupied.

Palmer sits left of the podium, several rows back, Ross and Lowe seated on either side. The briefing room filling with troopers, officers, and brass, he watches Monroe pace in front of the ceiling-to-floor curtains forming a backdrop. Palmer's known Monroe since he was a cub, just out of the academy, admiring his equal parts work ethic and political savvy. Wearing his dress uniform, Detective Commander Captain Jefferson Monroe's an imposing figure; tall and sculpted with close-cropped black hair and clean-shaven brown skin complementing his charcoal-gray uniform and deep-chestnut leather accoutrements.

At forty-five, Monroe's already among the highest-ranking Black public safety officers in the country and a strong candidate to replace Superintendent Brisbane in a few years. His difficult ascension has opened the doors of opportunity for younger troopers of color. Still, some would argue the opportunity he seeks is more self-serving than altruistic. As he watches Monroe walk back and forth, Palmer observes the crimson piping on his shirt and the stripes down his pant legs, streaks of blood on a troubled soul.

Once the briefing begins, Monroe provides updates on the recent discoveries before taking questions. Afterward, he seeks out Palmer. "Can you hold on, Frank? I've got additional information I'd like to share with you. Just let me kiss some ass for a few minutes, and I'll meet you upstairs in Steve's office."

Stricker slithers over, acknowledging Ross and Lowe with a nod. "Hi, Frank. What did Monroe say to you?"

"Hello, Trooper Stricker," Ross says, noticing Palmer's disinterest.

"*Detective* Stricker!" Tugging at his belt from the sides, Stricker's fingers brush his holster. "Did he tell you we're taking two teams down to Bryant College tomorrow to start combing the woods around the school? Think there might be more bodies there?"

Palmer reaches for a cigarette. "Didn't see where there were any found around Slatersville Reservoir, Detective Stricker."

"Up to seven, huh? Got a few missing, too. How many does he need to pass the Boston Strangler? Seven more?"

Palmer taps a cigarette against the pack. "Well, *Detective* Stricker, that assumes the Boston Strangler was the perpetrator of all thirteen murders. There were those of us involved in the case who believe the patterns were inconsistent with the behavioral profile of one killer. That said, myth and popular culture are pervasive, and simple minds will find convenient solutions more satisfying. Whether DeSalvo murdered one, thirteen, or any number in between, is irrelevant. He's dead. Whitey and the Winter Hill Gang saw to that. So, I don't care about the count, and you shouldn't either. What we should care about is the growing number of grieving families." Palmer pats Stricker's shoulder. "But I'm sure you'll keep us updated, won't you, Dean?" He lights his cigarette and walks away, leaving a cloud of smoke for Stricker to choke on.

Upstairs, Palmer takes a seat in Metcalf's office, Ross and Lowe stand by the door, and Metcalf sits behind his desk. Monroe comes in a few minutes later, turns his chair backward, and faces Palmer. "We're taking a lot of calls, Frank. A lot of dead ends, but we're following up on the credible ones and pulling some common threads. I didn't want to share this information downstairs because I'm concerned about leaks, but I made sure Brisbane knows."

Metcalf sets an ashtray near Palmer. "This is some interesting shit, Frank."

Monroe nods. "We've had a dozen callers say they've seen a small orange car at four crime scenes. Seven provided additional details, calling it a small, orange foreign car, while three identified an orange Datsun 510. All describe the car as having a lot of dings and rust. A number observed the car driving around the parking lot at Lincoln Park in North Dartmouth."

Lowe leans close to Palmer's ear and whispers. "Chief, Gonzalez drives a beat-up, orange Datsun 510."

Palmer waves Lowe off. "Please continue, Jeff."

"Some of the same callers, along with others, report seeing a tall, well-built or pumped-up, Latino in his forties or fifties walking around several of the locations, including Lincoln Park, Hunt's Mill, and Roger Williams. Most said they saw him holding binoculars. A few witnesses described him as scary while others pointed out a white T-shirt and tattoos on his biceps."

Palmer flicks his cigarette over the ashtray. "That sounds like Gonzalez, all right. What else?"

"There were also a number of callers who saw a very tall or very large White man with black hair. Said he was wearing a blue uniform and walking by himself. They mentioned things like a delivery driver uniform, sanitation worker, or mechanic. He was spotted at Lincoln Park, Hunt's Mill, Roger Williams, and Stepstone Falls. The only other consistency is a tan or brown, maybe a tan and brown, AMC Pacer seen by several witnesses at two locations: Lincoln Park and Hunt's Mill. It's a brand-new model just released earlier this year and very different looking, so it stands out."

Palmer taps his temple with his finger. "Steve, can you get several search warrants from Judge Landis tomorrow? Ross will provide you with the background information we have on Jericho Simon Gonzalez, one of the groundskeepers at Bryant College. He drives a beat-up orange Datsun 510 and has a prior for voluntary manslaughter. I want to search his apartment, car, and the maintenance building at Bryant. I think they call it the Shed. We can do all three while he's working tomorrow."

Metcalf waves Ross over. "I'm on it, Frank."

Palmer rubs his chin. "Agent Lowe, I need you to head down to the DMV tomorrow morning and have them check their records for any AMC Pacers registered since they were released. Have them search for primary color brown or tan. Let's cross-check the results with students, faculty, and staff at Bryant. If you come up empty, check with the Massachusetts DMV."

"Chief, Lumen doesn't own a car," Lowe says.

"I didn't say we were looking for Lumen's car."

Monroe watches Lowe exit, looking back at Palmer with concern. "You think we might have him?"

Palmer stares at Monroe, brows furrowed. "Maybe."

"What's troubling you, Frank?"

"The binoculars and the Pacer."

"Why?"

Palmer presses his cigarette into the ashtray. "If you were the killer, would you walk around an amusement park with a pair of binoculars? The Pacer would also attract attention, right? So, why would the killer drive a recognizable car or have an unusual object with him?" He shakes his head. "Something tells me we're gonna need a smoking gun on this one, gentlemen."

# 66

# A PRIVATE NIGHTMARE

## TUESDAY, 14 OCTOBER 1975

*P almer takes a deep breath in the cool, promising first light of morning; the smell of oak and wet grass fills his nostrils, throat, and lungs, temporarily replacing the sting of tobacco.* Standing just outside the Shed's office entrance, flanked by Ross and Lowe, he notices the dark rings around their eyes and the stubble on Lowe's chin. For an instant, he thinks he may be pushing them too hard but knows the killer won't rest. So they can't either. Not until they stop him.

"Thank you for meeting with us so early, Mr. Griffin," Palmer says.

Griffin's smile is cautious. "As I said last week, Investigator Palmer, anything I can do to help."

"I appreciate that." Palmer reciprocates with his warmest grin. "State troopers will be canvassing the surrounding woods for the next couple of days. You should've been notified sometime over the weekend. Is that correct?"

Griffin nods.

"I understand Detective Monroe will be briefing you on what to expect and police protocol." Palmer waits for Griffin's acknowledgment. "In addition, I need to inform you we'll have an investigative team searching this facility and a vehicle in the parking lot. Search warrants have been provided to President Archer and are available at the office based on his discretion."

"Are you looking at one of my guys as the killer?" Griffin places his hand across his chest. "Because I can vouch for any of them."

"We're just following every possible lead at this point, Mr. Griffin." The orange glow of Palmer's cigarette pierces the remaining darkness like a searchlight. "What we know is a young girl's body was found on the grounds, there's another local girl who's been missing more than a month, and the parents of an incoming student from Pennsylvania just reported their daughter missing as well. We need to pull every thread to unravel this case."

"I understand."

"What I need from you is simple." Palmer looks over Griffin's shoulder and sees Lumen walking up the road. "There will be two search teams here today. One will be starting along the access road here. They won't need support. Please ensure your men assist the team on the opposite end of campus today. They'll be searching behind the dormitories and gymnasium where the girl's body was discovered last Thursday. I don't want any workers near this facility. Our investigative team will need at least the morning to conduct their searches here."

"Yes, sir."

Palmer steps to the side of Griffin. "Good morning, Mr. Lumen. You're at work early." He scans the brightening sky above the tree line. "Looks to be a nice one." His eyes settle back on Lumen. "Enjoy your day, gentlemen."

Walking back to the Shed parking lot, Palmer picks up a sheet of paper—a Halloween party announcement—lying on the ground. He considers the public fascination with ghosts, skeletons, and corpses while watching troopers filter through the trees in search of a private nightmare. Even after the Halloween decorations have been taken down, the candy is gone, and the public's interest has subsided, his hunt for monsters and battle with demons will persist. Crumpling the announcement, he tosses it in a nearby trash can.

Palmer leans against his car, lights a cigarette, and, like an expectant father, waits in silent anticipation, though no celebration will follow what might be delivered here.

Forty-five minutes later, Stricker, standing on the opposite side of the access road, waves him over.

Palmer pretends not to notice.

After several failed attempts, Stricker bustles over. "Morning, Frank."

Palmer's eyes remain focused on the trees. "Dean."

Stricker blocks Palmer's view. "Any word from the northwest search team? Think we'll find anything?"

"I don't know, Dean." Palmer walks toward the Shed. "I'm sure you'll let us know if you do."

Stricker hustles to keep up with Palmer before stepping out front. "Heard a rumor you think the Pastoral Predator's here on campus. That true?"

"That what they're calling the killer?" Palmer navigates around Stricker. "You pay attention to the headlines and rumors, Dean. I'll investigate the truth." He speeds up, leaving Stricker in his wake.

At the Shed, his back to Palmer, Lowe leans on one of the work trucks.

Palmer places his hand on Lowe's shoulder. "Are all the groundskeepers accounted for and occupied elsewhere?"

Lowe looks over his shoulder. "Oh, hi, Chief." He turns to face Palmer. "Griffin has them all working behind the dormitories and gymnasium. Pretty messy back there with all the mud. Should keep them busy into tomorrow."

"What time's the investigative team getting here?"

"Supposed to be here by eight thirty."

"Has Gerry radioed with any updates on Gonzalez's apartment?"

"Yeah, the team's just waiting for the other roommate to leave for work. Ross confirmed his work schedule yesterday, so they should be starting soon."

"Okay, stay with the investigative team when it gets here. I'll be checking on the two perimeter-canvassing teams. I'll take the handheld with me. Keep me posted."

After checking on the northwest team, Palmer walks back to the Shed parking lot, resting against the trunk of his Bonneville. A cool breeze tickles the trees, wrestling the weakest leaves from their sanctuary. Turning up his jacket collar, he crosses his arms. An hour later, Monroe joins him.

Monroe buttons his uniform coat. "Must be rain coming. Breeze is chilly, huh?"

Offering the slightest nod, Palmer looks longingly at the fur around Monroe's neck.

"Forensics confirmed the cause of death for the Delaney girl," Monroe says.

"What did they say?"

"Looks like asphyxiation but can't be certain. The skin tissue and vital organs pretty much melted into the swamp. We're officially linking it, given the approximate timing, location, and similarities to the killer's M.O."

Unfolding his arms, Palmer digs out a cigarette. "I believe that's a safe assumption."

Monroe rubs his hands together. "Hotline's received a few more calls about the AMC Pacer. One caller remembered talking to a tall male with gelled dark hair. Told them the guy had just parked a du-al-tone, brown-and-tan, two-door Pacer in the Roger Williams parking lot when he tried to ask how the guy liked his car. But the caller said the guy was in a hurry and just said, 'It's great,' as he jogged away."

"There may be a link there, but I still can't help wondering why the killer would drive such an obvious vehicle. Have you taken a look at one?" Palmer shakes his head. "It's a shitty-looking car."

"Don't imagine brown would make it look any better, then." Monroe laughs.

"Should get some registration data this afternoon or tomorrow morning." Palmer brushes a leaf from his hair. "I'm gonna head over to the northwest team. I've seen enough of Stricker's fat ass."

Palmer takes the long route, walking the southwest perimeter across the townhouse parking lots. He pays particular attention to the cars out front of Suite Fifteen Barrington.

A little past ten, Lowe's voice comes across the handheld. "Chief?"

"Yeah?"

"I think you'll wanna see this, sir."

"I'll be right there."

Back at the Shed parking lot, Monroe and Lowe stand near the open passenger door of Gonzalez's orange Datsun. Kneeling outside the passenger seat, a white-gloved agent is bagging evidence.

Monroe backs away from the door. "Hey, Frank, we found the binoculars."

Palmer leans over the kneeling agent. "That's a connection, but not a strong one. Was that firearm retrieved from the car?"

Monroe nods. "The revolver was also in the glove box."

"Well, it's not smoking, but it's a gun."

"No gun was used in the murders."

Palmer tilts his head, looks at Monroe. "I know. So who's Gonzalez looking for?"

Stepping back, Monroe shakes his head. "You don't think he's the killer, do you?"

"Impossible to tell at this point." Palmer stares into the woods. "He may be, or he may be looking for the killer." He turns to the white-gloved agent. "Where are the cartridges?"

The white-gloved agent stands, holding two sealed bags. "There are no cartridges."

"What about in the gun?"

"There are *no* cartridges."

 

℗almer finishes his noon call with Gerry and stares at Lowe leaning against the front fender of the Bonneville. Facing away from him, Palmer can see Lowe needs a haircut, the young agent's wavy hair with perfect bounce suffering wind exhaustion. Palmer thinks back to when he himself was the youngest member of the team, concerned with his own looks. Watching Lowe wait on his instructions, Palmer wonders if the kid's next in line.

Grabbing a nearly empty pack of cigarettes from the dashboard, Palmer steps out of the car. "How's your wife handling the long nights?"

Lowe tilts his head, brows raised. "It's a lot with the kids," he says, shrugging, "but she knew what she was signing up for."

"For your sake, I hope she always remembers." Palmer pats Lowe on the back. "Let's see if we can close this one down so you can get back to your family." He shakes his head. "Unfortunately, kiddo, it may get a lot worse before it gets better."

Lowe looks to the gravel at his feet. "What did Agent Ross have to say?"

"Gerry's headed here. They found nothing in his apartment other than a few neatly folded white tees and a Bible with some scribbling in the margins. Ross said you could bounce a quarter off the bedcovers, and a crucifix was the only item on the walls in his room. No papers. No magazines. No mail. His toiletries were stowed in the nightstand. Not even a radio. He's clearly not materialistic and appears to be Christian. For a disorganized killer, he's certainly structured in his personal life."

"There was nothing in his locker either. Even his beat-up car's meticulous inside." Lowe shakes his head. "You're not thinking he's the killer, are you?"

Palmer digs out the only cigarette in the pack. "Can't tell, but I fear the vultures in the press will rush to judgment when they get a name and look into his past. And they always do. Some of the best investigators work for the papers." He crushes the empty pack, tossing it on the driver's seat. "He may be the killer, but there are still a lot of loose ends. Speaking of which, have you heard anything from the DMV yet?"

"I have to call at four thirty; see where they stand. After all, it is the DMV."

"What about the used gloves in the Shed?"

"They were picked up by one of Ryan's labbies about thirty minutes ago."

Palmer sees Stricker approach, bouncing on the gravel. "Hey, Frank, you seen Monroe?"

"I think he headed back to the barracks." Palmer lights his cigarette. "Why? What's going on?"

Hands on his knees, Stricker's panting. "We found skeletal remains under the leaves. Clothing's still evident on the corpse."

"Let's go take a look." Palmer taps Lowe's shoulder. "You go with Ross after he gets here. Head downtown and talk to Metcalf. Find out where he stands with the arrest warrant and when he's gonna paste a blue."

"Who?" Stricker, still panting, straightens up. "Who's the arrest warrant for?"

"C'mon, Dean, let's go see what your boys have dug up."

Stricker follows Palmer. "Who's being arrested?"

Palmer walks at a brisk pace past several troopers chatting along the road, straight through the trees to where two more troopers are standing about a hundred yards in. Stricker struggles to keep up.

Palmer crouches next to the skull. "Anybody touch the remains?"

A young trooper steps forward. "A couple of us removed a few leaves to confirm the remains."

"Was anything else moved?"

"No, Investigator Palmer, we were extremely careful."

Palmer takes a stick and brushes away several leaves. "Have forensics and photography been called in?"

Stricker motions the troopers to leave. "One of my boys called it in right after the discovery. Anything you can tell?"

"It's tough to determine when this may have occurred. I can tell the body's in advanced decay. It hasn't quite become dry, so I'd venture a guess of five to eight weeks, but I could be off."

"Think it's the same bastard?"

"Maybe, but not the same M.O."

"How do you know?"

"This is a female, though I have no way of estimating her age." Palmer uses the stick to point at the skull. "But this one was shot."

Stricker leans over the remains. "Damn."

Palmer stands and tosses the stick. "Alright, get Monroe over here. Your men need to finish up. They may be needed at a new location tomorrow or Friday." Leaves crunch under his feet as he makes his way back to the road.

"Hey, Frank," Stricker calls to Palmer, "who's getting arrested?"

"A killer, Dean. A killer."

# 67

# THE PASTORAL PREDATOR

## TUESDAY, 14 OCTOBER 1975

M o listens to the collective buzz of his coworkers on the drive to lunch. He silently joins in their speculation about the police presence, the prospect of more grisly discoveries like the one last week, and what their boss knows that might explain the reasons for today's anomalies. Why was the crew cab already waiting for them at the gymnasium lot this morning? Why didn't they all meet at the Shed for the drive to lunch? Why are they supporting the search team at the far end of campus and not the one across from the Shed? When they arrive at the restaurant, they continue to speculate, talking soft enough to assume their boss doesn't hear. Mo listens.

Reading at a separate table, Griffin ignores their whispers.

Mo pulls a chair next to Griffin. "Game three tonight."

Griffin takes a sip of coffee. "Mm-hmm."

"You think they can win?"

"Yup."

"I hope so. Cincinnati's really good at home."

"That's right, son." Griffin folds the paper and stands. "Listen up, boys. As you know, we have some guests on campus." He holds up his paper, showing them the headline—*Manhunt: Pastoral Predator—Freak of Nature.* "They're looking for this guy."

"That dude's prolific!" Sprinkles says. "As my mama always says: *If you're gonna do something, anything, no matter what that be, do it right and be the best.* He's the best."

"Be that as it may," Griffin says, "the state police and federal investigators will be on campus through tomorrow, possibly Thursday."

Theo points at Griffin. "They think there's something going on here, huh? Maybe looking for more girls' bodies?"

Griffin glares at Theo. "Guys, I'm talking. You can all ask your questions when I'm done." He takes a prolonged sip of coffee. "We'll be available to the authorities, as needed and as directed, for the duration of their investigation. As you know, they've started in the woods on the northwest side, behind the dorms and gym where the gunshots over on Mr. Gunderson's property can typically be heard, and on the east side near the Shed. They'll access Gunderson's property from our side, as two of the missing girls they're searching for are Bryant students. There are a couple of ponds on his property, so they should be back there a while. Our job's to assist the authorities in their search while ensuring the safety of the students, faculty, and visitors. All events and practices in the athletic fields are being suspended until their investigation's complete. This will keep everyone away from the back of the campus and traffic off the access road allowing the search teams to operate uninterrupted." He pauses, taking a long look at the crew. "That's what I've got."

King leans forward. "They think the killer's on campus?"

Griffin taps his fingers on the newspaper. "That never came up. I wouldn't know. Sarge, you got a question?"

"Yeah. What's the school doing to protect the female students?"

"President Archer mentioned a notice will be going out to all students and staff informing them of the police investigation. The school's also hiring private security to patrol the campus day and night until the killer's caught. We'll be changing out the walkway lights to brighter bulbs over the next few days, and students will be restricted from using the outer walkways and paths in the woods."

Juanito's voice is shaky. "Are they searching any buildings? What about the lockers in the Shed?"

"They have the ability to search wherever they choose, including the lockers in the Shed, but they're not looking for Playboy or pot." Griffin leans forward. "Why, Juanito? Is there something you're hiding in your locker? Do I need to investigate?"

The conversation continues, growing more gruesome and less relevant. Mo doesn't ask questions. He'd prefer to discuss tonight's game but is left watching his coworkers' animated faces and listening to their speculation. He notices Griffin glancing alternately between his paper and Flatbush.

Flatbush remains silent throughout, his face stoic, listening and watching his boss's subtle gestures and movements. He's been around dangerous criminals and engaged in violent crimes. He's conditioned to understand the nature of fear, premature judgment, and irrational responses. Intermittently, he locks eyes with Griffin. Each time, his boss is first to look away. Flatbush is savvy enough to know the score. His history will be resurrected in connection with any discoveries made on campus. His past, skin color, and silence will conspire. Yes, he knows the score.

A little after one, with the crew getting up to leave, Sarge puts his hand on Griffin's shoulder. "Anything else we can do, boss?"

Griffin looks past Sarge and to the background where Flatbush is standing. After several silent moments, he answers. "Pray."

Each game of the World Series is an event at the Thompson home. Kay's parents have invited Mo and Carlton over to watch game three. Carlton's coming back from Wellesley after a long holiday weekend with his mother, so Kay picked Mo up at the townhouse.

The large console in the living room's a giant magnet. Even as he sits in the dining room, enjoying an early dinner with the Thompsons, Mo can't take his eyes off the TV. After dinner, he heads out to investigate the surrounding area and calm his nerves. The Hillcrest Estates are a recent suburban housing development and Mo walks along newly paved community roads, following several quiet, wooded paths before arriving back at the Thompson residence soon after the pregame begins. Hoping for a better outcome, Mo sits in a different spot than he did when watching game two with Kay's family on Sunday. By the time Carlton arrives, the game's already begun. Mo scarcely manages a nod.

Mrs. Thompson watches Mo wedge himself into the edge of the family's white fabric sofa, a bag of Cheetos resting between his lap and the armrest, a can of Sprite in his left hand, and his uniform stained from a day's toil and sweat. She winces and hands him a paper towel.

Midway through the game, the home team's down by four. Mr. Thompson sulks on his chair, Carlton has his arm around Kay's slumping shoulders, and Mo's lodged himself deeper into the sofa. Mrs. Thompson, standing in the doorway, closes her eyes, placing the palm of her hand over her forehead.

Other than Mrs. Thompson, the mood in the house improves when the Red Sox tie the game. Mr. Thompson sits at the edge of his chair, Kay's hands are clasped in prayer, and Mo's less visible than the Cheeto dust on the armrest.

A heroic comeback is spoiled when the home plate umpire does not call interference on a sacrifice bunt. The resultant furor on the field fuels rage among Red Sox fans that only grows when Cincinnati later scores the winning run. Game over, Mr. Thompson stomps out of the room, Kay resists a peck on the cheek from Carlton, and Mo emerges from the crevice in the sofa. Mrs. Thompson scurries back into the living room, escorting the two young men out. Neither notice the fabric cleaner in her hand as they're shuttled to the front door.

With the Red Sox trailing in the series, there's little to rejoice on the ride back to the townhouse. An oldies station plays 1950s rock and roll, Carlton taps his fingers on the steering wheel, and Mo broods over the injustice of human error in sports. Between songs, a news update further dampens the mood:

POLICE DISCOVERED SKELETAL REMAINS AT BRYANT COLLEGE THIS AFTERNOON. THIS IS THE SECOND BODY TO BE DISCOVERED AT THE SMALL PRIVATE SCHOOL IN NORTH SMITHFIELD. POLICE HAVEN'T IDENTIFIED THE REMAINS OR WHETHER THEY CAN BE TIED TO THE KILLER NOW KNOWN AS THE PASTORAL PREDATOR. IF LINKED TO THE PREVIOUS MURDERS, THIS WOULD REPRESENT THE EIGHTH DISCOVERY IN JUST OVER A MONTH.

Carlton's thankful Kay's home with her parents.

Mo's relieved when the music comes back on.

# 68

# MR. WILLOUGHBY'S TOYS

## WEDNESDAY, 15 OCTOBER 1975

M*o does not look forward to Wednesday lunch with the same enthusiasm as previous weeks; the incident at Langford's house over the weekend, police activity on the school grounds, and last night's game three loss undermining his usual anticipation.* Standing at the entrance to the dining hall, he reads the letter from the president's office while waiting for the professor to arrive. Eventually, with the dining hall filling up, he decides to go through the lunch line alone, locating a table with two unoccupied chairs and an abandoned newspaper.

Once seated, Mo opens the sports section. He continues to feel the sting of an umpire's decision costing his team the game. Recognizing Red Sox fans will not soon forgive or forget, he wonders if the umpire is sad knowing his decision hurt so many people. Reviewing the box score, he considers how much worse losing must be for the players as they leave the field and how *they* might feel this morning.

The pitcher who took the loss, Jim Willoughby, had been called on to throw more than three innings last night, one of his longest outings of the season, facing the Reds and the pressure of pitching in the World Series. The run he allowed was unearned, and the loss undeserved, but recorded, nonetheless. He can still picture the arguing on the field after the controversial call, and Willoughby's head hung low. The pitcher's slow walk to the dugout after the play reminds Mo of the Willoughby couple from Remington Baptist Church and a fateful visit to their home when he was almost twelve and a half.

By early spring 1963, Sunday morning church services were no longer K&E marketing events. Gone were the days of driving the pickup, Ken preferring to take the Caddy in recent months. After dropping Grandma Cleveland off at Sumerduck Baptist, Mo and his father would head to Remington for their weekly spiritual nourishment. Ken insisted he better understood the rantings of Pastor Bainbridge, but a majority of the congregation in the hearty country church suspected a more salacious motivation.

Sitting in the back row with his son, Ken gazed upon the worshippers like a flock ready to be fleeced. One female parishioner in particular consistently attracted his attention. Seated by her husband was an exotic, brown-haired beauty in her mid-twenties with caramel skin and dazzling green eyes.

Mrs. Willoughby was young and alluring, European features accented with southeast Asian flare. Born out of wedlock to a Burmese mother who died during childbirth and an already absent British infantryman, she was a victim of Burma's crude system of orphanages and the Japanese occupation during World War II. She survived the war, spending six horrific years on the streets of Rangoon before being brought to America by a family living in Alexandria, Virginia. Her savior, a Korean War veteran, was scouting base locations when introduced to the thirteen-year-old girl at a makeshift brothel on the outskirts of the Burmese capital in late 1951. She was adopted under lenient Burmese legislation the following year.

"Good morning, John." Ken's words went in the direction of Mr. Willoughby, but his eyes were drawn in the direction of Mrs. Willoughby's curves as she crossed the fellowship hall.

"Hi, Ken. What's up?" Mr. Willoughby ran his hand under his belly, above where the belt buckle hung at a ninety-degree angle, staring at the floor. He wasn't young, a full two decades older than his wife.

"Not much," Ken said, his eyes returning to Mr. Willoughby in time to follow the motion of his hand. "Looks like business has been treating you good."

Nodding, Mr. Willoughby released a soft grunt. "Ain't easy owning a deli, working around meats and treats all day."

Ken gave Mr. Willoughby a playful nudge. "I hear you, John. But it buys some nice toys, don't it?" He nodded in the direction of Mrs. Willoughby.

The two men shared a laugh.

Mo recognized Mr. Willoughby's smile from the deli. He stood between the men and wondered what toys Mr. Willoughby had at home, hoping he might one day be invited over.

Mr. Willoughby's smile faded. "Yeah, but I'd like to go back to my younger days. All that mattered was booze, babes, and boxing." For Mr. Willoughby, his wife was a trophy placed alongside the bronzed gloves and plaques on his dusty, decorated shelf.

The conversation extended a few short minutes in a cordial yet nondescript manner until Mrs. Willoughby approached.

Ken cleared his throat. "How's the back porch door holding up?"
She continued past them. "It's fine."

An air of feigned disinterest hung between the two men as she shimmied away. Mo's eyes followed his father's to Mrs. Willoughby's floral-pattern dress and the pronounced rise and fall of its hem.

Ken swiveled around, following her into the church sanctuary. "How about that roof leak? You need me to come by and repair it?" Ken's voice faded as they proceeded out to the parking lot. He glanced at Mo, saying, "Get in the car, Son. It's time to go." His attention then shifted back to Mrs. Willoughby's needs.

Mrs. Willoughby held a hand up to shield her eyes from the sun. "Alright, I'll see you Wednesday morning..." Noticing her husband watching as he walked over, she spoke a little louder, "to repair the roof."

"I'll swing by Tuesday so I can match the shingles and pick 'em up at the supply house," Ken said.

Mrs. Willoughby nodded while Ken retreated to his truck. Walking toward Mr. Willoughby, her hand dropped to her side.

Mo saw her look back at his father and wink. He wondered if the sun only affected one eye.

Like weeds in a garden, as quickly as old sins are washed away, new ones sprout. Mrs. Willoughby had been a staple of local gossip for several years, rumors of marital infidelity a favored topic among decent womenfolk in these parts. Wives of men between the ages of twenty and sixty paid particular attention to any sign of communication between their husbands and the 'town Jezebel.'

For her part, Mrs. Willoughby avoided any involvement in clubs or organizations, preferring intimate engagements and the luxuries afforded by her husband's noble shop. Mr. Willoughby's deli closed at ten on weeknights and eleven on Saturdays. Nosy neighbors watched with prurient delight as cars with solitary male occupants arrived and left the Willoughby property on a nightly basis. It was clear to onlookers Mrs. Willoughby did not discriminate.

One such vehicle, with growing frequency, was Ken Lumen's Cadillac.

On the last Saturday in May, two months after Mrs. Willoughby's wink, with Grandma Cleveland visiting her sister in Charlottesville and his hand bandaged from a wolf spider bite, Mo hung his good hand out the window as his father drove along Sumerduck and Union Church Roads. Just after Sumerduck Run, before Red Cedar Road, Mo's father pointed to an elegant country manor, conspicuous against the early evening sky.

Larger than many of the farmhouses in Southern Fauquier, the Willoughby home was a white, two-story structure with fluted columns and a large wraparound porch littered with weathered rocking chairs and porch swings accented with throw pillows. Altogether, it was a comfortable-looking home demanding children to fully exhaust its five bedrooms and numerous charms.

The gardens at either end of the house were substantial, though not well-maintained—flowers interlaced with weeds to create an aura both sanctimonious and sacrilegious. A patch of roof shingles replaced by Ken was still evidenced by its darker gravel mix, presenting itself as a stain upon the landmark—one that only time and weather would allow to fade.

The evening was pristine, with cloudless sky and breezeless calm. Even the dirt kicked up by Ken's Cadillac couldn't disturb the gentle quality of this picturesque evening.

As Mo stepped out of the car, sterile serenity surrendered to audible turmoil coming from inside the house. He watched his father stand by the open driver's door, staring at a yellow Oldsmobile behind the house.

Motioning his son to leave the passenger door open, Ken was drawn to the front of the house by the sound of a woman's muffled crying.

Mo followed his father onto the porch. "What's that noise, Dad?"

Ken raised a finger to his lips as his only response, his entire focus on the sounds coming from inside. Approaching the front door, they heard another distinct voice, masculine and breaking through tears. His father stretched his finger toward the doorbell but froze a hair's breadth away.

They heard the man's voice clearly. "Get out! Get out, you whore!"

The woman's voice pleaded in response. "Stop it, please. Stop it!"

His father's finger retreating from the doorbell, he gripped the doorknob instead. Turning and pushing, Ken thrust himself into the center of the scene.

Distracted by the unexpected disturbance, Mr. Willoughby hesitated before realizing the significance of the intrusion. "Is it him?" he demanded through tears.

"What does it matter?" Mrs. Willoughby replied. Her eyes sought solace under her palm.

"Is it him?! Tell me, you whore!"

Mrs. Willoughby did not respond.

Mo stood next to the main staircase and leaned against the rail post. He could see tears escaping from under Mrs. Willoughby's curled fingers.

Mr. Willoughby stood over his wife, his fist raised. "Tell me, or I'll beat it out of you!"

Mrs. Willoughby's head moved very little, an imperceptible nod.

Mr. Willoughby lunged at Ken, hands clenched, tears redirected across his sideburns. He stopped just short of where Ken had assumed a defensive position and fell to the floor, letting out a tortured shriek followed by profuse crying. "Please. Just take her away. Take her from my sight." After a brief moment of unrestrained tears, he cried, "Why, baby? Why?"

Glancing above where Mr. Willoughby's huddled, shaking body lay crying on the floor, Mo saw cobwebbed trophies and tarnished bronzed boxing gloves seated on a dusty shelf. He looked around for toys. But he saw none.

Stepping forward to console the broken man, Ken reconsidered, turning instead to his wife. "Come with me," he said, helping Mrs. Willoughby out of the chair and guiding her through the front door. "Come on, Mo. Let's go."

Listening to Mrs. Willoughby sob on the ride home, Mo struggled to understand what the events at the Willoughby home had to do with his father. Although he recognized the couple from church and knew Mr. Willoughby as The Man Behind the Meat Counter, he seldom recalled his father saying much to either of them.

Arriving back at the Lumen home, Mo stood in the doorway while his father escorted Mrs. Willoughby to the living room, stood her by his recliner, and removed her sweater. Noticing Mrs. Willoughby's swollen tummy, Mo thought it might be the source of her pain.

Ken helped her into his chair. "You okay?"

Mrs. Willoughby nodded.

Ken looked to the doorway. "Mo, get some water for Miss Clara."

As he turned, Mo heard Miss Clara's words to his father. "What have we done?"


Finished with the sports section, and still waiting for Langford to join him, Mo stares at the headline: *Pastoral Predator Claims Another Victim; Second Body Found on Bryant Campus.* Choosing to ignore the article, he continues to think about Mrs. Willoughby—Jake's mother—the unwelcome houseguest whom he'd called Miss Clara. She had been in his life only briefly, but after she arrived, everything was different. And after Jake was born and she left, his father would never be the same. Recalling the umpire's missed call last night, he considers again how one person's decisions can impact so many lives. He wonders if Miss Clara ever feels bad about abandoning

Jake and his father.

Langford arrives after Mo has finished eating. "Hey," he says, looming over Mo, holding no tray, "I only have a few minutes." He sits very close and speaks in hushed tones. "This is strange, huh? All these police around campus?"

Mo looks up at Langford and nods, sliding his chair away.

Langford's eyes dart around the room. "Police are all over my town, too. Two girls are missing from here and another two around Slatersville. I think they're getting closer to the killer."

"I hope so. I had to start work really early today. I was starving by noon. Did you watch the game last night?"

"No, I didn't have time. How are you doing?"

"I'm okay. I hope the Red Sox win tonight."

"Me too." Langford picks up the front section of the paper, pointing to the headline. "This is crazy, right?"

"I know," Mo says. "He's hurting a lot of people."

Sliding his chair back, Langford stands. "I'm sorry, Mo, I've got to go. I'll see you next Wednesday. Maybe the Red Sox will be World Series champions by then." He looks out the window and across the campus, tossing the newspaper back onto the table. "Maybe they'll get this guy, too. And all this will be over."

# 69

# IMPRISONED BY IGNORANCE

## WEDNESDAY, 15 OCTOBER 1975

P*almer has a perfect view.* From the corner of Flower and Whelan, he can see the Woonasquatucket River, Merino Park, and, most importantly, Two Whelan Road. He's been sitting in his Bonneville with Ross and Lowe since three, waiting for more than an hour. At the other entrance to the complex, Monroe waits on the corner of Bodell and Whelan in an unmarked vehicle. Metcalf's car and a half-dozen cruisers are situated where Whelan dead ends into Route 6, while a handful of blues are positioned in Merino Park.

Familiar with stakeouts, residents of the project are quiet this afternoon. Stones, bricks, and bottles laying silent along the side of the road, school bus drivers feel a little safer on days like this, parents breathe a little easier. Imprisoned by their own ignorance, gang members and drug dealers watch from the safety of their brick and glass perches—jailbirds wondering whose turn it is to feed the pigs.

Amid all the enforced calm, Lowe brings Palmer up to speed on information from the DMV. "Eight hundred forty-one AMC Pacers have been registered across Rhode Island since late February. Four hundred thirty-two are X two-door models with forty-seven registered as either brown or tan as the primary color. Cross-referencing those registered owners against the list of Bryant College students, staff, and faculty resulted in one match: Michael Dean Langford, a professor of humanities. He lives in Slatersville."

"Now that's interesting, isn't it?" Palmer tosses his spent cigarette out the window. "Do we know how tall he is?"

"DMV provided a copy of his license listing him at six-four. He's a forty-four-year-old Caucasian with dark brown hair and brown eyes."

"Gentlemen, I believe we may have another person of interest." Palmer taps out a fresh cigarette. "After we're done here, Gerry, head over to the station. Talk to Metcalf. Find out if any new information has been called in." Palmer lights his smoke. "Lowe, I need you to follow up with forensics. See if they've been able to confirm the identity of the skeletal remains. Then, check with ballistics. Find out if they've identified the bullet gauge. Ask them if Gonzalez's gun has been fired recently. I'm gonna visit Osmond, let him know we need a full rundown on this Professor Langford as soon as possible. I want to personally oversee the boys back at the office working this tonight."

Lowe points out a tall, pencil-thin Black man with a well-rehearsed stagger. He's wearing a white tank top, patched blue jeans, and an ear-to-ear grin. "Take a look at this character. Is he coming to talk to us?" He unclips his holster, feeling for the grip.

Reaching back, Palmer grabs Lowe's arm. "Settle down, kiddo. He's not packing."

The man tips his purple velvet fedora as he struts by. "Good afternoon, gentlemen." His smile widens. "I do think I smell bacon in the air today." He moves on.

Lowe reclips. "Wouldn't want to raise my kids in this neighborhood."

"Be thankful you don't have to," Palmer says. "Parents here worry about more than murder. Sometimes a quick death's preferable to a long, painful life." He turns on the radio:

POLICE CONTINUE TO SEARCH FOR THE KILLER KNOWN AS THE PASTORAL PREDATOR. THE BODIES OF EIGHT YOUNG WOMEN HAVE BEEN DISCOVERED...

Ross turns the volume down. "Pastoral Predator, huh? Kinda has a nice ring."

"Seems like it doesn't take long once the national news gets hold of a story," Lowe says.

"Shh! Here he comes." Palmer takes a final puff, flicks his cigarette. "Gerry, radio the others."

Moments later, a mobile blue-and-red light parade converges to a single point; nine vehicles screeching to a halt in front of Two Whelan. A dozen shouting blues spill out with their guns pointed. The target places his grocery bags on the ground, raises his arms, and drops to his knees. His eyes stay focused down. He does not protest. He does not plead.

Several officers secure the cuffs, lifting him to his feet while another reads him his rights.

Metcalf steps forward. "State your full name."

"Jericho Simon Gonzalez."

# 70

# METCALF'S LUCKY HORSESHIT

## THURSDAY, 16 OCTOBER 1975

*P*almer can see the exhaustion in Monroe's forlorn eyes and crumpled *shirt.* Walking over, he pats Monroe on the back. Glancing at Metcalf, he sees the police chief's stubble crossing over to beard.

Monroe shakes his head. "Gonzalez will not talk. Son of a bitch is tough as an overcooked steak. Can't be intimidated. You can see he's done hard time. Keeps saying he's not the killer but won't say another goddamned word. Nothing. He's not gonna crack. Had him in the box all fucking night before the bastard finally said he won't talk without a lawyer. Could've just said that in the first five minutes. Then, I'd have gotten a full night's sleep."

Palmer leans forward to attract Monroe's focus. "Did he seem ornery or agitated?"

"He doesn't seem anything. He's not ornery. He's not agitated. He's not scared. He just gives us his name, date of birth, where he was born, and nothing else. Just keeps insisting he's not the killer."

"Did you try asking if he knows who the killer is?"

"That would imply we don't think he's the killer." Monroe buries the knuckle of his index finger under his lip. "But we believe he's the killer, right?"

Sliding out a cigarette, Palmer lays the pack on Metcalf's desk. "I don't believe anything, Jeff." Palmer pats his pants pockets, looking to Metcalf. "I know you got a light in your drawer there, Steve. Can you toss it over here, please?"

Metcalf shakes his head. "Haven't smoked in thirteen months,

Frank."

"Save the horseshit for someone else." Palmer holds out his hand. "C'mon, give me the matches."

Opening his desk drawer, Metcalf lights himself a Lucky before tossing the matchbook to Palmer. "I started again when this bastard showed up."

Palmer strikes a match. "Uh-huh." He turns back to Monroe. "I'm of the opinion Gonzalez knows who the killer is, or at least thinks he knows. He doesn't have any ammunition, so either he intends to scare someone, or he doesn't trust himself not to fire the weapon. Either way, it seems to suggest someone who's not inclined to kill—at least not anymore. But he knows something. What he's got, I can't figure out, but he's got to know something."

Monroe rubs the back of his neck. "The press is already running with this. They're digging for a name. You know they'll work until they find a bone."

"Forensics validate the gunshot wound to the forehead yet?"

"They did, just a short time ago. Ballistics also reported the entry and exit holes conform to a .38 caliber from close range. That would match the load of the Smith & Wesson Model 12 found in Gonzalez's glove box. They added that the entry and exit holes could also, dependent on distance at time of shooting, be consistent with a caliber anywhere from a 9mm to a .357, but they need the bullet or casing to confirm. They were able to rule out a .22, so it was no hunting accident."

Metcalf snickers. "Doubt there are many hunting accidents at point-blank range through the head."

Monroe stares at Metcalf before continuing. "I sent a team to search for the bullet. We don't expect to find a casing. That would have required the killer to empty the revolver chamber. He's not taking time to bury the bodies, or even hide them, so it would seem unlikely. Also, CSM did conduct an exhaustive search of the immediate area, and no casing was discovered. Unfortunately, finding the bullet's gonna take some time. Searching under all that groundcover this time of year's like looking for a blind surgeon. At the recommendation of ballistics, they're fanning out in a radius of five-yard intervals from where the victim was found. They established the maximum distance at twenty-five to thirty yards after passing through the skull. Ballistics is still evaluating the gun. They'll need the casing to determine chamber marks and firing pin impression for a conclusive match. Again, not thinking that's likely."

Palmer leans back. "It's possible, based on the killer's pattern, the victim was shot elsewhere before being dragged to where we found the body."

"Which makes finding the bullet even more difficult."

"But it might help locate a casing if the firearm used was a pistol rather than a revolver."

"Let's focus on finding the bullet; see if it's a match to the revolver. Looking for a casing at this point would require more resources than we can afford." Monroe stretches his neck from side to side. "There was another girl reported missing late Tuesday night. This one's young, Frank. Fifteen."

"Kidnapping, maybe?"

"Not much reason to think so. Both parents were home when she left to walk to her friend's house around five o'clock. The family lives in the Hillcrest Estates in Smithfield."

"Christ, another one in Smithfield." Palmer turns to Metcalf. "When did the tail get attached to Gonzalez Tuesday?"

Metcalf flicks into the ashtray. "We got approval for an unmarked around five in the afternoon. They waited in front of his apartment building for Gonzalez to arrive home from work." He looks up, his eyebrows raised. "He didn't get there until nine thirty."

Palmer, cigarette hanging from his lips, claps his hands. "Son of a bitch."

"We've got a crew out searching the woods between the family and friend's houses." Monroe rubs his neck. "God, let this one be found alive. I don't want our boys to discover this little girl's body. They're already suffering fatigue."

Metcalf reaches for another Lucky before realizing the one he's holding is only half-smoked. "Even when we think we're getting closer, the bodies keep piling up."

"And on that somber note," Monroe says, throwing his hands up, "what good news do you have for us, Frank? We already know the Sox tied the series last night."

"We believe we've found the owner of the Pacer." Palmer points at Lowe. "The kid here got the registration data from DMV yesterday afternoon. One of the brown or tan Pacer two-doors was sold to a Bryant College professor back in February. His name's Michael Dean Langford. He's listed as six-four with brown hair."

Metcalf slaps the desk. "Geez, Frank, why didn't you tell us yesterday?"

"Because I didn't have enough information." Palmer pulls an envelope from his inside jacket pocket. "Talked to Osmond late yesterday afternoon and spent the night with the guys down in research burning the midnight oil. Turns out Langford was questioned about a missing woman four years ago. Maria Costas Souza was one of the crew members working on his property in Slatersville when she went missing. There was nothing to go on, and Langford was never listed as a suspect. The case is still unsolved. One of a handful of young women who went missing around Providence between late 1969 and early 1971."

"Yeah, I remember," Monroe says. "The women were all of loose morals, and the murders were spread out across eighteen months. The bodies were never found. Wasn't a big outcry from the public for closure."

"I was assisting on the Marfeo and Melei mob hits. As you know, the Providence Crime Family was a high priority for the Bureau at the time, and the missing persons cases around Providence were never linked." Palmer hands the envelope to Metcalf. "In light of this information, and taking into account the two missing girls from Slatersville, you think you can get warrants for Langford's house, property, and car?"

Metcalf nods. "Jesus, a college professor."

"Yes," Palmer says, crushing his Marlboro into the ashtray, "I think we need to pay the humanities professor a visit."

# 71

# DARK CLOUDS APPROACHING

## FRIDAY, 17 OCTOBER 1975

M*o, like the rest of the team, loves Friday morning donuts.* In truth, they all love donuts anytime, but the end of a stressful week generates greater appreciation when Griffin brings a dozen from Dunkin' along with coffee. It's chilly outside the Shed first thing in the morning as each worker selects a donut, grabs a coffee or milk, and parks himself on a tree stump.

Griffin stands at the front corner talking to several officers, his Red Sox cap in his back pocket. He sips coffee and nods. When the officers talk among themselves, Griffin looks over to Mo and winks. The head groundskeeper's head shaking, lips curled, tells Mo this is all his boss has to say about last night's game five loss. His coworkers aren't talking baseball either. The events of the past week drive discussion as they wait for Griffin. Mo focuses on the conversation between Sprinkles and Sarge.

Sprinkles holds his donut just below his mouth. "What you think they be talking about?"

"I don't know," Sarge replies. "But where do you think Flatbush was yesterday?"

"I'm thinking he's the killer, being he's all quiet and mysterious and all."

Mo agrees Flatbush is quiet but doesn't think it's a good reason for him to be the killer.

"It could just be coincidence," Sarge says, "but the news is reporting they have a suspect, and it's someone from here at the school.

I guess it could be a professor, or a student, or someone on staff."

"I'm telling you, it ain't no professor. It's always the workers. It's Flatbush, for sure."

"What about the skeleton they found here Tuesday?"

Sprinkles scrunches his forehead. "Huh?"

"Well, the body they discovered Tuesday was just a skeleton, and Flatbush arrived in February."

"How long does it take to skeletize after we die?"

"I think once you're a skeleton, there ain't any change for a long time." Sarge rubs his chin. "And when they dig bodies up years later, they still have some dried flesh on them."

The two donuts in Mo's stomach churn, his thoughts turning to his father's burial in February. He tries not to picture his father's mummification or his mother's skeleton.

When Griffin approaches, the speculation ends and the workers come to attention. His face is sullen. "Alright, guys, I'll get right to the point. Flatbush was arrested Wednesday afternoon for illegal possession of a handgun. He served time for manslaughter years ago, so he's restricted from owning, or carrying, firearms." He lowers his head. "I didn't know this when I hired him. I was informed yesterday morning in President Archer's office."

Theo raises his hand. "He the Pastoral Predator?"

Griffin waves his hand. "I'll get to that. Just be patient and hold any questions until after I'm finished. I have a lot to get through. He grew up in New York, fought in the Pacific near the very end of World War II, and was honorably discharged just as the Korean War started in 1950. When he got back to New York, he found a job as a sanitation worker.

"Early '55, he started dating a woman and wasn't aware there was another guy until he saw them together at a dance hall. From what I understand, a fight broke out after he walked over to confront her. Flatbush, as you know, is strong. He beat the guy up pretty good, but his anger and a single punch to the head caused the woman's brain to hemorrhage. She was dead before the ambulance arrived.

"The case was big news at the time, so I was able to look through microfiche of old New York papers at the Brown University Library.

He was found guilty of voluntary manslaughter, though it should have been involuntary, which is a lesser conviction. It seems, from the articles I found, the more severe verdict was a result of prejudice. The girl was White, and he was tried before an all-White jury."

"Dang!" Theo exclaims.

"1950s America, gentlemen," King proclaims. "Ain't no different today. Just take a look at all that bussing stuff up in Boston. They don't want any of us mixing up with them White folks, in their schools or at their parties."

After an abbreviated nod, Griffin continues. "He got the maximum sentence of ten to fifteen years. *And*, because he had some prior arrests for minor offenses like drug possession and disorderly conduct, he was sent to Attica."

"That place is nasty," Juanito says. "My uncle spent time there. It's where all the really bad dudes go."

Sarge points at Griffin. "Where that big riot was, right?"

Griffin nods. "But Flatbush wasn't there at that time. He was paroled in '64, completing two-years probation in New York before moving to New England. He's been working odd jobs and moving from state to state for the past nine years. He moved to Providence in February and started working here immediately after. The school did a background check on him, but they can't automatically deny an applicant just because he has a record. Their review determined he was 'low risk,' and I was not made aware of his criminal background. I hired him based on his experience working in yard maintenance."

"So, the school hired a killer," Sprinkles says.

Griffin glares at Sprinkles. "No one's saying that. He's being held because he had a gun in his glove box. Unfortunately, that's very serious for a convicted felon, so he's probably going to jail, anyway. But it doesn't mean he's the killer."

"But he *could* be the killer, right?" Sprinkles nods, glancing around at his coworkers.

Griffin shakes his head, his eyes downcast. "They searched all over the Shed, his apartment, and his car, but they didn't find anything connecting him to the murders. However, there's some

circumstantial evidence, and that's what the authorities are building their case around. We know from the news the killer subdues
his victims with a blow to the head. Also, Flatbush moved into Providence at the beginning of this year, after a couple of years living
in the Hartford area." He pauses for a few seconds. "In my heart, I
don't believe he *is* the killer, but he's got an uphill battle."

Juanito raises his hand. "I've been working with him two days
a week for the past six months. Ain't seen nothing tells me he's a
maniac."

Griffin motions for quiet. "You're all gonna get the opportunity
to share your thoughts with the investigators. They want to talk to
anyone who's been in contact with Flatbush, so you're all going to
be interviewed between this afternoon and tomorrow. When they
come over in a few minutes, they'll tell each of you where to go
and what time you'll need to be available. There's nothing to worry
about. None of you are in any trouble. They're looking for information to help solve the case. It may turn out your answers help find
the killer and clear Flatbush."

King raises a fist. "I'll help Flatbush. He's already paid the price
to the man."

Pulling his hands to his mouth, Theo rubs them together. "What
kinda questions you think they'll ask?"

"I'm guessing they'll ask how you know Flatbush," Griffin says.
"They'll want to know whether you had any outside contact with
him socially, like going to dinner or doing anything on the weekend, or whether you ever saw him anywhere other than work. They
might ask about his personality; whether he ever got angry or did
anything out of the ordinary, stuff like that." He looks at Theo with
a reassuring nod. "Just answer their questions honestly. That's the
best way to approach it. If you lie, then they'll think you have something to hide."

Mo watches Mr. Griffin wave the officers over, wondering what
information *he* could possibly offer about Flatbush to help the
police. He checks his Timex, counting the hours and minutes to
game six. He worries about the dark clouds approaching and the
chill in the air.

# 72

# SOPHISTICATED
# INDIVIDUALS

## FRIDAY, 17 OCTOBER 1975

*P*almer *admires the architectural flair of Langford's house—The Beast* *appreciates the perfect monster's lair.* Old-world flourishes remind Palmer of his parents' Victorian in Cambridge. His childhood home had almost two acres—one too many when it came time to mow. The document in front of Palmer states Langford's got sixty-four. He may admire Langford's house, but he has no interest in his property—at least none beyond investigative.

Palmer spots Langford walking up Slatersville Road, the professor's pace quickening when he realizes there are several vehicles, including two police cruisers, parked in front of his house.

Langford checks his pulse as he turns into the driveway. "Can I help you, gentlemen?"

Metcalf steps forward. "We're looking for Michael Dean Langford, a professor at Bryant College."

"I'm Professor Langford."

"Good morning, Professor. I'm Providence Police Chief Metcalf. I have with me Rhode Island State Police Captain Monroe and Chief Investigator Agent Palmer with the FBI. We have search warrants for your property."

Langford, hair disheveled, is wearing jogging pants and a Bryant sweatshirt. "What's this in connection with?"

"There are two young women missing from the area, Professor Langford," Palmer says. "We're here to search your house and property. We understand you have significant acreage out back."

Palmer shares a sly glance with Metcalf while Langford reads.

Langford takes a step back, begins rocking. "I don't quite understand what this would have to do with my house, Investigator Palmer."

"Multiple witnesses have reported seeing your vehicle near key locations in the investigation. We're just following up on those reports. It's strictly procedural."

"Of course. I want to help however I can, but I have class this morning. I need to take a shower before I leave."

"Absolutely, Professor, we want to disturb you as little as possible. We can start with your car while you shower."

"Thank you, gentlemen. I'll get the keys."

By the time Langford emerges from having showered and dressed, over a dozen squad cars and two-dozen uniformed officers are there. Talking to a group of them, Monroe points to the rear of the property while others walk toward the house and garage.

"I didn't expect so many officers," Langford says. He's dressed in a wide-lapel, gray-flannel leisure suit and a blue, wide-striped oxford shirt with checkerboard ascot.

Claws receding, Palmer hands Langford his car keys. "You do own a substantial piece of land."

Langford fiddles with the keys. "I'll be back at noon. Do you think you'll be done before then?"

"I think we'll be here most of the day, Professor, and maybe into tomorrow." Palmer licks his thumb and forefinger, pinches his cigarette. "It's a lot of ground to cover." He looks around the driveway. "You have a beautiful house. Where do you keep the trash?"

"Out back, behind the garage."

"Thank you." Palmer steps away. Turning back, he points a fresh cigarette at Langford. "If you don't mind, what exactly *does* a professor of humanities teach?"

"We focus on the classics: language, music, philosophy, religious studies, and culture."

"Sounds like it would help build quite a sophisticated individual." Palmer places the pinched cigarette in his coat pocket. "I had enough trouble getting through criminal psychology."

"You're something of a celebrity, Investigator Palmer. Lots of people recognize you from the papers and TV." Langford opens the door of his Pacer. "I'm sure you're very sophisticated."

Twenty minutes later, Palmer stands to the side of the access road along Langford's woods, looking to the sky. Early morning sun has given way to ominous clouds, and a heaviness in the air promises rain—a lot of it. Palmer doesn't mind the rain, thinks it washes away urban grime, and helps unearth evidence. He enjoys the calm before the storm, equating it to knowing a puzzle's solved while laying down the final satisfying pieces. Smoking a cigarette, he stands next to Stricker, anxious for the rain to come.

Stricker leans against a tree with his hands in his pockets. "Looks like there's a storm brewing. Supposed to rain like hell the next couple days. Not sure how they'll get game six in tomorrow night."

"It's curious, Dean," Palmer continues to look up, "how much we fear the prospect of pain and disappointment, yet we welcome it with even the slightest glimmer of hope."

"You mean like the parents of those missing girls?"

Palmer rolls his eyes. "Yes, just like those parents. They wait and hope. They wait and believe that waiting's a good thing because it gives them hope. They wait because there's no choice. And they hope because there's no alternative." Palmer looks at Stricker. "Sometimes their anxiety's met with relief. But, more often, it's just another tragic loss."

"So, you think Boston's gonna lose?"

Palmer buttons his coat, shaking his head as he walks away. "Yes, Dean. I'm worried about baseball."

# - 73 -

# THE MEN WITH
# NO WINGS

## FRIDAY, 17 OCTOBER 1975

M o's interview looming, his workday ends early. Back at the townhouse by ten with dark clouds rolling in, he gazes out his
bedroom window, watching the first drops bounce off the ground
and build until the sound of a million drums fills his ears and
rain sweeps across his window. The suddenness of the rain's force
reminds Mo of a rare trip to the movie theatre just before Christmas
seven years earlier. His father slept through the movie in what, by
then, had become an indiscernible cycle of inebriation and hangover. The feature was forgettable, but he and Jake enjoyed the
animated short preceding it and its memorable song. This morning, looking out his window, he sings the only line he recalls—*And
the rain, rain, rain came down, down, down.*

Back then, Mo thought he was like Winnie the Pooh, and Jake
was Piglet. So, when he saved enough money, he bought his brother a plush toy of Pooh Bear. His younger brother slept with it right
up until they moved in with the Branch family. Staring at the rain,
singing to himself, Mo remembers that sunny day in the Summer
of '69 when they walked with their father and Earl Johnson along
Main Street in Warrenton, Jake squeezing his new stuffed toy.

That same hot and humid mid-August day in 1969, three hundred
miles north, on the hillside of a dairy farm in upstate New York, a
crowd of over four hundred thousand gathered to celebrate peace

and music. Meanwhile, twenty-five hundred miles west, on a run-down ranch outside Los Angeles, a young man named Manson was arrested and later released due to a misdated warrant. And much farther away, nine thousand miles east, in the jungles and villages of Southeast Asia, more than half a million American boys were embroiled in a generationally divisive conflict. But in a rural Northern Virginia hamlet, eighteen-year-old Maurice Lumen enjoyed a rare day out with his family, his father temporarily distanced from his own battles.

Jake pulled his father's shirtsleeve. "Daddy, can we get some candy?"

"Yeah, Dad, can we?" Mo reached into his jacket pocket and pulled out two quarters his grandmother gave him for doing household chores. "I can pay for it."

Jake held his Pooh Bear up so his father could see. "Can we get some taffy?"

Their father released an unintelligible grunt. With the help of Earl, Ken was making a final effort to clean himself up.

Jake took his father's response as a yes, jumping up and down in excitement.

Across the street, several teenagers called out to them from a stone wall in the town center. "There goes Slow Mo and the darkie! Hey, Slow Mo, don't sit on your shit-colored brother, you stupid elephant."

The older townsfolk stood by and stared.

"Boys! Stop it!" Earl waved his hands at the unruly juveniles. "Go home to your families and leave us alone."

The town bullies began to chant, "Slow Mo! Slow Mo!"

A rock passed by the back of Mo's neck and hit a brick on the foundation of a nearby store. Walking faster, he held Jake's hand tighter.

The sound of stone hitting brick and the sharp words struck Ken like a bayonet. He stopped, spinning around to confront the chanters. "Go do the devil's work elsewhere and leave my family in peace!" But his words, ignored, evaporated in the heat against a wall of ignorance. At this, he summoned up the strength to make a stand, walking toward them. "To what end are your words and your rock throwing? Why d'ya take pleasure insulting my family and throwing stones? We ain't done you no harm." He addressed the bystanders. "And why d'ya older folks stare and do nothing?" Wall still standing, and witnessing no change in the behavior of either the bullies or the bystanders, he descended into a profanity-laced tirade.

Mo cried out in pain when a stone struck him on the right temple. His father chased after the local miscreants, unsuccessful in catching even a single one. But in defending his family's honor amid public humiliation, Mo's father salvaged a brief measure of dignity. Breathless as he rejoined Earl and his sons, resigned to the truth he could no longer shelter his children from every injustice, Ken muttered, "Earl, I need a goddamned drink."

Mo sits by his bedroom window waiting for his escort, curious why people cast stones and use hateful words. He wonders what happened to that Winnie the Pooh stuffed bear. Did Jake grow tired of it? Did he leave it in the rain? Did it get washed away in the Rappahannock? And, just for a moment, he wonders if the police are searching in the rain and how horrible it must be to tread through all that mud because, as his dad would tell him when he was young—*Mud sticks to you like your past mess-ups*. And still, through all his singing and thinking and wondering, the rain comes down.

Noon, Mo hears a knock at the front door and is greeted by two uniformed police officers. Having never been in a police car before, he's unimpressed with the grated prisoner partition and the cold vinyl seats. He pictures Flatbush sitting alone in a dank jail cell. Concepts as complex as misunderstanding, injustice, and blind hate do not cross his mind.

The Providence Police and Fire Headquarters exterior is an uninspired example of early twentieth-century municipal architecture, while the interior's inhospitable, functional, bland. To Mo, it looks like an airport terminal he saw while watching a television show with Jake. Following the officers down a long corridor with windowed doors and runway lighting overhead, he imagines looking for his seat on a jet airliner, headed off to some tropical paradise with exotic animals.

When they arrive at door 117, Mo enters a large, open room with windows along one wall that he pictures as a hangar. He's greeted by two hatless men with no wings on their coatless chests. The Men with No Wings have the somber look of wear and defeat, diesel stains running down their white dress shirts to the elbows. He follows them to a collection of desks lined up as if on a tarmac waiting to depart, the roar of voices crackling and discharge of cigarette smoke competing for air space. He's instructed to sit down and informed the purpose of the interview. Encountering a prolonged blank stare, one of The Men with No Wings explains he may know the subject by his nickname 'Flatbush.' Mo nods, knowing he's not going anywhere interesting.

Because he doesn't know Flatbush outside of work, Mo finds the interview repetitive, apologizing several times for either not understanding a question or not being able to answer. He has an easier time addressing questions about his fishing trip with Mr. Griffin and Professor Langford, though he's confused when told Flatbush had been there. In an interview lasting twenty minutes, he provides a continuous stream of polite answers, in most cases replying, "No, sir."

When the interview concludes, The Men with No Wings thank Mo and tell him he's been very helpful. They walk him back to the same corridor and point to the same two officers. Mo expresses gratitude and follows the officers, happy to be departing.

Staring out the window of the cruiser, Mo observes streams of water collecting along the sidewalks, the city's drainage system struggling to manage the sheer volume of this storm's first volley. He thinks about the diverted water at Bryant and the deer carcass he buried with Juanito. With all the rain, is the deer still buried? Is the mud sticking to its body? Do deer go to heaven? How does God judge whether a deer has been good or bad? What about a cute little bunny? He thinks about his mother reading him *The Velveteen Rabbit* at her bedside. Are raindrops God's tears bringing His formerly living creatures back to life? Are flowers symbols of God's great love? On this late afternoon, with the rain pouring down, he thinks and thinks and thinks.

# LANGFORD'S CEMETERY

## FRIDAY, 17 OCTOBER 1975

P*almer's soaked.* Despite his gabardine trench coat and umbrella, the rain comes down at angles that saturate. He's undeterred. The rain brings hope. And promise. And he needs it.

Dodging puddles, Palmer paces the access road along the edge of Langford's woods. Watching raindrops bounce off shallow pools, he waits for the morbid call of discovery, curious what Mother Nature will unearth, undress, or untangle. He waits patiently. And the rain keeps falling.

Nine becomes four in a slow, steady march, interrupted by coffee deliveries, piss breaks, and hand-cupped lighting of damp cigarettes. Palmer marks time by his discarded cigarette butts floating in the puddles. The yellow coats of the search teams no longer visible, he ventures into the woods, hearing his name before he gets very far.

"Frank!" Stricker's voice channels through the trees. "Frank!"

Palmer's pace quickens. "What did they find?"

"Looks like two female bodies, clothed, not far apart from each other."

Palmer follows Stricker deeper into the woods, resting a knee on the ground next to one of the bodies. Sticker looming over him, rain falls like tears from his umbrella.

Monroe approaches, moving with purpose. "Lieutenant Stricker, call in CSM and get your men back in there unless you want to do this in a swamp. It's gonna rain all weekend. I've got it from here."

Stricker walks away, head down, grumbling.

Monroe watches Stricker disappear into the mist before turning to Palmer. "How long you figure, Frank?"

Palmer looks up at Monroe. "Can't be certain, maybe a week. There's redness near the temple on this one."

"Looks like our killer."

Palmer nods. "Let's go take a look at the other one."

"Your boys are right behind me. We booked Gonzalez this morning on possession of an unregistered weapon. He'll be held without bail until his case comes up, which won't be for a while." Monroe curls his lip. "Dental records of Violet Rose Rollins, the missing first-year Bryant student from Columbus, Ohio, matched the gunshot victim. Search team's still looking for the bullet at the crime scene. Rain's not helping."

Palmer crouches over the second body. "Both are fully clothed. I don't see any visible breaks, and they each have a contusion on the left side of the temple. Looks to be two more for the bastard."

Monroe sighs. "What do you want to do about Langford?"

"His car was clean. Did they find anything in the house or garage?"

"They found size twelve and a half Sears Craftsman work boots and a pair of garden gloves in the hall closet. We're sending them to forensics."

"Did they check the garden behind the garage?"

"I'm sure they searched the garden. Why?"

"I'm curious whether he has any of those Chinese orchids."

Ross and Lowe arrive moments later, along with even heavier rain. Lowe stops at the first body, staring.

"Lowe," Palmer says, snapping his fingers, "look over here. Listen to me. Take a few soil samples from Langford's Garden. Send them back to the lab. Look through the pictures in the back seat of my car and find the photo of the base and stem of those orchids. See if he has any."

Palmer pauses, distracted by several indistinct voices deeper in the woods. A thirty-something trooper with adolescent eyes emerges through the trees. "Captain Monroe, sir?"

"Yes, trooper, what is it?"

"Detective Stricker thinks you should come over, sir."

Monroe looks to Palmer, eyebrows raised. "Let's go."

Palmer points to Ross. "Gerry, you stay here until CSM arrives."

In a clearing a hundred yards deeper into the woods, Palmer squints through sheets of rain. Five football-sized stones are aligned with rectangular depressions collecting rainwater below each.

Monroe looks at Palmer, his head at an angle. "Ancient burial ground?"

Palmer scans the scene. "Not judging by the rusted shovel leaning against that tree over there."

"I sent two men to get shovels," Stricker says.

Monroe passes his hand over the graves. "No one touches this site until we get photos. Have someone see whether the forensic photographer's here and get the rest of your men to finish canvassing the property." He turns to Palmer. "Frank, can you stay here? I'll be back in a few minutes. I've got to let them know we need more resources."

By five thirty, all five shallow graves have been unearthed, silent skeletal remains lying in the mud of each. Unlike the two corpses found in the mud earlier, these don't look like they'd float away. There's an eerie quiet hanging over the intermittent sound of latex and plastic, a dozen men in bunny suits methodically collecting evidence.

Four hours later, rain of biblical proportions dumping across the access road, the last of the remains are placed in a coroner station wagon and scooted away. Palmer stands on the gravel, sullen, sodden, and watching taillights fade until they disappear, and only his Bonneville remains in the distance, and he's alone.

In the road.

In the rain.

And in the darkness.

- 75 -

# FIVE HEADSTONES

## SATURDAY, 18 OCTOBER 1975

Palmer's descent into the mind of a monster makes him nocturnal. And he never naps. Along with nicotine and caffeine, Visine becomes a staple of the chase. After three weeks deprived of meaningful sleep, Palmer bathes in the stuff. Saturday afternoon, he walks into Metcalf's office, squeezing droplets in his eyes.

"Hey, Frank," Monroe says, kicking out a chair, "grab a seat. Metcalf and I questioned Langford for almost four hours. Made him sit in there for a couple of hours alone this morning before heading in. We just let him go. Put a twenty-four-hour detail on him."

Palmer reaches across the desk, grabs an ashtray. "What was he wearing?"

"Brown-and-white cardigan with tan chinos, black loafers, slicked-back hair, and glasses."

"Likes the Roaring Twenties fashion, doesn't he? I didn't notice him wearing glasses yesterday. Did you?"

Monroe nods then shakes his head. "I didn't."

Palmer lights a cigarette. "Where were his hands?"

"Had them on the table during the entire interview, palms down. Said a few times he was cold and rubbed the top of one hand with the other. His fingers would shake a little, kinda like he was playing the piano, when we talked about the bodies on his property."

"How did he sit?"

"Both feet on the floor during most of the interview. Crossed his legs when discussing his classes or friends."

"When will I get a copy of the transcripts?"

"Should have them by six. I'll let you know as soon as I do."

386

"Any update from ballistics on the gun?"

"Ballistics doesn't believe the .38 Special Model 12 found in Gonzalez's glove box has been fired in several years, if not longer. The search team found a bullet this morning, twenty-five yards closer to the access road on almost a straight line from where the body was discovered. It went to forensics to match against the exit hole. It'll go to ballistics once it's confirmed. The area was all woods up until five years ago, so it could be from hunting. We don't know enough yet."

Rubbing his thumb across his lower lip, Palmer thinks for a moment. "The two girls on Langford's property identified?"

"Yeah, they were identified as Loren Sophia Navarro, age twenty, and Georgia Jewel Minsk, twenty-three. They were the two missing girls from Slatersville. Minsk went missing on September twenty-seventh, Navarro a week ago, on the eleventh."

"When we were standing by the five graves, I noticed CSM taking out personal effects along with shoe and clothing remnants. Have they been able to identify any of those remains?"

Monroe rubs the top of his head. "This part is mind-boggling. Forensics said it appeared their personal items had been folded and placed alongside their bodies, based on the position of the footwear and some polyester and nylon remnants. But, Frank, here's where it gets *really* bizarre. Forensics hasn't confirmed any of the dental records yet, but we know the identities with almost certainty because the killer buried each with their purse or handbag intact. Each had personal identification with them. I've never seen anything like it in my twenty-one years on the force." He opens a folder and begins reading: "Karen Anne Boyd, thirty, Woonsocket, Rhode Island, missing September 1969. Cynthia Starr Finley, twenty-nine, Providence, Rhode Island, missing April 1970. Janice Leigh Sinclair, twenty-seven, Cranston, Rhode Island, missing July 1970. Lynnette Love Lippett, thirty-two, Providence, Rhode Island, missing September 1970. Maria Costas Souza, thirty-three, Pawtucket, Rhode Island, missing May 1971."

Monroe looks up, rubs his eyes. "All but Souza were known prostitutes. Souza was the one who was working on Langford's house when she went missing."

"That's a first." Palmer flicks his ashes into the ashtray. "If Langford's the killer, it wouldn't make sense to bury his victims with identification unless he wanted to be caught."

Monroe closes his eyes and shakes his head. "There's more."

Hearing a knock at the door, Metcalf calls out, "Come in." He gestures to Ross and Lowe. "Have a seat, gentlemen."

Monroe nods as they pass. "Forensics took the boulders from each shallow grave. Turns out they were headstones. The initials of each victim were painted in white underneath."

Ross looks at Palmer in disbelief. "What?"

"Hold on, Gerry." Palmer waves Monroe to continue.

Monroe grabs his glass of water. "When I spoke with forensics, they said there's damage to the C2, C3, or C4 vertebrae on all five victims. Chipping and possible clean break from cartilage displacement suggests blunt force trauma with a sharp object."

Metcalf tugs his ear. "A shovel, maybe?"

Monroe downs his water in a single gulp. "They did a preliminary analysis of the fifty-five-inch shovel and determined there are splatter stains on the wood handle near the metal socket and soaking along the top of the shaft. Stains along the rusted edges of the round-tipped blade also appear to be consistent with splatter patterns. Although there's no way to determine if the stains are, in fact, blood after several years of weathering, it's quite possible the shovel was used as a weapon. The staining at the top of the shaft could've come from shoveling with bloodied hands after the murder or might suggest the victim was murdered prior to decapitation."

"Anything else?"

"No, that's everything."

Palmer angles to look around Monroe. "Lowe, what were you able to determine about the shovel?"

"The shovel matches the one we found in Langford's garage. It's a Craftsman manufactured by..." Lowe checks his notes. "Ames Shovel and Tool Company in North Easton, Massachusetts. We've contacted Ames for production years, quantity, and distribution data. We know Langford has a Sears credit card from the search of his home. Sears is searching credit data to see if two or more were sold to Langford prior to the first victim's murder. We expect that information tomorrow."

Palmer points to Ross, "What have you found out about the work done to Langford's house?"

Ross pulls out several pages from his trench coat. "Langford kept all the house renovation receipts in a shoebox in his bedroom closet. From those, I was able to compile a list of two prime contractors, one interior and one exterior, as well as fourteen subcontractor companies that worked on the house between spring 1969 and fall 1971. From police records, we know Maria Costa Souza worked for Klauber Construction at the time of her disappearance. I went to Pawtucket around seven this morning to speak with the owner of the company. He has a small finish carpentry firm specializing in custom exterior woodwork. He distinctly remembers the job due to the historic nature of the house and, of course, the missing worker."

"What could he tell you?"

"The owner mentioned they were there for a couple of months, working on porch railings, eave corbels, the widow's walk, and everything ornate on the exterior trim. The company had four employees at the time, including Souza. All worked on the house at some point. The owner was questioned at the time of Souza's disappearance, along with the three employees, and employment records were provided to the authorities."

"Police records would have those interviews documented," Monroe says.

Ross scans his sheets. "I pulled them about five hours ago. There's not much in there, except for one worker mentioning Souza's friend coming to the worksite. I called Klauber again to schedule another visit a little after one. I asked Klauber about Souza's friend, and with some coaxing, he admitted to hiring her friend and paying him under the table for a few months around that time."

Palmer leans closer to Ross. "So the friend's name doesn't appear on payroll, but why didn't the workers mention him at the interviews?"

Ross places the papers on Metcalf's desk. "I asked Klauber why neither he nor any of the workers ever mentioned this cash employee at the interviews. He admitted to warning them about losing their jobs if he lost his license and was forced out of business for paying someone under the table. I haven't been able to talk to the former workers yet. None work for Klauber anymore."

Palmer leans back, setting his cigarette in the ashtray. "Did he give us the name of this former worker?"

"Said he didn't know the worker's name but recalled Souza and the other employees calling him 'Flatbush.'"

Metcalf slaps his desk. "Gonzalez, that son of a bitch!"

Reaching for his cigarette, Palmer shows no emotion. "Gentlemen, this case is far from closed." He takes a prolonged drag, releasing a billow of smoke. "What we have is a lot of circumstantial evidence placing Gonzalez at the scene of many crimes, including the five from several years ago. His past also has negative implications. But all this amounts to suspicion. It's becoming apparent the gun found in his glove box isn't tied to what we believe may have been the first of this recent killing spree—the Rollins girl with the gunshot to the head. It is *possible* the first isn't tied to the others, but I believe it *is* connected, making it difficult to tie the murders to Gonzalez just yet."

Metcalf looks out at the pouring rain. "What about his work gloves and boots? The orchid trace evidence?"

"We know from my discussion with him on the eighth, and his interview on Thursday evening, Griffin purchased nearly two dozen size twelve and a half work boots from the Sears at Midland Mall. He gave all his employees a pair over the past two years. He also acknowledged giving his buddy Langford a pair when he first purchased them and another last week."

"Maybe we can get warrants to inspect all the boots," Lowe says.

Palmer shakes his head. "Won't get those without probable cause for the other workers. We've analyzed Gonzalez's boots and found almost nothing. He must clean his boots with a toothbrush. Langford's are in with forensics now, but they're swamped, so we may not know anything for a day or two. He also just got them from Griffin, so may be nothing there."

Lowe pulls out several photos. "The trace evidence from the endangered Chinese orchid will also be inconclusive because it's certain to be on all the workers' clothing along with Langford's gloves and boots. Griffin acknowledged having given Langford seeds sometime in the past, though he doesn't remember exactly when. There was visual confirmation of the base of the orchids residing in Langford's Garden, which appears well maintained, and stems were found in a compost pile in his backyard."

Palmer lifts his cigarette, stopping before it reaches his lips. "So, it appears we have two primary suspects, but, in fact, we may have more. I read the transcripts from the Lumen kid's interview yesterday afternoon. He confirmed having gone fishing with Langford and Griffin at the end of August, consistent with Griffin's statements on Friday afternoon. In the interview, he acknowledged Langford as a friend. Says he slept over a couple times and went for walks. He wore his work uniform to the interview, and several callers into the hotline have noted seeing a large or very tall man in a blue work uniform. Didn't recall seeing Gonzalez when they went fishing, saying he went for a walk. Also said he never saw Gonzalez, or his car, at Langford's place. The kid says he loves to walk alone in nature."

Metcalf retreats to his chair. "Damn, Frank, with so much going on, I haven't had time to read the transcripts of yesterday's interviews."

"I haven't gotten through them all either," Monroe says.

Palmer shrugs before continuing. "I looked at Agent Lowe's notes from last week on Lumen's housemates. None have criminal records, including the one who appears to have left the townhouse—Boulet. Of mild interest, one of the housemates—Dufresne—is quite tall by his Massachusetts driver's license, listing him as six-four. I wanna get this Lumen kid back in as soon as possible. I need to see where else he's been and how well he knows Langford." Palmer points at Monroe. "Think you can get him back in here for questioning tomorrow?"

Monroe nods. "I'm sure I can, Frank. What about the Dufresne kid and the other roommates?"

"Let's focus on Lumen for now. We can bring the others back in once I get a better handle on his dynamic from the Lumen interview. Also, check to see if any callers reported seeing a turquoise or bluish-green Caprice."

"Is that Lumen's car?"

Palmer shakes his head. "Lumen doesn't own a car. That's Dufresne's car."

"You see these kids as viable suspects?"

The room falls silent as Palmer considers the question. "Of the five women from four-plus years ago? No. Those could be Gonzalez, Langford, or both; maybe even someone else. Just not enough substantive evidence at this point." He pauses, taking a puff and exhaling. "But it could be any of them, a combination, or one working with someone we haven't identified yet for the recent murders. I'm not ruling out anything or anyone at this point, but my gut tells me we're looking in the right places. They all meet the physical requirements and, in some way, connect to Gonzalez and Langford. We don't know enough about Dufresne at the moment. We don't know whether he's been to any of the murder locations or even if he has a pair of Craftsman boots or gloves with trace orchid material. All we know is he lives with Lumen. We need to get more information from Lumen. Following that, we need to see whether Dufresne fits into this case if he does at all."

Metcalf taps his desk with a knuckle. "You really think it's possible two or more could be working together?"

"Not necessarily, Steve, but I've seen it before. Couple of years back, I got called in by the Texas Rangers to work with Houston Police on the 'Candy Man' case. Dean Corll had those two teens, Brooks and Henley, help him lure and capture more than two dozen young men before Corll subsequently tortured and murdered them."

"You see similarities?"

"I'm merely envisioning possible scenarios. At this point, I know we need more information about the bullet, and we need to, somehow, locate the gun." Palmer checks the notes sitting on his lap. "And I need to talk to this Maurice Leroy Lumen."

# A FLOWERLESS FIELD
# OF BLOOD

## SATURDAY, 18 OCTOBER 1975

Mo *returns from the Unistructure to a cold, empty townhouse, his housemates having gone home to spend the stormy weekend with their families.* Restricted by the killer's actions from walking the campus paths and precluded from walking off-campus due to the heavy rain, Mo instead spent the morning in the cafeteria, laundry room, and library, checking mail before heading back. He was surprised to find an unexpected package addressed to him in the mailbox, his name written on a slip of paper sticking out the middle pages of a book. But he couldn't find anything indicating who gave him the present. Sitting on the sofa back at the townhouse, examining the cover of *Watership Down*—a rabbit staring off to the left—he likes it but thinks it may also be judging him.

Between afternoon and early evening naps, Mo lifts himself from the sofa only to change stations, his dozing a race to end the solitude, albeit more a series of sprints than a marathon. By seven, the sound of the doorbell's a welcome distraction.

Kay stands under a shiny umbrella on the front door landing, her smile bringing joy to an otherwise depressing evening. "Hi, Mo."

Mo rubs his eyes. "Hi, Kay."

"Can I come in?"

"Sure, yes, sorry."

"I figured you'd be alone, possibly bored, and thought maybe you'd like to get something to eat. Would you like to go somewhere?"

Mo nods, his eyes wide. "Yes, please. I'm starving."

"Okay, grab a coat. It's chilly out."

"My raincoat's at work. I'll be okay. Let me put my boots on. I'll be right back."

Sharing her umbrella, they walk to Kay's car. It's a short walk, but Mo enjoys each time their arms brush. Kay opens the passenger door and hops over a puddle on her way to the driver's side. Through the rain-distorted windshield, Mo follows her progress across the cascades of water.

*Sister Golden Hair* is playing on the radio when Kay starts the car. "Carlton loves this song," she says, stretching her damp blond hair through her fingers before tying it back in a ponytail. She stares at the radio dial. "Sometimes, I feel more like the sister he never had than his girlfriend." She shakes her head. "What do you feel like for dinner?"

"I could eat almost anything. Do you like pizza?"

"I do, but I don't want to eat at Tony's or anyplace where televisions will be on. I just want to have a night where I don't have to hear about the Pastoral Predator."

Mo nods. "I had to go to police headquarters yesterday to tell them what I know about Flatbush. They called *again* just before you got here." He shrugs. "I need to go back tomorrow afternoon because they have more questions."

"Yeah, I heard about yesterday's from Carlton. I wonder what more they want to know. We did go to a lot of places where the girls were murdered." Kay sees Mo's head hang down. "But let's not talk about it tonight, okay?"

"Okay."

"How about Chinese?"

"I like Chinese."

"Good. I know a place in town."

With the torrential rain, Pearl's Authentic is quiet for a Saturday night. Mo and Kay sit in a booth and chat.

"The first thing I noticed about you, other than how tall you are, is your watch," Kay says. "I've never seen you without it. Did you buy it for yourself or was it a present?"

Mo pulls the flexible metal wristband. "My grandmother gave it to me for Christmas three years ago."

"What was your grandmother like?"

"She was just like my mother. She came to live with me and my father after my mother died, and she was a really good cook."

"So, the watch is very special then?"

"When she gave it to me, we were at my aunt and uncle's house. After we opened all the presents, everyone was heading to the dining room to eat, but Grandma Cleveland fell when she tried to get out of her chair." Mo's lips curl and quiver. "The next week, the doctor said she had cancer. She died last year."

Kay puts her hands on Mo's. "That's so sad. At least you got to spend some good years with your grandmother. That's a good thing."

They converse over dinner, exchanging pleasant dialogue centered on family and the prospects of the hometown team. Afterward, Kay takes Mo bowling. Mo hasn't bowled since Jake was born but isn't concerned about his score. Instead, he focuses on Kay's lane approach when it's not his turn, each time appreciating her petite frame in snug-fitting bell-bottom jeans and white sweater. As the night progresses, his enthusiasm swells. After several games, they return their shoes to the counter. A black-and-white television's situated on the back wall, news of the Pastoral Predator irresistibly on display:

IN LATE-BREAKING NEWS, POLICE BROUGHT IN BRYANT COLLEGE PROFESSOR MICHAEL DEAN LANGFORD FOR QUESTIONING TODAY. EARLIER, AUTHORITIES REPORTED DISCOVERING TWO FEMALE BODIES AND THE SKELETAL REMAINS OF FIVE OTHER FEMALES ON THE HUMANITIES PROFESSOR'S SIXTY-FOUR-ACRE PROPERTY BEHIND HIS EAST SLATERSVILLE HOME LATE YESTERDAY. POLICE ARE SAYING THE TWO MORE RECENT VICTIMS APPEAR CONNECTED TO THE MASS MURDERER KNOWN AS THE PASTORAL PREDATOR WHILE THEY CONTINUE TO INVESTIGATE THE OTHER FIVE. POLICE ALSO SAID LANGFORD IS COOPERATING AND NOT CONSIDERED A SUSPECT AT THIS TIME.

Kay holds her hand over her open mouth.

Mo stares at the screen in silence.

"My God!" Kay turns to Mo. "I had him in class."

Mo's chest begins to ache, the sweat from bowling resurfacing.

Moving to a table, they sit.

Kay tilts her head, pointing to Mo. "Didn't you sleep over his house?"

Mo nods.

"Did he act strange?"

"Not really."

"Did the guy who works with you ever sleep over?"

"Flatbush? No, not when I was there."

"What a tragedy. All those poor girls and their families. When you went to the police station yesterday to answer questions about Flatbush, did they ask you about Professor Langford?"

"Only whether I remembered seeing Flatbush when I went fishing with Professor Langford and Mr. Griffin, but I told them I don't."

"Where did you go fishing?"

"Georgiaville Pond. It's not far from the school. I went for a walk, so Flatbush probably stopped by when I was gone."

"Well, there hasn't been a report of a girl's body being found there, so that's good." Kay's hands tremble. "I hope they weren't working together. How long did they question you?"

"About twenty minutes, I think."

"Do you like Flatbush?"

"Yes. He's quiet, but he seems nice. Mr. Griffin doesn't think he's the killer."

"What about you, Mo? Do you think he may be the person who's killing all these girls?"

"I don't know, but I hope not. He seems nice to me."

Kay rises to her feet, hands still shaking. "Okay, let's get you back. I need to get home, too. I don't want my parents getting worried after they hear this." She pauses, looking at Mo and shaking her head. "We just can't get away from this, can we?"

In the entryway of the townhouse, Kay places her arms around Mo's chest. Feeling the residual tremors from the news report in her warm hug, he responds by pulling her off her feet and closer. She gives him a peck on the cheek. "Goodnight, Mo."

"Goodnight, Kay." Weightless in his arms, her hair soft against his cheek, Mo closes his eyes and takes in her scent, embracing her the way he hugged his mother, the way he did his grandmother and Mrs. Harrington. But he never held them off the ground. Never felt the intense warmth of their bodies. And never felt their heartbeat pounding like the hands on his Timex. He wants her to stay, keep him safe from every creak in a wall or settling of the floor, protect him from the anxiety sure to surround him when she leaves. With a surge of emotion, Mo's words slip out effortlessly, as they had in the past. "I love you."

"Try to get some sleep," Kay whispers back. "I love you, too."

Mo waits for Kay's car to pull away before closing the door, retreating to the living room—to the silent and unsympathetic living room—restless and awake. *Watership Down* stares ominously from the sofa cushion. He wraps himself in a blanket, props his feet on the sofa, and rests the book against his knees, opening to where he had stopped earlier.

Mo reads the words of the smallest rabbit, Fiver, warning the others that something very bad is coming. He looks up from the book, shivering as he imagines himself as a rabbit staring out across a flowerless field of blood. He reads very slowly. He reads even though he does not want to. This book's not at all like *Charlotte's Web* or *Stuart Little* or *The Trumpet of the Swan*. It's not about pigs or spiders or mice or swans. It's about rabbits. And it's scary. And it's boring. And he doesn't understand.

Recalling his father's favorite book is about a whale, he thinks it might be more interesting, maybe easier to read. He leaves the comfort of the sofa and retrieves the paperback from his father's shoebox under his bed, returning and rewrapping himself. He reads for several minutes, stopping at the word 'circumambulate,' deciding *Moby Dick* is no easier to read than *Watership Down*.

When Mo sets the book down, all the pages fall to one side, revealing handwriting inside the front cover. Discovering a short note addressed to Ken and signed 'Clara,' he reads the words before dropping the book to the floor. The edges of the sealed envelope containing his father's letter hang tantalizingly out the center pages. Hands shaking, he removes the blanket and reaches for the envelope. Ripping the edge, he pulls a single sheet of paper out the side, unfolds, and reads the letter, dated 7 November 1971—Jake's eighth birthday:

*Son,*

*If your reading this letter I'm probably dead. There's some things I need to tell you that'll help you learn from my mistakes. Your mother was the love of my life and she loved you too. Sure wish she'd been there to raise you. Sorry I couldn't be the father you needed after Jake was born. I forgot about what was really important when everything went bad.*

*You need to know Jake is not my son and he's not your real brother. He's got another father who never knew. Miss Clara asked me to raise him and I did because I use to care about her. I'm sorry I lied about this but thought it might be good for you to think you had a brother. I kept him hoping one day his mother would come back. It got harder to deal with the shame his being in our family brought us. I hated myself for it and punished you. I apologize. Love Dad*

Uncertain how to react, Mo refolds the letter and slides it back into the envelope before inserting it behind the front cover of *Moby Dick*. Drying his eyes and dragging himself into his room, he places the book back into his father's box.

Resting his head against the edge of the bed, Mo thinks about all the lies and secrets. His mother taught him not to lie; his father kept secrets, Mo the product of their collective human frailties. He's not sure who to blame—his father, Jake, Clara, Dr. Cross, Mr. and Mrs. Branch, Emily, Sam, Grandma Cleveland, or Mrs. Harrington. He wonders if everyone tells lies and keeps secrets. Did his *mother* lie to him? Does *Kay* keep secrets? Do all lies become secrets? Do secrets get carried to the grave? Do children bear the burden of their parents' secrets? Does he carry the awful secrets of his father, and his father's father, and his father's grandfather? What secrets does he himself carry? Finally, he wonders if the stench along the Rappahannock after a flood is the smell of carcasses being washed clean of lies and secrets as they're carried downstream. And what happens to the ones buried in the dirt and the mud? Do they lie under a flowerless field of blood?

Returning to the sofa, Mo opens *Watership Down*. He continues to read with great difficulty, his eyes sleepy and dry. Despite the challenge, he reads because someone—someone mysterious—gave it to him. But it will take time—a lot of time—and he will need someone to explain it to him. Maybe the mysterious person will explain it to him. Maybe Kay will. It seems different and scary. He doesn't want to be scared when he's sleeping alone in the townhouse. So he puts the book down and pulls the blanket over his head, leaving the light and television on as an extra layer of protection while he falls asleep thinking about his mother and Kay, whales and rabbits.

# DARK WATERS

**SUNDAY, 19 OCTOBER 1975**

Mo stares out the sliding doors behind the townhouse early Sunday morning, trying to remember the last time he did not say his night-time prayers, but he is distracted by the swollen stream pressing against the back patio steps. In his loneliness, he wishes Sam would float by on a raft, smiling and waving, or Louie would pass by, gently bobbing in the water and playing his trumpet. But as the steady rain turns into a cloudburst, the flooded stream becomes a raging river. The water, and Mo's thoughts, turn darker. He fears he'll see his father's black-haired critters cut loose and floating, their stench carried downstream, or maybe the bodies of those young women the police think Flatbush or Professor Langford killed passing by on their way to the Rappahannock.

Gazing beyond the rising water, Mo looks for promise in the forest, but forty-eight hours of relentless rain is condemning, casting judgment upon the landscape and all who venture to disturb nature's balance. For two days and two nights, there are no World Series games. For two days and two nights, there are no new murders. For two days and two nights, there are no resolutions. And, on the third day, Mo rises—he rises with the hope of sunshine and baseball, falling into despair with the reality of more rain and more questions. Staring out the sliding doors, abandoned by the distraction baseball provides and disturbed by the rain's accusation, Mo prays.

Mo sprints to breakfast, unprotected from the deluge. Reading the sports pages, he discovers he'll have to wait two-and-a-half more days before the World Series resumes. On the front page, he counts how many times Gonzalez's and Langford's names are used in the headline story, wondering what new questions *he'll* be asked.

Mo's disappointed when Kay's father picks Mo up for church without Kay.

After service, Mr. Thompson speaks with Mo in the back of the church. He's not interested in discussing baseball. "Kay tells me you know both suspects in the Pastoral Predator case."

"Yes, sir." Hoping Kay's father would ask him to watch game six at the Thompson home, Mo is surprised by Mr. Thompson's serious tone.

"Do either of them seem like they could do the things we hear about on the news?"

"No, sir, I don't think so."

"Kay tells me you're going back down to police headquarters to answer more questions this afternoon."

"Yes, sir."

"You know, Mo," Mr. Thompson folds his arms and moves closer, "it hasn't escaped my attention that you arrived here a couple of months ago or that you walked around our neighborhood the night the Dumont girl went missing."

Mo takes a step back, staring at Mr. Thompson with eyes wide. Kay's father, with his shoulders raised, seems much taller than his six-foot frame.

"Honey," Mrs. Thompson says, placing a hand on her husband's shoulder, "we talked about this with Kay this morning."

Mr. Thompson glances at his wife before turning back to Mo, his tone less stern. "Alright, Mo, come on. Let's get you home. Don't want you to be late for your interview."

# A WOLF IN SHEEP'S CLOTHING

## SUNDAY, 19 OCTOBER 1975

*almer peeks into the interview room through the door's small window.* He sees Lumen's elbows on the table, chin in his palms, and his blank stare focused on the recorder in the center of the table. He waits until one thirty before thrusting the door open, clearing his throat as he enters. "Good afternoon, Mr. Lumen."

Startled, Mo looks up at Palmer, Monroe entering right behind. "Hello."

"I apologize, Mr. Lumen. Have you been waiting long?"

Mo looks at his Timex. "I've been here for almost half an hour."

"Again, I apologize for our tardiness." Palmer takes off his coat, lays it on the back of a chair. "We've been conducting a lot of interviews the past several days. Sometimes, we lose track of time." He places a pack of Marlboros on the table.

"It's okay."

"Mr. Lumen, it seems I owe you another apology for making you come back for more questioning today." Palmer pulls the cellophane tab around the pack, removes the top. "Last time, you were asked questions about your relationship with Mr. Gonzalez. We brought you back today to ask about your relationship with Michael Dean Langford."

Mo's eyes shift between Palmer and Monroe. "Okay."

"I'm turning on the recorder. Answer all questions completely without using nonverbal gestures, understand?"

"Yes, sir."

After Mo states his name and date of birth, Palmer tears the foil off the top of the pack, taps out a cigarette, and begins. "Mr. Lumen, what can you tell us about your relationship with Mr. Langford?"

Palms down on the table, Mo's fingers tremble. "He's a friend."

Cigarette between his index and middle fingers, Palmer looks at Monroe and taps the table. He waits for Monroe to exit. "What types of things do you do with your friend?"

"We go fishing, I slept over his house a few times, and we've had lunch at school."

"What do you talk about?"

"We talk about the Red Sox, but he's not as big a fan as Mr. Griffin or my other friends."

"So, what do you talk about besides baseball?"

Monroe reenters, placing an ashtray on the table.

Mo shrugs. "I'm not sure. I guess we talk about our families and friends and his house."

Palmer lights, releasing a waft of smoke. "Did you have any discussions about the Pastoral Predator?"

"Not really. He'd read the newspaper, but I wasn't interested, so I'd just think about baseball."

Palmer is surprised by Lumen's interest in the home team just two months after arriving but has no immediate desire to leverage this angle. "What can you tell us about your lunches with Langford?"

"They were at noontime on Wednesdays, and we would eat for about half an hour. Sometimes he would invite me to sleep over."

"Did he ever ask you where you were going on the weekend when you would be at lunch or visiting his house?"

"I think so."

"And what places did you go?"

"I went a lot of places with Carlton and Kay. Brian and Trevor went once, too."

Palmer asks Lumen to clarify his relationships with the people he named before turning to locations. "Would you remember all the places you've gone?"

Mo sits up straight, pushing out his chest. "Yes, sir, I look at the signs and make a memory of everywhere I've gone with my friends since I got here."

"Excellent, Mr. Lumen." Recognizing his subject's eagerness to discuss this topic, Palmer rests his cigarette in the ashtray and leans toward him. "Do you remember going to Hunt's Mill?"

"Yes, sir."

"Who did you go with?"

"Carlton and Kay."

Palmer asks Lumen the same questions for each location a body was discovered. Each time, Lumen responds affirmatively and politely, including who went with him.

Monroe watches over the scene like a prison guard during an inmate visit.

"On Friday, you told the detectives you didn't recall seeing Mr. Hernandez at Georgiaville Pond the day you went fishing with Langford and Griffin. You stated he may have been there when you went for a walk. We verified this with Griffin, and your story checks out." Palmer lifts his cigarette from the ashtray, takes a short puff. "Did you ever go for walks at any of the other places you visited?"

"Yes, sir, I always go for walks when I go someplace new. I like to look at the different flowers and trees."

"Were you alone when you went for these walks?"

"Yes, sir."

"This is important, Mr. Lumen. Do you remember telling Langford you were going to Hunt's Mill or Lincoln Park or Stepstone Falls or Stillwater Scenic Area or Roger Williams Park?"

"Yes, he would ask me where I was going and who I was going with. I remember saying I was going to Lincoln Park and Roger Williams Park, but I'm not sure about the others. Maybe. Probably."

"Did you ever see Langford at any of the places you visited?"

"No, sir."

"Do you know what his car looks like?"

"Yes, it's a new Pacer, and it has two brownish colors. He likes his car a lot and cleans it every weekend."

"Did you ever see his car in the parking lots or around the places you visited?"

"Only if I went with him."

"But not when you were with your other friends?"

"No, sir."

Palmer cycles through the same series of questions with respect to Gonzalez. After which, he settles back, considering Lumen's presence at the murder scenes, asking himself whether this polite, intellectually naive young man could somehow be involved. But he doesn't sense rage in Lumen's fear. Or if there is rage, it's well disguised. "Alright, Mr. Lumen, let's go back to your relationship with Langford. Griffin told us Langford drove you home after fishing at Georgiaville Pond. Is that correct?"

"Yes, sir."

"Did he drive you straight home?"

"No, sir. I went to Professor Langford's house. That was the first time I went."

"Do you remember what you talked about?"

"Not really. He asked some questions about my family."

"What about your family?"

"About my mom and dad and my brother Jake and why I live here now."

"Why do you live here now?"

"Because my dad died and my brother was adopted by the Branches, but they didn't want me, so I had to leave Virginia and come to Rhode Island."

Palmer notes the pace of Lumen's blinking quickens. "Why did they want your brother and not you?"

Mo responds through clenched teeth. "Because Emily said I did bad things, but she was the one who did bad things to me, and Mr. Branch and Mrs. Branch believed her."

Palmer watches Lumen's hands shake. "Alright, Mr. Lumen, it's okay. Is Emily one of the Branch children?"

Mo's hands clench to fists. "Yes, sir."

Sensing anger in Lumen for the first time, Palmer picks a little more at the wound he's opened. "How old is Emily Branch?"

Mo pulls his hands down to his lap and straightens up in his chair. "Fourteen."

"You don't like Emily, do you?"

"I used to pray she would be okay and stop hurting me."

With Lumen's entire body quivering, and concerned he may shut down, Palmer backs off. "I understand, Mr. Lumen. Let's return to your relationship with Langford. Did he ever introduce you to any of his friends besides Griffin?"

"Yes, the first time I slept at his house, there were five of his other friends there."

"Did you notice anything strange about Langford's friends?"

"No, they were really smart and talked a lot, but I think they were okay. Professor Langford told me he wasn't going to be their friend anymore, but I don't really know why."

"Langford didn't explain why he wouldn't be friends with these five individuals anymore?"

Placing his hands back on the table, Mo interlaces his fingers, his knuckles still white. "He did, but I can't remember why. I think it was because of me and Mr. Griffin, but I didn't understand. I'm sorry."

"That's fine." Palmer uses the last bit of lit tobacco from his cigarette to light a new one. He asks a series of questions about Langford's friends before returning to Langford. "What did you do after Langford's friends left in the morning?"

"I went for a walk, and then we went fishing before I went home."

"Where did you go fishing?"

"Olney Pond."

Palmer leans forward and rests his cigarette in the ashtray. "Did you go for a walk at Olney Pond?"

"Yes, sir."

"And did you walk alone?"

"Yes, sir."

"Do you remember if you might've seen Gonzalez's car any-where, either when you went for a walk at Langford's house or Olney Pond?"

Mo shakes his head. "I wasn't looking at the cars."

"Is Langford good friends with Griffin?"

Mo lays his hands on the table. "They go fishing sometimes."

Palmer realizes Lumen relaxes when Griffin's name is used in the conversation. "But Griffin didn't go with you and Langford to

Olney Pond?"

"No, sir."

Retrieving his cigarette, Palmer leans back. "Do you know if Griffin sleeps over, or has ever slept over, Langford's house? Did he sleep over on any occasion when you did?"

"Mr. Griffin told me he's never been to Professor Langford's house."

"So, would you say your friendship with Langford is better than Griffin's?"

"Mr. Griffin was friends with Professor Langford before I was. He introduced me to him."

"Since Griffin introduced you to Langford, who do you think has spent more time with Langford?"

"I'm not sure. Probably me."

"So, is it fair to say you are now better friends with Langford than Griffin is?"

Mo shrugs. "I guess so."

Palmer's questions encourage Lumen to explain his interactions and exchanges with Langford by continuing to weave Griffin's name into the dialogue to keep the subject at ease.

Each time, Mo provides sincere responses with little emotion. When he's asked about his relationship with Gonzalez, and whether he had seen either of their cars at specific locations, Mo's response is always the same, "No, sir."

After twenty minutes, Palmer begins a new line of questioning. "Mo, did you ever go to Griffin's house?"

"Yes, sir."

"How many times?"

"Three."

"Do you like going over Griffin's house?"

"Yes, sir."

"Did you eat there?"

"Yes, sir. Then, we would play games."

"Would you eat and play games inside the house or outside?"

"Inside. We'd play games like *Sorry* or *Chutes and Ladders*."

Pausing for a few moments, Palmer takes a few drags while staring at Lumen. By this point, he's well aware of Lumen's emotional attachments, knowing that Kay, his fellow townhouse residents, and Griffin relax him. At the same time, the mention of Langford or the Branch family—especially the daughter Emily—increases his anxiety. "Did you ever see Langford's Pacer or Gonzalez's Datsun outside when you were at Griffin's house?"

"No, sir."

"Did you go for a walk on any occasion when you went to Griffin's house?"

"No, sir."

"Why not?"

"Because it's a Colored neighborhood."

Monroe takes a seat at the end of the table. "To be clear, you mean a Black neighborhood, correct?"

Mo is surprised by Monroe's sudden entrance into the conversation. After a brief pause, he answers. "Yes, sir."

"Why wouldn't you take a walk in a Black neighborhood?"

"My dad always told me to be careful of Black people and don't be out alone in the Colored neighborhoods."

"Why is that, Mr. Lumen? Why can't you walk around a Black neighborhood?"

"Because they might hurt me because I'm White."

"You grew up in Virginia, correct? You lived there until a couple of months ago?"

"Yes, sir."

"Does everyone in Virginia feel the same way you do about Black people?"

"Yes, sir, uh, I don't know about that, but we lived in a White neighborhood and didn't see Black people around much. I only talked about it with my dad, though."

"Unfortunately, a lot of people feel the same way here in New England." Monroe leans toward the recorder, wrapping his fingers together and placing his hands on the table. "What about you, Mr. Lumen? Are you scared of Black people? Are you afraid of *me*?"

"I'm a little scared because you're a policeman, but I liked my friend Sam back in Virginia, and I like Brian at the townhouse here, and my Black friends at work, and Mr. Griffin and his family. They all seem nice to me."

"I'm glad to hear that, Mr. Lumen. I truly am." Monroe sits upright, looking at Palmer with a wry smile.

With Monroe's concerns addressed, Palmer offers him a conciliatory nod. Hoping to settle Lumen back down, he returns to a source of comfort. "Now, Mr. Lumen, Brian refers to Brian Covington, your housemate, correct?"

"Yes, sir."

"Why do you like Brian?"

"Because he's funny, and he's nice." Mo rubs the side of his face. "He has a lot of girls who like him, too, but he doesn't bring them home anymore."

"Why is that?"

"Because Carlton doesn't want girls at the townhouse unless they're like Kay."

"Why would Carlton be concerned about Brian's girlfriends?"

"Because they only come over once, and some of them would say bad things."

"You mean like swearing or using profanity?"

"No, sir." Mo pulls his hands down to his lap, tapping his thumbs together. "Because they would say mean things."

"What kind of mean things, Mr. Lumen?"

Mo pushes the seat of his pants into the chair and leans over the table. "Like calling me an idiot or a retard or telling me to bark like a dog."

Palmer watches Lumen rest his palms on the edge of the table and push his chair back a few inches. "Were these girls also saying mean things about the other housemates?"

"No, sir."

Palmer pauses to fill Lumen's water glass and watches him take a drink, Lumen's shoulders hunched. Palmer wonders what Lumen would think of Peggy and Pauline. Would he see them as someone like Kay or the girls who were mean to him? "Mr. Lumen, do you go to church?"

Mo rubs his neck. "Yes, sir."

"Where do you go to church?"

"I go with Kay's family to Saints Peter and Paul."

"Have you ever seen either Gonzalez's car or Langford's car in the parking lot of the church or anywhere near the church?"

"No, sir."

"Have you ever gone back to the Thompson home after church?"

"Yes, sir."

"And what do you do after church at the Thompson residence?"

"I have lunch with Kay's family and watch TV."

"Have you ever gone to the Thompson residence for anything other than lunch after church?"

"Yes, sir."

"Do you remember when those were?"

"I watched two World Series games with them: game two last Sunday and game three on Tuesday night. Mr. Thompson's a big Red Sox fan."

"Did you ever go for a walk on any of the occasions you went to the Thompsons' home?"

"Yes, sir, one time."

"When was that?"

"On Tuesday. I was nervous about the game, so I went for a walk. My mom always said it's good to walk off your nerves."

Palmer watches Lumen's eyes light up when he mentions his mother. "That's right, Mr. Lumen. Did you see either Gonzalez's car or Langford's car when you went for your walk?"

"No, sir."

"Think very hard, son," Monroe says. "We've had multiple sightings of vehicles fitting the descriptions of their cars in the area that evening, so please try to remember."

Palmer witnesses Lumen's brows furrow and eyes fall to his hands. It appears to him that Lumen doesn't like being called 'son.' Maybe he doesn't like being called son by Monroe, or maybe he doesn't like being called 'son' by a Black man. He wonders if Lumen inherited some of his father's prejudice or if he's just afraid.

Monroe taps the table in front of Lumen. "Did you see either of their cars?"

Mo stares at Monroe for a short time, trying to remember, before answering. "Maybe."

Monroe leans into Lumen. "Maybe? Which car?"

"Cars went by while I walked—a few. A-And maybe I saw one of them, but I don't remember. I don't really look at the cars when I'm walking."

Frustrated, Monroe raises his voice. "What time did you get back from your walk?"

Mo sinks into his seat. "A little after the pregame started."

Palmer places his hand on Monroe's cuff. "So, a little after seven?"

"Yes, sir." Mo relaxes, preferring Palmer's calm manner.

Monroe rises to his feet and stands by the door, shaking his head and glaring at Palmer.

Palmer offers Monroe a reassuring nod before continuing. "Who else was at the house when you returned?"

"Kay and her parents. Carlton came, too, but he got there a little after the game started."

"And the game started at eight thirty, correct?"

"I think so."

Palmer straightens up, feeling Monroe's eyes still piercing through him. He considers Dufresne's relationship with Lumen, his access to the locations where the murders occurred, his mobility, and his motives. He does not perceive the same anxiety in Lumen as when they're discussing Langford. "Carlton was always with you when you went with Kay, wasn't he?"

"Yes, sir."

"Does Carlton know where Professor Langford's home is located?"

"He dropped me off at his house once."

"Do you know how many times Carlton went to Langford's house that you're aware of?"

"Only that once."

"Did you ever see Carlton's car any other time you were at Langford's house?"

"No, sir."

"And you never saw Gonzalez's car when you were at Langford's house?"

"No, sir."

"One last time, Mr. Lumen, think very hard, Gonzalez's car was seen in the immediate vicinity of Langford's house on a number of occasions over the past six weeks. Did you happen to see Gonzalez's orange Datsun?"

"No, sir, I'm sorry. I don't really notice cars when I'm walking, and I don't look at them when I'm inside someone's house."

Palmer leans back and taps the table. "Alright, Mr. Lumen, that's all we have. Detective Monroe will take you back to the officers who brought you here so they can drive you home. If we have any further questions, we'll contact you. Thank you."

Mo stands next to Monroe. Before exiting, he turns back to Palmer. "Can I ask one question, sir?"

"Yes, you can." Palmer straightens up, hoping Mo will have something significant to contribute.

"Do you think Professor Langford or Flatbush is the killer?"

Palmer settles back and takes a long drag, blowing smoke across the table to where Mo had been sitting. "We can't answer that today, Mr. Lumen. We're just collecting as much information as we can right now. That's why we had you come down for questioning." He looks to see if Mo has any other questions. "Thank you again. You've been very helpful."

Palmer lingers in the interview room, tapping his fingers on the table. In the aftermath of their conversation, he sees Maurice Lumen as everyone else does—a respectful, affable young man with limited maturity and intellect. Unlike everyone else, Palmer knows Lumen's now a central figure in the investigation and could be a wolf in sheep's clothing—a monster. But why was The Beast not aroused? Could Lumen be the subject of a monster? Or is he well-cloaked? He replays the interview in his mind. While Lumen seemed indifferent when Gonzalez was mentioned, why was he uncomfortable discussing Langford? Is there a connection between

Lumen and Langford? Why was he so anxious when answering questions about fourteen-year-old Emily Branch and the young women who weren't like twenty-year-old Kay Thompson?

Palmer thinks about Peggy and Pauline back in Ohio—about the same age as Emily and Kay. He also considers how similar Dayton is to Providence: with declining populations and about fifty miles from a significant metropolis and a major league baseball franchise. He wonders if the girls are rooting for Cincinnati in the Series. He wonders if they think about him. He wonders if they go jogging on the local trails. But mostly, he wonders if there's someone like Gonzalez or Langford or Lumen lurking in the woods.

When Monroe returns, Ross and Lowe are in tow. They stand around the table staring at Palmer, his shoulders slumped, head in hands, taking deep breaths through his nose.

Palmer runs his hands down his face and realizes he's not alone. "There's no shortage of suspects on this one, is there, gentlemen?"

Monroe pats Palmer on the back. "It's okay, Frank. We're all feeling it."

Palmer pitches forward. "Cut the sentimental horseshit, Jeff. I'm trying to get rid of a headache."

"We all are." Ross laughs at his own joke.

Monroe backs away. "Hey, sorry I got a little uptight in there." He shakes his head. "Lumen kid's answers just frustrated the hell out of me."

Palmer nods. "It happens. Any new information?"

Monroe curls his lip. "The bullet we found at Bryant *is* the one used in the murder of the Rollins girl. Forensics matched the fired bullet footprint to the exit wound, and ballistics confirmed the bullet's a 9mm—not a match to the gun found in Gonzalez's glove box. In addition, the spent round's well-tarnished, indicating it's an older bullet, maybe more than a decade old."

Palmer straightens up. "That means the gun that fired the bullet is probably a pistol."

"That's true."

"Then we need to get the team back there to search for a casing."

"I'm on it. Let me go make a call."

"Jeff, wait up." Palmer scratches his head. "I'd recommend having them make a straight line from where the body was found to the walking path along the access road. Have them look up to thirteen feet left and right of that line. I believe thirteen feet is correct but confirm with ballistics that's the maximum spent shell ejection for a 9mm pistol. Tell the search team to start from the trail and check for any footpaths in the woods that cross that line. I'm sure I saw a few, but I can't remember if they cross. If my hunch is correct, they should find the casing just as they enter the woods or near any path along the line to where the bullet was found. They should be able to pinpoint a few high-probability thirteen-foot circles to conduct their search. I'm hoping they can find the shell quickly."

"I'll oversee the search team myself in the morning," Monroe says. "What do you make of the kid's interview? Lumen seems harmless, but he's been everywhere the murders have occurred."

Palmer nods and pulls out a cigarette. "And then some. I recommend you also get a search team out to Georgiaville Pond."

"I was thinking the same thing."

"It won't solve a whole helluva lot since Langford and Gonzalez were there, too."

"You think this Lumen kid's capable?"

"God, I hope not," Palmer says, lighting and releasing a short, quick burst. "If this kid turns out to be the killer, it will alter criminal investigation as we know it." He stares at the wall. "Jesus, just imagine, a polite young man with the mental capacity of an eleven or twelve-year-old filled with sufficient rage to murder at least ten young women with no apparent sexual motive."

"He's a full-grown man, Frank."

"With the mind of a pre-pubescent."

"He's big and physically capable."

"There are a lot of angry eleven, twelve, and thirteen-year-old kids out there. Regardless of size, any of them are capable with a gun." He looks at Monroe, his eyebrows raised. "You wanna think about hunting down young kids?"

Ross taps the table with his finger. "What about the Co-Ed Killer in Southern California?"

Palmer settles back into the chair. "I researched the Kemper case for profiling. He's tall alright, something like six-nine. Shot his grandmother when he was fifteen because she reminded him of his mother, whom he hated. Then he shot his grandfather to spare him the pain of seeing the dead grandmother. However, *that* didn't make him a mass murderer." Palmer takes a thoughtful drag, blowing the smoke out his nose. "His more recent murder spree focused on young hitchhikers. Those were accomplished by an adult sexual predator with an extremely high IQ and diagnosed paranoid schizophrenia. There have been some young murderers in the United States, but not mass murderers like the Co-Ed Killer or the Pastoral Predator. I don't see the high intellect, paranoid schizophrenia, or sexual maturity in Lumen." He shakes his head. "No, unless he killed someone close to him down in Virginia and his lack of intellect is an elaborate disguise, I wouldn't be inclined to compare him to Kemper."

"Let's pray he's not another Kemper." Monroe stands, walking past Palmer. "We'll get a team out to Georgiaville Pond tomorrow morning. I'll give Stricker a call and tell him to get his team ready."

"Have the team at Georgiaville focus on the side of the pond opposite to where the main trail is located and start looking within ten feet of the water's edge. If there's a body there, it will have been dragged from a path and left near the water."

Monroe grabs the door handle. "I'm on it."

"One more thing, Jeff."

Monroe turns back, his cream-colored eyes tinted red. "C'mon, Frank, we've only got so many resources."

"Sorry, we're gonna need some interviewers to talk to Lumen's housemates and the Thompson girl tomorrow. I need to understand the relationship between Lumen and Dufresne."

"Are you gonna sit in any of those?"

"I won't be here." Palmer takes a final drag, exhaling as he presses his cigarette into the ashtray. "Gerry and I are headed to Virginia in the morning. We need to speak with a Mr. and Mrs. Branch in Sumerduck."

# THE STORM INTENSIFIES

## SUNDAY, 19 OCTOBER 1975

M*o slogs to the dining hall with the weight of Mr. Thompson's words hanging over him and the gravity of Palmer's questions dragging him down.* Taking advantage of a late afternoon break in the rain, he wades over to the Unistructure for an early dinner, knowing The Lady Behind the Lunch Counter doesn't work on weekends, so there won't be the same food selection. After a bland meal, he exits the dining hall and is greeted by a familiar face.

"Hey, dummy, remember me?" Veronica's flanked by two female friends. Her brown hair is pulled up in a messy bun, every word she says is drenched in disdain. "Veronica?! Brian's friend?! Remember?!"

Mo nods and walks away.

She calls out behind him. "I think they have the wrong guy! I think it's you! I think *you're* the killer, you big retard!"

Mo spins back on his heel, taking a single step toward Veronica. He stares into her suddenly terrified eyes, his hands clenched. "Shut up! Why do you do this to me? Shut up!"

He feels for his gloves, heart racing, fighting back tears, but it's raining hard outside, and there's nowhere he can go to relieve the pain. He sets a course for the library, considering how the accusations and isolation have returned—just like it was in Virginia, exactly as it happened with Emily—his banishment set in motion by one final confrontation four months earlier.

After the fight in the schoolyard, Mo spent a great deal of time alone. On schooldays, Mrs. Branch kept him busy with menial chores. Once finished, he'd read or nap before lunch, spending the afternoon passing time until Paul came home. On rainy days, he watched reruns of his favorite old shows with Dion. But when it was nice outside, he enjoyed convening with nature along the Rappahannock. Listening to the water navigate rocks, he and Dion waited patiently by the river's edge for the school year to end.

Four weeks after the schoolyard incident, two weeks into summer break, a rejuvenating summer rain skated down windowpanes, leaving the Branch children housebound. The boys played Yahtzee with Mo and Jake in the living room while Emily and Mary watched television. The Branch parents found space cleaning out the garage.

"Come on, Emily, play with us," Peter said.

Emily waved her brother off. "I don't want to play. Be quiet!"

Mary, snuggled between her big sister and a Raggedy Ann doll, put her finger over her mouth and uttered, "Shh…"

The boys did nothing to dampen the sound of dice shaking in the plastic cup.

Emily's face cringed. Her body quivered with each roll.

Mo watched her closest on his own turns, shaking vigorously.

Though his face remained expressionless, even Dion seemed to relish annoying the older Branch daughter.

Emily stomped over to the television and raised the volume. "Shut up, all of you! Go play upstairs. I can't hear my show."

Mo got up from the floor. "Let's go, guys."

Instead of retreating to the sofa, Emily confronted the boys, her body arched forward, arms folded, and eyes glaring. "Yes, listen to the freak, go upstairs!"

Paul poked at Emily's leg with his foot. "Don't call him a freak!"

Spit flew from Emily's mouth. "He *is* a freak! A big dummy!"

Paul jumped up, running across the room. "Stop it! I'm gonna tell Mom and Dad!"

Emily gave Paul a dismissive wave. "Go ahead! They know it's true!"

Mo turned his back to Emily, motioning Peter and Jake to follow.

Emily pushed Jake from behind, bumping Mo into the bottom post of the staircase railing. "Get going!"

Peter grabbed the bell-bottom leg of his sister's jeans. "Stop it, Emily!"

"You're gonna be sorry you did that!" Emily reached back and pulled her brother's hair.

Peter howled in pain, yanking his sister's arm down by the wrist before letting go.

From behind, Jake grabbed Emily's other arm and spun her around.

"Stop it!" Mary cried from the sofa, tears rolling down her face. "Stop it!"

Emily slapped Jake across the face. "Let go of me!"

Jake released Emily's arm and stepped back.

Emily followed with a kick to his leg.

"Ouch! Stop it, that hurts!" Jake tried to get away.

Mo pushed between them, holding Emily away. "Stop hitting my brother!"

Emily lunged at Jake. "Let go of me, you retard!"

Hand clenched around the back of Emily's shirt, Mo held her away.

"Try this, Slow Mo!" Emily's knee found Mo's crotch.

By the time Mo looked up from his crouched position, the living room was silent except for Mary's crying. Mr. and Mrs. Branch, mouths open, stood with Paul at the far end of the room with Emily lying motionless next to the fireplace hearth, blood seeping from her head.

Mr. Branch rushed over to Emily's side. "Margie, call for an ambulance!" Placing Emily on the sofa, he used a throw blanket to control the bleeding.

The children stood in grave silence.

Mo saw a stream of blood creep in a crooked strip of recessed cement on the fieldstone hearth. He wondered if it would leave a stain.

Mr. Branch whispered into Emily's ear. "You're okay, honey. Daddy's here. Daddy will take care of you."

The ambulance arrived, and Emily, still motionless, was lifted into the back on a stretcher. Mr. Branch jumped in with her. Mo, recalling his father's lifeless body seven months earlier, hoped Emily's fate would be different, if only for his own well-being.

The evening meal was a somber event, the boys and Mary eating pizza when Mrs. Branch broke an uncomfortable silence. "Who started it?" Her voice was calm.

"Emily said our game was bothering her," Peter said, "so we were heading upstairs, but she came over and pushed Jake. She was kicking him, so Mo got in between them. She tripped over my leg and hit her head on the fireplace."

Mrs. Branch shifted her glare to the other side of the table. "Is this true, Mo?"

Mo shivered at the convicting tone of her voice. "Yes, we were playing."

Mrs. Branch's voice rose. "Did you push Emily?"

"I don't remember."

"It just happened a little while ago." Mrs. Branch shook, her face red. "How can you not remember?"

Mo looked down at his half-eaten slice of pizza, voice trembling. "I don't know. I don't remember." Then, the phone rang, offering Mo a reprieve.

Mrs. Branch hurried over, listening for a few moments before exclaiming, "Thank God!" and weeping into the receiver. She hung up and leaned her head against the wall, wiping away tears of relief before announcing, "Emily's going to be okay. She'll spend tonight in the hospital and come home tomorrow." With that, she went upstairs.

Mary and the boys finished their pizza in complete silence.

Mo wasn't hungry. He knew Mr. Branch would be home soon.

And the storm had not yet passed.


In the library, Mo sits at a desk in a quiet corner and cries. Forehead resting on the back of his hands, his sobbing is heard far enough away to attract the attention of a concerned student. She approaches him, placing her hand on his shoulder.

Distracted from his grief, Mo looks up. The dim ceiling light shines through her golden hair. "I'm sorry," Mo says, brushing his sorrows from the side of his nose.

"You have nothing to be sorry for." Her voice is delicate and familiar, but Mo doesn't know from where.

"I'm sorry if I've disturbed anyone."

"Sometimes, it's okay to disturb others if it helps you let go of the pain." She rubs his back before withdrawing.

Her shadow remains over Mo as he rests his head back on his hands and falls asleep. He heads back to the townhouse just before midnight, the sting of Veronica's insults and accusations softened by the kindness of an angel in the library.

# HANGING PROMISES

## MONDAY, 20 OCTOBER 1975

M o endures another evening alone in the townhouse, suffering another restless night on the sofa. Unable to sleep, he leaves early—too early to encounter campus security, too early to walk the woodland paths, too early to eat at the cafeteria. He sits on the front doorstep, waiting for daylight, checking his Timex, and expecting the sun. But the sun does not come. He's not sure the sun will ever come again. Taking a different path to work, he walks through the center of campus under walkway lighting. There's no movement this early, and he's alone. Again.

Mo's thoughts match the pre-dawn landscape—gloomy and desolate. Mo sidesteps puddles, navigates mud buildup, folds his arms around his chest to keep warm, and thinks about yesterday: Mr. Thompson, Investigator Palmer, and Veronica—all with questions and accusations.

Approaching the wrought-iron archway, Mo does not avoid it. He does not think anything from his past could be worse than the pain and loneliness he feels right now. He runs his hands along the metal, cold and wet, as he passes through, arriving safely on the opposite side without apparent change—mood still somber, outlook still bleak. He wonders if the past is present in each stride. If every stream, river, lake, and pond feeds into the Rappahannock. If the Rappahannock drains into the ocean. And if, like the floating carcasses, he is destined to offer a temporary scent before slipping under the water and becoming part of the landscape, in the trees and groundcover, the flowers and shrubbery.

Sitting on a stump outside Griffin's office, in the cool, damp darkness, Mo knows creatures are stirring in the woods, just as there are students in their dorms and security on campus. Still, he sits alone, feeling increasingly isolated.

Griffin arrives early enough for the remaining darkness to shroud Mo sitting fifteen feet away. Unaware of Mo's presence, he passes by, tugs at the office doorknob, and repeatedly kicks the metal plate. "C'mon," Griffin says through gnashed teeth, "open up, you prick." He pulls and kicks harder.

Mo walks behind Griffin, his arms still wrapped around his shivering body. "Good morning, Mr. Griffin. Can I help?"

Griffin jumps. "Geez, Mo, I didn't see you there."

Mo notes Griffin's wrinkled brows. "I'm sorry. Are you okay?"

"I'm fine, but all the rain's really swollen this door tight." Griffin kicks the door one last time. "Let's go through the garage." He grumbles as he stomps the mud off his boots.

Mo's glad he can't understand what his boss is saying. Inside Griffin's office, he watches the head groundskeeper sit and fling the morning paper on his desk. Unlike other mornings, Griffin doesn't reach up for the work schedule. Instead, he stares at the newspaper, his shoulders slumped, eyes downcast. Mo wonders if all the rain has dampened Griffin's spirits.

Mo sits opposite Griffin. "Game six tomorrow night."

Griffin nods, his eyes fixed on the paper.

Mo sees the word 'Predator'. He places his hand over the partial headline. "Looks like Tiant's pitching again."

Griffin continues nodding, looks up at Mo with weary eyes.

Mo rubs his neck. "They have to win tonight."

"Mo..." Griffin's voice breaks, "I don't feel like talking baseball right now."

Mo pulls his hand back, looking down at the paper. The headline typesetting has grown larger, a stain expanding across Griffin's desk. He mutters, "Okay."

Griffin taps his fingers on the desk. "Look, son, I'm shorthanded today, and a lot of work needs to get done on campus. The boys have all been called in for questioning, so I'll be working with whoever's available throughout the day until I go in this afternoon."

"I'll be here all day. I'll work extra hard."

"No, Mo," Griffin says, shaking his head, "I need you to go home."

Mo slumps in his chair. "But I can help."

"Son, I need you to go home so the others can get some work done. You'll be a distraction, and we've already had enough distractions lately. You've got enough on your *own* plate."

Mo stares at the jagged red lines in Griffin's eyes, the head groundskeeper's voice and words sounding more like Mr. Branch's the evening Mo was banished to his office. He places his palms on Mr. Griffin's desk. "But I want to help. I can work away from the others. Please, sir."

Griffin walks to the other side of the desk, placing his hand on Mo's shoulder. "You *are* helping. I know the police questioned you again yesterday, and they may bring you in again." He pats Mo's shoulder several times. "You need to be available to help them catch this killer. We can handle the work here. Go home. I'll see you next Monday. I'll make sure you get paid. Just try to relax and enjoy the rest of the World Series." He steps back. "Go ahead, get going before the boys get here."

"Yes, sir." Mo rises from the chair, arms hanging listlessly by his sides. He drags his feet as he exits.

Griffin calls out, "Mo?"

Mo looks back through the doorway, hope lifting his shoulders, and notices several new uniform shirts hanging in plastic on the back of the exterior door, 'Mo' embroidered on the name patch. A brand-new Red Sox cap hangs just above. "Yes, sir?"

Office light shining off Griffin's now-glazed eyes, he says, "This is family, son. We're all behind you."

Finding little solace in Griffin's words, Mo sulks away. Plodding along the access road, his coworkers drive by and wave. He can't even lift his arm to reciprocate.

When Mo crosses the threshold, the townhouse is like an island—remote and surrounded by water. Daylight finally coming through the windows, he lies on his bed to nap, feeling isolated and knowing he can't walk off this anguish.

# 81

# DION

## MONDAY, 20 OCTOBER 1975

*P almer has not slept in days, so with Ross gently snoring in the seat beside him, he takes advantage of a short flight, a courtesy pillow, and the cabin wall.* And Palmer sleeps. Time in the air from T.F. Green to Washington Dulles is ninety minutes—long enough to dream. So Palmer dreams. He dreams of Santa's Village and Leonardo's Pizza and Franklin Park Zoo. He dreams of Marilyn and Peggy and Pauline. And he dreams of their house in the suburbs and the branches in the backyard and the dining room table. In his dreams, he and Marilyn are together, and the girls are young and happy. But he never sleeps long. And when his dreaming is done, Palmer's alone. Always alone.

Palmer's shaken awake by the force of rubber meeting runway. He and Ross rent a car and arrive at the Branch home midmorning, where Mr. and Mrs. Branch come outside to welcome them. Palmer bends down to greet the family pet, compliments their two-story colonial home, and takes note of their freshly washed station wagon and carefully tended gardens as they enter the house.

The interior of the Branch home is also well maintained. Passing through the kitchen, Palmer glances at a coffeepot on the stove, noting how the sun radiates off its immaculate stainless-steel shell and onto the spotless linoleum floor. The crystal of a chandelier above the dining room table refracts unencumbered light onto the ceiling, and the glass windows of the china cabinet have no fingerprints. Although he knows there are children, there is little to suggest they live here. He's certain there are no rodents in this home—at least not of the garden variety.

Seated at the table, and after several minutes of pleasantries, Ross begins. "We're here to gather information about Maurice Leroy Lumen. Are you comfortable answering questions about Mr. Lumen?"

"Agent Ross," Mrs. Branch says, "we have no secrets here. Of course, we'll answer all your questions."

Palmer's response is measured. "Mrs. Branch, what I've determined in twenty years on this job is that everyone has secrets."

Mrs. Branch sits back and folds her arms. "Hmph."

Ross opens his notepad, beginning the interview with a series of straightforward questions verifying Lumen's having lived with the Branches and establishing the timeframe of his arrival and departure. After some dialogue around the younger brother, the interview begins in earnest.

Ross flips through several pages. "Based on the information you've provided, Mr. Lumen and his brother were left homeless after their father passed. You also stated that Mr. Lumen's mother died many years ago. Since they're half-brothers, why is it that Jake did not go to live with his mother?"

Mrs. Branch brushes her nose with her finger. "Mo's father raised Jake when his mother ran out on him. It was quite a source of gossip locally, and the business their father started with Earl Johnson failed as a result."

Ross turns to Mr. Branch. "Was Earl Johnson a family friend in addition to being a business partner?"

Mr. Branch nods. "He and Ken were friends a very long time. I believe they fought together in Europe."

"So, Mr. Johnson would know Maurice Lumen fairly well?"

"I think so, but I haven't spoken to Earl in several years."

"Does Mr. Johnson still live in Sumerduck?"

"Yes, he has a house on the other end of Sumerduck Road, near Rock Run." Mr. Branch picks up a pitcher in the center of the table. "Would either of you like some more water?"

Palmer shakes his head.

Ross holds a hand over his glass. "We understand that Jake was taken in as a foster child, but how is it that his adult brother was permitted to stay with you?"

"We agreed to take Mo along with Jake at the behest of my wife's friend, Janice. She feared he would fall through the cracks in the system."

"Who is Janice?"

"Janice Harrington was the sixth-grade teacher at Sumerduck Elementary for many years."

"Why would she be concerned about Mo's welfare?"

"She taught Mo years ago. She died last month, just a couple of months after being diagnosed with cancer."

"I'm sorry, I still don't understand why she would be so concerned with Mo's welfare."

Mrs. Branch leans forward with her palms on the tablecloth. "She was his mother's friend from childhood, a generous, God-fearing woman who had a soft spot for children with special needs. That's how we came to know her. She and her husband have a son with muscular dystrophy."

Ross nods as he scribbles. "Now, Mr. Branch, you mentioned Mrs. Harrington feared Mo would fall through the cracks in the system, and Mrs. Branch, you just stated she had a soft spot for children with special needs. Maurice Lumen's not a child, so what are his special needs?"

Mr. Branch opens his mouth to speak but stops when Mrs. Branch places her hand on his. "Mo had a major seizure when he was eleven," she says. "Dr. Cross was amazed he survived. Mo seemed to be normal at first, but as time passed, it was clear he wasn't keeping up with his classmates, so he wasn't able to finish grade school. He's quite large, and many parents didn't want their children to go near him. His father and grandmother tried to protect him from the cruelty of a tight-knit community, but some of the local children would call him 'Slow Mo' and other disparaging words. Very mean." She checks her cuticles. "And with Jake being so dark-skinned, well—"

Palmer dusts his hand across the tablecloth. "So, he has an intellectual deficiency?"

"Yes, he's mentally retarded and has an emotional handicap. He doesn't fit in well."

"Mrs. Branch, we've met with Mr. Lumen. He seems to be fitting in quite well in Rhode Island. He's clearly immature for his age, but he's made many friends and appears to be functioning well given his newfound independence. There also seems to be a genuine innocence in the way he communicates and how he talks about others." Palmer leans forward. "So, I'm curious, what do you mean he doesn't fit in well?"

Mrs. Branch falls back in her chair, staring with her mouth agape and hand over her heart.

Mr. Branch squirms in his seat. "I'll answer this one if you don't mind. Mo seems to be a nice boy, but there were anomalies, some of them quite disturbing."

Palmer relaxes into his seat, turns to Mr. Branch. "Do these anomalies have anything to do with his no longer living here with his brother?"

"Yes, there were several incidents where Mo's actions resulted in one of our children, or children at the school, getting hurt."

"I thought you said Mo stopped going to school. Certainly, he wasn't in school earlier this year?" Palmer pulls his pack of cigarettes out, showing it to Mr. Branch.

Mr. Branch nods, his lips pursed. "Go right ahead."

Palmer observes Mrs. Branch's alarmed stare. "Do either of you have a match?"

Mr. Branch rubs his wife's hand. "I'm sorry, we don't smoke."

"Can I use your stove for a moment?"

"Sure, just go right through there."

Palmer lights his cigarette, taking the circuitous route through the living room and around the staircase as he walks back. Approaching the table, he releases a billow of smoke directly into the chandelier. "Why was Mo at school earlier this year?"

Mrs. Branch winces. "He would walk with Jake and our children to and from school each day."

"I thought you said he didn't fit in well? But now you're telling me he walked to and from school with the kids?"

"*Well*," Mrs. Branch harumphs, "he did. That is, he did until he got into a fight with a number of the eighth-grade girls."

Palmer stares at the tip of his cigarette. "Can I please have an ashtray, Mr. Branch?" He turns back to Mrs. Branch. "How old is your oldest daughter?"

"Emily just turned fifteen earlier this month."

"And what grade is she in?"

"She started high school this year."

"So, she was in that eighth-grade class when the incident took place earlier in the year?"

"Yes."

"Is it fair to say Emily is friends with some, or most, of the other girls in her class?"

"Emily's very popular at school, yes."

"And would Emily have had any reason to dislike Mo or not like his being here?"

Mrs. Branch shakes her head. "Emily didn't dislike Mo. She saw Mo touch a young boy at school inappropriately."

"Alright, Mrs. Branch, I can understand how that would be disturbing." Palmer takes a bowl from Mr. Branch and places it on the table. "Did the child's parents report the incident to the school or the authorities?"

"No."

"Did Emily tell you she saw Mo touch the boy inappropriately?"

"Yes."

"Did any of your other children say they saw Mo touch the boy inappropriately?"

Mrs. Branch looks at her husband. "I don't remember."

Palmer flicks his ashes into the bowl. "Mrs. Branch, we can wait here until the children come home from school."

Mrs. Branch scoffs and crosses her arms.

Mr. Branch frowns at his wife. "None of the other children, or any adults, saw Mo touch him. The boy said Mo didn't even go near him. Our boys told us it wasn't true, and Emily admitted later she may have seen it incorrectly. I'm sorry, my wife was badly hurt by the whole chain of events leading to Mo's departure."

"That's understandable," Palmer says, offering Mrs. Branch an apologetic nod. "I'm sorry for your suffering." He turns back to Mr. Branch. "Was anyone hurt in the incident at school?"

"Emily had her hair pulled. Mo had some scratches. I don't think any of the other girls were hurt."

"Sounds like Mo may have gotten the worst of it." Palmer takes a puff and exhales. "Tell me more about this chain of events leading to Mo's having to leave."

"My wife and I were out in the garage on a rainy day in late June. The kids were out of school and playing in the parlor. Our youngest boy comes out yelling for us to come over. When we walked in the door, Emily was on the floor near the fireplace bleeding from her head, and Mo was standing over her. Kids said he pushed her, and she tripped over my oldest son's legs."

"But you didn't see it happen or what caused it?"

"They were having some kind of argument over the boys playing too loud while she and Mary were trying to watch TV."

"But you didn't see what happened, correct?"

Mrs. Branch slaps the table with her palm. "We saw the *result!*"

Palmer acknowledges Mrs. Branch with an unemotional glance before turning back to her husband. "Are you a Redskins fan, Alan?"

"Yes."

"You watch the games?"

"I do, sometimes."

"Well, then you know it's common in football for the referee to see the punch thrown in retaliation and not the instigating one. Are you familiar with this?"

Mrs. Branch slams her apron on the table. "Are you implying my daughter hit Mo *first?!*"

"What I'm suggesting, Mrs. Branch, is that Emily has two doting parents who may be inclined to overlook their daughter's instigation, choosing instead to place blame on the one they wish to accuse."

Mrs. Branch storms out of the room.

"I apologize again for my wife. We were both very frustrated at the time. Whenever anything bad would happen, Mo would lie and say he didn't remember. She had hoped we were done with him."

"Is his brother, Jake, still living with you?"

"Yes, we finalized the adoption last week."

"Then, Mr. Branch, how could you and your family be done with Mr. Lumen? Wouldn't Jake be entitled to see his brother?" Palmer takes a long drag.

"Uh, yes, we were, um, talking about maybe taking a-a family trip." Mr. Branch clutches his glass of water. "We were thinking possibly next summer so Jake could see Mo."

Palmer exhales, releasing a thin stream of smoke just above Mr. Branch's head. "But we both know that trip won't take place, don't we, Mr. Branch?"

Mouth hung open, Mr. Branch's focus falls to his hands.

Palmer leans toward Mr. Branch and places his elbow on the table, resting his chin on his hand. "Let's discuss Mo's banishment. How did he end up in Rhode Island?"

"Because Jake was in the adoption process at the time, and family placement services was aware that Mo was also in our home, we were required to report if we wanted to remove Mo from the household."

"Was it because Mo's departure could have an emotional effect on his brother?"

"Yes. My wife and I also informed Mrs. Harrington before notifying social services. We explained to her that Mo was a danger to our children. She asked for time to try and place him. She was afraid he might, as my wife stated earlier, fall through the cracks in the system. She must've already known she was very sick and was concerned he might be institutionalized or left to fend for himself. She told us the state has very few resources available for special needs adults in rural areas, and she worried he might end up homeless. She felt very strongly he deserved better."

"Did you and your wife, Mr. Branch?"

Mr. Branch looks at Palmer, scrunching his eyes. "Did we what, Investigator Palmer?"

"Did you and your wife feel very strongly Mr. Lumen deserved better?"

"Enough to let him stay here in my office until Mrs. Harrington found him that job in Rhode Island."

"And where is your office?"

Mr. Branch rubs his temples. "Out in the garage."

Palmer runs a finger along the edge of his brow. "Did he sleep alone in the garage?"

Mr. Branch stares at his coffee cup. "No, we let Dion sleep out there with him."

Ross jerks his head, one eyebrow raised. "Who the hell's Dion?"

Mr. Branch's shoulders slump.

Palmer flicks his cigarette. "I'm guessing that's the family Labrador that greeted us when we first arrived. Is that correct, Mr. Branch?"

Mr. Branch nods, his head hanging.

"It was very humane of you and your wife to allow Mr. Lumen to stay in the garage with the dog, Mr. Branch." Palmer picks up the bowl. "Can I wash this in the sink for you?"

Mr. Branch takes the bowl from Palmer and places it back on the table. "My wife will take care of it."

"Thank you. Can we see the garage?"

Palmer and Ross follow Mr. Branch to a detached garage behind the house.

Palmer notices rot creeping around the doorframe with cobwebs in the window and top corner of the door. Inside, dust collects on the floor, desk, and stacks of document storage boxes. "So, Mr. Lumen stayed here for how long?"

"About a month and a half, from late June until he left in mid-August," Mr. Branch says. "I don't think anyone's been in here since he left."

"What were the requirements for his departure?"

"In order for Mo to leave the state, he had to pass psychological and physical tests."

"Where were these tests performed?"

"Fauquier Hospital in Warrenton."

"Did you accompany Mr. Lumen?"

Mr. Branch nods. "I drove Mo to his tests."

"Would you remember the name of the psychologist who evaluated Mr. Lumen?"

"Yes, his name was Dr. Winchester."

"Thank you, Mr. Branch. Can Agent Ross use your phone?"

"Of course." Mr. Branch escorts Ross back to the house.

Palmer walks outside and down to the river. The trees are almost bare, leaves scattered and drifting on the water. He imagines Lumen sitting alone on a big rock near the edge, his feet in the water and looking to the far bank. Listening to the sound of the water passing by, he can hear his daughters' laughter as they'd jump into the potholes and dip in the frigid waters of a popular swimming hole in Shelburne, Massachusetts, along the Deerfield River. Marilyn and the girls loved walking across the nearby bridge of flowers in late spring. Although he had little interest in the bright floral display, Palmer loved watching their smiling faces. Picturing Lumen walking along the river, looking at the flowers and the trees, he asks himself a single question: *Is it possible for someone to enjoy beautiful things and choose to destroy them?*

Palmer hears the porch door slam and returns to the front of the garage, where Ross is waiting with Mr. Branch.

"His secretary says Dr. Winchester has an opening at one thirty." Ross taps his watch, raising it to his ear.

Palmer points to his wrist. "That why I wear a Timex and not some overpriced Swiss brand. It's twelve fifty. We have time for just a few more questions, Mr. Branch, if it's okay with you."

"I'll answer any questions I can for as long as is necessary," Mr. Branch says.

"Excellent." Palmer points behind the garage. "By the way, what river is that?"

"That's the Rappahannock. Mo loved to sit by the river during the day when the kids were in school."

"I can see why. It's very peaceful."

Reentering the garage, Palmer turns to Mr. Branch. "Where did Mr. Lumen sleep?"

"On a cot along that wall." Mr. Branch nods in the direction of a pile of old boxes.

"Where's the cot now?"

"It's stored up there." Mr. Branch points to the top of a loft ladder. "You can climb up and see it if you like."

Palmer ascends the ladder and looks around before peering down at Mr. Branch. "Did Mr. Lumen have anything with him? Anything he may have taken with him to Rhode Island?"

"Not much, just some clothes we gave him and a few pictures of his parents." Mr. Branch catches his breath, eyebrows raised. "I almost forgot…" He scratches his head. "Mo got a box of his father's personal items after Ken died. There was a gun and a box of bullets I took away from him." He looks at the ladder. "I hid them up in the loft. They must still be up there."

"Can you show me where those are?"

Mr. Branch positions himself near the top of the ladder and lifts a floorboard, his face just inches from Palmer's. Turning his head, he stares straight into Palmer's eyes. "They're gone. I put them right here. I never gave them back."

"Do you remember what type of gun it was?"

"Only that it was a handgun. I don't know much about guns. I'm not a hunter, and I don't believe in having them in the house with the children."

"Do you remember anything about the bullets?"

"They were in a faded, white box. Print wasn't English. Sorry, that's all I remember."

"That's alright, Mr. Branch." Palmer looks down at Ross taking notes. "You all set, Gerry?"

Ross finishes a few final scribbles before giving Palmer a thumbs-up.

Palmer descends the ladder after Mr. Branch reaches the bottom. "Thank you, again, Mr. Branch, this has been very helpful." He extends his hand. "Please tell your wife we appreciate her time. Again, I'm sorry this has been so hard on her."

Mr. Branch shakes Palmer's hand. "You're welcome." He pauses before releasing. "Agent Palmer?"

"Yes, Mr. Branch?"

"Before you go, can I ask one question?"

"Absolutely."

"Does all this have to do with the mass murderer up there in Rhode Island? The Pastoral Predator that's been in the news?"

"Yes, we're investigating all possible avenues and looking at the backgrounds of many individuals as part of the process."

Mr. Branch's eyes light up. "Do you think Mo's somehow involved?"

"That would be a second question, Mr. Branch," Palmer says, turning and heading down the driveway, "and I only agreed to answer one."

Mr. Branch follows Palmer and Ross to their rental. Palmer opens the passenger door and addresses Mr. Branch, standing forward of the car. "To be fair, Mr. Branch, I have one last question for you, and you don't have to answer it." He drops his exhausted cigarette into the driveway gravel. "If Maurice Lumen had been your son, would you have treated him the way you did and sent him away?"

As Ross backs the car out of the driveway, Palmer observes Mr. Branch solemnly shaking his head.


Palmer's not apt to notice birds, animals, or anything nature-related unless it pertains to an investigation. He enjoyed seeing the performing bears at Clark's Trading Post with his father but didn't venture to their pens. And his family went to the zoo when his daughters were young, but only to appease Marilyn. It disturbed him to see the animals in their cages; he felt cages were for the real animals—the ones on the street. So, watching the plastic bird on Dr. Winchester's desk bob up and down, he admires its red, velvet head, purple top hat, and the fact it's unconstrained.

"I'm sorry I'm a few minutes late, gentlemen," Dr. Winchester says. "I'm so glad Loretta showed you into my office. I see she laid out a few snacks."

"Good afternoon, Dr. Winchester. I'm Agent Ross, and this is Chief Investigator Palmer. Thank you for finding time to meet with us on such short notice. We know you must be very busy." Ross reaches for a Ring Ding from the side table between himself and Palmer.

"No problem at all. I hope I'm able to help." Winchester, realizing Palmer's eyes are observing the drinking bird, pushes the toy closer. "Quite fascinating, isn't it? A friend of mine gave it to me. Said it would go great with my Newton's cradle." He points to a shelf.

"I've seen them before but never perched on the side of the glass." Palmer sits up straight. "Hmm, interesting."

"Yes, I find having objects of interest in plain view can be a source of comfort for my patients; sometimes distracts them from their issues temporarily." Winchester slides it back to the corner of his desk. "How can I be of assistance?"

Ross opens his notepad. "We have a few questions about Maurice Leroy Lumen. We understand you evaluated him a couple of months back. He's a rather large twenty-four-year-old with a mental deficiency. You would've signed the release documentation allowing him to live and work in Rhode Island, is that correct?"

"Yes, I remember Mr. Lumen. I reviewed his file before you arrived. Very interesting case. How's he managing up there?"

"He's fine, Dr. Winchester. We're just doing routine background investigations on a number of individuals who may be related to a case we're working on."

Winchester leans forward. "Would that be the Pastoral Predator? It's been all over the news the past week."

"Yes, Doctor. Could we look at the notes from your interview with Mr. Lumen?"

"Because Mr. Lumen wasn't a patient of mine, I can discuss any of my findings for the state. Let me have Loretta make you a Xerox copy while we talk. This will just take a moment." When he returns, Winchester clasps his hands. "All set. Now, what would you like to know?"

"When did you interview Mr. Lumen?"

"I interviewed Mr. Lumen on August fourteenth, a little over two months ago."

"Did you find him agreeable during the interview?"

"Very much so. Mr. Lumen's quite amicable and very straight-forward. What he lacks in intellect, he makes up for in pleasantry."

"Did he answer all of your questions?"

"Yes, I interviewed Mr. Lumen for about forty-five minutes. He answered every question."

"Did he seem disturbed by any of the questions or express his emotions verbally or physically in any way?"

"He genuinely enjoyed talking about his family. Though both of his parents had died, he expressed sincere affection, as he did when talking about his brother, grandmother, and a teacher from grade school who was a close family friend." Winchester folds his fingers together. "But when we started talking about his time with the family he was living with—the Branch family—he was very different. He continued to answer every question, but his body language displayed considerable discomfort. I asked about the events leading up to his having to leave the household. It was clear the discussion was painful for him. In particular, he tensed up, even cried, when talking about the Branches' oldest daughter, Emily."

"Was he angry or disappointed?"

"A little of both. I sensed clear frustration, not only with how Emily treated him, but also because he couldn't remember the actual events themselves."

Ross reaches for another Ring Ding.

Palmer, brows furrowed, grabs Ross's wrist before turning to Winchester. "Would it be possible, Doctor, for him not to remember? Mr. Branch made a similar comment, referencing Mr. Lumen lying."

Ross shakes free of Palmer's grip and rests his hand on the arm-rest of his chair.

"Mr. Lumen suffers from psychogenic amnesia, a memory disorder resulting in episodic memory loss. In most cases, the afflicted individual will have difficulty remembering bad events, particularly those in which they play a central role. It tends to happen to individuals who have experienced significant emotional trauma and serves as a mechanism to protect them from future bad experiences or prevent them from having to deal with any guilt associated with their actions, which they may understand at the time to be bad behavior. The individual's memory normally recovers over time, and they ordinarily refrain from the negative behavior once they recall their actions. I explained all of this to Mr. Branch after interviewing Mr. Lumen."

"So, Mr. Lumen wasn't lying to Mr. and Mrs. Branch. He actually couldn't remember the events which resulted in his having to leave the Branch family?"

"Yes, I believe that's correct."

"Since a person with this memory disorder is disassociated from the guilt of his actions, would he be more likely to engage in bad behavior?"

"Clinical evidence doesn't support such a hypothesis, Investigator Palmer. The psychogenic amnesia, in and of itself, shouldn't present an issue. Coupled with clinical misogyny, however, it could be quite serious. That said, I didn't see the pattern traits consistent with misogynistic tendencies in our conversation." Winchester reaches for a glass of water. After taking a long, deliberate sip, he resumes. "Mr. Lumen was always within the level of acceptable emotional responses, and my final assessment was Mr. Lumen's a very affable and affectionate young man who experienced several highly traumatic events at a relatively young age. He also suffered the loss of key nurturing figures in his life, replaced by less accommodative relationships with subsequent females. This has created an overly simplistic view of two types of women: ones he loves, such as his mother, grandmother, and teacher; and all others, for whom he has little regard emotionally or builds up distrust, disassociation, or dislike."

Palmer pulls his pack of cigarettes halfway out of this pocket, staring straight at Winchester. "Could these key nurturing females in his life be replaced by new ones?"

Winchester shakes his head. "Sorry. This is a medical facility; there's no smoking allowed. To answer your question, it's possible but unlikely. His key nurturing figures were all women during his childhood development. It's doubtful he will be able to find females suitable to replace those as an adult." Winchester picks up a pencil and begins twirling it with his fingers. "In psychology, for sexually active men, we would refer to this as the Madonna-whore dichotomy. This differs from misogyny in that the individual doesn't hold contempt for all females but only those who don't measure up to the individual's view of acceptability. Unless the pattern were to be consistently reinforced in an environment where there's no perceived Madonna figure, and given his psychosexual development's stalled in the latency stage, I don't believe Mr. Lumen, given his intellectual limitations, is capable of hurting anyone. Therefore, I couldn't see any reason why he should have been held back from moving to Rhode Island and working a job commensurate with his intellect and abilities."

"So, Doctor, what I think I hear you saying is Mr. Lumen wasn't outwardly aggressive or abnormally enraged when you asked about his experiences with the Branch family and specifically the oldest daughter, Emily. Is that correct?"

"Yes, that's accurate."

"For the sake of my better understanding, what would happen if Mr. Lumen was afflicted with..." Palmer stretches his neck to read Ross's notebook, "clinical misogyny or misogynistic tendencies?"

"To be quite honest, for Mr. Lumen, an adult stalled in the latency stage, I don't think very much." Winchester lays down the pencil and straightens the nameplate on his desk. "Maybe some disagreements with women might irritate or agitate him, but not much else."

"But he wouldn't become violent?"

"No, Investigator Palmer, I do not believe he would. Again, Mr. Lumen's permanently suspended in the latency stage of psychosexual development due to his prepubescent intellectual maturity. His body and mind haven't entered the final stage—the genital stage. That would be the stage where violence could become an issue for a misogynist."

"But some eleven-year-old boys are already sexually active, and Mo was almost twelve when he had his seizure."

"That would be more common in an environment where boys are encouraged to accelerate their sexual awareness. We see this in tribal settings and among disadvantaged youth growing up in impoverished and predominantly minority neighborhoods. You might expect a younger boy in the roughest, largely Black, urban areas to be more sexually aware and active, rather than here in a predominantly Christian, White, middle-class community like Fauquier County." Dr. Winchester bows his head and looks through the frame of his glasses. "Mr. Lumen never mentioned anything relating to sex during our discussion, not even coincidentally. He was raised in a home where he was sheltered from the outside world by his father, grandmother, and much younger brother. It's clear he hasn't had sexual feelings about the women who have nurtured him and whom he adores, and he lacks the maturation to feel sexual frustration with those who have been emotionally insensitive."

"Is it possible, Dr. Winchester, he hasn't met a female closer to his own age whom he finds nurturing and potentially sexually attractive?"

"Anything's possible, I guess, Investigator Palmer, but I'd say it would be highly unlikely."

"I'm sure you're correct, Doctor, but if you'll humor me just a little longer, please." Palmer squeezes his shirt pocket. "If it's even minimally possible Mr. Lumen could find a female his own age he sees as nurturing, would he be able to have a sexual relationship with her?"

"I don't believe so. He would be tortured by a desire he cannot fulfill, neither physically nor emotionally."

"And could this torture lead to anxiety and rage?"

"I doubt any rage would be directed at the object of his affection."

"Would it be directed elsewhere, maybe toward females he finds undesirable? Possibly women with whom he feels emotionally disassociated?"

"Again, anything's theoretically possible, but I interviewed Mr. Lumen and, under the circumstances, he's reasonably well-adjusted and entirely nonaggressive. He even mentioned praying for those who have hurt him or been unkind, just as he prays for his mother."

Palmer lifts himself from his chair and walks behind where Ross is sitting, placing his hand on Ross's shoulder. "I think Agent Ross and I are all set. We thank you for your time."

Ross folds his notepad and reaches again for the last Ring Ding.

Palmer kicks the leg of Ross's chair.."Doctor, if you don't mind, I just have three final questions, and I'll be quick."

"Certainly, anything I can do to help."

"You've been doing this job for quite some time. How many individuals have you diagnosed with psychogenic amnesia over the years?"

"Oh, I don't know, maybe a couple of dozen, give or take."

"And of those you've diagnosed, how many have you also diagnosed with clinical misogyny?"

"Misogyny, in lesser forms, is quite common. However, I've never diagnosed anyone with both psychogenic amnesia *and* clinical misogyny. To do so, for an individual in the genital phase of psychosexual development, would be to identify an individual as capable of horrific crimes."

"Then, Doctor, if you've never diagnosed someone with both, what will happen when you're wrong?" Palmer steers Ross out of the room, leaving Winchester to his thoughts.

# 82

# FURY

## MONDAY, 20 OCTOBER 1975

M*o looks out his bedroom window, his mood matching the early eve-ning gray.* Passing the time at the dining hall and library, he finds that even the sports pages can't hold his interest after four days without baseball. He wonders how long the rain will go on. How long the sports pages will report the weather. How many more days until the series resumes. Game six is only twenty-four hours away, but he's heard the same story since Friday.

Following a late dinner, Mo's walk back to the townhouse is dark and wet. Though the worst of the storm's over, it continues to drizzle, and the severed streams running off his umbrella remind Mo of the waterfalls he's visited with his friends here in Rhode Island; comforting images when all around is bleak.

Visible in the distance, a car sits conspicuously at the edge of the townhouse parking lot. Smoke had escaped out the windows on both sides of the vehicle when Mo left earlier. Now, a white cloud rises from just one side.

Mo hears footsteps behind him and stops. The footsteps also stop. Looking back, he sees a man with a lit cigarette in a trench coat standing fifty feet back, smoke following the contour of his hat. Coat collar up, The Cigarette stares menacingly through the distance and darkness. Mo resumes his march to the townhouse, moving faster and forgetting about the waterfalls. Up ahead, the safety of his dark, lonely townhouse is disturbed by light—light from his bedroom. Mo walks faster, more afraid than he has ever been. The Cigarette keeps pace.

Mo's fear subsides when he enters the front door, his mood

improving with the welcome sound of his friends' voices in the rear of the townhouse. Walking through the hall, he scans his bedroom, turns out the light, and closes the door, continuing to the living room where Carlton is seated on the sofa with Trevor and Brian on the love seat and chair.

"Hey, uh, M." Carlton's fingers tap the armrest. "Crazy stuff about your friend, uh, Professor Langford, huh?"

Mo nods, scratching his head. "Hi, guys. Did anyone go into my room?"

Carlton's eyes narrow, brows furrow. "W-why would anyone go in your room?" He chuckles.

Brian and Trevor shake their heads.

Mo looks in the direction of his bedroom door and shrugs. "Where's Kay?"

"She, uh, said she was tired tonight. It was a wicked busy day at her father's store with people getting stuff to clean up after the weekend." Carlton looks at Trevor and Brian, his fingers tapping faster. "There's only about four minutes until the end of the second quarter, and then we'll talk. We're watching O.J. and the Bills play the Giants." He points at Mo's hand. "Hey, M, whatcha got there? Is that a card?"

"Jake sent me a birthday card. I got it in the mail today." Mo holds it up, a giant elephant sitting on a tiny stool with an under-sized party hat on the cover.

Carlton rubs the armrest. "Jake's your brother, right? Is your birthday today? How old?"

"Yeah, uh, no, it's tomorrow. Twenty-five." Mo walks to the kitchen and tosses the card in the trash.

At halftime, Trevor comes back from the bathroom in time to catch the end of a news report providing the latest on the Pastoral Predator. He turns to Carlton. "Did you tell him where we were today?"

"No, we were waiting for you," Carlton says, motioning toward Mo. "We should take him to McGuinn's for his twenty-fifth birthday tomorrow after the game."

"That would be cool," Brian says, "but I have to head back home.

My ma needs more help in the yard. I only came back to get some fresh clothes. Sorry, Mo."

Trevor stares at the floor and rubs the back of his neck. "Me, too. The electricity's out, so the sump pump hasn't been working. My father asked me to give him a hand cleaning out the cellar."

"Geez, you guys suck." Carlton looks over at Mo. "Well, nothing is stopping us from celebrating after the game."

Trevor glares at Carlton, still rubbing his neck. "We should tell him."

Carlton nods, lips pursed. "The police had the three of us come down for questioning today. We were there most of the afternoon. They asked a bunch of questions about Professor Langford and the Gonzalez guy. They asked whether we had seen you with them or if we had been anywhere with you and them." The lines in his forehead become more pronounced. "They asked a ton of questions about you, Mo. They wanted to know when you went for walks, and for how long, here at school and when we went places." His eyes grow narrower. "I think they think you may be a suspect."

Mo cocks his head back. "Like Flatbush and Professor Langford?"

"I'm not sure, but it sounds like they think you're important in the case. It could be that one or both of them are following you or something, or maybe one of them is trying to set you up, but they asked a lot of questions to all of us. I was in longer than B or T because we've been to a bunch of the places where the girls were murdered." Carlton rubs his hand along his forehead. "I guess they could think I'm a suspect, too, but they said it was just an interview and not an interrogation. They also said you're not a suspect right now. I asked them straight out, but I think they're investigating everything, so you're in their sights, and maybe me, too. It's getting scary. Did you see the green Fury outside with the two guys in it?"

Mo sits at the edge of the sofa. "I think they're following me."

"We got your back, Mo," Trevor says. "I think they know it's either Langford or Gonzalez or both, but they're trying to figure out how you fit in the mix. I wouldn't worry too much about it."

"Yeah, we told them you couldn't be the Pastoral Predator," Brian says. "We said you're a great guy and super laid back." He turns to Carlton. "By the way, I still think Foliage Flogger would've been better."

Carlton waves off Brian. "I did see Jim going in after I finished. I'm sure he wasn't kind."

The color drains from Mo's face. "Did Kay have to go in?"

"Yeah, she went in this morning. I saw her come out. Looked like she had been crying."

Mo's rattled by the thought of Kay crying. Looking away from his housemates, he begins shaking. "Maybe I shouldn't have gone for walks." He feels for his gloves. "I'd like to go for one now, but it's too late, and those guys out there scare me."

Carlton nods. "Yeah, I think maybe not tonight."

The ring of the house phone shatters a moment of awkward silence. Trevor answers and motions to Mo.

Mo plods over and puts the receiver to his ear. "Hello?" A few single-word affirmative responses follow before ending with, "Yes, sir." He hangs up, realizing, for the second time, not all phone calls are good ones.

Trevor waits for Mo's blank stare to dissipate. "Who was that?"

"It was a police officer." Mo releases the receiver. "I have to go in for more questioning tomorrow."

Trevor walks over, pats Mo on the arm. "You'll be okay; you'll see."

Mo stares at the floor.

Trevor gives Mo one final pat. "Well, I better go grab my stuff."

"Me too," Brian says.

When Trevor and Brian return to the living room, they each have a duffel bag. Without saying a word, Mo sits on the sofa watching a game he doesn't understand, sad that his friends are leaving again.

Trevor hands Mo a baseball card. "Here you go. I know it's the last one you need for your Red Sox set."

Mo takes the card. "Did you get a double? I can go get my cards to trade."

"No, I just wanted you to have it. I still need a few to finish my set, so it's fine if I need one more. I'll eventually get it." Trevor winks. "I always do." He puts his hand out. "I'll see you in a few days, right?"

Mo shakes Trevor's hand. Looking into his friend's eyes, Mo notices the same jagged red lines that were present in Griffin's this morning.

Brian reaches for Mo's hand. "See you later, M."

Mo doesn't remember shaking hands with any of his housemates before. It reminds him of Mr. Branch's handshake at the Greyhound station the day he left Virginia.

"Alright, guys," Carlton says, "we'll see you in a couple of days." He turns to Mo. "I'm gonna turn in. It was torture clearing out my mother's basement, and I'm beat." With his head down, he follows Trevor and Brian to the front door before climbing the stairs.

Mo shuts off the television before trudging to his bedroom. Silence, like a delicate shroud, blankets the room. Mo stares at the stack of baseball cards on his nightstand, struggling to take his mind off the car outside, the investigator's questions, the murders, the coincidences, and his walks.

Mo wonders if he's a suspect. He wonders if Investigator Palmer thinks he's a suspect. Does Investigator Palmer believe he's the killer? How can anyone kill? Could he kill? His father killed. But he had never thought about killing anyone. Well, not *really*. Maybe he hates Emily and would like it if she were dead. But kill her? Not *really*. And what of Veronica and her mean words? What about *that*? Could he kill *her*? No, not *kill* her. Just walk away. And for an instant, for just a split second, he thinks, *Maybe I am the killer. But wouldn't I know? Would I know?* But he doesn't know.

And after all his questions, Mo, again, finds himself looking outside his bedroom window.

The Fury remains.

# 83

# EVIL

## MONDAY, 20 OCTOBER 1975

*P almer stares into the mirror, examining the creases in his forehead and the lines on his face.* Standing at a sink in the Providence Police and Fire Headquarters bathroom, he sees he's aged. Just in the past three weeks, he's aged—forty-five going on sixty—and he knows it. Reaching down into the deepest recesses, seeking to understand the motivation of a monster sucks the life from his body, corrupts his mind, and tortures his soul. Walking in the shadows of his own controlled depravity, skating the edges of societal norm, Palmer communicates with evil.

And evil talks back.

And he listens.

And it consumes him.

Palmer splashes his face and heads into the police chief's office, where Metcalf, Monroe, and Lowe wait in collective silence. He reaches into his shirt pocket and digs out a Marlboro. "Good evening, gentlemen." Walking to the far end of the room, he rests against Metcalf's desk. "Agent Ross and I had a productive day."

"We've got some information to share as well," Monroe says.

Palmer lights, reaches across the desk for an ashtray, and drops in the match. "You go first then, Jeff."

"The search team found a casing off the path where you suggested. It's gone to ballistics for detailed analysis, but their preliminary review suggests the casing is quite old. This is consistent with the appearance of the spent bullet found last week. They're digging deeper into historical manufacturing data to find a match."

Palmer pinches his nose, forcing air through his ears. "With any luck, we may have a better idea of the gun that fired that bullet soon. Ross is still in Virginia to meet with a friend and business partner of Lumen's father in the morning. We're hoping this guy will shed some light on a gun Lumen's father left him when he died earlier this year."

"You're thinking Lumen has the gun?"

"He might, but I want to verify the type of gun he may have brought with him from Virginia before we request a search warrant. We've got to have strong probable cause on this one, given we already have two prime suspects, one in custody."

"Understood." Monroe flips the page of his notepad. "The Georgiaville Pond search team found skeletal remains along the water on the backside of the pond where the hiking trail ends. Forensics is looking at dental records, but we believe it's likely the Belanger girl who went missing seven weeks ago."

Palmer rubs his eyes. "You'll wanna get a search team back over to Hillcrest Estates. Search any bodies of water within a thirty-minute walking distance from the Dumont house and the friend's house she was going to see."

"I'll call Stricker and let him know." Monroe squeezes the back of his neck. "We're also looking into another missing persons report. It's another Bryant College student. Told her roommates earlier in the week she'd be leaving Friday morning and heading home for the weekend. She was last seen at her townhouse before walking to an off-campus variety store late Thursday afternoon. Apparently, she thought it would be safe to go alone because the news was reporting we had the killer in custody."

Palmer wriggles his finger in his ear. "If this girl's linked, it means Gonzalez isn't the killer, or at least he's not working alone."

Metcalf looks up from his notebook. "Two sick bastards working together?"

"It's very rare," Palmer says, "but we can't rule out a connection between Gonzalez and Langford, Lumen and Langford, or Gonzalez and Lumen. Maybe even all three."

Monroe rubs his five-o'clock shadow. "We need one of them to talk. Gonzalez doesn't say anything, Lumen talks but says nothing, and Langford's too wily. Between the three, I don't trust Langford."

Palmer flicks his cigarette over the ashtray. "What about the Dufresne kid? What did he and his roommates have to say?"

Monroe leans his head against his knuckles. "Dufresne substantiated pretty much everything Lumen said yesterday. He seems to genuinely like the kid, referred to him as a friend several times. Says he and the housemates were bothered at first with Lumen being there, but his girlfriend, Thompson, made the difference in getting them to accept him."

"Did Dufresne mention any incidents involving Lumen?"

"He said there were several situations where Boulet's negative behavior led to Lumen being hurt emotionally, with one final episode leading to Boulet punching Lumen. Apparently, the others had to pull Boulet off Lumen. Based on what I've seen from the transcripts, the others offered similar explanations of the events. Dufresne also said one of Covington's female friends said some mean things to Lumen, but it was early on, and the Covington kid later agreed not to bring his female friends to the townhouse after that. Said Lumen absorbs punishment, then walks it off."

"What about Boulet?"

"He was asked to leave the house after the fight with Lumen. The roommates felt he'd never be able to accept Lumen living there. Boulet was the only one who had anything negative to say. He was visibly upset talking about Lumen and anxious throughout the interview. According to the other three roommates and the Thompson girl, Boulet has alcohol and anger issues."

"What was the consensus on Lumen?"

"All but Boulet say they've never seen him angry or aggressive. Didn't even fight back when Boulet was whaling on him. Boulet had no specific incidents of Lumen being aggressive. Just kept saying he doesn't trust him, thinks he's dangerous. Dufresne, Bohan, and Covington all appear to think of Lumen almost like a younger brother, and Dufresne's girlfriend loves the kid, thinks he's really sweet. Straight out said she couldn't imagine him hurting anyone."

"Anything stand out?"

"Only one real revelation. Everyone who went to Lincoln Park with Lumen recalled seeing Langford at the amusement park. Boulet didn't go." Monroe runs a knuckle under his lower lip. "Langford never said *anything* about going to Lincoln Park in his interrogation."

Palmer massages his forehead. "Doesn't help Langford's case, does it?"

"Nope. I genuinely don't trust the professor."

"I don't either," Metcalf says. "Just too, I don't know, slippery with his answers. Seems pretentious."

Palmer pushes himself from the edge of the desk, picks up the ashtray, and sits in a chair on the opposite end. "From the transcripts, it does seem Langford's guilty of something, even if it's just unbridled arrogance. I still don't think Gonzalez is the killer. The gun with no bullets? The binoculars? Just doesn't make sense. But he did kill a girl years ago with a single punch, so he's fully capable and has a past. It seems, at this point, he would *have* to be working with someone. Again, that's extremely rare."

"Lumen's very suspect," Monroe says. "He's the only one who's been, even by his own admission, to every location where the bodies were found and where he had time alone. But we have no concrete evidence, and the consensus seems to be that he's not capable. Frankly, I don't want it to be this kid. I'd rather it be Langford or Gonzalez."

Palmer taps his cigarette on the edge of the ashtray. "But let's not overlook Dufresne. All we really know about him is that he's tall, lives with Lumen, and has been to many of the murder sites at the same time Lumen was there. He has a car, so he's more mobile than Lumen. In addition, we know he flipped from emotionally insensitive toward Lumen to becoming good friends with him, taking him on weekend outings with his girlfriend." Palmer blows a cloud of smoke over the desk before continuing. "I always consider the possibility of a killer creating a smokescreen, using some other hapless or unsuspecting individual as a shield to take the fall if things go south. That could be Langford's angle with Lumen, but it could very well be true for Dufresne, too."

Palmer stands and walks to the window, watching his exhaled

smoke spread against the pane. "Gonzalez won't crack, and Langford's obviously lying. We need to know why. I have to get inside Lumen's head again tomorrow, and I need to figure out Dufresne." Palmer points his cigarette at Monroe. "You notify Lumen?"

Monroe runs his hand along his knee. "We called earlier, right after you called from the airport. I'll send someone out in the morning to bring him in."

"We need to identify him as a suspect and let him know at tomorrow's interrogation. I'll bring Lowe in with me to see how Lumen reacts to a younger presence in the room. He's intimidated by us, but he may find refuge in a younger guy. I also want the Dufresne kid back in for more questioning on Wednesday. We need to squeeze him a bit more."

"We'll notify Dufresne tomorrow and schedule a time for Wednesday. What *did* you learn about Lumen in Virginia?"

Palmer turns from the window and sits next to Monroe. "We don't have everything we need yet. In addition to the father's former business partner, Agent Ross will be talking to the principal at Lumen's elementary school before flying back tomorrow afternoon. Meanwhile, I think we all need to get some sleep."

"Yeah, right," Metcalf says. "C'mon, Frank, we all know you don't sleep."

Palmer smiles. "I was using the royal 'we.' I didn't say *I* was going to sleep."

Monroe edges closer to Palmer, raising his eyebrows. "Frank, what do you have?"

Palmer leans into the ashtray and stubs his cigarette. "We received information about a possible handgun Lumen may have brought with him from Virginia, we gained insight into society's unequal and unjust treatment of individuals with disabilities, and we learned something about psychological disorders."

"But what does it all mean?"

"It means we need to get some rest because we have a lot of work to do. It also means we discovered a lot about Maurice Lumen's traumatic path to Rhode Island."

# A SUBJECT OF INTEREST

### TUESDAY, 21 OCTOBER 1975

Palmer sits in the interrogation room contemplating the two puzzles in front of him: the Times crossword and the Pastoral Predator. Focusing on the latter, he believes he has the four corner pieces—Gonzalez, Langford, Lumen, and Dufresne—and is working the edges. But key pieces are still missing, and he's unsure which image will appear when it's finished. He evaluates the layout of the investigation and the position of the authorities in this massive manhunt.

Reading the next crossword clue—*wander aimlessly in search of pleasure*—Palmer embraces the mind of The Monster, the sickness of the mind, and the symptoms of the sickness. He pencils the letters, *g-a-d*, into the boxes while considering Lumen's loss, wondering how his own path might've been different had his mother been taken from him at eight instead of twice that age.

Lowe opens the door to the interview room and shows Lumen inside. "I believe you've already met Chief Investigator Palmer." Pulling out a chair, he instructs Mo to take a seat before sitting on the opposite side of the table. "Chief, Mr. Lumen has brought a stack of baseball cards with him. He'd like to know if it's okay to have them in the room."

Palmer's seated at the end of the table. "Absolutely," he says, pointing to the stack of cards Lumen's placed on the table. "Who did you bring with you?"

"All my Red Sox cards."

"Looking forward to game six tonight?"

"Yes, sir. It's been five days. I can't wait anymore."

Palmer speaks through his exhaled smoke. "I feel the same way.

There's a lot of anticipation and anxiety out there, isn't there?"

"Yes, sir."

"Who's pitching tonight?"

"Tiant," Mo says, showing Palmer the pitcher's card. "He's already won both games for the Red Sox."

Palmer takes a casual glance. He knows showing an interest in the Red Sox is a sure way to get Lumen relaxed. "Hopefully, he'll win a third and send the series to a seventh game."

"I hope so. I don't really like the Cincinnati Reds. Do you?"

"There's something good about every team and every city." Palmer pauses, staring at the ashes he's tapped free from his cigarette. "But, no, Mr. Lumen, not really. I don't care for Cincinnati." He shakes his head. "Well, let's get to the matter at hand, shall we?"

"Yes, sir."

"Once again, I must apologize for requesting your presence on such short notice." Palmer starts the recorder. "We're here today because our investigation has identified you, Maurice Leroy Lumen, as a significant subject of interest and possible suspect. In addition to your previous interviews, we have had conversations with many individuals and witnesses who have helped establish your presence at all known crime scenes. We've also established that you have a connection to both primary suspects." Palmer pauses to watch Lumen's reaction—stoic, witless. "Therefore, this interview represents an interrogation, and you have rights under the law. Have you been read your rights under the Miranda Act?"

"Yes, sir, when Agent Lowe picked me up this morning."

"If at any point you would like to speak to an attorney, you have that right. Do you understand?"

"What's an attorney?"

"A lawyer."

Mo nods then shakes his head. "No, I don't have one."

"But you understand you can request an attorney at any time, correct?"

"Yes, sir."

"You are allowed to make a statement before we begin questioning." Palmer leans in. "Would you like to make a statement?"

"No, sir, I wouldn't know what to say." Mo rubs the back of his hands, the hairs sticking up like weeds in an open field. "It's very cold in here, sir."

"I apologize, Mr. Lumen. Unfortunately, the energy crisis caused oil to soar, and the bill to heat this building must be extraordinary. Would you like a coffee before we begin?"

"No, sir. I don't like coffee."

"We'll be here for some time, so if you get thirsty, there's water on the table. If you'd prefer something else to drink, all you have to do is ask."

"Thank you." Mo places his arms around his chest.

Palmer spends forty-five minutes revisiting the discussion from their previous interview. Once again, Lumen's polite and direct, providing accurate yet nondescript responses and offering little in the way of additional information or productive clarification. Palmer understands Lumen's limitations and doesn't read the emotionless responses as a defense mechanism. Instead, he sees Lumen as sincere, and the young man's answers reflecting a genuine lack of attention to details that wouldn't concern a preteen.

Palmer pours water and gestures, filling Lumen's glass after he nods. "By all accounts, you are amenable and likable. You've made a lot of friends here in a very short time. Mr. Griffin, Professor Langford, your coworkers, and your housemates all speak very highly of you. Even when you've had to deal with adversity, virtually no one has seen you respond in a negative or aggressive manner." Palmer's tone shifts to accusatory. "But you harbor some anger, don't you?"

Mo takes a sip of water. "No, sir. I don't think so."

Palmer leans forward and glares. "What about Emily Branch? Are you angry at her?"

"I try not to think about her." Mo sets the glass down, picks up the stack of baseball cards, and lowers his hands onto his lap, interlacing his fingers around the cards.

Palmer slides his chair a bit closer. "But sometimes you do, right? Sometimes, you get angry when you think about her?"

"Sometimes."

"When, Mr. Lumen? When do you think about Emily Branch?"

"When I pray at night. Sometimes I pray for her, or I pray she won't be mean to her brothers and Jake."

"What other times do you think about her?"

"Sometimes when people say mean things to me." Mo wipes the sweat collecting in his palms onto his pants while still clutching the baseball cards. "Sometimes, when someone asks me about her."

"What do you *do* when you think about Emily?"

"I don't know. Sometimes I get really sad." Mo's face shows the strain of an hour's questioning. "Maybe I get a *little* angry."

Palmer makes a fist and positions it in Mo's line of sight. "Do you want to hurt Emily when you get sad or angry?"

Mo looks down and squeezes the cards tighter. "No, I ask God to make her better. I ask God to make her nicer. I ask God to take care of her."

"Take care of Emily how?"

"To not be able to bother me or anybody else anymore."

Palmer studies Lumen's eyes. "But she can't hurt you now. Emily can't hurt you from so far away, right?"

"No, but she lies and gets Jake in trouble, and then he can't write to me." Mo blurts the words out, pain evident in his eyes. "She just does things to hurt me."

"Does that make you angry? When Emily does things to hurt you, even though she's far away, does that make you angry?"

"Sometimes."

"How do you get rid of the anger?"

"Sometimes I walk, or sometimes I watch the Red Sox, or I read."

"Do you know the color of Emily's hair?"

Mo stares at Palmer, tilting his head and furrowing his brows. "Dark hair?"

"Is that a question, Mr. Lumen?" Palmer reloads. "What's the color of Emily Branch's hair?"

"Brown, I think."

"You *think*, or you *know*?"

"I think it's brown. At least I know it's dark."

"When you went out to walk off your anger, did you ever talk to, or come across, a girl with brown or dark hair?"

"I don't know. I don't pay attention to people when I'm walking." Mo reflects for a second. "There was one girl who came over when we both saw a deer. That was when I first got here."

Palmer rests his cigarette in the ashtray. "Were you walking around the grounds at Bryant College?"

"Yes, sir." Mo's eyes follow the thin blue stream rising from the tip of Palmer's abandoned cigarette. He envisions his parents' souls ascending to heaven.

Palmer asks Lowe to retrieve a binder from Metcalf's office before readdressing Mo. "Did you talk to this girl?"

"No, sir. I don't think so. Maybe a couple of words. I don't remember. She came over and put her finger over her mouth so I'd be quiet, and we both looked at the deer until it ran away."

Lowe returns, sliding a thick three-ring binder in front of Palmer.

Turning the binder so Mo can see, Palmer believes he may be close to a much-needed break, though he still doesn't feel the rage in Lumen that is typical of the monsters he's hunted. "Was this the girl?"

Mo looks at the photo. "No, sir. I don't think so."

"Take a closer look." Palmer moves his chair nearer to Mo, looking at the photo alongside him. "Do you think it could be this girl?"

"No, sir."

Undeterred, Palmer flips through one photo after another.

Mo looks at each, his answer always the same. "No, sir."

Saving the girl who was shot at Bryant for last, Palmer's thumb presses hard against her photo as he places his hand on Lumen's shoulder, hoping to feel the connection between predator and prey. "Okay, now look at this one very carefully. Do you recognize this girl?"

Mo stares at the photo, dropping his head closer and closer. "I'm sorry. I don't."

Palmer's shoulders fall back hard, his chair sliding away from Lumen. "Would you recognize her if you saw her again, or a photo of her?"

"Yes, sir."

"How can you be so certain, Mr. Lumen? That was two months ago. You've stated you can't remember if you spoke to the girl."

"Because I've seen her jogging on campus when I've gone walking since then. Sometimes she waves to me as she goes by."

"When was the last time you saw The Jogger?"

"A couple of weeks ago, before the police came. No one was allowed to be on the roads or paths after that."

Palmer sighs, running his fingers through his hair. "Alright, we can check it out. I don't suppose you know her name?"

"No, sir. I never talked to her."

"But you could point her out to us?"

"Yes, sir."

Palmer, sounding defeated, looks down at the recorder. "I don't suppose you know what color this girl's hair is?"

"Yes, sir," Mo says, taking a prolonged sip of water. "She has brown hair."

Palmer allows Mo a bathroom break. With his return, Palmer jumps back in. "Alright, Mr. Lumen, let's talk about these trips you've taken with your friends over the past two months. Have you ever seen either Mr. Gonzalez or Mr. Langford while you were out walking either at Bryant College, Langford's house, or any of the other locations we've discussed?"

"No, sir. Not unless Professor Langford was there with me."

"Have you ever seen either of their cars—Langford's two-tone, brown AMC Pacer or Gonzalez's orange Datsun 510—at any of the locations you've gone for a walk?"

"No, sir."

"Not at Bryant College or Roger Williams Park, Lincoln Park, Stillwater Pond, Georgiaville Pond," Palmer flips through some notes. "Hunt's Mill, Olney Pond, Stepstone Falls, Langford's house, or near the Thompsons' house?"

"No, sir. Only in the parking lot at work or when I was with Professor Langford."

"Alright, Mr. Lumen, I only have a few remaining questions, but they're important ones." Palmer leans forward to ensure eye contact. "You have visited every location at key times when a young female was murdered, having had time separate from the people you went with at each of those locations." Palmer pauses, leaning in a little closer. "Given all the facts, at least on the surface, there's room for suspicion." He hesitates again, continuing to stare into Mo's eyes from less than a foot away. "Do you believe either Gonzalez, Langford, or both may have been following you over the past two months?"

Mo breaks from Palmer's eyes, looking down at the table. "I don't know." He runs his thumb along the edge of his baseball cards.

"Can you think of anything that might explain why either Gonzalez, Langford, or both would follow you over the past two months?"

"No, sir."

"Is there anything you might have done to either Gonzalez or Langford to make them want to set you up as the killer?" Detecting confusion in Lumen's silence and blank stare, Palmer restates the question. "Did you do anything to Gonzalez or Langford to make either of them angry at you? Any reason for either of them to make it look like *you're* the killer so that *you* would take the blame for *their* crimes?"

After a brief pause, Lumen responds. "No, sir, I don't think so."

Palmer's breathing is rhythmic, his words unsympathetic. "Okay, then, Mr. Lumen, one final question. If none of the scenarios we've discussed here seem likely in your estimation, are you the killer known as the Pastoral Predator?" When Lumen fails to respond, Palmer inches closer and rephrases the question.

Staring first at his cards and then at his watch, Lumen straightens himself, looks his accuser in the eyes, and responds. "No, sir."


Alone, Palmer doesn't leave the interview room until he's completed his crossword. After which, he tucks the sports section under his arm and heads upstairs to Metcalf's office, where Monroe and the Providence Police Chief are waiting. He tosses the paper on Metcalf's desk. "That was interesting."

"That good, huh?" Monroe smirks.

"Lumen kid might have anger issues, but I don't think he'd remember them. It's still hard to believe he could be responsible for the murders."

Monroe nods. "I have an update for you. They found the Dumont girl's body near the water tower just outside the Hillcrest Estates."

Palmer presses his cigarette into the ashtray. "Not like I don't know, but tell me again how old she was?"

"Fifteen."

"Fucking bastard." Palmer digs around the pack in his pocket for a cigarette.

"I also have some interesting news about the bullet casing," Monroe hands Palmer a document. "Turns out the one we found is from a bullet manufactured in 1944 by Ruger for the Nazis. The imprint matches war munition stamping. That bullet's more than three decades old!"

"Holy shit." Palmer tilts his head away from Monroe, his eyes wandering around the room. "The Branch father said the bullets Lumen got from his father were in an old, faded white box. He said the wording was in a foreign language." Palmer stands up, begins pacing. "Branch also told us Lumen's father and his partner, Earl Johnson, fought in Europe together." He stops at the window before turning and staring at Monroe. "I think we may have the break we need." Tired of fumbling for a cigarette, he pulls the pack from his shirt pocket. Finding it empty, he tosses it in the wastebasket.

Metcalf opens his drawer, pulls out two Luckies, lights one with the other, and hands it to Palmer. "You think Lumen has the gun?"

Palmer takes the cigarette, inhales, and releases a dark cloud. "Maybe. Can you send someone downstairs to find Lowe? He was supposed to call Ross and come up here right after. He should've been here by—"

Lowe knocks and enters. In a huff, he says, "Chief, I just got off the phone with Ross." He pauses, sensing heightened anticipation in the room. "Earl Johnson says the gun was a Nazi SS Walther pistol Lumen's father recovered on a German battlefield in 1945."

Palmer grabs Lowe by the elbow. "Did he say whether Lumen's father also had a box of Nazi bullets?"

"Yes," Lowe responds, staring at Palmer slack-jawed. "How did you *know* that?"

"It's not important right now." Palmer turns to Metcalf. "Steve, I need a search warrant for Lumen's townhouse and the Shed."

Metcalf rolls up his sleeves. "You'll only get the Lumen kid's bedroom and common areas. I know Landis; he won't allow you to search the other kids' bedrooms without probable cause. The Shed shouldn't be an issue."

"That's fine." Palmer points to Monroe. "I want to be there when they find the gun and cartridges. I'll be back in time to talk to Dufresne. Just bring him in early. Have him wait alone in the interview room. I want him anxious when I arrive."

# A WORTHLESS SPECK

## TUESDAY, 21 OCTOBER 1975

*M*o *has never felt so small.* Several months earlier, lying in the dark on his tiny cot with only Dion by his side, he felt isolated and unappreciated, but never small. After today's interrogation, lying awake in his bed with sunshine flooding through the window of his lonely room, he waits for his only accessible friend, feeling insignificant.

With accusation right outside and abandonment all around, Mo doesn't feel like reading or looking at his baseball cards or even eating. He thinks he may never do those things again, imagining himself withering away and becoming a speck on the drywall. There, he would listen to Carlton, Trevor, and Brian speculate on where he's gone until they'd stop and forget he was ever here. Then, Investigator Palmer would not be able to find him, he thinks. But neither would Kay. And he imagines himself screaming as loud as he could, trying to attract her attention. But she wouldn't hear him. And all his screaming would cause him to fall to the floor with all the other worthless dust, swept up and hauled to the incinerator by Mr. Griffin. And Mr. Griffin also wouldn't hear him holler until his minuscule voice makes his minuscule throat hoarse, and he's mute. And not even the imperceptible trace of ash his speck becomes would be sufficient to enter God's kingdom. And he loses everything and everyone.

Lonely and afraid, Mo passes the time praying in his bedroom until Carlton arrives. Praying for the Red Sox. Praying for Investigator Palmer to find the Pastoral Predator. And praying he will not become a worthless speck. He prays until he falls asleep. And he sleeps until he hears the entrance door open, at which point he sprints out, turns on the television, and takes a seat on the sofa, still silently praying. A few minutes later, Carlton comes downstairs, sitting on the other end of the sofa.

"Hey, M," Carlton says. "See you got your lucky spot. How you feeling about tonight's game? Think they'll win?"

Mo is relieved when Carlton sees him. "I think so. Tiant's pitching again. They've been winning when he pitches."

"That's true."

"The field's still soggy, but—"

"Oh, hey, yeah, um, Kay's not gonna make it tonight. She's, uh, watching the game at home, so if it doesn't go well, she can just go to bed."

"Can we go over to Kay's house to watch the game?"

"No, I don't think so. Kay wants to watch it with her dad. I also believe she wouldn't want to be rude by going to bed if we were there. She really wants the Red Sox to win for her dad."

Mo raises his eyebrows. "Do you think she'd change her mind if you tell her it's my birthday today?"

"That's right! Happy birthday, old man." Carlton hesitates before continuing, rubbing his arm. "No, I don't think we should disturb Kay tonight. But remember, I'm taking you to McGuinn's after the game. How's that sound?"

Mo sits up straight. Eyes wide, he nods. "If they win, do you think Kay would come with us?"

"I'm pretty sure she'll just want to go to bed after the game. She has work in the morning and tomorrow's her twenty-first birthday, so we have a big date tomorrow night."

Mo slumps back into his seat, "Okay, I hope I get to see her for her birthday. I want to give her something."

"I'm sure she'll like anything you give her."

They watch the game in silence. It's a tense battle, seesawing back and forth, still tied after nine innings. A little after eleven, they head to McGuinn's to watch the extra innings and celebrate Mo's birthday. The green Fury follows close behind.

McGuinn's is packed. Many of the patrons are Bryant students and they're partying hard. Excusing his way through the crowd, Mo settles near the bar, accepting Carlton's birthday present, a pint of beer, and enjoying an unimpeded view of the television. He takes a sip, grimaces, and hands the mug back to Carlton.

By the time the game enters the bottom of the twelfth, Mo's nerves are shot, believing his very existence hangs on every pitch, every out, every squandered opportunity. The announcers discuss the game in a historical context, wondering where it stands among the greatest of all time. Mo soaks up every word like a drunk wringing a bartender's towel over his mouth.

On the second pitch of the inning, Mo holds his breath, listening to the announcer's excited voice: *There it goes, a long drive, if it stays fair...home run!* He watches the Red Sox catcher round the bases. Initially high fiving, then brushing away enthusiastic fans, Fisk weaves his way down the third base line before jumping onto home plate and into the arms of his teammates. *We will have a seventh game in this 1975 World Series.*

Jumping up and down in celebration, McGuinn's patrons shout, scream, and fist pump, spilling more taxable beverage than revolutionaries at the Boston Tea Party. Though he doesn't like the smell or the soiling of his uniform, Mo's not going to complain. Carlton starts singing *Happy Birthday*, with many in the pub joining in, cheering, recognizing, saluting. Mo looks at his Timex. It's a little after midnight on the twenty-second and no longer his birthday. At twenty-five years and one-day old, Mo feels, if only momentarily, accepted, appreciated, and part of something bigger than himself—bigger than a worthless speck.

# RAGE

## WEDNESDAY, 22 OCTOBER 1975

P*almer parks his Bonneville outside Suite Fifteen Barrington before dawn and rolls the window down a crack; coffee steam and cigarette smoke seep carelessly out.* Across the parking lot, he can see the plainclothes officers assigned to tail Lumen bleeding twice the steam and smoke through their green Fury's lowered windows. Staring at the townhouse-style dormitories, the row of windows and entry doors remind Palmer of *her* apartment building. It had only been once, in a moment of inebriated weakness, but he's never been able to shake the memory. Like the courtroom prison officer after a guilty verdict, the mail slot in Lumen's townhouse door drags him back to a desolate place—back to that late-February morning in 1969.


Several months earlier, Palmer had requested removal from the Bureau's ongoing investigation into the New England Crime Family. He hadn't agreed with Agent Rico's tactics or close association with mobsters Whitey Bulger and John J. Kelley. The ensuing internal turmoil had taken its toll by the time he was reassigned to help track down the Cape Cod Casanova in Truro.

Once deployed, he let the stress and booze take over. But mostly, he let The Beast consume him. Osmond warned him not to go out, but Palmer was in the mind of The Monster. And he couldn't sleep.

She was convenient, willing, young—much younger, nearly two decades' worth. She meant nothing to him, just a way to relieve tension, possibly a vessel to get deeper inside the mind of a young sexual predator. He couldn't know for sure. Leaving the following morning, he looked back, ignoring the name above the mail slot on her door. He didn't need to know. She's a ghost now—one still haunting him.

It took eighteen months to tell Marilyn. He begged. She tried. But a year later, Marilyn and the girls were gone. He'd discovered the distance between the girls and himself was more than the eight hundred miles measured on a map.

This morning, staring at the mail slot in the front door to Suite Fifteen Barrington, Palmer knows his primary focus, as it has been since that night, is to control the damage, even as he serves out his sentence.

Lumen leaves for breakfast at seven, carrying his laundry and transistor radio. At seven thirty, Palmer knocks on the door and hands the warrant to Dufresne, who gets picked up for questioning at eight. Three officers commence searching five minutes later while Palmer and Stricker stand in the hallway outside Lumen's bedroom.

Stricker stirs his coffee. "Must be getting closer, Frank, huh?"

Palmer opens the closet door under the stairs. "Not sure, Dean. We'll see."

Stricker pushes the closet door closed. "Let them do their job, will you?"

Palmer glares at Stricker. He wants to tell him to fuck off, but he chooses not to be an asshole today—today, he'll control The Beast. There's rage in this townhouse, but on *this* day, he's not going to succumb. "Alright, Dean."

Stricker tugs at his belt. "That's better. Can't be any bodies *here*, right?" Stricker angles his head to look up the stairs. "What are we looking for anyway?"

"We're looking for the gun used to kill the Rollins girl here on campus." Palmer cringes as the words slip out. He reminds himself he's being charitable.

"Really?" Stricker darts over. "You think the killer lives *here*?"

*I'm trying*, Palmer thinks to himself, *but Stricker's an ass.* He rubs his palm across his forehead. "No, Dean, we're here because I'm looking for a more affordable apartment outside the city." He shakes his head and walks into Lumen's bedroom. Stricker follows.

A young officer, a tall six-pack with droopy eyes and half a mustache, walks over carrying a box. "Not much in here, Detective Stricker. Just uniform shirts and pants hung in the closet, and several pairs of socks and some underwear in the nightstand drawer along with a Bible and another book, *Watership Down*. There's a few framed photos, a stack of baseball cards, and a transistor radio on the nightstand, and this box from under the bed."

Stricker taps the side of the box. "What's in here?"

Wearing protective gloves, Six-Pack fingers through the box. "Some more baseball cards, a few old photos—I'm guessing of his family—a paperback of *Moby Dick* with an envelope inside, and this little, silver, coin-like thing with a heart on it."

"What's in the envelope?"

"Looks like a letter from his father."

"Hold it here, please, so I can take a look." Palmer stands alongside Six-Pack and reads to himself. "Hm, *that* must have been a surprise." Palmer steps away while running a knuckle across his lips.

Six-Pack opens the front cover of *Moby Dick*. "You may want to see this, sir."

Palmer leans in and reads the note:

*Ken,*

*I never wanted the medallion or the baby. I'm giving you back the medallion, it's yours anyway. The baby is not. His father is a poor Negro from Tinpot Alley named Sam. We should've aborted when you and I talked to the doctor. Now the baby has no mother or father. His best chance is for you to raise him. I'm placing him in your care. Love him like your own and forget me.*

*Clara*

Palmer rubs his temple. "Jesus!" He inspects the red-hearted medallion. "Take a photo of this and the notes."

By nine thirty the search is complete. With the investigative team gone, Stricker stands next to Palmer at the foot of the staircase.

"No gun," Stricker says, smirking.

Palmer stares up the staircase. "Yup. Keen observation, Dean." He places his foot on the first step.

"The warrant doesn't permit us to go up there, Frank."

Palmer lifts the other foot.

"Frank!"

Palmer's fingers compress around the grooves of the handrail. Knuckles turning solid white, The Beast growls. "Fuck!"

Stricker takes a step back, his eyes wide.

Glowering, the redness in Palmer's eyes radiate like lightning from his dark pupils. He releases the handrail. "I gotta go downtown for an interview," he says.

Palmer exits to the front landing and reaches into his shirt pocket. Ripping the top of a pack open, he pulls out the last Marlboro, crushes the empty pack, and tosses it behind a bush. Catching sight of the mail slot in the door, he thinks back to The Girl Who Moved One Stool Over and the eight-hundred-mile divide she created. As he steps off the landing, a single word, almost inaudible, escapes his lips. "*Bitch.*"


Thirteen cigarettes. Thirteen cigarettes across three hours. Twelve cigarette butts discarded with no remorse. Twelve cigarette butts lying in a bed of ashes—one for each girl in the killer's count. And one for himself, still squeezed between his fingers. Ross and Lowe are gone; sent home to Boston to watch game seven with their families. In seven hours, they will know. In seven hours, that anxiety will end. But the pain and suffering may linger. Palmer knows tonight may just lead to more loss. He knows tonight may result in more disappointment. But he'll watch the game anyway, hoping The Monster watches, too.

Monroe and Metcalf walk into Howard Johnson's. They knew they'd find him here.

Monroe places his hat on the booth hook. "Hey, Frank. How you holding up?"

Palmer shrugs.

Monroe sits beside Palmer and pats his forearm. "Stricker told me about the Lumen search. Said it didn't go as expected."

Palmer shakes his head. "I was sure we'd find the missing piece. Damn Dufresne kid had nothing new to add either. Every time I thought he was going to say something important, he'd talk about Lumen needing to watch tonight's game and hoping the Sox would win. Sounded almost cryptic at times."

"He does seem to really like the kid," Monroe says. "It's hard not to; a young guy like that going through so much shit at a young age. To be honest, I was half hoping they *wouldn't* find the gun today."

Metcalf taps a spoon on the table. "Does seem like his house-mates and coworkers care about him." He waves the waitress over. "Hey, doll, can we get three coffees, please?"

Palmer presses his palm above his right eye. "I need to cut out the caffeine. I got a headache that just won't go away, and I either gotta get some sleep or get a drink." His lips curl into a coy smile. "Maybe get a drink or two to help me sleep."

"You need some sleep, Frank. You look beat."

"I will. I'm gonna drive back to Boston in a little while, have a couple of shots, and watch the game before heading home. I wanna try and sleep in my own bed tonight." Palmer closes his eyes and cups the back of his neck. "We may not have the killer yet, but we're close. Gonzalez is in a cell, Langford and Lumen are under twenty-four-hour surveillance, and we know where Dufresne lives. It also seems like the missing persons reports have tapered off. He's not necessarily caged, but we may have him cornered. Let's all get some rest tonight, enjoy the game, and blow off a little steam. Maybe he'll make the mistake we need tomorrow."

# AN OCEAN OF DESPAIR

## WEDNESDAY, 22 OCTOBER 1975

M*o's growing isolation yields no pity.* Entering the townhouse after another dinner alone, he's shaken when Carlton greets him with a wide-eyed and silent stare. Not long after, aware his friend and roommate is avoiding him and believing accusation has again crept into his home, Mo decides to leave.

Under the watchful eyes of his detail, Mo heads back to the Uni-structure. Mrs. Harrington's Saint Christopher medal now hangs around his neck day and night. And he needs it. The Cigarette follows on foot with his partner seated in the Fury. Mo feels guilty by association, guilty by coincidence, and guilty by preoccupation. He's not angry. He understands anger might get him into trouble. Instead, he tries to distract himself with baseball, but judgment is a disturbance swirling all around him.

Upon Mo's return, Carlton confronts him at the entrance to the downstairs bedroom. "Kay's not coming over tonight. I'm taking her out for her birthday and our anniversary." His face is ashen. "We figured you'd wanna watch the game by yourself here at home."

Mo's face falls further. "I'm not going to see Kay tonight?"

Carlton rubs the side of his neck. "She, uh, doesn't want to watch the game. Says she'll be too nervous. She's, um, working late, and we have a reservation for dinner. Then we're heading over to a special place for us. I'll be home pretty late."

Mo steps toward Carlton. "Can I go? I can bring my radio and listen to the game."

Carlton backs into the hallway. "But you've been looking forward to this. It's the decisive game. You'll wanna watch it, right?"

"It's okay. I don't mind listening."

Carlton steps toward the base of the staircase. "I really think you should stay and watch the game. I'm gonna head upstairs and get ready to go."

"But I didn't get a chance to get anything for Kay's birthday."

Carlton hurries up the stairs. "It's alright. You can get her something later and give it to her when you see her."

Moments later, water rushes through pipes to the upstairs shower. Mo heads to the kitchen to wash the dishes, letting the water run hot. He hears Carlton curse and mutters, "Serves you right." Washing his hands, Mo sees the glare of his Saint Christopher medal in a dinner plate. *This will work*, he thinks. When the shower turns off, Mo realizes he has little time. He kisses the medal as he rushes to his bedroom. Opening the nightstand drawer, he removes the jewelry box. After polishing the medal on his shirt, he rests it on the ball of cotton inside, allowing the thin sterling chain to slither into the corner of the box. As it has protected him, Mo believes the medal will be a permanent guardian over Kay.

Back in the kitchen, Mo corners Carlton, handing him the jewelry box. "Here, give this to Kay, please."

Placing his sweater and notebook on the counter, Carlton opens the tiny box. "Oh, Mo, that's so thoughtful. She'll love it." He looks into Mo's eyes, then swiftly back at the gift, clearing his throat. "I'll give it to her on the boardwalk when we're alone."

"Thanks, Carlton. Tell Kay I wish her happy birthday."

"I will. Hopefully, I'll see you tomorrow morning before you leave." Carlton's lip quivers. "I hope the Red Sox win so you can enjoy that tonight. Watch it for me." After hugging Mo, he grabs his sweater and exits without looking up.

Once again, Mo's alone. He opens the sliding door and spills out onto the back porch. Staring at the thin strip of lawn and lining shrubbery separating the townhouses, he sees a minimalist garden in an ocean of despair. He weeps. He will do his praying and pleading in solitude tonight.

Tangled within hopes and heroics, sights and spectacle, shouts and screams, genuine drama will unfold tonight. And, while history will record an outcome, time will diminish the struggle, honoring the victor and overlooking the vanquished. Such is the nature of sport.

Mo's impressed by the powerful Reds lineup, but he won't be rooting for any Cincinnati players tonight—tonight, he's pulling for Boston and New England as their drama unfolds.

Sitting in his lucky spot on the sofa and holding his stack of Red Sox cards, Mo is ready to watch the game. He doesn't like that the cards now have worn edges from yesterday's interview, but he's glad to have a complete set. He wonders what Trevor will say when he sees them, but he'll worry about that tomorrow. For the next few hours, his focus will be on the game.

For the second straight night, Boston builds an early three-run lead, and Mo is cautiously optimistic. With two outs in the bottom of the sixth, Boston's starting pitcher tempts fate once too often, and a Cincinnati home run cuts the lead to one. The following inning, the Reds tie the score.

Seeking to relieve his stress, Mo heads to the kitchen for a glass of water. Splashing his face, he notices a green notebook, upside down and open on the counter. Knowing it's Carlton's, Mo spins the notebook around, intending to close the cover and take it upstairs. However, considering his friend's behavior earlier in the evening, he wonders what secrets Carlton may be keeping. At the top of the page, he sees today's date and just below, a list of girls' names entered into a hand-drawn table, including rows for age, date of disappearance, and location. Mo's eyes grow wide as he recognizes several of the names from the news.

Near the bottom of the page, a bulleted note:

- Kay, 21st Birthday, Cook Pond Boardwalk, Fall River

Underneath, two additional bullets:

- Gun—top dresser drawer—wrapped in towel.

- Police station tomorrow morning—hand over Mo —reward money.

Mo stands in quiet disbelief, brain overloaded, struggling to grasp the gravity of his discovery. Rushing to his room, he reaches under the bed for his father's shoebox. Unable to find it with his blind hand, he leans sideways and places his head on the floor to peer underneath, spotting the misplaced box on the opposite side. He hurries around and retrieves the box. It's too light. He knows what he'll find even before he removes the cover—no gun.

Sprinting upstairs, Mo finds his father's Walther, as expected, in the top drawer of Carlton's dresser. The clip's loaded save one round. As he swings around to exit the room, he sees a stack of newspapers on the side of Carlton's bed with dozens of clippings lying on top.

Mo descends the staircase and races out the front door, searching frantically for the green Fury. It's not there. His breathing heavy and dysrhythmic, he charges back through the hall. Rifling through the kitchen counter drawers, he slams each back in place until he locates the telephone book. Tearing pages out as he flips through, sweat pellets form on his brow. Finally, he reaches for the phone.

Panting, he struggles to get the words out "I-I-I need a taxi."

He listens, then responds, "Bryant College campus." Several excruciating seconds pass. "Yes, I'll be in front of the Unistructure in five minutes. Please hurry."

He doesn't hear or see the ballgame in the living room. Stopping by his bedroom, he grabs money out of his father's shoebox. He moves as fast as his body will allow, reaching the Unistructure just as the taxi arrives. With students staring at televisions, and under cover of darkness, there are no witnesses as he plunges into the rear passenger seat.

But the driver stares at him in the rearview mirror. "Where you headed?"

"Cook Pond Boardwalk in Fall River," Mo says before catching his breath. "As fast as you can."

# MONSTER'S WARM BREATH

*Palmer stares at the scotch in his tumbler.* The game's on every screen at McEnaney's, but his interest is fleeting. Finishing his drink, he considers what The Monster might be doing. Is he watching? Is he prowling? Is he even in the area anymore? He taps the bottom of his tumbler on the counter and pushes it to the bartender's side.

A cherry-red fingernail crosses the path of his eyes and rubs around the top of his empty glass. Looking up, he smiles. But he's not drunk, and he's not digging up skeletons or hunting ghosts tonight. He shakes his head. Cherry smiles and walks away. The tears in Cherry's black nylons tell him she'll be back. But it'll have to be a Saturday night, and Bernie will have to be a lot quicker with the bottle.

Palmer feels a slap on his back accompanied by a familiar voice.

"Thought I might find you here."

"Hey, Harry, figured you'd be watching the game at home."

"I was." Osmond checks Palmer's eyes. "You okay?"

"I'm fine. Just nursing a couple of shots during the game." Palmer points to his empty tumbler. "Bernie's pouring slow tonight." Recognizing the look in Osmond's eyes, he straightens up. "You didn't come here for a drink, did you? What's going on?"

"You might want to get to your car and wait by the phone. I just got a call from Metcalf. His boys lost Lumen."

"What? How?"

Osmond shakes his head. "They figured he wasn't going anywhere while the game was on, so they left to get coffee. Driving back up the entrance road, they saw a taxi speeding in the opposite direction. One of them went around to the back of the townhouse to make sure he was there. When they didn't see him, they checked the front door. Lumen left it unlocked. He's gone."

"Son of a bitch!" Palmer jumps from his stool, grabbing Osmond's shoulder. "Let's go!"

"No, Frankie, I took the promotion so I wouldn't have to do that anymore."

Palmer doesn't wait for Osmond to finish his sentence, making a beeline for the exit. Running back to the parking garage, he feels the cool air on the shopwindows staring at him. With each long and determined drag of his cigarette, he feels the warm breath of The Monster. Unlocking his car door, he sees the puzzle pieces falling into place. And staring at his car phone, he shares the anxiety of the Pastoral Predator. He knows they're both hunting tonight.

# THE SECOND DEATH

## WEDNESDAY, 22 OCTOBER 1975

M o sits in the back seat of the taxi gripping his father's *Walther.* He knows steel is hard, cold. But somehow, this steel gun casing is harder and colder still. Maybe it's the design: the smooth, hollow barrel, the intentionally textured grip. Possibly, it's the purpose: the icy disposition of a cold-hearted killer, the calm, cool manner of a professional hitman. Most likely, it's the perspective: impersonal, detached, unsympathetic, the distance occupying the space between momentarily connected parties. To Mo, it doesn't matter why, only that it *does.*

As Mo presses his father's handgun against the cool vinyl seat, his forefinger falls, unintended, inside the trigger guard, sending a chill that channels through his chest. Staring at the hands of his Timex, he's bewildered when critical minutes pass faster than the excruciating tick of each second.

His instincts as a premeditated killer are unqualified, but his concern for Kay's safety is unquestioned. He must watch over her. He must protect her. He will kill for her. The gap between innocence and vengeance diminishes with every mile of his fare.

Mo doesn't hear the radio, doesn't listen to the game; his thoughts overtaken by passion and rage, focused on justice and retribution. He grips the pistol tighter, feeling every pronounced groove of the handle against his ungloved and anxious palm.

Crossing the Taunton River on Braga Bridge, Mo thinks back to the Rappahannock and Kelly's Ford Bridge, to fishing and hunting with his father. He hopes his father will be by his side and help steady his hand tonight. Caged within the forged steel beams of

Braga Bridge, Mo prays. Silent lightning christens the night sky, etching tortured reflections in the restless waves below.

The surrounding night grows more suffocating as they navigate from highway to street, boulevard to thoroughfare, lane to access road, darkness shattered by mute bursts of electrical discharge as they reach Cook Pond.

Mo doesn't see or hear the amount of the fare, dropping several twenties onto the front seat. As he steps away from the car, lightning reflects off the Walther, alerting the driver to its destructive intent. The vehicle speeds away.

Staring down a central pathway through several rows of maples and oaks, Mo can barely make out two seated figures in the faint reflection of distant light on the water. He avoids the manicured footpath in favor of camouflage within the trees. Pressing forward, he's veiled in darkness and obscured by nature.

A curious whitetail emerges near the water's edge, the doe's eyes ablaze. In her condemning glare, Mo feels the full force of his fury and the weight of his weapon. He thinks back to the panicked stare of the doe he couldn't shoot and his father's words of encouragement as he knelt, young and afraid, in the dark, cold, and damp woods. He recalls the loss of his mother not long after. With only Kay left, his father's words propel him; his mother's love compels him.

Emerging from the trees, Mo steps across a clump of weeds and onto the far end of the boardwalk, mere yards from where Carlton's hands encircle Kay's neck, his thumbs resting on her jugular notch. Kay is trembling, head down, imploring Carlton to listen. Mo treads softly, approaching Carlton from behind.

Kay's weeping intensifies. Struggling to breathe, she looks up and canvasses Carlton's eyes, negotiating, pleading, begging. Her protests unheeded, she attempts to pull away, catching Mo's resolute eyes staring down from above her boyfriend. Weak, shaking, breathless, she mouths, "*Mo.*" Her eyes grow large, then close—her body slumps.

Carlton's hands drop to his side, chin resting against his chest.

Kneeling beside Carlton, Mo feels the vengeance of more than a dozen female victims pumping through his veins. He sees the collective terror in their eyes in Kay's motionless body. And smells the fear of their final breaths in the cool midnight air. They summon him. He presses the muzzle just below Carlton's right ear and pulls the trigger.

For Carlton, there's only sound—a single thunderous blast that penetrates his skull and ends his suffering.

Lightning reveals the Saint Christopher medal lying helpless between Kay and Carlton's lifeless bodies, the words 'Pray for Us' reflecting in Mo's eyes. A stream of blood weaves its way through the sterling chain and toward the water. Mo follows its course along the boardwalk, his gaze extending across the pond. Another strike reflects the whited-out windows of an abandoned mill on the opposite side, reflecting dozens of unwavering eyes in the gently rocking waters.

Sirens shatter silence, a radio blares from an open door, and lights approach through the convenient pathway. Mo spins around to address the disturbance, thrusting himself into the spotlight— the focus of a parade of torches converging. The warm glow of 'Lumen' glistening on his name patch offers a fleeting refuge. He hears yelling. Unable to discern any words, his arms remain by his side, hand still gripping the Walther. More yelling, but his attention's focused on the wind whistling through the trees, carrying a faint, recognizable voice emanating from behind the approaching posse. The confident evenness of the announcer's play-by-play is, as it has been recently, a source of comfort in these anxious moments: *Cincinnati, with two down, has runners at first and third, one ball, two strikes on the batter.*

A half-dozen police officers edge closer, their collective and disjointed shouting replaced by a single voice. "Settle down, son. Drop the weapon and hold your hands up."

Confused, recognizing the voice, Mo feels his father's guiding hands help steady the gun in front of him. *"Daddy?"*

Mo loses his balance when the first bullet grazes his left knee. Falling, a second bullet lodges into his brain. He drops the Walther on the deck just before his head slams against the blood-soaked lumber. His arms, limp, offer no cushion.

*There's a looper... And, the Reds have the lead.*

Unable to move, eyes open, thoughts spreading like dandelion seeds helicoptering from his youthful breath, Mo lies in perfect recollection. He sees his father sitting in his recliner, watching television and drinking with Earl, and his mother standing in the downstairs bedroom, surrounded by vases filled with lavender and talking with Mrs. Harrington. He sees Mr. Griffin and Flatbush standing next to the Bryant archway, smiling and laughing, and Kay with her arms around him, whispering in his ear. He sees Grandma Cleveland seated at the table, her hands outstretched and no longer worried, and Sam on a raft floating downstream with Trevor listening to his baseball stories, Louie following right behind and playing his trumpet. And he sees Jake holding Pooh Bear and waving from the opposite bank behind the Branch house, Dion sitting by his brother's side.

Individual thoughts turn into a flood, crashing like waves against the storyboard of his life. Memories stroll, then sprint, into darkness before trickling into the pond and the water that will drift downstream, dumping into the Rappahannock with all the black-haired critters and other carcasses before washing away the sins of his father and his father's fathers. And as Mo succumbs to the deluge, breathing becomes more difficult, every gasp a struggle to remain conscious.

Officers come closer. They stare. Mo's eyes close. Thunder finally, mercifully, follows lightning, almost simultaneously, and a light rain blesses the scene, insufficient to wash away the stain of multiple streams of blood where they cross. Memories fade into a sea of silence. All is still, finally, and without explanation.

Throughout the great, vast somewhere, in houses and dormitories, parks and public buildings, cathedrals and country churches, there will be expressions of joy, notes of appreciation, and prayers of thanksgiving. Everywhere, there will be the satisfaction that comes with justice—retribution in response to disturbance. But, here, in this dimly lit, gravely cold, unholy, and blood-drenched setting, a cry of salvation rises up to the heavens.

While the first death requires no witnesses, the second death must be presided over by judge, jury, and executioner. With his final self-driven breaths, Maurice Lumen hears the heartbeat of the watchful deer, sees the light reflect off the purifying water, and feels his father's gun under his still-beating chest.

# A HOPELESS SEARCH
# THROUGH THE DARKNESS

### THURSDAY, 23 OCTOBER 1975

P *almer arrives forty-five minutes after the drama unfolds.* Stepping out of the Bonneville, he hears a voice rise above the sirens and emergency radios.

"We have a pulse here!"

Looking over the crime scene, Palmer takes a drag from his cigarette. In the background, news vehicles contribute to the mounting chaos. After assessing the situation with local police, he walks to a pool of tired and hungry reporters. "We won't be answering any questions tonight," he says. "There will be a press conference tomorrow. We'll release the time and location in the morning." His pace is hurried as he separates from a dissatisfied press corps.

Palmer makes his way down the slope. Pulling the barricade tape over his head, he overhears an exchange between two officers.

"If that kid survives," the first officer says, "it'll be a miracle."

"No, if that kid survives," the second one says, "he'll be a vegetable."

Ninety minutes pass in a heartbeat. Lightning and thunder having long since ceased, chaos surrenders to the serene landscape. At the edge of the woods, Palmer stands just off the boardwalk and lights a cigarette, a fine mist settling on the water. Ross and Lowe approach, but he ignores their presence, staring instead at the hazy outline of the King Phillip Mill along the far bank.

Lowe stands a few feet away. "Chief, you wanna talk to forensics? They're packing up and wanna know if you have any more questions."

Palmer doesn't acknowledge or alter his focus.

"Alright, then. We'll let them know they can get going." Lowe walks away.

Palmer releases a cloud of smoke. "The kid's done a good job, Gerry. Might be something there."

"He likes working with you," Ross says. "*That's* something."

Ignoring the weeds at his feet, Palmer continues to stare over the water. His eyes focused on distant light to the west, the thin stream of smoke rising from his cigarette cannot fully veil his pain. He wonders if Marilyn and the girls celebrated Cincinnati's victory.

Ross pats Palmer's shoulder. "It's okay, boss. We got him. When did you know it was Dufresne?" Ross waits for a response that does not come, several long moments seeping into the pond. "Stricker told me you tried to go upstairs yesterday morning."

Palmer gives Ross a sideways glance. "How's the girl?"

"Sounds like she's gonna be okay. Shaken up pretty bad, though."

Palmer nods, takes another drag, and resumes his hopeless search through the darkness.

Ross kicks a rock near his foot. "Too bad about the Lumen kid, though. He ended up doing our dirty work. You must be glad it's over."

Palmer draws a final shot of nicotine through his filter, inspecting the fading glow at the tip. He knows Lumen got a monster alright; Dufresne's not gonna harm any more girls. And they got Lumen. But Gonzalez is behind bars, Langford's under surveillance, there are still five unsolved murders, and a hysterical young girl is insisting it wasn't her boyfriend. The Beast is quiet. But not for long.

Palmer flicks his cigarette into the water, the lines on his forehead like shore-bound waves. Thoughts drift to his daughters until they are swept away with fear, relentlessly drawn to another monster and the resulting disturbance that will occupy his mind.

*And baseball is, as it has always been, merely a distraction.*